SWIFT VENGEANCE

Visit us at www.boldstrokesbooks.com

By the Authors

Jean Copeland
The Revelation of Beatrice Darby
The Second Wave
Summer Fling
The Ashford Place
Spellbound
One Woman's Treasure

Jackie D
The After Dark Series
Infiltration
Pursuit
Elimination

Lands End
Lucy's Chance
Rise of the Resistance: Phoenix One
Spellbound

Erin Zak
Falling into Her
Breaking Down Her Walls
Create a Life to Love
Beautiful Accidents
The Road Home
The Other Women

Closed-Door Policy (Novella in Hot Ice)

SWIFT VENGEANCE

by

Jean Copeland, Jackie D,
and Erin Zak

2021

SWIFT VENGEANCE

ISBN 13: 978-1-63555-880-7

This Trade Paperback Original Is Published By
Bold Strokes Books, Inc.
P.O. Box 249
Valley Falls, NY 12185

First Edition: June 2021

CREDITS
EDITORS: VICTORIA VILLASENOR AND CINDY CRESAP
PRODUCTION DESIGN: SUSAN RAMUNDO
COVER DESIGN BY TAMMY SEIDICK

Acknowledgments

Thank you, Vic Villasenor, for guiding us through this fun and sometimes frustrating process. This was truly a team effort, and we couldn't have done it without you. Thank you, Cindy Cresap, for catching all the last-minute glitches. Bold Strokes Books for indulging our whimsical story ideas so the three of us could collaborate. Thank you to our readers for always being willing to come along for the ride.

Dedication

For all the women who've been told
they were too much, not enough, or to tone it down.
Don't dull yourself for anyone.

CHAPTER ONE

*A*sphalt crunched in her mouth, leaving small tears on her gums, coating her teeth with blood. The smell of spilled gasoline and burnt rubber was sickening, burning the insides of her nostrils and turning her stomach. She struggled to look down at her leg to see where the blinding pain was emanating from. The more she struggled, the more intense the throbbing became. She lay her head down on the ground, watching the brilliant red, white, and blue lights bouncing off the dampened street. She couldn't marry the simplicity of the lights with the extraordinary anguish she felt in every part of her body.

Fragments of the last twenty-nine years flashed through her mind. There was no logical order to the birthday parties, graduations, first kisses, and heartbreak that rose from somewhere in her subconscious. When she'd heard of life flashing before your eyes, she thought it might be with more grandeur. Or maybe it was because she hadn't done anything worth memorializing.

Hands were pulling at her body, and sentences were being exchanged. She should probably be more interested in what was said, but she couldn't focus on anything but the pain. The struggle to stay conscious had grown too great. She gave in to the blackness, letting it swallow her whole.

Brittany blinked in the darkened room. She hadn't been able to shake the dreams since the accident a year ago. They came to her night after night, an unwanted visitor there to remind her how far she'd come and how far she still needed to go. When she spoke of the nightly occurrences aloud, she lamented their interference in her life. But that wasn't entirely true. Another part of her, a darker part, one that she didn't want to confront, found comfort in the nocturnal repetition. It tethered her to her anxiety, an excuse to remain in the predictable life she'd created for herself. She knew what to expect every day, and there was comfort in that. That comfort kept her safe.

She reached for the water she kept beside her bed and knocked it over before she realized her fingers were trembling. She didn't have the chance to push herself out of bed to remedy the mess before the light to her room turned on.

"Are you okay?" Amy's voice held trepidation and concern.

Amy and her girlfriend, Lena, had taken Brittany in after her release from the hospital eight months ago. Brittany was grateful for their friendship and their care, but a part of her hated herself for needing it for so long.

"Yeah, I'm fine." Brittany walked into the bathroom and retrieved a towel from the rack. "How did you even hear the glass hit the carpet?"

Amy leaned against the doorframe. "I didn't. You were talking in your sleep."

Brittany was so tired of seeing that look of pity on everyone's face.

"Is Laura back?" She wanted to talk about anything but her PTSD.

Amy sat on the bed. "Yeah, she got in about an hour ago. She and Lena are already forty-five minutes into an argument about her college class load."

She put her hand on Brittany's arm, and Brittany forced herself not to pull away. "Lena's only hard on her because she loves her."

Amy sighed. "Try explaining that to a nineteen-year-old."

"You were nineteen once, too." Brittany forced a smile, searching for a bit of normalcy with her.

Amy laughed. "I don't remember that, and you have no pictures to prove it."

Brittany dabbed the last bit of water from the carpet. "Well, Laura is lucky to have both you and Lena. I am, too. I know I don't say that often enough. But I'm not sure what I would've done without you guys the last several months."

Amy kissed the top of her head. "No thanks are necessary. We're happy we were able to help."

"You know what I'm going to miss the most when I finally move out?" Brittany smiled as Amy's eyebrows lifted. "Free food from Lands End. I'll probably starve."

Amy laughed as she stood and walked to the door. "Chloe hasn't paid for a meal there her entire life. I think you've finagled your way into the same category."

Brittany pretended to wipe sweat from her forehead. "Thank God. That alone was worth almost dying."

Amy smiled, but it didn't reach her eyes. Brittany had taken the joke too far. She'd known it when she said it and wished she could take it back. The accident hadn't only affected her. It had taken a toll on the people she loved as well. None more so than Amy, who had sat by her bedside every day for months. She'd come to every appointment and had picked up every prescription, and she'd driven her to physical therapy and sat with her while she cried and sweated her way through the first few weeks when the pain had been more than she could've ever imagined. She'd never be able to repay Amy for all she'd done, and even if she could, Amy would never accept anything in return.

"We still going to lunch with your aunt on Friday?"

Brittany fell back onto the bed, intentionally dramatic. "She's confirmed twice already."

"I've always liked your aunt."

Brittany turned off the light next to her bed. "Well, I'm happy to share the crazy in my family with you."

Amy chuckled. "Night, hun."

"Night."

Brittany practiced her breathing exercises, hoping to put her mind in a peaceful place before falling asleep. She pushed past the odd tingling that started behind her eyes and washed over her body; her body that had been like a stranger to her for the last several months—feeling, doing, and healing without her consent or input. This was just another anomaly to add to the ever-growing list.

Chapter Two

December 26th–Journal Entry 468

I had a therapist as a child who would set up toys for me. She wanted me to act out my thoughts and feelings with the dolls. I understood, even at five years old, what she was trying to accomplish. She wanted to see where the darkness hid. She wanted to find the cause of it all. There had to be a reason, after all. Normal children didn't behave like me. That's what I heard my father tell her anyway. I wouldn't say she gave up on me. No, that wouldn't be fair. Giving up would imply there was something to fix, something to save. There was never anything in me to save. I've felt the wickedness simmering under my skin, in my bones, my blood, my whole life. Even when I try to cobble together my earliest memories, it was there—the need to inflict pain, to watch people suffer. I've heard people throw out titles like psychopath, deranged, evil, and dangerous. But I don't really like any of those. They seem arbitrary—afterthoughts of things I've done and the ways I've behaved. Nouns and adjectives strung together before or instead of my name to try to make sense of what I am, simply because the truth is too much for most people to comprehend.

I am free. I'm not tethered to the societal norms that give most people a false sense of security. My actions have no real consequences because I place no power in the hands of society. I'm not tied down by guilt, remorse, or the need to appease. I see no virtue in curbing my natural instincts for the benefit of others. Why should I? Society is a construct in our minds, designed to keep the strong leashed and the weak on pedestals. That line of thought doesn't serve me. Why would I waste my time here, bending to the whims of others when there is so much out there to see and feel?

The first time I watched the life drain from someone's eyes, I knew what true power was. God isn't the only one who gets to decide who lives and dies. Everyone on this planet makes that decision every day. A guy cuts in front of you in line, and you sheep dull your animal instincts to rip the jugular from his throat. Why? Because you've become lazy and complacent. Not me. I can see it before it happens. I can picture laying him out on my table, taking my knife to his chest, and sliding it down his body. The idea of watching his skin split open, and his blood accumulate at my feet is the closest I will ever come to religion. We all have this power. It's not my fault that so few of us comprehend it. And it's not my fault that so many of you find it repulsive. The animal kingdom is brutal and unforgiving—I've simply taken my place within it.

God creates all things; that's what your books say. So in that line of thought, He created me. He put me here to find you, to hunt you, to make you realize how far astray so many of you have gone. I'm the world's greatest predator. You don't know what I am when I stand next to you at the bank, when you pass me on the street, or when you deliver my pizza. You don't realize that you've survived these encounters because I've let you. There is no other reason. I've been gifted with good looks, intelligence, and the ability to mimic your pathetic emotions. You never see me coming because you've removed yourself from this world. You live a mundane existence, buried in your phones and binge-watching shows. But I'm here. I'm waiting for you, for my opportunity, for my perfect moment. Make no mistake. When it's presented to me, I always take it.

I witnessed a hit and run a year ago on the streets of San Francisco. The motorcyclist that was hit lay on the ground, her blood pooling around her. I watched her emotions shift from horror, to pain, to acceptance. She touched the blood with her fingertips, seemingly mesmerized by the situation. I sometimes wonder if she lived or died, and whether or not she is aware of the peacefulness that engulfed her face when she accepted what was happening. It was beautiful. The moment death taps on a person's soul and promises an eternity of unknown. The moment when they're forced to question every choice they made that led them to this point. I wanted to dip my hands in her blood and run them across her face. I wanted to help her bathe in her reality, her choices. But that wasn't my destruction to revel within. You think I'm a monster—such hypocrisy. You all do wicked things to each other every day. At least I own who I am.

I've found my next toy, the woman who'd wronged my father and me years ago. He was so deeply affected that he took his own life. I cannot fathom how someone like him gave life to someone like me. But revenge is something I can understand, and I will serve it to her. She will know that her fate is no one's fault but her own, and it could have been avoided had she behaved differently. Once I'd found her, I studied her for quite some time and have deemed her unworthy to continue in this existence. It is as simple as that. I make these decisions with the same amount of decisiveness with which you choose your morning cereal. It will be because I choose to make it so.

It won't be long now, friend. Not long at all.

Chapter Three

Leslie ambled into the Second Wave, the local pub she and Alice owned on Swift Island, New England's most popular LGBTQ getaway. They'd purchased the place a year ago and renovated it into a modern island hangout where everyone from millennial hipsters to Stonewall veterans could enjoy the welcoming atmosphere. The Second Wave offered fabulous piped in playlists, mixing and mingling among eclectic patrons, and three taps of custom-made, local beer courtesy of Nereids Brewing, a small women-owned island microbrewery. The owners had convinced Alice and Leslie early on that they were about to take on the whole East Coast, and that if they were savvy, they'd take them up on the offer to partner with them selling craft beers labeled exclusively for their new establishment.

As Leslie moved toward Alice, she brushed her hand along the square, high-top tables for a sense of support. Engrossed in stringing lights around the mirrored backsplash above the liquor bottle collection, Alice clearly hadn't heard her light footfalls as she approached the bar. Leslie smiled. Mother Nature continued to treat Alice graciously. In her early seventies, she was lithe, steady, and energetic with remarkably youthful skin. "Clean living," Alice said whenever anyone complimented her on a timeless beauty that belied her true age.

"Hey, lover, be careful up there," Leslie said. "There's only room for one invalid in this marriage."

Alice turned, still clutching the lights, and laughed. "You're lucky you're so cute. Otherwise that gallows humor of yours would really get on my nerves. Where's your cane?"

"I don't need it." Leslie picked up the dangling end of the rainbow lights and held it for Alice.

"You may not *need* it, but it certainly doesn't hurt to use it."

"It'll only be in the way while I'm helping you decorate." She flashed her angelic smile that her wife never could resist. "Besides, I thought you loved my gallows humor."

Alice stopped and glanced down from her small stepladder. "Okay, I admit that I do. It's my favorite of all your stroke side effects."

"Touché," Leslie said. "I can't wait for my niece to arrive. Toni's going to love helping out."

"She's coming on the first ferry tomorrow morning, right?"

"Yes," Leslie said, her heart swelling with joy. "I'm so glad I was able to convince her to spend the rest of the season with us. She's had such a rough time since her breakup."

Alice nodded as the glimmer of haunting familiarity flickered in her eyes. "She knows that you and I are no strangers to matters of the heart. I'm looking forward to all of us spending time together."

Leslie glanced around at their pub. It had been a lot of work running the place, and while it was physically taxing at times, using her mind and body as Alice's business partner had brought a new vitality to her in the four years since her stroke. Together, they'd reveled in all the best parts of life in New England running their bar on Swift Island.

"I can't believe we're over halfway through our first season already," Leslie said.

Alice descended the few steps to the floor and caressed Leslie's shoulder. "Hard to believe, isn't it? Sometimes I'll look around when the place is packed and just marvel at the fact that we actually did it." She pressed her warm lips against Leslie's forehead, something that always made Leslie swoon. "I've never felt closer to you than I have these last three months. It almost killed us, getting used to the rigors of owning a business, but it's been wonderful doing it alongside you."

Leslie sighed and slowly fell into Alice. Melancholy momentarily swept over her as Alice wrapped her in a warm hug.

"Are you okay?" Alice asked.

"Yes," she replied into the softness of Alice's light hoodie. "Just a little fit of emotion. You know, the one where you're in the middle of enjoying a euphoric moment together, and then you remember how many years we'd lost."

Alice pulled her tighter and rubbed her back. "I know, my love. But what do we always say to each other when that happens?"

"Better this time that we have than none at all," Leslie said robotically.

"We can't steal back the lost years," Alice said. "But we can savor every moment we have now. And we still have many more to come."

Leslie pulled back to look Alice in the eyes. "Why are you so goddamn logical?"

"You know why. I worked in insurance for a hundred years."

"It was rhetorical, but yes, it's clear you worked in insurance." Alice glared at her. "Like I said, you're lucky you're cute."

"I'm lucky all around." Leslie gently cupped Alice's face and kissed her on the lips. "If this island didn't get so cold in the winter, I'd make sure we never had to leave."

"I have a reservation. One ticket."

"Identification, please."

Toni pushed her ID under the glass partition. She glanced to her left, where a sign read, "ROUGH SEAS TODAY." Her throat tightened and she swallowed, hoping to dispel the feeling. She wasn't a fan of boats or the water, but a ferry ride was the quickest way to get to Swift Island, where her aunt, Leslie, and her wife, Alice, had decided to rehab an old pub. Their decision surprised the family, but they seemed happy, so who was she to question it? And when she reached out and said she needed a soft place to land for a while, they seemed to understand without question. She bit down on her lip as she watched the attendant hold up the plastic and check to make sure it was really her. She smiled, raised her eyebrows, and shrugged. "It's me. I promise."

He eyed her. "Your hair is red in this picture."

"I know. It grew out." She pushed her dark locks over her shoulder. She'd curled it that morning, but the wind was wreaking havoc on it. She knew she should've pulled it back, but she was trying every second of every day to just *be better*, to not be such an emotional wreck. Getting her heart broken had proven to be quite the blow to her self-esteem.

"Your ID says Antoinette. Your ticket says Toni. They really should match."

"Yeah, well, it's a nickna—"

"Whatever." He waved his free hand. "Here's your ticket." He pointed at the sign. "Rough seas. Don't forget the ginger chew." He pushed a yellow sucker under the glass.

"Thanks." Toni snatched up the ticket and the sucker. "I'm heading to see my aunts."

"Lady, I don't need to hear your life story. The ferry picks you up down there," the man said with his gruff voice around a fat cigar held between dry, cracked lips. He motioned toward the end of the pier before he removed the cigar and coughed, a puff of smoke billowing around him.

She turned and rolled her eyes. Not at the man. Well, a little at the man and his piss-poor customer service skills, but more so at herself. Because, *of course,* she was oversharing. She hated the part of herself that always felt the need to tell everyone everything, especially when she was nervous. And right that second, every nerve in her body was buzzing with dread over the hour and a half ferry ride to the island. It had been years since she visited her aunt, and right now was a perfect time to getaway. She needed the escape, considering the last year and a half of her life had been loaded with nothing but drama.

As she pulled her suitcase behind her, she wondered, fleetingly, if she'd survive the ferry ride. All she could remember from being on a boat years ago was barely making it over the side when she threw up.

The ticket-taker ripped her ticket and handed it back, also alerting her to the rough seas.

"Are rough seas normal for this time of year?" She heard the worry in her voice, so she knew he could, as well.

The older man nodded. "Unfortunately, yes, dearie." He gave her a small smile. "August in the Atlantic is no joke. Welcome to New England." His eyes twinkled. "You'll be fine. I promise. Captain Taylor is the best captain we have."

"Great." She pushed out a breath as she rolled her suitcase by him and headed onto the deck of the ferry. She found a space for her large bag near the front of the cabin then quickly found a seat near the side and middle. She slid across the bench to the window and pulled her sweater around her shoulders. Aside from oversharing, being nervous also made her feel as if her body was turning into an iceberg.

"Good morning, lovely passengers, and welcome to the Swift Island Ferry. As a reminder, the seas are a bit rough today. A crew member will be coming by with ginger suckers if you'd like one."

Toni closed her eyes and took a couple of deep breaths, in, out, in, out, before she opened her eyes and graciously accepted another sucker. Hopefully, she wouldn't need them. *Hopefully.* And if she perished, she was going to blame Penn Tucker for everything, which wouldn't be a stretch. It was Penn's fault Toni's heart got broken. It was Penn's fault she left Colorado. It was Penn's fault she said yes to a marriage proposal. It was Penn's fault she got in over her head with a woman she knew she shouldn't trust.

Oh, who was she trying to kid? She wanted out of Colorado and that one-horse town more than anything, and Penn provided the perfect escape plan. That's what had made the marriage proposal so appealing that starry night after too much tequila and exactly the right amount of sex. Penn knew how to be irresistible, and Toni loved being blinded by the intense light of her attention. Penn sure had a way of making her feel like a queen.

Until, that is, she didn't. And when Penn decided she was done with Toni, she crumpled her up and threw her away, just like she'd done to all the women before her. And like all the women before, Toni was left alone to deal with a broken heart, broken trust, and broken self-worth.

Yeah, she could have gone back to Colorado and licked her wounds at the Main Street Pub, where Benjamin would have been more than happy to help, but the idea of being trapped again made her skin crawl. And it wasn't just about going back to a guy, to Benjamin. No, it was the idea of being trapped in a town where everyone knew everything about her. It was being a cashier at the general store for the rest of her life. It was about going back to everything she'd run away from to begin with.

The ferry jerked, and Toni immediately felt her body tense up. An older woman behind her chuckled as she leaned forward. "Honey, don't worry. It won't be nearly as bad as you're assuming."

"I hope you're right," Toni said with a smile. When she glanced out the window, she tried to focus on the horizon.

As the ferry got farther and farther from land, and the water got choppier and choppier, the more her body started to warm up. Her stomach was starting to churn. She knew what that meant. She pulled her sweater from her shoulders and leaned her head against the window. The coolness of the glass felt amazing. She continued to breathe deep.

Her mind flashed back to Penn, to their last fight, to how horrible Penn had treated her, and the thought made her feel even worse. She grabbed a sucker from her bag and pulled the wrapper off, quickly pushing it into her mouth. It was lemon and ginger, and even though she didn't understand the reason behind why ginger settled a stomach, she was never more grateful than she was that moment.

Just focus on the horizon, Toni. Don't you dare throw up. You can do this without ralphing. You can do this. It's easy. You can freaking do this.

Brittany doubled over, her vision going black. She patted the cold, hard tile, trying to anchor herself to the familiar. Then came the vision of hands in front of her, covered in red liquid. It wasn't thick enough to be paint—it was sticky, like blood. The hands moved under the flowing water of the sink. A whistling noise came next, a happy tune. The hands were clean now, and they shook off the last droplets of water before they reached for a blood-stained knife on top of a stainless-steel counter that they cleaned with precision and familiarity. When the task was complete, the knife was placed into a leather roll with several others.

Brittany was silently screaming for it to stop, but she was powerless to do anything but watch. She could see and feel everything that was happening, but she knew it wasn't happening to her. It was like she was seeing through someone else's eyes. Although, even in her current state, she knew the idea was ridiculous.

Her vision came back into focus, and she stared at her hands. She opened and closed them, willing them to give her answers. She desperately wanted the words to describe what had just transpired, but there were none. There had been so many changes since her accident. Some physical and some mental. Was this another side effect? Was she starting to have hallucinations? It couldn't be possible she was having visions now, on top of everything else. But it had felt so real…

Her ears were buzzing, and heat started to crawl up her neck and across her face.

"Are you okay, dear?" Aunt Patty kneeled beside her on the bathroom floor. "Should I get Amy?"

"I…I'm not sure what just happened." Brittany pushed herself off the floor and stared at herself in the mirror. "It's like I was watching…"

Aunt Patty came up behind her, putting a hand on her shoulder. "What did you see?"

Brittany leaned down into the sink and splashed water on her face. "I don't know how to begin explaining it. You're going to think I'm crazy."

Amy peeked into the small bathroom. "Are we having lunch in here?"

Brittany stared at Amy in the mirror. "No, I'll be out in a second."

Amy took another step into the bathroom. "If this is too much, I can take you home."

Brittany gripped the sink hard. The cold porcelain against her fingertips made them go white. "It's not that. I just need a minute."

Amy looked like she wanted to stay but nodded to her aunt and walked out.

Aunt Patty said nothing as she stood next to Brittany and rubbed her back, her countless gold bracelets clanging against one another as she soothed her.

Brittany watched her aunt in the mirror. The lines around her eyes and mouth were proof of years full of laughter and sunshine. Her short, styled cut didn't have a single hair out of place. Her leopard print jacket was probably a holdover from the 80s, but it was one of her aunt's favorite pieces. Most of the family thought Patty was an old kook, but Brittany had always been fond of her. She'd spent countless nights sitting in her aunt's backyard while Patty smoked cigarette after cigarette, recalling her mischievous youth.

"I saw something, and I'm not sure if I'm just losing my mind," Brittany said.

Aunt Patty turned Brittany to face her. She put her hands on her cheeks, and Brittany was momentarily comforted by the familiar scent of cigarette smoke from her fingers. "Are you ready to tell me about it?"

Brittany shook her head. "Not yet."

"Then let's go have lunch; time with Amy will relax you," she said as she opened the door and motioned her to follow.

The idle chitchat did exactly what her aunt had hoped. Brittany felt slightly more at ease, but what had transpired pulled at the edges of her mind. She didn't understand what had happened, but it would be impossible to ignore. She stared at Amy and her aunt and decided there would be no one else she could trust with what happened.

"I had a weird hallucination." Brittany blurted it out before she could change her mind. Both Amy and her aunt stopped talking and waited for her to continue.

The words poured out as she tried to make sense of what she'd seen. To their credit, they didn't look at her like she'd lost her mind. They sat with rapt attention, waiting for her to finish.

"It wasn't a hallucination," Aunt Patty said when Brittany had finally stopped talking. "It was a vision, and one I don't think you should ignore."

"A vision?" Brittany pinched the bridge of her nose. "What does that even mean?"

Aunt Patty reached across the table and put her hand over Brittany's. "You have the sight." She squeezed her hand when Brittany looked up to protest. "I've told you about this before, and I think you should listen to me now. This gift runs in our family. Not everyone has it, but it's there. Perhaps your accident awakened it in you."

Brittany rolled her shoulders, needing some of the accumulating stress to fall away. She had heard her aunt speak about *the sight* since she was a child, but she had always chalked it up to her eccentric personality.

Brittany took a deep breath. "I don't know what that means." She shook her head. "You think I mysteriously woke up with the ability to see what? The future? The past? What?"

"I don't know, sweetheart. I don't know what it means for you or someone else. I just think you should pay attention." Aunt Patty smiled at her.

"What can I do to help?" Amy asked.

Brittany picked up the napkin from her lap and tossed it onto the plate. "Can you just take me home? I need to lie down for a bit."

Aunt Patty pulled her purse off the back of her chair. "You two go, I'll take care of lunch." She held Brittany's cheeks when she leaned down to kiss her good-bye. "The visions always mean something, but you'll have to figure out what that is. I'm here if you need anything. I love you."

"I love you, too." Brittany kissed her aunt's cheek and followed Amy out to the car.

"You okay?" Amy pulled onto Market Street, heading home.

Brittany snorted. "Sure. I'm having some type of psychic visions about someone with bloody hands and a big ass knife, and I'm going home where I live with my ex and her partner. Just another day."

Amy squeezed her leg. "Maybe it's worth considering."

Brittany stared at Amy, unsure of what she was hearing. "Do you honestly believe her?"

Amy shrugged. "I think there's a lot we don't know and don't understand. I think you suffered a near-death experience, and no one fully understands what that entails." Amy took her hand. "I also think you're one of the smartest and most logical people I know, and if there's any other explanation, you'll figure it out."

Amy was always pulling for her. The last several months had proven that particular endeavor to be a daunting task. Amy saw the potential in her when Brittany felt as if there was none left. She hadn't always been this way, neither of them had. There was a time when Amy was the cynic, and Brittany saw all the potential in the world. Amy had changed after Lena, and Brittany, after the accident. She needed to get her head together and her life back on track, to be the person Amy remembered—that she remembered. She just wasn't sure how to go about that yet.

She squeezed Amy's hand. "You're a good friend, Ames. Thank you."

Amy pulled into a parking spot at Lands End, Lena's family restaurant. "I just need to run inside for a moment, and then I'll take you home.

"No problem." Brittany got out of the car and walked to the railing to look out at the ocean. The midafternoon sun danced across the whitecaps, creating a sea of diamonds.

She breathed in deeply, hoping the crisp salt air would help clear her thoughts. Instead, cold blackness slid through her like oil and she felt like she was slipping into the mind of another. This time, the view was broader. She was on a ferry boat, pulling into a pier. There were excited passengers everywhere going about their business. Women were grabbing bags and heading to the forward portion of the boat. The air was chilly, but the sun was hot, beating on her neck. She scanned the people waiting on land for their arrival. No one stood out, but coldness overtook her body. It felt almost like hatred, which would be misplaced as she felt no recognition for anyone near her. A surge of violence flared, and she felt the person hold back an impulse to attack.

Brittany wanted desperately to yell at everyone to run. She wasn't sure why, or how to explain it, but it seemed imperative. But there was nothing she could do. She was stuck, anchored to herself through whoever this other person was. The need for sheer violence was alarming. She watched as several women descended the stairs of the ferry and walked to the pier. Brittany wanted to force the eyes she was looking through to scan the area. She needed to see something, anything that could pinpoint the location. Her intense need to determine her location was continuously eclipsed by the growing visceral anger the person was emitting. Her heart rate increased as the person she seemed to be invading grew eerily calm and focused.

It was disorienting and almost painful—a crushing need to be wherever this was consumed her. Someone needed protection. Someone needed a warning. Someone needed to know what she saw—what she felt.

Brittany heard the loudspeaker of the boat. "Enjoy your time here at Swift Island."

She practically fell over backward a moment later. She looked around frantically, surprised that she was still in the parking lot of Lands End. She bent over and grabbed her knees, breathing heavily. The urge to throw up from the sudden change bombarded her senses, but she managed to hold it together. Her skin crawled with the lingering remnants of hatred and violence.

She didn't notice Amy come up beside her. "Are you okay?" Amy rubbed her back.

Brittany wiped her hands down her face, still trying to make sense of what was happening. "I think I need to go."

Amy pulled her shoulders, forcing her to make eye contact. "Go where?"

"Swift Island," Brittany said and then turned to vomit over the rail.

CHAPTER FOUR

Leslie rolled her golf cart as close to the dock as she could without ticking off Gus, Swift Island's curmudgeonly dock keeper. She was so excited for the ferry to arrive with her niece, Toni. She'd said good-bye to her daughter, Rebecca, and her family a few weeks ago, and she missed them terribly. Spending a couple of months with Toni would be a perfect way to end the season, especially since she'd suffered such a painful breakup and sounded so dejected on the phone. If any two people on earth knew about punch-in-the-gut heartbreak, it was Leslie and Alice. Once they'd cracked open a bottle of rosé, she knew Toni would cajole her into retelling the story of her star-crossed romance with Alice decades ago, but Leslie didn't mind. She'd always been a sucker for a happy ending.

"Mrs. Burton," Gus said, startling Leslie out of her reverie. "Haven't we discussed that you can't park this golf cart here?"

"Good morning, Gus." Leslie shot him a deadly sweet smile. "Are you having a bad morning?"

His craggy, sunburned face melted into softness. "Well, no, not particularly. But janitorial services are sure earning their pay this morning with that choppy water out there."

"Hmm, those white caps are something, aren't they?" She batted her lashes at him.

He averted his eyes from hers as he cleared his throat. Despite being in her early seventies, her perky charm and baby-blanket blue eyes never failed to render men goofy in her presence.

"Well, uh, the ferry's docking now," he said in a more affable tone, "so just stay put right here until your guests disembark."

"Oh, absolutely, Gus. And thank you."

He shook his head at her as he walked away.

"Toni," she shouted as she gingerly climbed down from the cart. "Over here." She waved her arms in the air like she was guiding an airplane.

"Aunty Leslie," Toni shouted back. She dropped her bags and nearly lifted Leslie off the ground her hug was so firm.

"You look beautiful as always," Leslie said. "I hope you feel even half as good as you look."

Toni shrugged, then seemed to manufacture a smile. "I'm much better now that I'm here and can see your gorgeous face."

Leslie slid over to the passenger side while Toni loaded her bags into the back of the cart. "Now don't forget to call your mother and tell her you made it here. This morning she emailed me an article about a ferryboat capsizing."

Toni chuckled. "I have a better idea. Why don't you do it for me?"

"Toni." Leslie pretended to scold her. "When did you become such a fresh kid?"

"You know I love my mom, but she likes to talk. She'll keep me on the phone for an hour, and I just want to sit quietly on a still object until my stomach settles down."

"Oh, dear. That ferry ride can be tough. But I'll bet you anything Alice has a drink recipe that'll help that."

"One of the many reasons I'm excited to hang out with you two."

"Well, you have us for the next three months."

When they pulled into the pebble-covered driveway, Leslie smiled at the "Welcome, Toni" sign and the mylar martini glass balloon whipping with the smaller balloons against the edge of the front porch. "Looks like the welcoming committee's home from work early."

"This is amazing," Toni said. "Your house is amazing."

"Oh, it's just a little cape."

"But it's adorable. So beachy and quaint. I love it." A memory of pillow talk about getting a place by the water someday floated in, but she quickly banished it.

"Thank you." Leslie seemed to take enormous pride in her flower gardens and floral shrubbery. Their place really did look like the quintessential cliffside beach cottage.

Alice came charging out the front door to meet them on the stone walk. "Get over here, you," she said, her arms outstretched. "It's so good to see you."

After the major hugfest, they went inside, got Toni settled into her room, then stepped out onto the back patio overlooking the Atlantic.

Toni and Leslie sat on the cushioned wicker love seat, and Alice relaxed in a chair beside them.

Alice crossed her legs and sipped her iced tea. "I know we promised not to interrogate you about your breakup, but I just want to know how you're really doing?"

Toni sighed. "I'm angry and exhausted and ready to stop feeling this way." She gazed out at the ocean and watched the waves reflect the early afternoon sun. "I couldn't have picked a better place to start the journey."

"I'll say," Alice said. "This island is crawling with lesbians."

"What's that expression?" Leslie said. "The best way to get over someone is to get under someone else?"

"Aunt Leslie." Toni's mouth hung open in amused surprise. "I can't believe you said that."

"Don't look over here." Alice stood and gave her a playfully stern glare. "She didn't get that from me," she added as she went inside.

"Is that what you did when Alice wouldn't go back with you in the eighties?" Toni said it softly so Alice wouldn't hear through the open sliders.

"Hardly," Leslie said. "I went back to dating men. Occasionally."

"Ah, the beauty of bisexuality," Toni said.

"Not really." Leslie grew pensive. "My heart belonged to Alice. It was just less painful to go out with men, less chance of me comparing them to her."

Toni squeezed her aunt's hand. She recognized her own fragile emotional state in Leslie. Funny how even though she and Alice eventually got their happily ever after, the memories were still vivid, the longing still palpable.

Alice returned with a bowl of fresh mixed fruit. She brushed her hand across Leslie's shoulder before sitting, and Toni watched as Leslie instantly melted into her touch. That simple touch cleared all the dark clouds away.

"I love your love story," Toni said. "I never get tired of hearing it."

"If anything, I hope it gives you hope, Toni," Alice said. "After I lost Maureen, I was in a terrible space. It's bad enough to lose someone you love, but then to believe you'll never experience intimacy and companionship anymore? I'll admit I'd given up. Then out of nowhere, I get a Facebook message from your cousin Rebecca."

"I was good enough to have had a stroke," Leslie offered.

"Yes, you were, honey," Alice said sweetly, then turned to Toni. "Sometimes I disagree with her doctor when he said she didn't suffer any permanent cognitive damage."

"Good thing I don't have my cane beside me," Leslie replied, playfully shaking a fist at her.

"You two are something." Toni dug into a dish of fruit salad and wanted so hard to believe that she would have that someday, too. She just hoped she didn't have to wait until she was seventy to find it.

It was close to eleven when Toni finally decided she'd had enough of Alice's lemon drop martinis. She thought her tolerance would be much higher than the four she devoured. Especially since she was used to drinking at a higher altitude than sea level.

Boy, was she wrong.

She stumbled into the small bedroom, knocking her knee against the footboard, and stubbing her toe on her discarded shoes from earlier. "Mother *fucker*," she muttered, followed by a low hiss. She fell back onto the bed, held her toe, and rubbed it as if her life depended on it. She could feel tears in her eyes but refused to let them out. She'd shed enough tears in the past two weeks and she wasn't about to cry over a stupid stubbed toe.

No way. No how.

She saved those tears for memories of Penn. She wanted to kick herself for letting the memory of their discussion about a beach home into her mind earlier. She needed to stop thinking about her. There was no way Penn was still thinking about her, so why the hell did she keep letting the memory of Penn's hands, mouth, body, invade her mind?

"Stop." Her voice sounded so loud in the small area. She turned to the window next to her bed and pulled the curtain open. She had a view of the Atlantic and of the moon shining brightly over the seemingly never-ending body of water. She pulled a deep breath in and held it for one beat, two, before she slowly let it out. "You've got to move past this, Toni. You've got to heal."

"Toni?"

Shit. "Aunty, I'm so sorry. I thought you were asleep."

"Talking to yourself isn't a crime you need to apologize for." Leslie leaned against the doorframe. Her smile was illuminated by the moonlight still streaming in through the window. "We'll help you get past it. If there's anything Alice and I know how to do its work through things."

Toni didn't fight the small smile as it worked itself to the surface. "I believe that."

"Good. You need something to believe in. And you need to believe in yourself, as well."

"You know what else I believe in?"

"What's that?"

"Pancakes for breakfast." Toni raised her eyebrows and tilted her head. "Huh? Right?"

Leslie's laugh filled the small room. "That can certainly be arranged." She pushed off the doorframe. "Get some sleep," she said with a wink as she pulled the door closed.

Toni plopped onto the bed and sighed, relaxing into the big fluffy pillows. She was so much stronger before all of this and she intended on getting back to that person. She'd known Penn was trouble the second she laid eyes on her, and she'd walked into it anyway. Maybe her biggest fault was that she gave people the benefit of the doubt too often.

Especially dark-haired individuals with gorgeous eyes. First Benjamin. Then Penn. The time had arrived to focus on her own soul, spirit, and mind. Unless, of course, she happened to find some other beauty on Swift Island, since it was, according to her aunt, crawling with lesbians.

Toni sighed and chuckled. Lesbians. Who would have ever thought she'd go that route?

As she drifted off to sleep, she imagined herself free from heartache, free from stress, and finally alive. It was a really great dream.

Chapter Five

An automobile. A plane. And now a fucking ferry. Brittany pulled her backpack into her lap as she settled into her seat on the Swift Island Ferry. It'd only been three days since the vision, ample time to talk herself out of the mission—yet here she was. Was this the craziest thing she had ever done? Rushing off to an island clear across the country she knew absolutely nothing about in search of the source of visions she also knew nothing about?

Brittany chuckled as memories of her youth flooded her mind. Nope, it wasn't the craziest thing she'd done. But this in particular wasn't just crazy. It was impulsive and dangerous, and what if she got herself into a jam she couldn't find a way out of?

That was probably the biggest fear floating around in her already jumbled thoughts. What if she got hurt? Again? After finally healing from an accident she honestly wasn't sure she'd ever heal from.

There were moments in her life when she let her impulses take over, and they weren't always bad. After all, being a journalist meant taking chances, going after the story when no one else saw the point. Or going after the big break when everyone else was clamoring for it. Either way, she knew what it took to be the best. And lately? Lately, she was far from the best. The accident broke her not only physically but mentally, emotionally.

"Don't forget spiritually," her aunt Patty had said as Brittany got out of the car at the airport that morning. "Your spirit is sometimes the last thing to heal, my dear." Her gold bangles danced as she pulled Brittany into a hug. "Go find what's tugging at that damaged spirit. You'll be happy you did."

As Brittany focused on the sea and the horizon, her aunt's analysis of the situation bounced around her head. She was having visions.

Fucking visions!

And not just any visions. Oh, no. She was having visions with blood and... *Ugh.* Brittany's stomach churned. From motion sickness or the flashback of bloody hands and water, she wasn't sure. She pulled the yellow ginger sucker from the left front pocket of her jeans and unwrapped it, jamming it into her mouth. She was not going to let herself get sick on this damn ferry. No way.

She looked around at the other passengers, some who sat silently, others involved in conversation, and many played on their phones. There was a woman and two boys toward the front, one of them fast asleep leaning into her arm. The other's nose was stuck in a handheld video game. Brittany wondered why they were headed to Swift Island. Why was anyone on this ferry headed there? What was so special about this island? The limited knowledge she'd been able to acquire from her research about the island was that it had become a summer haven for the LGBTQ+ population. That was about the only thing she was looking forward to. Otherwise, it seemed like any other East Coast fishing town. That was the other thing she was excited about. Fresh seafood. She could get it any time in San Francisco but rarely did. So she was going to take advantage of it now.

The first thing she planned on doing was find a place to get a drink, a lobster roll, and French fries. She'd decided when she boarded the plane back in San Francisco to have at least one thing to look forward to every day while she was on the island. Not only was this trip a chance for her to figure out what the fuck was going on with the damn visions, but it was also a time for her to get back on her feet and stand tall again. She needed the time alone to figure herself out.

And maybe she'd be able to decide how to get past everything that had happened in her life.

Her accident.

A career that was wonderful but stalled.

And a love life that wasn't just stalled—it didn't even have a battery.

The trip to Swift Island wasn't only about discovering the source of the visions. She knew it had to be about more than that if she was going to do something so impulsive, and yes, crazy. This trip had to be about her, too, and she vowed to make sure Swift Island would jump-start the person she wanted to be.

And, maybe, heal her stupid spirit.

Brittany's eyes widened as she saw the island appear out of the clouds in the distance. She pulled in a deep breath and held it for one count, two, three before she pushed it out slowly. *This is it. This right here starts the rest of your life, Brittany. Let's do this.*

Swift Island was just as picturesque as the photos Brittany had seen online. She understood the appeal the instant she disembarked from the ferry. The sea air was crisp, even in late summer. The sky was a blue she'd only seen a few times in her life. A California blue sky was something to behold, yes, but the blue above Swift Island seemed almost dreamlike, as if it was its own color in a box of Crayola crayons.

After renting a scooter and checking into her small rental unit that was a lot closer to the water than she'd realized, she took to the streets in search of a much-needed drink. And the food. *Can't forget about the food.*

She bounded up onto the uneven sidewalk as she headed down the main drag, Swift Street, which was littered with a variety of shops. Typical for an East Coast town, but these stores seemed to have a lot of personality. Bookstores with pride flags waving proudly, souvenir shops with outlandish T-shirts, bait and tackle shops, coffee shops that promised the best cup of coffee the island had to offer, and, of course, old pub after even older pub.

Her mouth watered at the thought of a chilled glass of some lovely dark brew, and Brittany ducked into the first old pub she saw, *Governor Seaman's.* She took one look around at all the old, grizzled men lining the bar top and decided she could wait just a bit longer for that beer. Definitely not the place she wanted to relax into. She left as quickly as she entered and pushed on to the next block. A freshly painted building caught her attention.

The sign above the door read, *The Second Wave.*

"Hmm…" She pressed her hands and face to the glass, hoping for something different than her last short-lived venture. Everything inside looked newer, and the place was bustling—and not just with grizzled old men with beards. She pulled back and checked the sign again.

EST. 2018

The ornate wooden door was propped open, inviting the passers-by in, so she shrugged, said, "Screw it," and walked inside.

Everyone turned and looked at her, which irritated her until she realized she sort of stuck out like a sore thumb. Even in August, she didn't leave home without her leather jacket, and today was far too warm for such attire. She shrugged it off her shoulders and hung it on the back of a barstool before she sat down and made herself comfortable. Well, as comfortable as she could possibly be alone in a different town on a strange, remote island.

As she sat, she took in her surroundings. Rainbow colored lights were strung across the ceiling rafters. In the corner hung a variety of United States flags with pride stripes, instead of the typical red, white, and blue. Other LGBTQ+ flags were dispersed along the opposite corner. The pictures that decorated the rest of the space were all different sizes—black-and-white photos, old-timey colored ones, movie posters professionally framed, including a *9 to 5* poster and *The Big Chill*. The decor was an eclectic mix, but for some reason, it really seemed to work. The place was packed, too. She reached across the bar to the caddy with menus and pulled one out, admiring the logo on the front before she flipped the trifold paper over to the back.

Welcome to the Second Wave

Founded on the inclusive ideals that make Swift Island great, we are ardent about quality craft beer for everyone. With help from local brewmasters, we hope to provide the world with a taste they will never forget. From our excellent beer to our mouth-watering morsels, once you've tasted the wave, we're sure you'll be back for seconds.

Brittany felt herself smiling at the picture of two older women, hand in hand, under the welcome message. They were adorable, and for the first time since being on the island, she felt the weird weight on her chest budge.

"Well, hello there, weary traveler. What can I get for you?"

Brittany jerked her attention to the voice across the bar top, and that weight that had previously budged? Yeah, well, it grew wings and was about to fly away at the sight of the bartender. She was absolutely gorgeous. Long luxurious waves of dark hair with big curls were pulled away from her pale face with a barrette. Her smile, which was breathtaking, reminded Brittany of being a kid again and finally realizing she was a lesbian. That ah-ha moment sprang to life all over again. She opened her mouth to answer the bartender, but all that came out was an, "Uh…" She couldn't stop staring at this woman's sea-green eyes. If the bartender wasn't feeling like a piece of meat, Brittany would be surprised.

The bartender smiled, though, and her eyes twinkled. Then she grabbed a bottle of something and sprayed the spot a couple of spaces to the left of Brittany and started to wipe it down. "We have our three Second Wave brews on tap. But the rest of the menu is a lot of local brews from the mainland. They're bottles and cans. We also have a couple of appetizers. Take your time." And as she leaned to reach the farthest side of the bar top, Brittany let her eyes travel the length of her from the white tank top she was wearing all the way down to the tiny black cutoff shorts.

Brittany blinked quickly three times and said with force, "I'll take the Amber Waves of Ale." She felt so stupid for the way she sort of shouted her order, but dammit, she couldn't seem to get her bearings. She went from feeling completely comfortable to completely baffled in a matter of seconds. All because of a hot girl. *Jesus, get yourself together, Brittany.*

"That's definitely a good one."

The bartender slid a cardboard coaster in front of her, then picked up a pint glass, pushed it onto a water sprayer plate near the tap, and began filling the glass. Brittany's mouth was watering. Of course, she wasn't sure if it was from the excitement about the beer or her teenage boy hormones running rampant. When the bartender set the glass on the coaster, she made eye contact. Once again, she found herself captivated by the color of the woman's eyes. The blue of Swift Island's sky had impressed her earlier, but that color had nothing on the bartender's eyes.

"Are you going to try it? Or just stare at me?"

Whelp. That's embarrassing. "Oh, shit, sorry." Brittany scrambled to grab the beer. When she lifted it to her lips and took the first sip, she knew she'd made the right choice. Hell, the minute she saw this woman standing in front of her, she knew she'd made the right choice. The beer was an added bonus. Being called out about staring, though? She could have lived without that.

❖

"How's it going up there, Toni?"

Toni sighed as she leaned against the countertop in the back of the pub. "The bar top is pretty busy. I was totally getting checked out by a new chick in town."

"Oh?" Leslie walked over to the door to see out to the restaurant. "Is she cute?"

"Aunty," Toni said softly. "I'm so not in the right place to even be thinking about that."

Leslie gasped as she peered through the window of the door. "Honey, is that her?" She looked over her shoulder at Toni. "She's gorgeous."

"Oh my God, seriously?" Toni pushed away from the counter and breezed past her aunt. "Stop. Please?"

"Okay, fine. I'm just saying. It feels nice to be looked at every now and then, doesn't it?"

Toni rolled her eyes. "No." She was lying. It actually felt really good, and her aunt was right, the woman at the bar was beautiful. It wasn't like it'd hurt to let someone else melt her ice-cold heart just a bit. Not a full defrost setting on a microwave, but at least a little thawing.

She pushed past her aunt and went back behind the bar. A few customers needed refills, so she got to work, pouring brew after brew. Her first pour of the day two days ago was the worst pour on record, Alice had said. But now she was borderline expert. No head and a clean pour every time. Except, of course, when she knew someone was watching her. And she felt the weight of that new woman's eyes on her the entire time she was behind the bar.

Being looked at was something Toni had dealt with for most of her life. It didn't bother her most of the time. Heck, it wasn't bothering her at that moment, either. She actually kind of liked it. But liking something that was supposed to make her feel good so quickly after handing her heart over to Penn seemed like the wrong thing to do. *Penn threw your heart right back to you, though, didn't she?*

"Would you like another?" Toni flitted over to her new brunette customer. Her head was down as she feverishly scribbled notes into a spiral notebook. She slapped the notebook closed when she heard Toni, her eyes wide.

"I'm sorry, what?"

Toni smiled at the look of being caught on the woman's face. "Would you like another beer?" She slid a basket of pretzels over. "Name's Toni, by the way."

"Oh," she said softly. "Yeah, I'll take another."

"Do you have a name?" Toni grabbed her glass and placed it into the dishwasher bin before she turned and grabbed another. "Or do I need to keep referring to you as the new brunette customer?" Her full pink lips spread into a smile, and Toni definitely didn't overlook the twinkle in her light brown eyes.

"Brittany," she said and nodded. "Toni, hmm? Antoinette?"

She sighed. "Ugh, yes. Passed on from my great-grandmother. I was super happy to have such a unique name growing up."

Brittany chuckled before she took a drink of her freshly delivered beer. She placed it on the coaster, and Toni watched as she let her fingers slide down the chilled glass.

She glanced back up to Brittany, who was still watching her every move. "What brings you to Swift Island? You a writer or something?" She motioned to the notebook, and Brittany's demeanor instantly changed.

"Oh, yeah, um, no. I mean, yes. I'm a journalist, but I'm just here trying to…" Brittany paused, took a breath, glanced around the bar, and then locked her gaze back on Toni. "Figure things out, I guess."

"Hmm, sounds like there's a story there."

"You could say that." Brittany lifted her chin, pressed her lips together. "Speaking of stories, what's yours?"

"Smooth, very, *very* smooth."

"What?" Brittany's laugh filled the space around them. "I was only making conversation."

"Sure," Toni replied with her own chuckle. She leaned against the bar top, bracing herself against the sturdy wood. "My aunts own this place." She flipped the menu sitting in front of Brittany over and pointed to the picture of Leslie and Alice. "Leslie is my mom's older sister. And Alice is her wife." She smiled, recalling the memory of their love affair—proof that absence and time really do make the heart grow fonder. "I came to stay with them awhile."

"On a whim? Are you a bit of a free spirit?"

"Heartbreak will do that to ya." Toni shrugged after pushing away from the bar top. "And those notes you're scribbling, what are those about?"

"Is this like an eye for an eye or what? You show me yours, and I show you mine?" Brittany's arched eyebrow denoted her point, but before Toni could relent, she smiled and said, "I'm just trying to figure some things out. That's all."

The fact that Brittany was also trying to work things out on this island wasn't lost on Toni. She wasn't surprised, yet she definitely didn't expect that to be Brittany's answer. If anything, she thought Brittany would say she was working on an article or a story or maybe even a book. "It seems like Swift Island is the place to be to figure things out. You've definitely come to the right spot."

"That's good to know."

Toni's attention was pulled to a couple at the end of the bar, so she breezed over to them and took their order. Business was starting to pick up. It must've been getting close to dinner time. After she poured beers and punched in appetizers for the new couple at the bar, she turned to check on Brittany but she was nowhere to be found. Under her empty glass was forty dollars and her business card. On the back of the card she'd written, *Thanks for the company*, in chicken-scratch handwriting. The sentiment was small, almost minuscule, but Toni still found herself smiling at the note.

Chapter Six

May 22nd–Journal Entry 488

Trapped. All of you are trapped in your minds, your expectations, your social contracts. You blame your jobs, your spouses, your family—everyone but yourself. The truth no one wants to admit is that you're a product of your own impotence. You watch the days unfold in rapid succession without any challenge to your thoughts. You yell at your television sets, your podcasts, your politicians, and your activists. You curse your neighbors under your breath for things you lack, things you want. You refuse to take control over your own life because you're terrified of offending, saying the wrong thing, projecting unworthiness.

You point to people like me, and you whisper. You whisper to your friends about our lack of humanity. You sip your wine, share your philosophy about "others." You do this because you're terrified. You fear that one wrong decision, one misstep, one rage-filled evening could turn you into what you've deemed unfit—unhuman. So you watch your documentaries and read your books. You learn what you can about me because you believe knowledge is power. You think if you can understand me, you'll avoid becoming me. The truth, friend, is we're already more alike than you're comfortable admitting.

Oh, I see you. I watch you. I see you disparage the most disadvantaged in your society. You livestream yourself giving money to the homeless. You take pictures of your good deeds and post them on social media, hoping to gain approval—seeking the high of affirmation. But I see you. I see you mock the woman you don't like. I see you pass up the causes that don't fit nicely into what you've decided are worthy. I see you turn a blind eye to the struggles of sex workers, addicts, and the poor. I see you ignore the pleas of those who don't retain your innate privilege. I see you.

I choose people, too. I choose who is unfit. I choose who isn't worthy. I choose.

You think you're safe from me because I'm an outlier. I know you're in danger because I've accepted what I am. There is enormous freedom in that. Freedom that you're unwilling to take. Liberation from one's apathy is a truly beautiful thing.

I arrived on this island intent on finding my target. It didn't take long. I wasn't sure at first if it was her. It was her eyes that gave her away. There are lines around them now. Proof that her body is slowly beginning to abandon her spirit. Much like her selfishness caused my father to abandon me. She made a choice. All choices have repercussions. We all have to pay the Reaper when he comes to collect. I'm here now, and I'm coming for you.

Chapter Seven

Brittany walked the streets of her new temporary home to familiarize herself with her surroundings. People dipped in and out of the stores, excitedly giggling with their companions, while some walked quietly by themselves. She studied their faces, hoping to get an inkling of familiarity. Anything that would nudge her toward the visions that had led her here. When she'd decided to come here, it was because she had an overwhelming sense of impending violence. She wasn't sure who was behind it, or how she could stop it—she just knew it felt imperative.

Now, as she wandered through the streets, she considered again whether it was all in her head. She pinched the bridge of her nose. It was easy to recall the emotions she'd felt consume every nerve in her body. *There's no way that was a hallucination. It was too real.* But if the visions had led her here correctly, what was she supposed to do now?

It wasn't that she expected some large neon sign with an arrow to appear and point her in the right direction. But she had hoped, maybe foolishly, that if she followed her gut, it would lead her somewhere. The breeze coming off the Atlantic was different than back home. It smelled the same, even tasted the same on her lips, but the humidity made it seem heavier, sticky. It felt like putting on a damp T-shirt.

She sat down on a bench near the water to watch the tide change. She wasn't there long before she heard a woman curse loudly behind her.

"God damn it!"

Brittany turned to see an older woman kicking the wheel of a golf cart. "You okay?"

She pointed to a piece of paper on the plastic windshield. "Can you believe they gave me a parking ticket? I have a sign written right here that says it's okay to park." She pointed to a different piece of paper on the other side of the windshield.

Brittany examined the second. "It looks like you wrote that."

"I did, and they still had the nerve to give me a ticket."

Brittany laughed. "I'm not sure that defense will hold up in court."

The woman threw her hands up. "It should." She looked up and down the street. "I bet it was George. He's always been my least favorite. It's not like he doesn't know where to find me if it needed to be moved. Patrols this place like it's the streets of Boston."

Brittany couldn't pinpoint if it was her antics or the way she smiled, but she instantly liked this woman. "I'm Brittany, by the way. It's nice to meet you."

"Oh, I'm already aware of the new girl in town. I saw you at my pub, the Second Wave. It's nice to meet you officially. I'm Alice." She shook Brittany's hand.

"I thought you looked familiar." Brittany shook her finger at her. "You're on the menu."

Alice wiggled her eyebrows. "I may be a little too old for you."

"Oh, I didn't mean—"

"I knew what you meant, sweetie. Just let me have this." Alice winked at her. "I saw you sitting at the bar a little while ago. It looked like you even made a friend."

Brittany thought back to Toni, who'd immediately thrown her off her game. "I'm not sure what she thought of me. It was nice to talk to her though."

Alice pointed toward the bar. "Toni is as sweet as they come."

"I'll have to keep that in mind. Thanks."

Alice stepped closer and seemed to inspect Brittany's biceps, squeezing one of them. "Those things work on power tools?"

"I've been known to knock down a few walls in my time."

"Perfect." Alice pulled a pen from her pocket, plucked the parking ticket from her windshield, and scribbled on the back. "Be at our house on Saturday morning at eight. We have a few things we could really use help fixing. I'll feed you, water you, and give you free drinks at the pub. Deal?"

Brittany nodded as she received the ticket, overwhelmed by Alice's boisterous spirit. Had she just been steamrolled into helping with a home improvement project? She thought of declining but changed her mind. Maybe it would be beneficial to her search to get to know some of the locals. "I'll be there."

Alice flashed her the "okay" hand signal. "See you Saturday."

"Wait," she shouted as Alice pulled into the street. "Don't you need this ticket?"

"What ticket?" Alice smirked and drove off.

Brittany stood there for a moment in awe watching the golf cart chug off down the street. Alice was a character, all right, and one Brittany was happy to have encountered.

She headed back toward her small rental, feeling she'd undoubtedly made the right decision in coming here. She needed to be around people who didn't know about her or her accident. She wanted to find herself again, and the best place to do that was somewhere she wasn't known. No one to question her behavior, or worse, relentlessly check if she was okay. She could just be Brittany until she could figure out exactly who that was now.

"I'm sorry. Can you repeat that? I thought I just heard you say that you invited Brittany over to the house, and she'll be here in an hour." Toni tilted her head, hoping she was having an aneurysm that was jumbling words in her head.

Alice scooped the eggs out of the frying pan and into a bowl. "I'm being friendly to the new person in town. It's good for business."

Leslie sat at the table and sipped her coffee. "And you want to replace the front window."

Alice put the rest of the food on the kitchen table. "And I want to replace the front window."

Toni grabbed the plates and followed. "Are you trying to set me up? I feel like you're trying to set me up."

Leslie rubbed Toni's arm. "We'd never meddle, dear." She winked at Alice. "We need work done here, and Alice found someone to do it."

Toni sighed and let her head fall back. "You two realize I can see you. You're sitting right in front of me."

"You don't have to talk to her. You can stay hidden, tucked away—afraid to ever love again," Leslie said between bites of eggs.

Toni rolled her eyes. "Subtle."

Alice looked down at her watch. "Gosh, it looks like she'll be here in forty-five minutes. All that time to come up with a reason to leave—or shower."

Leslie shrugged. "Or go for a run. The options are endless."

Toni stood, pushing the chair back with more force than intended. "You two are criminal." She walked toward the stairs. "I'm going to shower," she said begrudgingly, hearing them laughing as she headed to the bathroom.

Toni looked at her closet and the limited selection of clothes she'd brought with her. *What says I'm happy to see you but may have other plans?* She pulled the towel off her head and tried on several different shirts. She was looking for aloof, yet friendly. *Wonder Woman it is.* She pulled the shirt on and stood in front of the mirror. The T-shirt was snug around her breasts but not tight around her waist. The sleeves were cut to show her arms but not scream that she needed attention.

"You should definitely wear pants," Alice said from the doorway.

"No, really?" Toni said. "Maybe you'll get a discount on labor if I don't."

Alice chuckled. "For someone who was mad that Brittany's coming over, that's a lot of shirts to sift through." She pointed. "But I insist on the pants."

Toni groaned. "You're enjoying this way too much. I'm not ready for this."

Alice tilted her head. "We're never ready."

Toni heard the door knock and Leslie welcome Brittany into the house. She looked over at Alice who was smiling broadly.

Toni pulled on pants while quietly cussing her aunts out under her breath. She didn't even understand why she was nervous. There was nothing to be nervous about. *Probably because Brittany's insanely beautiful and probably emotionally unavailable—which means you'll want her even more.*

She stood at the top of the stairs, watching Brittany talk to her aunts as they explained how they wanted the window. *Damn, she's just as stunning as I remember.* Brittany wore a tight black tank top that accentuated her well-defined arms. Her jean shorts were tight, hugging her hips and ass perfectly. Toni's mouth went dry. It was one thing to banter with a customer at your bar top. That was her world, her zone. She had control. It was quite another to have them in your home—especially a home where two of your favorite people were fawning all over her. She decided the only way out was straight through.

"Hi," Toni said as she came down the stairs. "What did they promise to get you here?" Toni took a step closer. She felt compelled to be closer.

"I'd like to say I did it out of the goodness in my heart, but it was the free beer."

Damn if this woman didn't have the most incredible smile.

Brittany held their eye contact longer than what she was used to experiencing. Typically, something like that would freak her out, and she'd be planning her escape. But that's not what she felt at all. Brittany's eyes were kind, soft, but there were secrets there. Secrets Toni suddenly wanted to discover.

A loud plop pulled Toni out of her reverie. She looked over to see Alice pointing to a large tool bag. "I think I have everything you could need here."

Brittany chuckled and rubbed the back of her neck. Perhaps she'd been caught up in the moment along with Toni. Toni couldn't decide if that was what she was hoping for or not.

"Guess I'll get started then." Brittany turned toward the bag.

"Okay. Let me know when you need my help." Toni pointed to the kitchen. "I'll just be over here." She turned to leave. "Even if it's just water. I can bring water. Lots of serving skills. You need water, and I'm your gal."

Toni walked into the kitchen, hoping Brittany didn't notice how red she'd turned. *What the hell.*

Leslie shook her head. "That was very…"

Toni flopped down onto the chair. "I know."

Leslie sat down and patted her leg. "It could have been worse."

Toni put her face in her hands. "I don't see how."

"Well, you didn't throw up on her."

Toni let her forehead rest on the table. "That's the bar? Not vomiting on someone?"

"Apparently."

Chapter Eight

Brittany watched Toni disappear into the kitchen. She had no idea she would be seeing her this morning and wondered how much of that was by design. Toni was just as lovely as she'd been a few nights before, but she seemed different somehow. It felt like there was more to the story.

"So, you didn't tell me Toni would be here." Brittany glanced over at Alice, who was pulling tools from the bag and laying them out on the table.

"Didn't I mention that?" Alice ran her hand through her hair. "Silly me. I just get so forgetful sometimes."

"Uh-huh. I don't buy that for one second."

Alice grinned and shrugged with one shoulder. "The details are a little fuzzy."

Brittany decided to let her off the hook and not push for more. They were clearly trying to play matchmaker, and she wasn't sure how she felt about it. Brittany from a year ago would've welcomed the prospect. Past Brittany was free from nightmares, not sleeping in her ex's spare room, and full of hopes and dreams. Current Brittany, the Brittany Alice was trying to set her niece up with, was much more of a mess. She was undoubtedly attracted to Toni, but that wasn't all that mattered. She didn't feel as if she had much to offer anyone—even herself

Toni was beautiful, yes. Her big curls and wild eyes were captivating. She seemed witty, fun, and probably a bit spontaneous. She also sensed a bit of pain bubbling beneath the facade. Brittany sensed her interest, veiled with apprehension. If she came on too strong, she could spook Toni and scare her off for good. All of that bumping around in her head, on top of her own issues—Brittany needed to stay clear.

"So, where are you from?" Alice leaned against the wall near the window.

"San Francisco. Well, originally from a small town in the East Bay, but I live in San Francisco now." Brittany inspected the window trim and picked up the pry bar from the table.

"I love San Francisco. It's a beautiful city. Haven't been there in ages, but I'd love to go visit." Alice tapped the window trim, indicating where to start. "You single?"

Brittany felt herself blush as she slid the bar between the trim and the wall. "You don't beat around the bush, do you?"

"I'm old. I don't have time for all that."

"I am single, and before you ask, yes, I date women."

"I already knew that. I saw the way you looked at my niece. I said I was old, not blind."

Brittany carefully removed the trim from the wall and placed the wood on the ground. "Touché."

"So, what brings you to Swift Island?"

Leslie walked into the room with Toni on her heels. "Stop interrogating her."

Alice grinned. "What would you like us to talk about, politics?"

Leslie took her by the arm. "Good Lord, no. Unless you voted for a man in the 2016 election?"

Brittany pried the next piece of wood from the wall. "I did not."

Leslie led Alice toward the kitchen. "Good enough for me."

After they were gone, Toni came in and handed Brittany a glass of water. "Sorry. They're actually very sweet when they're not auditioning women for the lesbian *Bachelorette*."

Brittany finished the last two pieces of trim. "I have no doubt." She pointed to the front yard. "Do you want to help me get the siding down so we can pop this window out?"

"Sure. I'd be happy to get away from prying ears." She raised her voice at the end of the statement, probably to make sure her aunts could hear.

Once they were outside, Brittany made quick work of the siding around the window. She could feel Toni's eyes on her, examining. "I'm actually glad I got to run into you."

Toni slid her hands into the back pockets of her jeans and smiled. "Yeah? Why's that?"

"I was going to do that bike trail and thought it might be more fun to go with someone." Brittany shrugged. "It would be even more fun if that person was you."

Toni bit her bottom lip. "I don't work tomorrow. We have a few bikes in the garage we can use instead of renting." She pointed to Brittany's pocket. "I'll give you my number. Text me around ten and I'll let you know where to meet me." She punched her numbers into the phone Brittany handed her.

"It's a date." Brittany wished she could take the words back when she saw the terrified look on Toni's face. "A date like a decided upon engagement that we will both attend. Together. But not necessarily together, together. Just together." She took the phone back and slipped it back into her pocket, thankful she had something to do with her hands.

Toni laughed and put her hand on Brittany's forearm. "I get it. I also understand things like time and schedules."

Brittany liked the way Toni's hand felt on her. Then came the overwhelming feeling that was becoming all too familiar. She was going to have a vision. *Jesus, not in front of her. Maybe I can hold this one off a little longer. Or not.*

"I have to go. Tell your aunt I'll be back tomorrow. I'm sorry. I forgot I had another thing." Brittany dropped her tools and made it around the corner before it started.

She placed her hand against the first building she could reach. This vision was different. She was more familiar with her surroundings. Instead of feeling an overwhelming sense of doom, she felt almost eager to try to pinpoint the source. Her stomach turned. The same vile hatred she'd felt before surged through her body. The street she recognized this time. Whatever she was seeing, or whomever she was seeing through was looking up at a sign, *The Second Wave*. She felt the heartbeat thunder in her head—the sound of blood pumping in her ears. There was more agitation growing, more anger. Brittany had never experienced so much darkness. A darkness that seemed rooted in a place so deep in the psyche, it could never be reached.

She tried to force her sight to the window in front of the pub. She desperately needed to see the source of the darkness. She willed the person to move, to take a step. She was so close, the glare from the window was shining in her eyes, but she couldn't force forward motion. The hatred was still there, but the person was in control, and they seemed focused. Brittany was still attached enough to her own senses to understand someone was in danger. But who? What was this thing or this person searching for? It ended then, with no warning, no easy exit. It was just over.

Brittany slid down the side of the wall. She wanted to run to the pub, to see if she could catch a glimpse of something to give her a clue as to what she'd just seen. But no matter how much she willed her legs to work, she couldn't move. She felt depleted. Her body and soul were exhausted as if something had sucked everything out of her. The same doubts she'd had since San Francisco slid to the forefront of her mind.

What if they aren't real? What if I'm losing my mind?

Could that be what was happening? Had the accident knocked something loose? She didn't think so, but there was no way to be sure. Whatever the truth was, Brittany had to get to the bottom of it. She had to get answers. Somehow, her soul depended on it.

"What do you mean she left?"

Toni blinked at her aunt. "I'm not sure how else to say that."

Leslie tilted her head. "Normally, I would appreciate your sarcasm, but in this instance, I'm actually worried. Was she okay?"

Toni crossed her arms. "Honestly, I'm not sure. She got really pale and looked almost like she fell into a daze. It was a little weird." She shrugged off what felt like concern. "Look. The last thing I need is to get involved with another unstable, emotionally unavailable, crazy person."

Leslie rubbed Toni's shoulder. "What if it was a medical issue? Give her a chance to explain. She seems very nice."

Toni huffed. "You know who else *seemed* nice? Penn. Penn seemed nice. You know who wasn't nice? Same person."

Leslie sighed. "You can't hold everyone you encounter responsible for everything bad someone else did to you. Everyone has their own story."

Toni threw her hands up and headed toward the stairs. "You two are supposed to be on my side."

"We are," they called out in unison.

Toni flopped down on her bed and stared at the ceiling until she relaxed. Maybe she should give Brittany the benefit of the doubt. Maybe she was being irrational. Maybe she was holding Brittany responsible for the sins of another. *Or maybe you should end this before it starts.* But even as she thought it, she knew she wouldn't. She felt a pull to Brittany, a draw to her that she couldn't quite put her finger on, and that was enough to let her explain. She could, at the very least, allow her that.

Then there was that way Brittany smiled at her. She had a way of looking at her and making her feel as if her attention was solely focused on her. *Until it isn't, and she takes off running.* Toni put her pillow over her face. *What are you doing?*

Leslie stepped into the doorway. "It's just a bike ride."

"We'll see if you're still saying that when I don't come home tomorrow because she turns out to be a crazy person."

Leslie chuckled. "You have so much of your mother in you."

"You mean my good looks and witty banter?"

"No, I mean your sarcastic comments and your cynicism." She sat down next to her on the bed. "Listen, if you really don't want to go, don't. I don't want you to do anything you aren't comfortable doing."

Toni sat up and put her head on her shoulder. "It's not that. I barely know her, and I'm comfortable around her. I feel like I could actually really like her." She flopped back down again. "That is what scares me."

Leslie patted her leg. "Listen kiddo, coming from someone who has decades' worth of 'should-haves,' take the chance. You miss a hundred percent of the shots you don't take."

Toni groaned. "Are you seriously quoting Michael Jordan to me?"

"Alice always says, 'Jordan's the greatest. Don't listen to the LeBron hype.'" Leslie walked out of the room.

Toni listened as Leslie padded down the stairs. The last thing she wanted was to spend a lifetime wondering "what if." Now, she just had to decide if she could manage another potential heartbreak. She wasn't sure she could survive another. Did Brittany have the potential to be the next big letdown? Brittany with her cocky smile, incredible arms, and smooth talk. Yes, she did.

CHAPTER NINE

The morning of the bike ride Leslie had cajoled Toni into coming into the pub to help with food prep for the lunch crowd. It wasn't that she and Alice needed the help. She just couldn't bear the thought of leaving Toni to wear a path in their wood floors contemplating all the reasons why this outing with Brittany was a terrible idea. Yet it was plainly obvious Toni had some sort of thing for her. Leslie couldn't blame her.

When Leslie first saw her tanned face and brown ponytail as she stood beside Alice in their living room, it was almost as though they were side-by-side versions of past and present Alice. Although she was gorgeous now as a soft butch with her short, salt-and-pepper hair, Leslie vividly remembered how struck she was by Alice's youthful beauty when they'd met in the 1970s. Same style brown hair, flawless skin, and feminist swagger as Brittany. She would've felt like a defective aunt if she failed to convince Toni to at least see where it led.

As if on cue, Toni emerged from the kitchen and joined Leslie behind the bar.

"Are you sure you don't need me for the lunch rush?" Toni asked.

"I'm sure, honey." Leslie brushed a stray strand of hair off Toni's forehead. "Go and have fun on your bike ride, and if she's not a complete head case, come back here for something to eat."

Toni chuckled. "Okay. I still have some time, so I'll hang out here." She poured herself a cup of ice water and leaned against the beer cooler.

"Perfect. I have to run to the ladies' room, and Quinn is supposed to arrive with our weekly delivery any minute. Would you mind?"

"Of course not," Toni said.

❖

No sooner did Leslie pass through the two-way door to the stockroom, a van pulled up near the side delivery entrance. Toni walked over and opened the door. "Hi. You must be Quinn."

"That I am," she replied. She hiked up her cargo shorts before rolling three small beer kegs onto a hand truck.

"Can I help you with that?"

"No, no. I got it." She rolled the hand truck down the small ramp and pushed it through the open door. "The usual?" she asked once inside.

"I guess…but I don't really know what the usual is."

Quinn finally looked up at her and smiled. But it was a weird one that was like an instantaneous combination of *Hey, now* followed up by *Oh, shit. That was so obvious.*

Toni recognized it because she'd been the recipient of it before in her single days before Penn. Ugh, Penn. But once Toni had fallen for her, she'd stopped noticing flirtation from other people. From then on it had been all about Penn, for a while anyway.

"The ladies usually have me install them," Quinn said. "Or is that your gig now?"

"Me? No. My aunts are fine with me serving the beers, but I don't think they'd want me finagling around with that stuff."

"Your aunts?"

Toni nodded. "I'm Leslie Burton's niece, Toni. I actually just arrived here a few days ago."

"Oh. How nice," she said as she flapped her T-shirt against the heat. "A little mid-summer vacation?"

"Actually, it's a little more than a vacation. I'm staying with them till the end of the season, so you'll be seeing me around here."

"That's great. Welcome to the island," Quinn said. Her glance lingered uncomfortably on Toni, then her eyes dropped to Toni's cleavage for a second. This woman was sort of cute in a nerdy way, but definitely not her cup of tea.

As if sent from heaven, Brittany walked in and waved from the entrance. "Ready to get your pedal on, or are you still on the clock?"

"Oh, no," Toni called across the bar. "I'm definitely ready."

She flashed Quinn a polite smile and extricated herself from the situation. After hurrying through an obstacle course of tables and chairs, she leapt over the three steps up and landed eye to eye with Brittany.

"You must really like bike riding," Brittany said.

Toni smiled, not wanting to share the details of her exchange with the flirty delivery woman. "Let me just say you're timing is impeccable."

"It's always nice to be greeted with a compliment," Brittany said. "Thanks."

They headed off on the mile or so walk back to Alice and Leslie's house to get the mountain bikes. Toni again marveled at how easy Brittany was to talk to and how relaxed she felt in her presence. Usually a jumble of nerves about everything, Toni responded to the good vibe she gave off. "So you're feeling okay for a bike ride?" Toni asked.

Brittany seemed perplexed. "Why wouldn't I be?"

"Yesterday, when you left so abruptly. I didn't know if you were sick or something."

"Oh, that." Brittany shrugged it off as though it was nothing. "I just get these headaches sometimes. It's nothing. I think maybe the heat got to me."

That was totally plausible. She'd clearly jumped to conclusions thinking Brittany was some sort of freak, and it made her smile. "It's hard to stay hydrated on these humid August days. We'll pack extra water for our excursion."

"I'm glad I didn't have to cancel," Brittany said.

"Me too," Toni replied.

❖

About an hour into their ride, they'd made it to the exact opposite side of the island to a scenic bluff overlooking the rocky shore. A smattering of small pines danced in the ocean wind, sheltering them from the full rays of the early afternoon sun. "This seems like a great place for a break," Brittany said. "What do you think?"

Toni agreed, and they sat on an outcropping of rocks and broke open fresh bottles of water from their bike bags.

"If I had known this spot would be so perfect, I would've suggested a picnic lunch and a bottle of wine," Brittany said.

"If I had known, I would've definitely agreed," Toni said.

"That's right. I forgot you only got here a few days before me." Brittany chugged from her water bottle. "This whole experience feels surreal when I stop and think about it."

"In what way?" Toni asked.

Brittany exhaled wondering how far in she should allow Toni. Psychic visions? Unexplained feelings of déjà vu even though she knew she'd never been to these places before? She'd better stick to the basics. "What I meant was it's so strange that I ended up here and am now having this wonderful moment of Zen. I was in a motorcycle accident and experienced a traumatic brain injury. Needless to say, my recovery has felt like an uphill battle."

"Wow. I'm so sorry," Toni said. "I never would've guessed—"

"That's the miracle part." Brittany turned her gaze out over the ocean. "I've managed to make an almost full recovery. But the old dome took a solid hit, so I still have some minor issues that may or may not be permanent."

"Like the headache the other day?"

Brittany paused, weighing whether or not she should just leave it at headaches for now. "Yeah, the headache." Maybe on the next bike ride.

Toni reached over and clutched her hand. "Well, if you get another one with me, don't be shy about saying something. I'll do whatever I can to help."

Brittany's spirit rose. Toni was so empathetic. Maybe that's why she felt this inexplicable connection to her. "I appreciate that."

"Are you getting hungry?" Toni asked.

"Very. That granola bar earlier didn't cut it."

"Aunt Leslie insisted we stop off at the pub for a late lunch. Think you can make it back to town or do you want to hit the Clam Shack on the way back?"

"I think lunch with all of you would be the perfect finish to this scenic bike tour."

Toni sprang up first and offered her hand to Brittany. She almost pulled her hand back when she realized how natural it had felt to take it. Almost.

After mounting their bikes, Brittany fell behind to let Toni lead the way back. She enjoyed watching Toni's calf muscles work as they pedaled along. Her shoulders looked so sexy as they glistened in the sun. She began to feel immensely grateful for the visions that had drawn her to the island. And to Toni.

"We're back," Toni said as she and Brittany slipped into the pub's small kitchen.

"Hey, you two," Alice said as she plated two orders of paninis.

"Did you have a nice bike ride?" Leslie asked as she piled mixed greens on the plate beside the sandwiches.

"Yes, and we're starving," Toni said. "Can you guys join us?"

Leslie looked at Alice, then Alice looked at David, the college student who did most of the cooking for them.

"What do you say, David?" Alice said. "Can you hold down the fort?"

He quickly shoved his phone in his shorts pocket. "No prob."

"No prob," Alice grumbled as the four of them took a table in the tasting room.

"How are you feeling?" Leslie asked Brittany.

"Oh, much better. Thank you. Sweet of you to ask."

"And it's not just because we need you to help finish the project at the house." Alice winked at Brittany.

"Oh, stop, honey," Leslie said. "You know we can hire David to help you finish if you're that impatient."

Alice grabbed Leslie's hand and laced their fingers together as if it were second nature. "You know I'm just teasing her."

Toni swooned. "You guys are so stinkin' cute. I can't stand it." She continued to stare at them trying to recall if she'd ever felt the bond with Penn or anyone else that Leslie and Alice clearly had.

"I agree," Brittany said. "You're making me wonder if I've ever truly experienced love before."

Toni whipped her head toward Brittany. "Right? If you knew their history, you'd probably say you haven't."

A blush fell over Leslie's face as Alice gazed at her. "I've learned the true meaning of soul mates, thanks to Leslie. We lived separate lives for most of our lives, but I can definitely attest to the old adage, 'the longer the wait, the sweeter the reward.'"

Brittany stared at Alice and Leslie in awe. If she'd first met them at a grocery store, they would've appeared to be two cute older ladies who wouldn't have left more than a second's worth of impression on her. But after observing them together for a little while, the chemistry they shared clearly told a different story.

"So are you guys going to share this mysterious history Toni's been telling me about or just keep me hanging?" Brittany said after the server took their orders.

"Oh, we wouldn't want to bore you kids with that." Leslie blinked shyly and cast her eyes down.

"Trust me," Toni said. "There is nothing boring about their story."

"Thank you, Toni," Alice said. "Leslie's entirely too modest. It all began in the mid-seventies during the height of the women's lib movement."

"And when the LGBTQ rights movement was still in its infancy," Leslie added.

"We were work friends," Alice said. "Both living as straight women at the time, and soon we became after-work friends when I invited her to a crochet group I had with a bunch of my feminist friends."

Leslie chuckled as she reminisced. "It was more like wine, grass, and brainstorming ways to smash the patriarchy—much to my initial surprise."

Alice's eyes lit up as she and Leslie regaled them. "She was so straitlaced at first, I was afraid the other girls were gonna accuse her of being a spy for Phyllis Schlafly."

"Ugh. That witch," Brittany said.

"Did you watch *Mrs. America*?" Toni asked Brittany excitedly.

"Yes," Brittany replied, not even trying to conceal her disgust.

"We did, too," Leslie said. "And we threw things at the TV during every episode."

"Anyway," Alice said. "Our connection was instant. And then one thing led to another, and we found ourselves madly in love."

"Phew." Brittany downed a hearty sip of her beer. "I fell for a straight woman once, too, but she stayed straight even after a couple of months of screaming out my name in hotel rooms."

Toni looked as though she were about to spray her sip of beer across the table. "That also sounds like a story I'd like to hear."

"Definitely one for another time," Brittany replied with a smirk and returned her attention to Leslie and Alice. "So then what?"

"I made a choice that I'd live to regret for the next forty years," Leslie said.

Toni seemed to wince at her aunt's sad recollection. Brittany felt the air change as a pall fell over their light conversation.

Alice threw an arm around Leslie's shoulder. "You had to because of the lack of LGBTQ legal protections back then." She looked at Brittany and Toni as if to validate Leslie's decision. "Her kids were young, and she was afraid Bill would take them from her if she left him."

"That's so sad," Brittany said. She then felt a rumble of pain shoot through her head. *Oh, no. Not now.* Not in the middle of this amazing, heart-wrenching story.

"By the time, I was ready to leave him, it was too late. Alice had moved from Connecticut to Boston and had fallen in love with someone else. It was then I'd realized I'd already asked enough of her."

As Brittany rubbed her forehead against the throb of pain, she casually noticed that Toni's eyes were all teared up. "Jeez, I didn't mean to bring down the room."

"Toni, are you crying again?" Alice playfully poked her arm.

"No," Toni said with a quick swipe under each eye.

Leslie reached across and took Toni's hand. "My niece is an incredibly sensitive woman."

"You don't say," Brittany replied.

"It's easy to get swept up in the tragic part, but I absolutely love how it all turned out," Toni said. "To me, it's just…magical."

"To me, too," Alice said.

Brittany heard the words, but another sharp pain rocketed through her brain, and she couldn't suppress a moan of discomfort.

"Brittany, are you okay?" Toni asked. "Is it another headache?"

"Yeah. Can you excuse me for a moment? I'm gonna splash my face with cold water." She jumped up from the table and headed to the bathroom. "Come on, Britt, you can fight this," she muttered to herself as she ran her hands under the faucet.

As the cold water hit her face, she experienced bright flashes behind her eyes. Dark images appeared, like film negatives of various places she'd just seen on the bike tour with Toni. Then the silhouette of a person. She tried to focus her mind's eye against the ache to see if she could make out any features of the person. But all she was able to decipher was that the figure's back was to her.

A knock on the door. "Brittany? Do you need any help?" Toni asked.

"No, no. I'm fine. Be out in a minute." With one last splash of cold water, she opened her eyes, and the severity of her headache began abating. What the hell was happening to her? And what was this island trying to tell her?

She shrugged off a slight bout of nausea from the migraine-like headache and took a few breaths to calm down. Once she felt stable, she opened the door and jumped at Toni standing like a security guard outside the door.

"All yours," she said as she held the door.

"Oh, I don't have to go. I was waiting for you."

"Why?" Brittany was puzzled as they headed back to the table.

Toni rolled her eyes. "To make sure you weren't going to black out and smack your head on the sink or something."

"Well, that's graphic."

"Fine," Toni said in a huff. "Next time I'll let you pass out on the bathroom floor."

Brittany couldn't help laughing as she grabbed Toni's arm. "Hey, I was just kidding. I think it's sweet that you did that."

"You do?"

Brittany was about to reply, but the warmth in Toni's eyes momentarily mesmerized her. After a nod, they headed back to Leslie and Alice.

The afternoon had vanished into dusk by the time they were through eating, drinking, and swapping stories. They walked out together, but Alice and Leslie went one way, and Toni followed Brittany over to her scooter.

"I had a great day," Toni said. "Thanks for inviting me on the ride."

"Thanks for accepting. After spending the afternoon with your aunts, I can officially say that all of your boasting about how amazingly cool they are is one hundred percent accurate."

"So, you'll never doubt my word again?" Toni flashed what Brittany could only interpret as a full-on flirty smile.

"I will not," Brittany said. She suddenly felt awkward around Toni after being with her most of day, which was curious. "But I gotta say, if you use your aunts as a benchmark for relationships, you have a tough act to follow."

Toni raised her hands playfully. "Tell me something I don't know."

"It's good to keep the standards high no matter what you do." Brittany fastened her helmet strap under her chin and turned on the quiet motor of her scooter. "Need a lift back?"

Toni furrowed her brows. "I don't know. Is it wise to take a ride on the scooter of a woman who admitted she's brain-injured from crashing her motorcycle?"

"Oh…what a burn!" Brittany let herself laugh, half at Toni's wit and half at her audacity to go there.

For her part, Toni looked mortified. "I didn't mean for it to come out like that. Honest."

After a few embarrassed chuckles, Toni accepted the ride back to her aunts' house.

As she drove, Brittany loved how Toni's arms felt wrapped around her waist. She thought it was a positive step. It would take more than a scooter ride to feel like herself again, but for the first time since she could remember, she felt really good.

Chapter Ten

Toni leaned back in the Adirondack chair on the front porch of her aunts' home, glad Brittany had accepted her invitation to share a bottle of wine. And glad she'd had the nerve to ask her. She eyed Brittany over the top of her glass of sauvignon blanc and tried to decipher how her subconscious had allowed her to do so. One minute, she was completely against meeting anyone because of the constant ache of her broken heart and the next...

The next, she was finding herself sinking deeper and deeper into light brown eyes and smooth tanned skin and *God, the most magnetic smile...*

Brittany sighed as she raised her wine glass to the sky. "Here's to you, Amy Winehouse."

"I'm actually floored you like her," Toni said. "I swear no one I knew back home liked her. They were all into godawful country music. Blech."

"Where is it you hail from, exactly? I've been trying to pinpoint your accent, and I can't quite put my finger on it." The small flickering fire they'd managed to build in the chiminea, and the dusk light seemed to make Brittany's eyes sparkle. The breezy air coming off the Atlantic had just enough of a chill to make them both shiver.

Toni swirled her wine, watching as it tornadoed inside the glass. "A small town in Colorado where the cattle outnumber the people." She glanced at Brittany. "My mom and dad moved there to help his mom run the town's general store. I had the lovely job of being the cashier. Sounds super glamorous, doesn't it?"

"We've all had jobs that didn't thrill us."

"Yeah, well, my life has been one long string of not knowing who the fuck I am." Toni swallowed. *Jesus, Toni, get your shit together.* "I am so sorry. I think the wine has gone to my head. I didn't mean to say that like that."

"Like what?" Brittany smiled, raised her glass to indicate a toast, and shrugged. "You're not the only person on this porch who struggles with who they are deep down."

Toni laughed. "I should feel comforted by this?"

"Absolutely."

She raised her glass and they clinked theirs together softly. "To hot messes."

"To hot messes, indeed. Long may they waver." Brittany drank and Toni couldn't seem to pull her gaze from the way Brittany's lips pressed against the glass, the way her throat moved as she swallowed, the glisten of wine on her lips when she pulled the glass away.

She fought against the impending lump in her throat as she forced herself to look away. She stared at the Edison lights strung from one side of the porch to the other. At the shiplap ceiling of the porch. At the red-hot wood in the fireplace. At anything to distract her from imagining how it'd feel to be that glass in Brittany's fingers, against her lips, surrounding her tongue.

"Are you…"

Toni snapped to attention. "Am I what?"

"Are you seeing anyone at the moment?"

She let out a single, "Ha!"

"Is that funny?"

"Oh, Brittany, it's hysterical."

Brittany smiled as she adjusted her seated position in the Adirondack chair opposite Toni and took another sip of her wine.

Full lips. Full wet lips. Full wet pink lips. God.

"Is there a story there?"

Toni nodded. "Isn't there always?"

"Can't argue with you there." Brittany took another drink, emptying her glass. She reached over and grabbed the bottle from the marble wine cooler and poured herself more. She motioned to Toni who couldn't help but nod for more. "You want to tell me about it?"

No. "Sort of."

"What's stopping you?"

I'll sound weak. "It's boring."

"I doubt that."

I'll sound pathetic. "How much time do you have?"

Brittany picked the wine up again and held it up to the light. "I have a half a bottle of time." She chuckled as she set it down, then sipped her wine again, her gaze never wavering.

"Well…" She set the glass on the arm of the chair and held it steady with the stem between her index and middle finger. She was having an even harder time focusing after a bottle and a half of wine and Brittany's light brown eyes rummaging through her soul. "I was originally interested in guys."

Brittany chuckled. "That doesn't surprise me."

"What? Why?"

"No reason." Brittany had a smirk on her face she tried to hide behind another sip.

"Mm-hmm." Toni smiled and shook her head before she continued with, "Last summer, I was helping this local rancher, who also happens to be my very dear friend, Elena, during herding season. And there was Penn, in all her cowgirl glory, fresh off the heartbreak train."

"She was heartbroken when you met her?"

"Yeah, she was actually dating Elena first."

"Oh, Jesus."

"I know. Right?" Toni sighed.

"So?"

"When the season was over and things settled down between Elena and her new girlfriend, Julia, Penn decided she was leaving. She came to the store, asked me if I wanted to escape that one-horse town with her, and I didn't even think twice about it. I left in the middle of my shift." Toni laughed when Brittany's eyes widened. "I've always been a little bit of a wild child."

"Hell, I guess so."

"But my mom was super okay with me spreading my wings. She never wanted me to be stuck in that town."

"What happened between you and this Penn woman? And, by the way, what kind of a name is Penn?" Brittany grabbed a few more small pieces of wood and laid them gently into the chiminea as she squatted before the fire, waiting until the wood caught.

"Penelope." Toni shook her head, remembering how much she'd hated her real name. "We had a whirlwind romance, she proposed to me, and of course, I said yes, and then two weeks later, she left me in the middle of the night when we were at a hotel near Great Falls, Montana."

"Wait." Brittany glanced over her shoulder, braced herself on the chair with her left hand, and scrunched her face. "You were engaged? And she just fucking left you there?"

"Yep."

"With no explanation."

"Yep."

"And no ride?"

"Yep." Toni smiled. "And no money, either."

"Holy shit." Brittany made her way back to the chair. She propped her feet on the wooden ottoman. "I'm so sorry. No one deserves that kind of breakup."

"Tell me about it." Toni laughed mirthlessly. "I had no interest in staying there either. I wasn't going to be the new, heartbroken, gay girl in town."

"Oh, how I understand that." Brittany laughed. "When I rolled into the pub, every person in there stared at me like I was—"

"Like you were hot." Toni realized what she said a full beat after she said it and immediately, her hand shot in the air. "Like, not hot but like warm hot. Like, you had a leather jacket on. In August. Not that you were like hot *hot*. Not that you aren't hot because you absolutely are, but I just mean... Jesus. I'm going to shut up." She wanted to crawl under the porch and never come out. *What the hell, Toni! Why don't you just fling yourself off the cliffs right into the fucking Atlantic?*

"You're adorable," Brittany finally said after Toni was through with her internal berating.

She felt her entire face flush and heat spread throughout her body as if she was sliding into a hot tub. She shook her head. "I have no idea why drinks keep going to my head so fast here. The night I arrived, I had some lemon drop martinis, and it felt as if I had drunk a whole bottle of vodka."

"Some, hmm?"

"Yeah, like, I don't know, four?" Before Brittany could reply, headlights came up the driveway and up pulled the golf cart with Alice driving and Leslie planted firmly in the passenger seat. She was carrying a growler of beer and a smile. "Well, well, well, look what the cat dragged in."

Leslie made her way from the golf cart to the porch and found a seat on the arm of Toni's chair. She moved her cane out of the way, tucking it behind the chair, and sighed. "Have you two been out here for all this time?" She looked between Toni and Brittany, the familiar scene of new beginnings plastered all over their faces. "Two bottles of wine, too? Brittany, I don't think you'll be going anywhere tonight."

"Oh, no, I'll be fine, Leslie. Thank you for your concern, though. I can always catch a Lyft."

Alice chuckled from her spot on the steps to the porch, her head leaning back against the railing. "Honey, Lyfts and Ubers are as sparse here as straight people. You'll be better off if we just drive you home on the golf cart."

"Absolutely not," Leslie said with a firm tone. "Your eyesight is atrocious this late at night. Brittany can have the pullout. Period." She noticed Brittany's eyes move from hers to Toni's then back to hers. "End of story."

"Okay, okay," Brittany said with a laugh.

"If you're complying only to get two old women off your back, I'd say you're learning really fast." Toni softly elbowed her aunt then leaned against her leg. "I wouldn't say no to you playing with my hair, Aunty."

Leslie shook her head as she caught Alice's gaze and held it for a few beats before she placed her hand on Toni's head. "You used to beg me to do this when you were a kid." She smiled, recalling the memory of a young Toni skipping through the house, asking for a snack-sized

3 Musketeers, and giggling as she peeled the chocolate off and ate the nougat by itself. "You were quite the handful back then."

"Toni was telling me she's always been a little bit of a wild child." Brittany took a drink from her wine, licked her lips, and smiled at Toni. "I'm sure there are plenty of stories about those very intriguing times."

"I have loads of stories." Leslie could feel the emotion as it formed in her throat for no apparent reason. She sniffled which Alice, of course, seemed to hear.

"You okay, my love?" Alice reached her hand out and placed it on Leslie's calf. "You need to get to bed?"

Leslie scoffed. "She's always trying to get me into bed with her." She followed up with a playful wink.

Toni chuckled. "I really do hope I have a relationship like yours one day."

"I agree," Brittany said.

Leslie, once again, noticed the way Brittany's eyes lingered for a couple of seconds longer on Toni. "Toni, why don't you show Brittany her accommodations for the night? Alice and I will be in shortly."

"I can really make it home just fine—"

"You can really stop pushing the issue and just go inside, please. I will not be responsible for you wrecking that damn moped." Leslie saw the way Brittany's demeanor changed momentarily before she nodded, a small smile coming to her lips. "Thank you." She watched as Brittany followed Toni inside, then turned to Alice. "I'm a genius, I tell ya."

"You are definitely upping your game in the matchmaking department." Alice ran her hand over Leslie's calf again. "I do love living our life together, just the two of us, on our little island. But I have to say, it's been a real breath of fresh air to have Toni here."

"She seems lighter, doesn't she?"

"Think it has anything to do with the handywoman I snatched up?"

"I think it has everything to do with that," Leslie said.

"You don't think we're pushing Toni toward something she may not be ready for?"

Leslie paused to consider the suggestion. "I suppose that's possible, but the chemistry between them is undeniable, whether it's exactly the right time or not. You remember how that goes, don't you, my love?"

"I remember it all too well." Alice's demeanor grew somber. "Falling in love with you was the most exciting thing I'd ever experienced. And the most excruciating when you said you couldn't leave Bill for me. I'd never wish that on anyone, especially Toni."

"I didn't mean to minimize the seriousness of our situation, darling. I was there, too. I had to live with the consequences of my actions for decades. But times are so different now. Women are so different now. Toni says she's not ready, but she certainly seems to enjoy the time she's spent with Brittany." Alice stared at her with a mixture of caution and adoration. "I will once again follow the love of my life into the great unknown." She leaned over for a kiss, then got up slowly. "You better be right this time, or I'm renting a room at Marjory's B and B if the shit hits the fan between them."

"I love you, Alice Burton." She accepted Alice's hand to get up.

"You better love me, Leslie Burton, because you're never getting rid of me."

Leslie kissed her again. "I am so thankful for that."

Not only had Alice completed her in ways she never even knew possible since the moment they'd become friends at work, she'd also become the reason for each breath Leslie took. She truly believed had Alice not shown up at her bedside when she'd had the stroke four years earlier, she never would've regained consciousness. If there was such a thing as soul mates, they were in mind, body, and spirit.

Leslie's biggest fear was that it was only a matter of time before all of those assumptions were tested, though. She knew Alice better than she knew herself, and for that, she was insanely grateful.

❖

Brittany switched off the light to the small bathroom that was off the living room. It was dark save for a small salt lamp that resided on the bookshelf next to an old tube television. She crept over to the bookshelf, secretly dying to know what kind of literature existed in an older lesbian couple's home. The salt lamp shed just enough light to see the familiar titles of *The Handmaid's Tale, A Room of One's Own, We Should All Be Feminists*. But there were other books, too. Ones Brittany knew of because they were the same ones she would sink into a comfy chair with, excited about the idea of escaping into a romance that spoke to her. Knowing these women, including Toni, were actual people with similar interests and desires made Brittany feel better about her impromptu and erratic decision to hightail it to this island.

"You can turn on a light," came a soft voice from behind her.

Brittany spun around, surprised to see Toni standing there, all smooth, toned arms and legs, in a white tank top and white boy shorts. Actually, surprised wasn't the right word. Brittany was completely taken aback, thrown off, and one hundred percent turned on by the sight standing before her. Up until then, the only way she'd seen Toni was completely put together and flawless. But now, even in the ambiance of the salt lamp, in nothing but her underclothes, Toni looked like a vision, an answer to a prayer Brittany didn't even know was on her mind, let alone in her mouth. She wasn't even sure if a god existed in this weird world. That moment solidified things, though.

There may not be a god, but there was most certainly a higher power responsible for Toni in that outfit.

She watched as Toni reached over and clicked on a lamp next to the pulled-out sofa bed. They both stared at the bed, and when Brittany took a chance and looked at Toni, she could have sworn they were having the exact same thought.

And it had nothing to do with praying, but rather taking that higher power's name in vain.

"I wanted to check on you." Toni's lips turned up into a small smile as she stood there, her arms at her side, her nipples erect. *What the fuck is she trying to do to me?*

"I'm good."

"No." Toni's laugh was tiny and quiet. Her hair was pulled into a haphazard bun atop her head. Everything about her was making it difficult for Brittany to remember why she came to Swift Island to begin with and it didn't have a thing to do with jumping headfirst into a fling with a woman, *a hot as fuck woman*, who was on the rebound.

"I know you're good, but are you okay with staying here? I don't want you sneaking out in the middle of the night. Who knows what kind of crazies are lurking around out there."

Brittany's skin prickled at the mention of crazies lurking in the streets. Toni had no idea how right she was, but this wasn't the time. It wasn't just because Brittany had no idea how Toni would react, but because she didn't want to ruin their night. A million thoughts of what she actually wanted to do with Toni bombarded her. They ranged from teeth on bare skin to nails down her back. Not a single one of them included Brittany's visions or the conversation it would require.

"I guess you're right." Brittany took a step closer to the pullout. She glanced down at the light blue comforter, the matching colored pillows, the way Toni had folded the left corner of the bed down for her. "I should probably get some—" Her sentence stopped, not of her doing, but as if it had a mind of its own.

"Sleep?"

She nodded.

"If you need me, I'm upstairs on the left."

That was a loaded statement. *Yes, yes, I fucking need you.* The desire coursing through Brittany's veins had been magnified by two bottles of a tasty sauvignon blanc and an even tastier white tank top and boy shorts. She finally made herself nod because if she stood there staring any longer, *she'd* be the crazy creep running around Swift Island.

Toni turned to leave but pulled up short before she spun back around. "I wanted to thank you."

"Thank me?" The sound of her voice startled herself. She was sure her voice had died right alongside her brain. "For what?"

Toni shrugged. "For being the person you are. Even if you aren't sure who that is." She smiled a smile that could have buried Brittany's heart as well, thrown in right on top of the casket holding her brain and her voice. "Good night, Brittany."

She left, and Brittany watched her succulent tan legs disappearing up the stairs as she took them two at a time.

As Brittany sank into the mattress, she sighed. Maybe this was what she needed.

And then the feeling of comfort was quickly replaced by the all too familiar shooting pain in her head. She rolled onto her side, covered her head with one of the pillows, groaned into the soft material, and rode out the next flashes: the pebble road, the Adirondack chairs, the chiminea, the easy conversation, as if she wasn't really a part of any of it.

And as quickly as it started, the vision stalled and the searing pain faded into the darkness. What did these flashes mean? How were they important? What was someone, or some*thing*, trying to tell her? Was it the higher power she didn't believe in? Or was it something else?

She needed to find out because collapsing into a pile of pain every time things in her life were going well was going to get real irritating, as well as real fucking awkward.

Chapter Eleven

It had been three days since she'd woken up on the pullout. Brittany had managed to sneak out before the sun came up, as well as before anyone else was up. She left a thank you note on the kitchen table and pushed the scooter to the end of the driveway before starting it. She hated being the person who left like that, but she'd needed to get her thoughts together.

The three days wasn't a timetable Brittany had set when she left that morning. They hadn't made any plans the last night they'd spent together, and Brittany hadn't texted to see if she could see her. If it had been "past Brittany," she would've texted the next day. But "current Brittany," the Brittany she was stuck dealing with, needed to pump the brakes. It was easy to get caught up in Toni and forget why she was here. Someone was depending on her. She just needed to figure out who. It had nothing to do with the way her heart skipped when she saw Toni. It definitely didn't have anything to do with how scared she was for Toni to catch a glimpse of how lost she felt. And it absolutely didn't have anything to do with Brittany's newfound fear of intimacy. Nope. *Keep telling yourself that.*

Toni had renewed Brittany's subscription to Heartache Weekly without a second thought. The only benefit to the updated subscription was there was no heartache. And hopefully, they'd keep it that way.

Brittany sat at her now normal spot at the bar at the Second Wave. She glanced up at the ceiling, the thoughts in her head sometimes too much for her to make sense of. She was trying to write everything down. Every detail. From what each vision meant to the way Toni's eyes lit up when she smiled. She gathered those roaming thoughts and, head bent, scribbled the latest entry into her spiral notebook.

Vision after vision. And all I can come up with is they have all taken place on Swift Island, all but one. Each flash is familiar, some are almost intimate, which freaks me out even more.

Am I seeing the future?

Am I seeing the past?

Am I seeing things of my past self? Or future self? Or is that the same goddamn thing?

Am I a basket case?

Is all of this from the TBI or do I really have a fucking screw loose? Or is this some generational family witchy shit?

I sit and scribble questions all day long and still no answers.

The only thing I can come up with is I'm either as crazy as a shithouse rat or I'm the next Miss Cleo. And while it would be fun to be a psychic, I have a hard time believing I have the sight or whatever Aunt Patty called it. Either way, I'm struggling to find clues. I don't know what the triggers are, and I feel like the more I try to understand this, the less and less it makes sense.

Aside from the frustration, it's also discouraging. I made the trek to Swift Island to figure shit out. I can't stay forever. I have to move forward with my life back home. I need to get back to work. I gave myself two months, and with the way things are going it will take two years.

So far, all this trip has done is remind me that I'm a raging lesbian with a primed libido who is stuck between begging for release and fearing the aftermath of said release. And also, I really like a woman in white boy shorts.

Fuck. What am I doing here?

"Another Amber Waves for the lady."

Brittany looked over at the voice that broke her attention, and in an instant, smiled away her irritation at being interrupted. "Leslie, hi."

Leslie pulled out the barstool next to Brittany and slid onto it. "How are you doing, my dear? We were sad to see you'd stolen away in the night the other day. Alice was all geared up to make her special banana pancakes. They're Toni's favorite."

The tug of heartstrings was all Brittany could feel after Leslie's intro, but the only thing she could offer was a smile. "I'm sorry. I really am. Sometimes I feel like…" She was having trouble coming up with the right word, but it sounded an awful lot like *intruder*. She wasn't made to feel that way. It was part of her DNA. She wanted to fit in all the time but also not fit in at any time. "The beauty of being an extroverted introvert," Aunt Patty had said with a grin one day after a lively tarot card reading. And she was right. Brittany loved talking to people, asking questions, pulling the real story out so the world could know it. But at the same time, she wanted to crawl into a hole and never face another human being again. Being a journalist was hard work. Being on was not only a necessity, it was required. These days, though, understanding everything wasn't a necessity so much as it was just a really great pipe dream.

"Like you're running a marathon with no end in sight and your bladder's about to burst?" Leslie said.

Brittany chuckled. "That's awfully specific."

"Not what you meant?"

"Not necessarily, but I feel as if I could totally wrap my head around how that feels."

Leslie didn't speak, just sort of watched Brittany. Her eyes didn't move, nor did she. Until finally she said, "I don't know why, but I sense a lot of good in you. A strange connection exists between you and us, and I'm including Toni in that. Ever since Alice first brought you into our lives, you've given off a really good vibe."

Brittany couldn't help but smile. She was always a sucker for a good compliment, but this one in particular had her thinking maybe the visions she was having weren't as horrible as she thought. Of course, blood wasn't a good thing. And how did her hands even get bloody? And why if she was putting off a good vibe, couldn't she just have some good flashes? Flashes that made her happy instead of anxious?

If she knew the answer to that, she wouldn't be in the predicament she was in.

❖

Toni did her third lap around the keg. With each rotation, she got a little closer.

"It probably won't bite you," Alice said as she leaned against the doorjamb.

Toni pointed at the silver cylinder. "You don't know that. These things can be temperamental, and the last thing I want to do is ruin another keg of beer."

Alice seemed to suppress a smile as she walked over to Toni's nemesis. She grabbed the red handle, pulled it out, and turned the coupler. She pulled the line out and motioned for Toni to take the empty one away and place the new one. When she did, she put the line back in, turned the coupler again, and pushed the handle down and back inward.

"There you go. All set." Alice slapped her hands together and crossed her arms.

"Okay, you're clearly some kind of wizard." Toni inspected the coupler. "Where did you learn to do that, anyway?"

"YouTube."

"Seriously? I thought I was the millennial."

"Well, you're not a very good one." Alice peeked her head out the door and then ducked back in. "Brittany is out there."

"I know." Toni rolled another keg over. "That's why I'm in here."

"That doesn't make sense."

Toni pulled the handle down and out and was quite pleased with herself when she heard the hiss. "I want to ask her out, but I don't want to just walk up and ask." Brittany hadn't texted or called in the last three days. It could be that she'd misread whatever was happening between them. Maybe Brittany wasn't interested. Maybe she'd just been being polite the last time they'd spent time together. It could be dangerous to ride bikes alone in an unknown place. Brittany could simply be very safety conscious. *Overthinking again. Perfect. You should start a podcast: How to Overthink and Never Get Anything Done or Add Any Real Direction to Your Life. Well, the title is going to need some work.*

Alice nodded. "How else would you do it? Sky writing?"

Toni chuckled as she released the coupler and pointed at her accomplishment. "I mean what am I supposed to say? I've never asked a woman out before." And she could—ask Brittany out on a date. What was the worst that could happen? *She says no and eliminates the speck of self-confidence you've managed to cling to over the last few months? Perfect.*

"Well, I can see why you're so concerned. No one told you the secret password for when you want to ask a woman out?"

Toni replaced the coupler into the new keg and closed it. "There's a password?"

Alice smacked her on the back. "No. It's the same if it's a man or a woman. There's no special trick. You two clearly got along. Just tell her you want to see her again."

Toni stood and brushed the dust off her knees. "What if she says no?"

Alice rolled her eyes. "Then she does. But she won't."

"She might."

Alice shoved her toward the door. "She won't."

Toni tripped into the bar area. Alice was stronger than she looked, and she made sure to shoot her a *knock it off* glance before she headed out toward Brittany.

Brittany was only forty feet away. That was plenty of time to let her mind wander to the multitude of ways this could go wrong. Brittany might just want to be friends. Toni might not even be her type. Then she thought back to the day and evening they'd spent together. Friends didn't look at you the way Brittany looked at her. She felt the excitement in her stomach start to bubble as she remembered Brittany's eyes on her, full of blatant desire. It had been palpable, but Brittany hadn't sought her out after.

She was only five feet away now, and she hesitated. Penn had looked at her with desire too. The chemistry with Penn had been so intense, it had finally blown up. What if it was the same with Brittany?

Brittany turned and saw her then. Her face softened, and she smiled so widely that her eyes lit up. Brittany was no Penn, and she needed to keep reminding herself of that.

"Hi there," Toni said. *Okay, so far, so good.*

"I was just thinking about you." Brittany leaned back in the chair. Her one arm draped over the top made her look even cooler and laid-back than Toni had remembered.

"Good things, I hope."

Brittany bit her lip, and Toni had to force herself not to sit down in her lap. *Jesus. Where did that come from?*

"Do you want to get dinner with me?" Brittany tucked a loose strand of hair behind her ear.

Toni coughed out a laugh. "I was coming over here to ask you the same thing."

"So, that's a yes, then?"

"Only if we can eat somewhere besides here or at my aunt's." Toni glanced over her shoulder to see if the two women in question were looking on, and of course, they were. "Prying eyes and all that."

Brittany leaned around Toni and waved. "Whatever you like. I'm not familiar with anything around here yet. Do you mind picking the place?"

"Not at all." She saw someone a few tables away raise their hand, trying to get her attention. "I'm off tomorrow. Pick me up at seven?"

"It's a date."

Toni smiled. "But not like a date-date, right?"

Brittany lifted her eyebrow. "No. This is definitely a date-date." She turned back to her notebook.

The confirmation startled Toni slightly, and she almost fell over the chair she'd accidentally walked into. *Smooth.* Luckily, Brittany hadn't seen, and she was only met with mild amusement when she arrived at the waiting customers. They rambled off their order, and Toni managed to get back to the bar without further incident.

She did her best to focus on all the customers that evening. But she was also keenly aware of Brittany. Every long stare out the window, like she was searching for something or someone. Every intense, concentrated look at her notebook, as if the answers to mysterious questions were hidden somewhere in the copious words she scribbled. Every woman who explicitly checked her out as they wandered by—Toni took it all in.

"Not a bad view, huh?" Leslie grabbed a towel and helped her dry pint glasses.

Toni grinned and glanced at her from the corner of her eye. "Not at all. You two really hit the jackpot with this location."

Her aunt laughed. "Yeah, it's pretty close to perfect." She handed her another glass. "The history makes it even more interesting. When we bought the place and started remodeling, we found all kinds of issues—faulty wiring, leaky roof, and parts of the floor had to be leveled. I thought it was too much of a project to take on, but Alice didn't see it that way." She stopped and put her arm around Toni. "She told me that we'd never find another place more perfect than this, and the effort to fix it up would be worth it in the end."

Toni put the towel and glass down. "Are we still talking about the building?"

"Were we ever?" Leslie rubbed her back and walked from behind the bar to take another customer.

Toni stared at the freshly painted walls, the perfectly lined pictures, and the glowing neon signs. She wasn't sure if new paint and some polished floors could fix her heart. She wasn't sure that a new electrical upgrade could fix whatever tormented Brittany. But that was the point her aunt was trying to make, wasn't it? Those issues still existed. They were still there if you looked closely enough or if you peeled back the new veneer. They just became harder to see because someone had taken the time to care for and repair the damage.

Toni watched as Brittany got up from her chair and moved toward the exit. Everything in her body screamed for her to go with her. She wanted to see where she was going. She wanted to know if she was meeting someone. She wanted to be near her. But she stayed rooted in her spot. She hadn't spent enough time repairing her own damage to go after someone else so blatantly. No matter how much her body wailed to do just that, her mind wouldn't let her.

Chapter Twelve

July 30th–Journal Entry 494

I came face-to-face with you today. There was no recognition in your eyes. You didn't seem to recall all our history. The endless days I spent in the darkness because my father was infatuated with you. The smell of mildew and dust would cling to my hair and skin for days after he'd finally let me out of the basement. I can still feel the heat that would radiate after each blow to my face. The blood that would pool in my mouth when he would come down after he heard me whimper. I run my tongue across my teeth and taste the lingering essence of copper. He was scared I'd give myself away. Scared I would alert you to my presence. It all comes back to me when I see you.

A therapist once asked me if I dream. Of course, I dream. I dream of the hours I tracked on the wall of that basement that turned into days and then weeks. I dream of the pain my body endured at the hands of the only person who was supposed to show me mercy. I dream of the scraps of food he'd put on the steps after the lavish meals you'd cook for him. I dream of the leaking foundation where I'd gather water to drink. I dream of how it will feel to place you on my table. I dream of my knife gliding through your now paper-thin skin. I dream of watching the life drain from your eyes as your body and mind give in to your fate. Do you think you'll remember me then?

You've made a good life for yourself here on this island. You've managed to banish your sins from memory. You've somehow made peace with your past. But did you really think you could escape me forever? Did you think I wouldn't find you? Do you really believe you're that special?

Things could have been so different for you. Things could have been different for me. But our paths, our fates, seem to be intertwined. All my training, all my studying, all my focused intent was to prepare for you. I wanted to be sure I could deploy the most painful experience imaginable for you, my friend. I'm ready now.

Are you?

CHAPTER THIRTEEN

Brittany ran her fingers through her freshly dried hair. "So, what do you think?"

"Pick me up and move me around. I can't see it all from this angle," Amy said.

Brittany picked up the phone and moved it around. "Is that better?" She put the phone back down on the bathroom vanity and started applying her makeup.

"You're as beautiful as ever, Britt." Amy picked up her wine glass and toasted her through the phone.

"Toni is different. I'm not sure how to describe it. It just feels different."

"Do you think she has anything to do with your visions?"

Brittany sighed. "I'm honestly not sure. I still don't have a real good grasp on what they all mean or what they're trying to tell me. It still feels like a warning. I really hope it's not a warning about Toni."

Amy scrunched her face, which Brittany knew meant she was thinking. "Does she have a kooky ex or anything?"

"The only one she's talked to me about is some asshole who left her in the middle of nowhere. I can't imagine she'd come all the way out here to torment her now. That seems counterintuitive."

Amy agreed. "What are your reporter instincts telling you?"

Brittany felt her face flush with frustration. "I can't tell anymore. I'm not even sure that what I'm seeing is real. It could all be a medical condition. Shit, I could just be losing my mind. Honestly, I'm not even sure I'd be able to tell the difference at this point."

"Hey," Amy said. "Don't talk like that. Your instincts are spot-on. They always have been. You're letting doubt cloud who you are. You work for one of the last reputable newspapers in the country. You've broken stories on drug cartels, corrupt politicians, and pedophiles in prominent positions."

"But, I—"

"No, let me finish." Amy was pacing now. "You're good at what you do because it's who you are. You were chasing leads when people told you there wasn't a story. You've pushed the envelope when everyone else was scared. You are a smart, brave, dedicated journalist. If there is something to these visions, and I believe there is, you will get to the bottom of it. I have no doubt."

"Amy." Brittany leaned her forearms on the vanity to get closer to the camera. "I love you. Thank you for always being you."

Amy leaned forward and kissed the camera. "I love you, too. Now get going. Don't you dare keep this woman waiting."

Brittany ended the call and slipped her phone in her pocket. She checked herself one more time in the mirror and headed out into the street with an extra bounce in her step. She was supremely grateful for her friendship with Amy, who always knew what to say and what she needed to hear.

Brittany moved through the streets, looking forward to her evening with Toni, but a part of her was still scanning the faces she passed. She was hoping to catch a glimpse of familiarity. She wanted an inkling of recognition. Hell, she'd settle for a jab in the chin if it pointed her in the right direction.

As she got closer to the house, her senses tingled. The hair on the back of her neck stood up, and she slowed her pace. She studied the passing faces with more scrutiny, but all she saw were smiling faces going about their evening. Still, she couldn't shake the feeling of impending pain, and what was that other feeling? Despair? She felt her stomach roll, and then as fast as it came, it was gone again.

Damn.

"You okay?"

Brittany's attention snapped into focus as Toni slid her hand up her arm. Immediately, she wanted to tell her what was happening, but where would she even begin? She had no idea how to accurately describe what was transpiring in her mind, much less in a way that wouldn't make her seem like a crazy person.

"Why are you down here? I was coming up to get you." Brittany knew she sounded like she was scolding her, and she winced. "I'm sorry. That came out wrong. I just didn't want you to think I'm some asshole who won't come to the door."

"I didn't want to spend the first thirty minutes of our date with my aunts looking at us like we're their next project." She thumbed in the direction of the house. "But if you'd like to go up there and chat with Chippa and Joanna Gays, I can make that happen."

Brittany laughed and didn't realize she'd taken Toni's hand until they'd already walked several feet. "Where are you taking me?" She was surprised how normal her voice sounded since her heart was clobbering her chest with the excitement of Toni's proximity.

Toni pulled her onto the sidewalk and through an overhang covered in ivy. "Right here."

Brittany read the sign: *Jane's Hideaway.* "That's on the nose."

Another couple stumbled out of the restaurant laughing. They were so caught up in their own conversation that they didn't see Toni and pushed her hard into Brittany. Brittany caught her before she stumbled. The couple called out their apologies as they continued down the street.

Toni slid her hands up Brittany's arms and onto her shoulders. The length of her body was pressed against her, and Brittany couldn't focus on anything but the way Toni's hands trembled at her neck.

"You look beautiful tonight," Brittany said because, at that instant, there was nothing more real or concise in her life.

Toni ducked her head slightly and took a deep breath. "I'm not sure anyone has ever looked at me the way you just did."

Brittany didn't think she'd ever met anyone so utterly unaware of their magnetism. Toni had confidence, but it probably came from a place of people only commenting on her looks. Brittany didn't think many people spent the time to search and appreciate everything else Toni had to offer. She decided at that moment she would be different. She would show Toni that it could be different.

"I'm starving," Brittany said because she could tell Toni was feeling a bit unnerved.

"I've brought you to the right place then." Toni beamed and pulled her toward the door.

She followed Toni toward the entrance and realized she'd gladly follow Toni anywhere she led.

❖

Toni sipped her wine and watched Brittany as she talked about her life growing up in California. She used her hands to speak, and every word was accentuated with a facial expression that revealed her feelings at the time of the memory. Brittany was funny, intelligent, articulate, and sexy as hell. Toni could see a proverbial brick or two from the wall she'd so carefully built around her heart fall to the ground and shatter.

The way Brittany would focus on her when she spoke, it was as if there was no one else in the world. The way Brittany methodically rolled her pasta onto a spoon before placing the fork in her mouth. The way she'd let her fingers linger on the glass of wine she held while she talked. It was all so mesmerizing. Penn had never asked about how she felt when Toni spoke of particular life circumstances, like Brittany did. Penn had never touched her hand in casual conversation while they were in public, like Brittany just had. Penn had never smiled when Toni was talking about something that particularly excited her, but Brittany's face lit up with enthusiasm. And Penn had never looked at her the way Brittany consistently managed to do.

"Do you want to go down to the beach with me?"

Brittany tucked the receipt for their meal into her pocket. "Yes. I would love that."

Toni took her hand when they left the restaurant like it was the most natural gesture in the world. She'd surprised herself by doing so, but it was entirely instinctive. It felt natural to be around Brittany. The thought scared her but not enough to put an end to their evening. She wanted more of whatever was unfolding between them. She needed more.

"So, you and Amy used to date?" Toni sat down in the sand and pulled Brittany down beside her.

Brittany leaned back on her elbows and crossed her ankles over one another. "Date is a strong word. We filled an emptiness for one another for a while. Then she met Lena, and we've been best friends ever since."

Toni looked at her. "You aren't jealous?"

"Not at all. Some people are meant to be, and those two are. There's nothing to be jealous of because Amy and I never had what she and Lena have. Not even close. I'm happy for her." Brittney wiggled her eyebrows. "Plus, I eat free at Lands End. I know that doesn't mean anything to you, but if you knew what I was talking about, you'd get it."

Toni leaned back and mimicked Brittany's position. "So, you believe in fate?"

"Don't you?" Brittany bumped her. "Your aunts are kind of proof of that."

Toni searched Brittany's eyes for something, but she wasn't sure what. She just knew there was an answer there somewhere. "I believe you play a role in your fate. You make choices, and your fate changes dependent on those choices."

"What choice are you trying to make now?" Brittany asked.

"Whether or not I should kiss you."

Brittany slid her hand around Toni's neck and pulled her closer. Their lips were close enough that Toni felt her breath against her mouth. Brittany's fingers rubbed gently against the skin at the base of her neck, and Toni felt every part of her body react. She closed the remaining minuscule distance between their lips and was met with a jolt of shared need. Brittany tasted like wine and salt from the Atlantic. It was both exquisite and intoxicating.

The kiss started with a bit of hesitation but quickly grew to mirror their growing attraction for one another. Brittany pressed against her mouth with tenderness and need. It was a combination that Toni had never felt intertwined. She let her hand move to Brittany's muscled leg, and she pulled her closer, wanting more of her body against her own. Brittany bit lightly on Toni's bottom lip, and Toni had to force herself to stay rooted to her spot. She wanted to climb on top of her. She wanted to pull off her clothes and run her mouth down her body. She wanted all of her.

Brittany broke the kiss first and rested her head against Toni's. "You're vibrating."

Toni felt slightly drunk from the flood of endorphins and didn't fully comprehend what Brittany was saying. "What?"

Brittany kissed her cheekbone down to her ear and bit slightly. "Your phone is vibrating."

Toni reached into her pocket and pulled out the device. She thought briefly about hitting ignore and crawling on top of Brittany, but seeing her aunt's name illuminating the screen, she thought something might be wrong.

"Hello?"

"Hi, sweetie. We just wanted to make sure you're okay. It's late. If you're having a good time, don't rush home. We just wanted to check." She was silent for a long moment. "I'm realizing now that I probably should have just texted. Forget I called."

Toni flopped down on the sand. It had been a long time since she needed to check in with anyone. "It's okay. I should've texted you and told you we were going to the beach. I'll be home in a bit."

"So, it's going well?"

Toni smiled and shook her head, because honestly, what else could she do? "Yes. It's going well. Still on the date."

"Okay, no rush. Say hi to Brittany for us. Bye."

Toni let the phone drop onto her stomach, and she covered both eyes with her hands. "I'm sorry about that."

Brittany sat up and pulled Toni to her feet. "Don't be. It's incredibly sweet that they worry about you."

"It is, and I'm lucky to have them," Toni said.

She took Brittany's hand and leaned toward her as they walked. Perhaps it was a good thing that her aunt had called. Toni wanted to take whatever was happening between her and Brittany slow. She wanted to take every precaution necessary to ensure this was happening for the right reasons and not just primal need.

Brittany walked her to her door and Toni felt like a teenager all over again. But she wasn't a teenager. She was a grown woman who wanted nothing more than to drag Brittany up to her bedroom, rip her clothes off, and dive—*Taking things slowly, remember?*

Toni stood on the top step and wrapped her arms around Brittany's neck, enjoying that they were now the same height. "Thank you for a wonderful evening."

Brittany kissed her softly on the lips. "I had a great time."

Toni put her hands on Brittany's face and kissed her again. She wanted Brittany to think about her the entire walk home and for the rest of the night. She wanted Brittany to go to bed dreaming of her. She wanted Brittany to feel what she was feeling.

"Good night," Toni said as she moved toward the door.

"Can I see you tomorrow?"

"You know where to find me." Toni waved one last time before she went into the house.

She stood there for a second, letting her mind catch up with everything her body was feeling. As it turned out, that was short-lived. Her aunts were sitting in the living room, smiling like a pair of Cheshire cats.

"Hi, honey. Did you have a nice time?" Leslie sipped her tea and winked.

"Yes. Very nice. Well, good night." Toni moved toward the stairs, hoping to avoid any more interrogation.

"You know, FYI, we wouldn't mind if you had an overnight guest," Alice said. "Just sayin'."

Toni and Leslie exchanged glances, then both looked at Alice.

"What?" Alice said innocently.

"Good night, my dear aunts." As soon as Toni was in her bedroom, she stripped off her clothes and pulled on her pajamas. The events of the evening ran on a loop in her head as she went about getting ready for bed. Brittany wasn't just a force to be reckoned with—Toni feared she may be *the* force, the one who could change everything she thought she knew about her world. The potential for that kind of shift was both exhilarating and terrifying.

Her phone vibrated on the table next to her. *Sweet dreams.*

She smiled like an idiot, and shook her head, trying to clear out the fog that Brittany brought to her mind. She forced herself to think about Penn and how that ended. Beginnings were always fun. But every beginning she'd ever had ended with her in tears. She wanted to let herself get caught up in what she was feeling, to let herself believe that this time could be different—that Brittany was different. She wanted all those things. But what she needed was to give herself a dose of reality.

Even with all those thoughts and doubts bouncing around in her head, she still went to sleep smiling, and excitement bubbling in her stomach.

CHAPTER FOURTEEN

Brittany tossed her phone down after texting Toni. She wished she'd FaceTimed her or called her or at least texted something other than *Sweet dreams* so she could keep talking with her. She was restless after their sexual near-miss on the cool beach sand and didn't want to lose that feeling. Since arriving on the island, she felt like she was flying in hyperspace, one minute taunted by piercing headaches and bizarre visions, the next floating in the euphoria Toni inspired whenever they were together. Even though they'd just met, she'd absolutely take the euphoria over the visions any day.

As she laid her head on the pillow in the darkness, she replayed their kisses earlier, the soft moistness of Toni's lips, the hunger in her eyes, the gentleness in her touch. She wanted to wake up tomorrow and just sit at the bar at the Second Wave and stare at her all day, but that would sort of undermine the whole purpose of her trip here. She needed to really explore the island tomorrow, hop on her scooter, and see where it took her. Maybe she'd find something along the way that would help her make sense of the holy mess rattling around in her head.

And by the end of the day, if it took her back to Toni, then so be it.

❖

The next morning, Toni stood at the bar slicing lemons, limes, and oranges as her mind traipsed along the shores of the recent happenings in her life. Funny how before coming to the island, whenever her mind had idle moments, it would drift to thoughts of Penn. Although still lurking in the background, Penn was becoming an afterthought, a ship in the distance, still visible but soundless and inconsequential. Now it was Brittany's voice and smile that wandered in first and pushed Penn out. She could really get used to that. If nothing else came of her rendezvouses with Brittany, at least she'd have that. And if she kept her expectations in check, she might even sail away from Swift Island by summer's end with amazing memories and a healed heart.

She caught herself smiling as Deana, their college student lunch server burst through the side door, clearly attempting to beat the time clock.

"Hi, Deana," Toni called out. "No need to break your neck punching in. I haven't even opened the doors yet."

Deana came running out from the back. "Sorry I'm late, Toni. I went for a jog this morning and took a wrong turn."

Toni laughed. "Well, I'm glad you found your way. Would you mind opening the doors for me and checking the tables for the beer list?"

"No problem," Deana said and got down to business.

Toni noted Deana's perfectly shaped ass tucked into her khaki shorty shorts. What else would she expect from a twenty-year-old scholar-athlete? Deana was good for business—sun-kissed skin, wispy blond, upswept hair, and the sweetest personality.

Just as the noon chapel bell rang across the island, customers started filtering in for lunch and the now famous fresh island brews.

"Hello?" Toni's ear pricked up as she recognized Quinn's voice. She was delivering some kegs, and Toni wanted to head her off before she made her way in and started ogling Deana.

"Hi, Quinn." Toni gave her an amiable smile.

"Is Leslie in?"

"Not yet. What can I do for you?"

Quinn looked away in what seemed like disappointment. "Oh, uh, well, we have a new beer I wanted her to try. I helped brew this one."

"Oh. Congrats. Well, seeing as though Leslie and I share the same bloodline, I think I can handle the tasting. What do you say?"

Quinn cracked a goofy smile. "Sure. Okay." She took off for the van as if she'd just pulled the pin on a hand grenade.

Toni suddenly felt bad for her. Maybe she'd judged her too harshly when they'd first met. Yeah, she was twitchy and socially awkward, but she seemed nice enough.

Quinn returned with a cold growler of Island Haze, the newest offering from the ladies at Nereids Brewing. "We think this is just what your bar needs."

Toni sipped a sample of the citrusy, hazy IPA and responded with a resounding, "Mmm."

Quinn's smile signaled pride in her work. "So can we put you down for a case? Or two maybe?"

"Let's go with two," Toni said after finishing the sample size. "Something tells me it's time for my aunts to get another tap line in here."

"Great. I've got them in the van." Quinn sprinted out again.

Toni felt good that she was perhaps helping Quinn move from delivery person to brewer. She wasn't sure what her level of contribution was, but it was tasty and would round out the Second Wave's craft beer offerings.

When Quinn returned, she had the two cases on a hand truck and a delivery slip for Toni to sign. As Toni reviewed and signed the invoice, she noticed Quinn glancing around, probably to check out Deana. "Here you go."

"Thanks." Quinn rolled the paper into a scroll and stuffed it in her back pocket. "So tell Leslie I said hi, okay?"

"You bet," Toni said.

As she watched Quinn lumber out the door, it dawned on her. *Quinn is crushing on Leslie.* Toni chuckled. All this time she'd thought Quinn was creeping on her, then Deana, but it was obvious now that Quinn was into older women. Leslie might have been in her early-mid-seventies, but she didn't look anywhere near it. In fact, without her cane, she could definitely pass for sixty. Maybe even in her fifties.

"You go, Quinn," Toni muttered to herself as she stocked the new beer cans in the bar's fridge.

The lunch crowd was picking up as Leslie and Alice arrived. Luckily, Toni was a born-bartender, and the two college girls they'd hired as cook and server were on the ball as well. But she and Alice made it a point to show up daily as ancillary help wherever it was needed.

"Look at you go," Leslie said as she approached Toni. "Need any help back there?"

"I'm doing fine so far," Toni said. "Try this." She poured Leslie a sample from the growler.

Leslie sipped and was impressed with the light hoppiness and bold citrus flavor. "It's delicious. What is it?"

"It's the newest IPA from Nereids Brewing. Quinn gave me this growler to sample, and I ordered two cases of it. I hope that's okay."

"Honey, if all your executive decisions are this scrumptious, you have carte blanche. Should we replace one on the tap with this?"

"Why don't we add another tap?" Toni said. "I'm sure Quinn would be eager to make that happen. I think she's got the hots for you."

Leslie slid the empty sample glass back to her. "What? What are you talking about?"

"Quinn, the beer delivery woman. She asked for you by name and seemed rather disappointed you weren't here."

Leslie pursed her lips at Toni's suggestion. "Aside from my wife, I am sure no one has the hots for me. I'd check your attraction barometer if I were you. It's clearly off."

"I'm sure it isn't," Toni sang in a teasing tone. "Somebody has an admirer."

"Uh-huh." Leslie smirked at her, hoping the blush she felt on her cheeks wasn't showing. "I'm going to see if my wife needs help in the kitchen. You have customers."

Toni gave her a salute, and Leslie went back to the kitchen. "How's it going back here?"

"Luisa and I have it covered," Alice said. "Have a seat and relax. I'll bring you out a wedge salad for lunch."

Leslie strolled over to Alice, who was stirring vegetables into a large pot of gazpacho, mindful of their other college student, Luisa's proximity. "You are too sweet to me. But I'm not here for lunch. I'm here to work. If you don't need me, I'll go out and help Deana."

Alice looked deep into her eyes as she stirred and whispered, "I always need you."

Leslie stared back at Alice, who never failed to make her swoon. "We have to get Toni out of the house again tonight," she said softly. "I want a romantic dinner, just the two of us with no distractions."

"I'll text Brittany. I have a feeling that won't be hard to arrange."

Luisa piped in. "I don't know who this Brittany is, but if you need someone to take Toni out, I'm your woman."

Leslie stared at their gorgeous, Columbian DACA student displaying a pearly white grin. "How old are you?"

"Nineteen," Luisa said.

Leslie shook her head. Didn't any of these girls date in their own age group anymore? "Why don't you take Deana out instead? We'll handle Toni."

"I'd rather handle Toni," Luisa replied with mischief in her dark eyes.

Leslie and Alice exchanged grins before Leslie headed into the dining room.

Brittany had spent the morning tooling around the island on her scooter, stopping at various artisan shops, a trendy coffeehouse, and the historic Lucinda Swift House, the first dwelling on the island and home of its namesake since the mid-twentieth century. She was intrigued by the lore the tour guide regaled visitors with and marveled at the courage of Lucinda and her former "housekeeper" Dessie Lloyd who had left her affluent Boston lifestyle for a quiet existence on the island owned by Lucinda's wealthy husband's family. She'd inherited it when TB made her a widow at forty in the late 1950s. The two women moved out to the island and allegedly turned the secluded family vacation spot into their own private paradise.

What widow from a stodgy, obscenely rich New England family wouldn't abandon her life of luxury and leisure to move with her African American "housekeeper" to a place it takes an hour to get to by ferry? Sure. Happened all the time.

Judging by the photos of the two women scattered around the home, Dessie was "keeping" more than just Lucinda's house.

When the tour was over, she checked her phone on her way to her scooter. A long text from Alice requested that she be a pal and take Toni out of the house for the evening as her lovely wife wanted a candlelit dinner.

She responded with, *Sure, I'd be happy to as long as Toni doesn't think I was paid off to take her out. Lol.*

I have a feeling Toni would want to accompany you tonight under any circumstances. Thank you! Alice even added a heart emoji to her reply.

Brittany shook her head and smiled as she started up her scooter and strapped on her helmet. She wheeled the scooter around and the tires peeled down over the shells and gravel on the long driveway. Her brief text exchange with Alice had jogged her memory of a dream she'd had of her and Leslie the night before. She couldn't remember any specific details, just that they seemed to be in a crowd or chaos of some kind. The more she thought about it, the less sense it made. After leaving Toni, Brittany expected that if she was going to dream about anyone it would've been her, not her septuagenarian aunts.

When she reached her final stop on her solo day tour, she decided the dream was just a random rehash of the day's events and probably symbolized the chaos of her emotions after having spent a romantic, albeit sexually frustrating evening with Toni.

As expected, Nereids Brewing was packed with an early afternoon crowd seeking tours and tastings. The building itself wasn't that big, and when she opened the door to the small tap room, a wave of warm air hit her. If the place had air conditioning, it wasn't on. The windows were all open in favor of a robust ocean breeze, but the sea of bodies made it feel oppressively hot. Her head started aching before she stepped fully inside. Maybe now wasn't the best time for a beer sampling in an overcrowded room with just a cranberry scone and coffee under her belt.

The pain switched from a mere ache to sharp thrum that was starting to nauseate her. She gave herself a quiet moment to focus her thoughts. Was this headache because this place was tied to anything she'd seen in the visions, or was it simple dehydration? She closed her eyes and relaxed her limbs. She wanted her body to tell her if there was something familiar here—something worth her attention. She wanted desperately to find another puzzle piece. The need to make headway of any kind was imperative. But there was no definitive response.

The headache wouldn't dull, and her senses wouldn't inform. Maybe there were too many people. *This shit should really come with an instruction book.*

She headed back to her scooter, guzzled what was left of her water, and wiped the sudden outbreak of sweat on her forehead. She'd leave the tour for another time. Another good excuse to get Toni to go out with her. But did she still need an excuse? After last night, it seemed that they'd moved beyond the need for pretense.

"You have got to be kidding me!"

"Oh, Julia, I wish I was." Toni bristled at the memory of Penn, then leaned back on the towel she'd spread out moments earlier on the beach. She had a rare afternoon off from the pub, so she was eager to catch some rays and relax. It was the first time she'd been on the beach since her night with Brittany and all she could think about as she lay there was how much she wished she was back in Brittany's arms again. Her infatuation had gone from a gentle pain to a full-blown ache in less than a month. She needed to talk it out. She needed to hear how stupid she was being. And if there was one person she could count on for that, it was her friend from back home, Julia. Toni laughed. "She literally bolted in the middle of the night."

"Holy shit. I thought Penn was a piece of shit before this, but now? She's like, the ultimate asshole."

"Believe me, up until I made it to my aunts' house, I regretted ever leaving Colorado with her. I fell so hard for her entire game. And she played me like a fool."

Julia chuckled. "You should've known. She did the same thing with Elena. Left in the middle of the night like some sort of thief."

"Seriously, though." Toni sighed. "Does everyone know?"

"Well…" Julia hesitated. "Yeah, everyone pretty much knows. I guess she still keeps in touch with a few people who, unfortunately, have no filter."

"Oh God."

"Now, come on. You were the one who had to remind me more than once that news travels around here like wildfire. You can't do anything without the entire town knowing your every single fucking move." Irritation dripped from Julia's words. "And not to mention, everyone gossips to me. Like I give a fuck about anyone else except for Elena, Cole, and you." Julia laughed once more. "So, anyway, tell me more about this weird little gay island you've managed to seek refuge on. And I mean gay *gay*. Not just happy gay."

Toni joined in with Julia's laughter as she situated herself so she was on her stomach looking out at the water as the waves washed onto the shore. For someone who thought she absolutely needed mountains to keep herself grounded, she was certainly digging the way the water and sand were helping her recover. "Well, my aunt Leslie is my mom's older sister. She's like this older feminist, and she dated men for a long time and then, all of a sudden, she rekindled her love affair with Alice and now they're married."

"How romantic," Julia said, sighing.

"Yeah, their entire story is like, oh, I don't know, the most amazing story ever. Seriously." Toni dug her free hand into the sand and pulled up a handful. As she let it slip through her fingers, she continued. "And this island? I can't even with how cute it is. There is so much to do, which is so crazy because the main drag is like a mile long."

"Sounds like home."

"Yeah, maybe that's why I've seemed to settle in so effortlessly."

"Anyone cute there? I mean, not that you need to jump into a new relationship—"

"Oh, no! Of course not. I don't want to do that."

"Wait a second."

"What?"

"That response was way too quick."

"What are you talking about?"

"What are *you* talking about?"

"Julia, seriously."

"Toni, *seriously*."

"Oh my God. Stop." Toni smashed her hand back into the sand. "Fine. I met someone."

"Ha! I knew it!"

"Whatever. You act like you know me so well."

Julia chuckled. "Yeah, well, I feel like I know you pretty damn well, considering."

"Whatever."

"So? Tell me about this new person! Girl? Boy? I want all the details."

Toni stared out at the water, the dark green color, the way each wave rolled in one after another with almost exact timing. "Her name is Brittany. And she's a journalist, but she's here sort of, I guess, trying to figure herself out."

"Yikes."

"No, not like that. I mean, she knows who she is. I think."

"All that really matters is that you know who she is." Julia paused a second. "Do you?"

Toni smiled. "I think so. She's so easy to talk to. And I feel comfortable with her. Y'know what I mean? Like, with Penn, I felt uneasy, as if the other shoe was going to drop. And it fucking did. In the middle of nowhere when she left me stranded like a goddamn idiot." She took a deep breath and held it for one beat, two, before she let it out as a gentle sigh. "But Brittany has this way of making me feel like we've known each other for much longer than we have. I hate to say this for fear of sounding like a lovesick idiot, but I kind of think we were meant to find each other on this island."

"Toni, honey, I think that's awesome. I really do."

She eased into the happiness for her in Julia's voice. "Thanks, Jules. I just don't want to fuck this one up."

"*You* did not fuck up the last one. I hope you know that. That was Penn. It will always be Penn. Not you. Or any other woman she catches in her vagina death web."

Toni laughed while shaking her head. "You really don't like her."

"Look, she tried to smooth things over with me after she made a move on Elena. She apologized. So I'll give her that. But now she's gone and messed you up, so she's back on my shit list. You don't screw around with my people. I'm an orphan with some real messed up abandonment issues so leaving someone in the middle of the night in east Jesus-nowhere? Not cool."

"Please make sure you beat the shit out of her the next time you see her."

"Oh, don't you worry your pretty little head about that. If I don't take a swing at her, I can guarantee that Benjamin will. Hell, even Elijah might this time. And I can tell you one thing, when Elena and I heard what Penn did to you, she looked like her heart broke all over again. Everyone here at the Bennett Ranch can't stand her. I promise."

Toni laughed as she and Julia sank into an easy conversation about life back home on the ranch. It was nice to hear about how things were going since she'd left all those months ago. She loved hearing about how Elena's demeanor had softened, how Cole's first year of college was going, and how old Benjamin was handling single life at the Main Street Pub. She hated to admit it, but she sort of missed the easygoing atmosphere of the town she'd learned to love. The only benefit of being on Swift Island was this town was turning out to be so similar. Everything here made her want to sink her toes into the sand and take a breath. A good cleansing breath that left a person feeling refreshed, invigorated, ready to take on the day, the week, the *life*.

While Julia was launching into another story about Benjamin's latest heartbreak, Toni's phone buzzed with an incoming call. She pulled her phone from her ear and saw that it was Brittany calling, so she quickly told Julia she'd have to call her back. To which Julia replied, "Already I'm second place. I guess first place was fun while it lasted."

Toni giggled and said good-bye before she switched over to the other call. "Well, hello there."

"Up for a drink?"

Toni sat up instantly. "Yes. Where?"

"Let's go to Pinewood Pub. I hear they have a mean plate of sweet potato French fries with pulled pork on top."

"That is quite the insider information."

"Yeah, well, I did some touring around the island today, and I'd like to expand both of our horizons."

"Sounds like a plan. I'll meet you there."

"Gimme an hour."

"Done." Toni hung up as she stood. She grabbed her towel and slipped on her flip-flops as she headed back up to the house, excitement fueling her every step.

Chapter Fifteen

The review Brittany had received about the sweet potato fries was spot-on. She knew after her first bite that she would never recover from the deliciousness of smoky pulled pork layered over crispy sweet potato fries and covered with white beer cheese and barbecue sauce. The appetizer dish was out of this world.

Of course, the company she was entertaining also added to the loveliness of the evening. Toni, with all her adorable bubbly personality traits that were making more and more appearances, was becoming exactly the type of person Brittany could see spending the rest of her life with. Not to mention she was hardly able to take her eyes off her because she was so fucking gorgeous. Especially that night. Her hair was pulled into a side-swept French braid, her face was completely free of all makeup, and her short jean shorts and loose black tank top were so laid-back, it almost had a calming effect on Brittany. She never felt this comfortable this quickly with another person before, and it seemed Toni was feeling the same way.

The night really was incredible so far and Brittany was unsure whether she should be thrilled with the direction it was going, or nervous.

"I told my friend back home about you today," Toni said softly as they walked up the driveway to Brittany's rental unit.

"Oh, yeah?"

Toni sighed. It was a wistful sound, as if she wished she hadn't let it slip that she was so interested in Brittany that she had to let it out to someone, anyone, including someone back home who must mean something to her.

"Yeah, and I have to tell you…" Toni paused as they continued to walk, their shoes crunching on the crushed shell drive.

"Tell me what?"

"You have been the most unexpected thing I've ever experienced." Toni let out a small laugh, so small it almost sounded unintentional. "Even more unexpected than Penn, and believe me, she came completely out of left field."

The statement took the wind right from Brittany's sails. Was it a compliment? It had to be. *Unexpected can't be bad…can it?*

"Brittany?"

"Hmm?" All that inner dialogue about being comfortable had decided to take a hike.

"It's a good thing. A really, really, *really* good thing."

Brittany laughed as she breathed out the air that was caught somewhere between heartache and her lungs. "Oh, thank God."

Toni joined in as she placed her hand on Brittany's arm. "I'm sorry. I thought my words were going to come out as much more meaningful than they did. And probably a lot smoother…"

"No, no." Brittany waved her hand nonchalantly, hoping to dispel the nerves as they crept closer and closer to the rental, her bed, and hopefully, the release they both seemed to be tiptoeing around. But was it too soon? It had to be too soon. Wasn't it? They were both so hesitant and for good reason. Because screwing this up now would be the worst thing they could do.

"Listen." With her hand still on Brittany's arm, she stilled her. "I need you to hear this. Can you look at me, please?"

Brittany wasn't sure what was about to happen or if she even had the capability to comprehend everything going on. She was so lost in Toni's entire presence these days that she felt almost as if she was in a constant daze. She blinked a few times so her eyes could adjust to the dark, as well as to Toni's features in the dimly lit drive. "I'm listening," she whispered. There was a voice inside her, though, screaming at her to not listen, to lean in and capture Toni's lips with her own. She wanted to tell the voice to be quiet, but it was hard when her body completely agreed with it.

"You came into my life at the weirdest moment. Like, I was ready to throw in the towel on love. I went back and forth between a guy back home and then, for some stupid reason, I fell for a person who was so lost and confused that she made me feel lost and confused. And I'm hardly the type to ever feel either of those things. Especially confused." Toni's voice sounded almost far away, as if Brittany was standing on the outside of this conversation with her ear pressed against the glass trying to listen in. "Then I came here, to this island, to try to heal and unconfuse myself and..." Toni took a breath, bit down on her lip, then released it. "You appeared, and I was so not ready to think, see, feel anything about anyone, especially someone new."

"I can understand that."

"I'm sure you can." Toni smiled a smile that screamed melancholy. "I mean, Penn really broke me."

"I know—"

"But," Toni paused, sighed, shrugged. "After meeting you, I couldn't stop thinking about you. About your eyes. And your smile. And the way you held that first beer I gave you, like it was this strange sort of lifeline, tethering you to the bar, the pub, the island somehow."

Brittany laughed a breathy chuckle. "Yeah, I was pretty shaky from the ferry ride that day."

"I completely understand that." Toni smiled again, and this time, it reached her eyes. "You make me excited about my future. I find myself wondering what tomorrow will hold. What our lives will look like in a week, in a month." Toni laughed. "I sound like a complete fool, don't I?"

"Not at all!" Brittany reached forward, placed her hands on Toni's arms, and squeezed lightly. "Toni, you have no idea how much I feel the exact same way." She smiled. "I, too, came here trying to heal, or at least to try to figure things out in my own life." *Because I'm seeing visions and I feel like a complete fucking lunatic.* "I so badly wish I could find the words to let you know everything that's going on inside me. All of these emotions and thoughts... I want to tell you everything and all at once."

"You can, you know."

"I know. I'm really starting to feel I can. I just think... God." Brittany shook her head and looked down at the crushed shells before she let go of Toni's arms and started walking again. "I don't want you to ever think differently of me." She heard Toni's quick footsteps behind her. "I don't want you to wonder how you got mixed up with someone who so badly wants to be who she knows she could be, if only her head would shut up and let her heart do the living." Brittany felt Toni's hand as it wrapped around her wrist and pulled her into Toni's arms. Toni's lips crashed into hers. Not violently but as if they were exactly like the waves on the beach. Their lips belonged together.

"I want you to take me inside."

Brittany pulled away from the kiss, and as soon as her eyes met Toni's, she felt the familiar searing pain of an impending vision. Only this time, when she saw the Second Wave, the window that looked onto the main drag, and the back of Leslie and Alice, there was nothing she could do to tell them to turn around, even though they were in terrible danger. She was screaming at them to turn around... "Look at the window! You have to look!" But her words and the sound of her voice was futile. She was looking around frantically, searching for clues, for anything that could lead her in the direction of where these visions were coming from. She stopped suddenly, though, when the vision focused on the window again, and a knife slid down the length of the glass. It was then the vision stopped, and she felt herself collapsing onto the crushed shells.

Somehow, Toni managed to catch Brittany before she fell onto the driveway that led up to the rental unit. She pulled her inside after finding a key in her pocket and flung her like a bale of hay onto the tiny love seat in the small unit. She rushed around like a madwoman trying to find a washcloth so she could wet it and place it on Brittany's forehead. She was absolutely floored by the number of headaches she seemed to have, and if she didn't know better, she would have thought they were getting worse. But of course, she had no real idea because aside from Brittany opening up a little about the traumatic brain injury, Toni really knew little else about her life.

How could she be so comfortable around someone she didn't really know all that well?

Once she found a washcloth, wet it with cool water, and placed it on Brittany's forehead, she texted her aunts. Alice immediately responded and said she was on her way in the golf cart. She sort of wished she wouldn't have said anything because of Alice's inability to really see well at night. But she needed the help. Brittany needed more than Toni's nonexistent expertise on passing out from searing headache pain.

"Okay, okay, so she just collapsed?" Alice asked as soon as she and Leslie arrived. "Just went down like a wet noodle?"

"No, not really. She sort of went rigid. I don't know. I sort of freaked and then I think my adrenaline kicked in."

Leslie placed her hand on Toni's back and rubbed lightly. "Honey, you did the right thing by calling us."

"I just didn't know what to do. And now she's sort of..." Toni motioned to Brittany, who was still passed out on the couch. "I'm worried about her." As soon as the words left Toni's mouth, Brittany opened her eyes. "Oh, thank God. Are you okay?" Toni knelt next to the love seat and placed her hand on Brittany's cheek. "You went down like a sack of potatoes."

"Oh, Jesus." Brittany tried to sit up, but Leslie and Alice both had their hands on Brittany's shoulders and made sure she didn't get up.

"No way, young lady. You're staying right there." Leslie perched on the arm of the love seat and looked down at Brittany. "How do you feel?"

Brittany sighed. "I feel fine. I promise. I just..." Her voice trailed off and she made eye contact with Toni. "I don't know why that one hit me so hard and so fast."

Toni's heart was beating like a jackhammer, and she was fairly certain everyone could hear it. "I'm worried about you."

"Do *not* worry about me. I'll be fine. I promise."

"Yeah, well, that's not really what it seemed like as I was dragging you into your rental unit and hoping no one thought I was some sort of nut." She wasn't used to being the concerned one. Typically, she was with people who did all the worrying, not the other way around. She wasn't super keen on having this nagging fear sitting inside her stomach.

"They're just headaches."

"But what if you get one while you're on that scooter?"

"I won't."

"How do you know?" Alice's voice was heavy with concern. "You don't know that, do you?"

Brittany's eyes moved from Toni's to Alice's. "No, but normally I can sense that they're coming."

"Well." Leslie placed a hand on the top of Brittany's head. "I'm pretty sure you should just come stay with us for the remainder of your trip. There's no need for you to be spending time alone when it seems like we could walk in here at any moment and find you passed out on the floor with a gash in your scalp."

"No, really, it's absolutely fine. I promise I'm okay."

"Oh, Alice, I think it's cute that this child thinks she has any say in this." Leslie smiled down at Brittany. "You can stay with us for free or continue to rent this for some astronomical figure. I am choosing free for you. So there you go." She stood and moved to the door with ease, her cane clipping on the tile floor. "It's settled. Pack your bags."

Toni smiled at her aunt, then looked down at Brittany. "You can always say 'no,' but why would you refuse the help of three sweet, vivacious women?"

"Ugh." Brittany sighed as she slowly sat up. She shook her head and let out a small laugh as she looked at Alice, then Leslie, then Toni. "Fine."

"Atta girl."

"I'll help you pack."

Fuck. Fuck, fuck, fuck. Brittany pulled her clothes from the small drawers in the even smaller bedroom of the rental and jammed them into her duffel bag. She raked her hands through her hair. This was not at all what she needed. She wanted to have space and not have to rely on anyone, but dammit, these visions were getting harder and harder to detect and even harder to steer clear of. She couldn't understand why it seemed there was literally no rhyme or reason as to why they were happening or what the trigger was. None of it made any sense. And as much as it was causing Toni, Alice, and Leslie to worry, it was getting even more infuriating to her. All she wanted was to understand them. To finally put the puzzle pieces together. Instead, she was falling deeper and deeper into the unknown.

She liked researching and figuring things out. It was in her nature as a journalist to get to the bottom of things. But this? All these stupid visions did was make her look like she was a lunatic who couldn't even be trusted to stay by herself.

Looking like an invalid wasn't cool. In fact, it made her angry at herself. She wished she could go back to the first time she had the vision to turn it off. Maybe then she wouldn't be haunted by the eerie familiarity of everything in the flashes.

And this last one? The sound of the knife scraping on the glass. Everything about that moment made her stomach churn. The eerie sound and the way the vision was directed at Alice and Leslie, made it seem more deranged. And getting to the bottom of why this was happening became more frantic because the rage the person felt was feral, like a snake about to poison its victim. She was freaking out. And if freaking out was making her collapse, she definitely needed to up her research game. She considered telling Alice and Leslie what she'd seen. The fact that their pub was in her vision was beyond unsettling, but tell them what, exactly? If they laughed her out of the room, it would make it more difficult to figure out why they were involved, and that could put them in more danger. Or it could spook them, causing them to change their habits. That could tip off whoever she was looking for, and again, put them in more danger. No, she couldn't tell them anything until she had more information.

"Okay." Brittany walked into the living area of the rental and looked around. "I got everything."

Leslie and Alice both beamed at her. Toni walked up beside her and leaned close to her ear where she pressed her lips against it and said softly, "This is actually a really good thing."

Brittany couldn't help the smile that sprang to her lips. "Oh yeah?"

"Yeah." Toni slipped her arm around Brittany's waist. "Let's go."

Chapter Sixteen

August 8th–Journal Entry 502

I read books about myself, well, books "experts" have written about people like me. They say that I have no concept of emotions. They say I'm not capable of feeling things like love, sympathy, or regret. They say it's because I lack empathy. An interesting phenomenon. How does one become an expert on people they've never met? These people presume to know the inner workings of another's mind. Then they have the nerve to call *me* the narcissist. I can feel. I feel the need to punish, the need to inflict pain, the need for revenge. But most acutely, I feel hatred. For instance, I hate you. I can feel it consume me when you're near.

I look at my knives a lot these days. I admire them. The sharpness of each blade. The shine of the silver. The way the handle feels so perfect in my hand. I have never wanted to cut someone or something as much as I want to slip this blade into your body. I imagine what your skin will look like when I split it open. I imagine the ease with which your flesh will betray you, allowing your insides to escape their casing. I imagine how your face will contort. I imagine the pain in your eyes.

I'm not sure how you live with yourself. I'm not sure how you look in the mirror without making yourself sick. Everything about you is grotesque. From the way you so easily ignored me to the way you go on about your days as if you are so much holier than anyone else around you. I watch you, not just from the shadows, but sometimes in plain sight. I see you, laughing and talking with people. I see you—and it makes me sick. You have no idea how much I can't wait to end it all for you. And every time I see that smile, I want to carve it from your face.

You disgust me. People think I'm the predator. What would they say about you if they were privy to my knowledge? If they knew you used people to get what you wanted? If they knew how you manipulated, deceived, and placated?

But there have been no repercussions for you. No day of reckoning. No revelation of who you really are to the people that love you. You've sidestepped your past, thinking it wouldn't catch up with you. But alas—here I am. The one you left behind. The one who didn't matter.

But I do matter. I have always mattered.

I am going make sure that the one thing I have always wanted to do will happen. I will kill you.

I will make you beg for mercy.

I will tell you how wrong you were.

I will hold you accountable for all the wrongs you have done in this world.

And just when you think I'm finished with you—I'm going to make you relive it all over again.

I think I'll use my large silver knife with the mother-of-pearl inlay on the oak handle. Yes. That's my favorite. That's the one I have always imagined slipping into your stomach, to watch it glide through your belly button.

You'll regret all your sins that day.

And by then, it'll be too late.

CHAPTER SEVENTEEN

Toni stood at the sink. It was just for show, really. She was pretending to do the dishes while she watched Brittany sit on the porch and scribble in her notebook. The morning sun highlighted the side of her body perfectly. In this lighting, she seemed to have a glow about her, and Toni felt her stomach flutter at the thought of running her hands through Brittany's hair. She wanted to feel her shoulders and let her lips explore Brittany's neck.

"See something you like?"

Toni jumped and dropped a glass in the sink. "Jesus. I need to get you a bell."

Aunt Leslie laughed while she helped her pick up the broken glass. "You could just go talk to her."

Toni waved toward the patio. "I'm not going to bother her while she's so clearly working on something."

"Oh, you two are past that now. Bring her a cup of coffee. That's always a good start."

Toni begrudgingly took a mug down from the cabinet. "You've really decided to pursue this whole matchmaking gig, huh?"

Aunt Leslie rubbed the sides of Toni's arms. "When I do something, I do it all the way." She winked at her.

Toni took a deep breath and filled the mug with coffee. She didn't necessarily like the idea of interrupting whatever it was Brittany seemed so intent on working through, but she wanted to be near her.

"Hi," Toni said as she handed her the mug. "I can come back if you're busy."

Brittany smiled and took her first sip. "Please, sit down." She closed the notebook. "Getting to talk to you is never a hardship."

Jesus Christ, this woman did it for her. Brittany had so much ease in her movements. She seemed so comfortable in her skin, so confident. Toni couldn't remember a time she felt that way about herself. Watching Brittany was like watching the ocean lap against the shoreline.

"You okay?" Brittany took her feet off the table and leaned forward, looking concerned.

"Yes. I just got lost in my thoughts there for a minute."

"Anything you want to share?" Brittany leaned back again, and the muscles in her legs flexed with each movement.

Get. It. Together.

"You just have an aura about you. You seem so confident and laid-back. I was thinking that I've never really felt like that about myself."

Brittany cocked her head slightly. "It must be a holdover from my life before the accident. I was confident and laid-back. But these days, I feel like I'm all over the place. My brain feels so foggy sometimes. It's like I can almost make out the shape behind the fog, and then it disappears." She ran her hand through her hair. "I must sound like a crazy person."

The vulnerability in her voice caught Toni a bit off guard. She wasn't completely sure what Brittany was experiencing, but she wanted to make it better. She wanted to give her something else to hold on to, anything else.

"Where was your favorite place to visit as a kid? Don't say Disneyland or something. I mean, where did you truly look forward to visiting?" Toni threw her a lifeline to change her train of thought.

Brittany tilted her head back and closed her eyes. She seemed to be giving careful consideration to her answer, and Toni felt another brick fall to the ground. Sharing with someone who gives a question so much thought is like a small gift. A gift she never knew she wanted to receive until Brittany handed it to her.

"My family owns a cabin up at Lake Shasta. We spent every summer up there. We'd swim, fish, and play board games. When I got old enough, my cousins taught me how to wakeboard, and then you really couldn't get me out of the water." She smiled, but it was to herself. "I'd spend months running around barefoot and sunburned. At night, we'd build a fire, and the whole family would sit around the pit and tell stories. The adults would drink, laugh, and talk about what it was like when they were growing up. My aunt Patty would regale us with fantastic stories. I always thought they were made up for entertainment. But now…"

Toni wanted to know everything. She wanted to visit that cabin in Lake Shasta. She wanted to see a small Brittany running around without a care in the world, her dark hair blowing behind her. She wanted to see Popsicle-stained lips and tan lines that could only be obtained by small children. Children who had no worries except the inevitable conclusion of seemingly endless summer days.

"But now what?" Toni scooted forward.

The joy on Brittany's face melted away into a type of sadness that Toni couldn't quite put her finger on.

"Nothing." She smiled at her, but it didn't reach her eyes. "That's enough about me. What about you? Where was your favorite place as a kid?"

Toni stared at her, trying to figure out why Brittany could be so open and honest one minute but shut completely down the next. It didn't seem that she was trying to hide something as much as it seemed like she didn't know how to deal with it.

Toni moved before she could talk herself out of it. She sat down on Brittany's lap and draped her arms around her neck. She watched as the pupils in Brittany's eyes dilated. Brittany ran her hand up Toni's leg until it settled on her waist. She wanted to be touching Brittany when she made another attempt at trying to figure out what storm was brewing under her demeanor. She wanted Brittany to feel their connection and know she could trust her. But now, sitting here, feeling her skin burn under Brittany's fingertips—she was struggling to focus. She watched Brittany's chest rise and fall more rapidly. They had agreed to take it slow, but now that was the last thing Toni wanted to do.

❖

Brittany had watched the sun drift into the Pacific Ocean until the colors merged beyond distinction. She'd seen Half Dome covered in snow on a perfect December morning. She'd been able to bear witness to the Northern Lights creating a glimpse of heaven. But nothing she'd seen had ever been more beautiful than Toni was right now. Toni's muscles tightened as she moved her hand along her body. She watched her lips slightly part when she squeezed her upper thigh. She could feel tension flame between them with each glance, each touch.

"You looked like you were going to ask me something when you came over here." Brittany hadn't meant to whisper, but that's how the statement left her lips.

Toni blinked at her. "I wanted you to tell me more about your aunt." She ran her hand along Brittany's neck and up into her hair.

"Do you still want to talk about my aunt?" Brittany leaned closer to Toni's mouth.

Toni slid her other hand to the spot between Brittany's neck and jaw, pulling her face closer. "No."

The kiss started slow, yet determined. Brittany wanted to take all of Toni in. She wanted to memorize every sensation, every feeling, every millimeter of Toni's lips. She felt the intensity building inside her. They should slow down, but nothing inside her would let that happen. She pulled Toni closer and was rewarded with a quiet moan. Her hands moved under Toni's shirt to her back. Her skin was warm, and it had everything to do with what was building between them and not the cool morning weather.

Toni's hand came down on her bare leg and slid up toward the hem of her shorts. She hadn't realized she sucked in a gulp of air at the movement until she felt Toni smiling against her mouth.

"I love touching you," Toni said as she ran her lips over Brittany's jaw.

Brittany was going to tell her that they should take this inside so Toni could touch her as much as she wanted when she heard the ring of a bike bell.

"Luisa?"

Toni stopped and stared at her. She looked a little dumbfounded. "Did you just call me Luisa?"

Brittany was still trying to reel her body in from her rapidly growing arousal. All she could do was shake her head and point to the driveway. "No. Luisa, who works with you? She's here."

Toni turned to look but didn't get up from her spot on Brittany's lap. "Is everything okay?"

Luisa crossed her arms, seeming angry. "I was stopping by to see if you wanted to ride into work together."

Toni's body stiffened. "What time is it?"

Luisa checked her phone. "Ten thirty."

Toni jumped up from Brittany's lap. "Shit. I'm going to be late." She leaned down and kissed Brittany. "Do not move. I want to pick this up when I get home." She kissed her again. "I mean, you can move. I don't expect you to be in this exact spot when I get back."

Brittany kissed her. "I know what you mean."

"Okay. Good. Luisa, I'll be right down." Toni ran inside the house.

Luisa leaned against the deck railing. "So, are you and Toni a thing?"

"I guess we are." Brittany wasn't sure what to call what was happening between her and Toni, but it felt wrong not to acknowledge it at all.

"Cool," Luisa said, but that wasn't what her tone insinuated. In fact, Brittany would venture to say that Luisa thought it was the opposite of "cool" because she knew enough to recognize the look on Luisa's face. She had a thing for Toni and wasn't expecting to find her, quite literally, in someone else's lap.

"You like working at the pub?" Brittany didn't want there to be any awkwardness, especially for Toni.

"What's not to like?" Luisa wasn't going to meet Brittany halfway and make this easy.

"You're right. Seems like a great place to work." Brittany stared at the door, willing Toni to reappear.

"It's supposed to be pretty busy today. Toni probably won't have a lot of time."

Brittany nodded at the unsubtle warning. "Good to know."

Toni came running out and stopped in front of Brittany. She kissed her again. "Tonight?"

"Absolutely." Brittany squeezed her hand as she walked away.

Brittany watched Toni head down the street on her bike. Now she had the whole day with nothing but her thoughts. Perfect. What could go wrong?

CHAPTER EIGHTEEN

Brittany showered, put her notebook and a few snacks in her backpack, and headed into town on a bike from the garage. It was a beautiful day, and the promise of what could happen tonight lingered in her chest. The anticipation was euphoric. She thought of nothing but Toni as she maneuvered through people on the busy streets. The way she smelled, the way she tasted, the way her body reacted to the slightest touch from Brittany. *Sigh.* It was going to be a good day.

Brittany had originally planned on going to the Second Wave but changed her mind at the last second when another small bar caught her eye. She wanted to take Amy's advice and follow her instincts. She got a seat outside so she could people watch and settled in with a beer.

She stared down at her notes. Words and ideas that popped into her mind were mirrored onto lined paper—descriptions of what she'd seen during the visions, along with all the feelings that came with them. She'd been pouring over article after article on her phone. Her Google search history was a mess. Between "psychic visions" and "possible serial killer motives," she was sure she'd probably been added to some sort of watch list. Even her notes made her feel discombobulated. She started to highlight certain words, phrases, that seemed to come up time and time again. Unfortunately, the word "crazy" was now traced over and over again, almost to the point where she tore through the paper. She couldn't really be crazy, though. Everything that had happened had to mean something.

The one piece of information she saw that made a little bit of sense, from a site called "You're Not Crazy, You're a Psychic" no less, was how actively summoning a vision might help a person get a grip on what was trying to be communicated through the vision. So, she was going to attempt it. Even though she was nervous she might pass out, or worse, vomit, there was a tiny flame of hope inside her that being in a public place would actually help her focus. She always did her best writing, best interviewing, best everything in public places. Maybe trying to summon a vision would garner the same results. She rolled her neck and tried to clear out all other distractions.

The noises swimming around her faded into the background. She focused on her breathing, counting as she inhaled and exhaled. She let her arms and legs go limp as she focused on the blackness behind her eyelids.

Then a flash. Something silver. It was hard and cold. She could feel it under the tip of her finger. It didn't matter that she knew it wasn't really there with her; it felt as if it were. There was the humming again. A joyous melody underpinned with the coldness of hatred and anger. But this time was different. This time, Brittany was in control. She hadn't been pulled here unwillingly—she'd gone under her own volition. That seemed to make all the difference.

Brittany took in everything she could. The room was dark and cold. Did it smell of hops? That couldn't be right.

Silver canisters. She couldn't tell what they were for. The smell of hops was back now, and something else; yeast, and a hint of chocolate. The person moved deeper into the room, and the canisters were clearly kegs. The person stopped walking, almost as if they'd sensed Brittany's intrusion. Hands began to squeeze her head so hard Brittany was sure she'd have bruises. She needed out.

She willed her arms to move. She pleaded with her body, her mind, any god to answer her call and remove her. Her fists clenched and unclenched. She started to feel the sunshine on her face, and then with a final wrench, she gasped. She opened her eyes and was grateful to see the people milling about the streets. She gripped the arms of her chair, needing to anchor herself to something. She had to know this was real. She needed to know *she* was real.

After a few minutes of letting the experience wash over her again, she began to sketch the scene. The darkness, the kegs, the silver canisters, the way the walls seemed to lead up to…nothingness. She scribbled what she smelled: hops, barley, dampness, mildew. She needed to make sure that she had it all right, didn't want to miss a single detail. She should have been more panicked, but she wasn't. She had been in control of this vision, and there was power in that. It didn't feel like something that was being done to her as much as something she was choosing to do. It was liberating.

The kegs. *What does that mean?* She scribbled in her notebook. The room could've been the backroom of any bar, brewery, or even a personal shed. Brittany ran her hands over her face in frustration.

The server walked up to the table. "Do you need anything else?"

"How many kegs do you keep stored in the back, like in general?" Brittany hoped she sounded curious and not like she was planning a heist.

The server looked confused. "Umm gosh, I'm not completely sure. I think it depends on the popularity of the beer. But they aren't just lying around in the back. We keep them in the fridge."

"Thank you." She put a twenty on the table. "Keep the change."

Brittany got on her bike and headed to her favorite bar. If she was going to make sense of what she saw, she was going to need a few more answers.

Toni was acutely aware of the cold shoulder Luisa had been giving her all afternoon. She wasn't entirely sure what she'd done wrong or how to fix it. Every time she'd smile at her, Luisa would roll her eyes.

"These are for table three." Alice handed her the piece of paper with the order scribbled on it.

Toni took six glasses out from under the bar top and started pouring. "Do you know what's going on with Luisa? She seems upset with me."

Alice leaned over the bar to get closer. "That poor girl has a giant crush on you. I'm sure finding you and Brittany this morning was a blow to her ego."

"What? How did I not know that?" Toni handed her the beers on a tray.

She shrugged. "I have no idea. It's pretty obvious. Maybe it's because you haven't noticed anyone but Brittany since the moment you laid eyes on her." She walked back to the table before Toni could answer.

Toni wiped down the bar top while considering what Alice had said. She thought she had been careful when it came to Brittany. They were doing everything they could to take this slow. They'd been seeing each other for over a month but still hadn't slept together. She didn't have anything to measure it against, but she was pretty sure she'd never taken things slower than that. But even as she thought it, she knew her aunt was right. Every spare moment was devoted to thinking about Brittany. When Brittany walked into a room, Toni found it difficult to breathe. Her skin would tingle where Brittany touched her long after they'd left one another. Toni could look at the spots where Brittany's hands had been and still feel them there. *Fuck.*

As if she summoned her, Brittany walked through the front door. Toni's heartrate picked up like it always did when Brittany was near. That cocky smile and easy swagger were always enough to make her skin prickle.

Brittany sat down at the bar. "Hey, I have a super weird question for you."

Toni leaned on the bar, wanting to be closer. "Is it about tonight?"

Brittany blushed slightly, and Toni wanted to pull her into the back office. "No, but I like where your head is at." She ran her fingers over the top of Toni's hand. "Where do you keep your kegs?"

Toni laughed. "That's not where I thought this was going." She stood and walked toward the swinging door. "I'll show you what we have back here. Come on."

Brittany looked around the back room like she was searching for something. Her hands were on her hips, and she looked puzzled. "Would there be any reason for someone to keep their kegs outside a cooler?"

Toni had no idea where any of this was coming from, but she was happy to help however she could. "Umm, not really. You'd skunk the beer. I guess if you were storing empty kegs, you'd keep them out of a cooler."

Brittany closed her eyes and tilted her head back. "Of course. Damn, I'm an idiot sometimes."

Toni put her arms around her waist and pulled her closer. "You're not an idiot." She kissed her chin. "What's this about, anyway?"

Brittany kissed her forehead. "Research for a project I'm working on."

Toni's internal temperature was rapidly rising from their proximity, and she wanted more. She kissed Brittany's jaw down to her neck. "I have a project you can work on."

Brittany pulled her in tighter, and the pulse on her neck quickened under Toni's lips. "How many more hours until you get off?"

Toni leaned back and raised an eyebrow. "Like from work…or?"

Brittany smiled and kissed her again. "You always taste so good."

Toni's heart was hammering so loud she was sure Brittany could hear it. Hell, she wouldn't be surprised if the customers could hear it. Brittany's lips were so soft, so enticing. Toni could easily spend hours kissing her. She wanted to spend hours kissing her.

"She'll be off at six. She doesn't have to close tonight." Alice pushed the door open and went back out into the bar.

"How long do you think she was back here?" Brittany laughed with her lips against the side of Toni's temple.

"Probably the whole time." Toni sighed. "I should get back out there."

"Okay. I'm going to make a few stops, but I'm cooking dinner for you tonight. Come home hungry."

Toni reluctantly let go. She checked her watch and was disappointed to see she had another four hours left of her shift. Four hours of thinking about Brittany and the sensual possibilities their night held. Four hours to consider all the ways she could potentially fuck this whole thing sideways. Four hours of hoping she wouldn't.

CHAPTER NINETEEN

B rittany pulled her bike up to the front of Riot Brewing, once again following her intuition. A delivery truck passed her, slowly cracking along the gravel drive. Brittany hopped on the bike and followed it around to the back. The driver got out and pulled the back door of the van open.

"Hey," Brittany called from twenty feet away. She didn't want to startle the poor woman.

The woman put her hand up to shield her eyes from the sun. "Hey. Can I help you?"

Brittany moved the bike closer. "This is going to sound really weird, but is this where they store all the beer?"

The woman smiled. "You planning a kegger or something?"

Brittany squeezed the handlebars. She felt foolish and needed something to do with her hands. "I've just always been curious about the process."

The woman nodded and took a step forward. "You can get a tour of the whole place. You just need to let them know up front."

Brittany stuck her hand out. "I'm Brittany."

The woman cocked her head but didn't move to shake her hand. "I'm Shea. Sorry. I'd shake your hand, but mine are covered in grease. I got a flat downtown."

Brittany peered around to look at the car. "You fixed it yourself?"

Shea nodded. "I learned a long time ago if you're gonna be in outside sales, you'll save yourself a lot of time and headaches if you can fix your own flats."

Shea walked over and pulled on a white door that rolled up into the ceiling. She opened the back of the van and took out samples from a cooler.

Brittany rolled her bike a few feet forward, wanting to get a better look. "How long have you worked here?" She wanted to keep the conversation going until she could see inside.

"I actually work for Nereids Brewing. We have a beer cooperative going with Riot." Shea turned and looked at her suspiciously. "You really aren't supposed to be back here. Safety reasons."

Brittany ignored the last part of her statement. "You live out here on the island, or…?" Brittany rolled a little closer. She angled her bike until she could see inside the small warehouse.

"Look, you're hot and all that, but I have a girlfriend."

Brittany saw the kegs lining the ground. They looked exactly how they had in her vision. The only difference was a large mural of sea gulls and a beach scene with pride flags flapping in the distance painted on the side of the wall. Maybe she'd missed it. She was, after all, poking around in someone else's brain. Surprisingly, that creeped her out less than making the whole thing up in her head.

"Okay. Well, thank you for your time." Brittany turned her bike to leave.

"I'm not saying I'm not interested. I just wanted you to know that I have a girlfriend. So, we'd have to keep this quiet."

Brittany put her feet on the pedals and gave her a quick smile. "I'll keep that in mind. It was nice meeting you, Shea." She didn't want to completely blow her off until she had managed to put all the pieces together. Brittany wasn't convinced she was in the right place—or the wrong place. She needed more information.

She headed back into town planning to do more investigating tomorrow. Right now, she needed to pick up a few things to make Toni dinner. She smiled to herself thinking about spending a few hours with Toni. She couldn't remember being this excited about anything in a long time.

Toni had hurried home after her shift and managed to shower while Brittany finished cooking. The dinner had been delicious. It was an excellent combination of tortellini, shrimp, and asparagus. But hell, Brittany could have fed her anything, and Toni still would have swooned. Brittany, in her tight jeans and a V-neck shirt. Brittany, who leaned forward on the table when she spoke, causing her breasts to push up against the fabric perfectly to accentuate her cleavage. Toni felt herself getting drunk on the dabs of perfume she knew Brittany had placed right behind her ears. She was hooked.

She clinked her wine glass against Brittany's on the couch after dinner. "Thank you for a wonderful meal."

Brittany sipped her wine. "Thank you for the wonderful company."

She was gorgeous in the soft light of the living room, and Toni found herself reaching to touch her cheek. "You really are beautiful."

Brittany leaned into Toni's hand. "You make me feel beautiful."

The excitement bubbled in Toni's core and spilled out into her chest. Her cheeks flushed hot from unadulterated need. "Come with me."

Brittany took their wine glasses and placed them on the table.

Toni stood and took her hand, leading her up the stairs. When they got to Toni's room, she shut the door behind her, and leaned against the wood.

Brittany wrapped her arms around her waist. "I've wanted to kiss you since you walked through the door."

Toni slid her hands under Brittany's shirt. She let her thumbs run against Brittany's stomach to the silky fabric of Brittany's bra. "I've wanted to kiss you since the first time we met."

Brittany lifted her arms, and Toni pulled her shirt over her head. She put her hand on Brittany's shoulder and traced her arm with the back of her hand. Her throat went dry as she moved her hands down to the belt loops of Brittany's jeans. She was mesmerized by the goose bumps she left on Brittany's skin everywhere she touched.

Brittany grabbed the bottom of Toni's tank top and pulled the fabric off. When their bare stomachs touched, another surge of arousal almost took Toni out in the knees. Brittany did things to her that no one had ever done before. She'd never wanted anyone more than she wanted Brittany now. Not even Penn. *Penn.* She slammed the thought away and focused.

Brittany kissed her neck and slowly moved up to her ear. "I want you."

She pushed Brittany onto the bed and crawled on top of her. The action of putting Brittany between her legs, of feeling her hips between her thighs, kicked up her need another level. Brittany ran her hands up Toni's stomach and around her back, pulling her in for kisses that were growing more feverish by the second.

Toni rocked against Brittany's hips and whimpered when her sex tightened against the friction. She raked her teeth down Brittany's neck and down to her chest. She could see Brittany's nipples hard against the fabric of her bra, and she wanted nothing more than to release them. She wanted to see, touch, feel, and explore Brittany in her entirety. She slid the fabric off to reveal one of Brittany's breasts, not wanting to waste even a second by unhooking it from the back. She put her mouth on the hard pink nipple and was rewarded by another thrust from Brittany's hips.

Toni felt her body shudder as another wave of arousal washed over her. More bricks fell from her wall. She wanted all of Brittany. She wanted to make Brittany hers. *Hers. Penn was mine once, too.*

Toni stopped moving, her body rigid, seized by panic.

Brittany grabbed her face, forcing her to look at her. "Are you okay?"

Toni felt tears on her cheeks. "I'm not sure I can do this right now."

Brittany pulled her down on top of her and hugged her. "It's okay," she said breathlessly. "We don't have to do anything you're not ready for."

"I'm so sorry."

Brittany kissed her cheek. "There is nothing to be sorry for. I don't want you to have any regrets. I don't want you to feel any pressure."

Toni sniffled. "It's not that I don't want you because God knows I do. I hope you know that."

"I know," Brittany murmured as she rubbed soothing circles on her back. "I know."

After several minutes, Brittany moved to get off the bed. Toni stopped her. "Can you just lie here with me? Will you just sleep next to me?" She didn't know if she was asking for too much, but the thought of Brittany leaving was too much to bear.

"Of course." Brittany curled up behind her and wrapped her arms around her. "I'm not going anywhere."

Until you go back to California, and I stay here. Without you.

Toni pushed her thoughts away and let herself be present in this moment. She didn't know what tomorrow would look like because of her decision. She wanted so badly to move on, let go of the past, but of course, she couldn't. Was she ever going to be able to? The thought that she'd never be ready, that some force would always be reminding her she wasn't worthy, carved a hole in her heart. She tried, though, to remember that she was exactly where she wanted to be. Even if her brain was having a hard time believing things might actually turn out okay. For once.

Chapter Twenty

Leslie peered at Toni as they sat at the kitchen table together. Something was different about the way Toni was holding herself these days, and she knew it was all to do with Brittany. It wasn't a bad thing, healing because of someone else, but healing at an alarmingly fast pace could be detrimental. Leslie sort of wanted to kick herself for pushing the two of them together so quickly. Maybe she should have held off on the matchmaking just a bit. At least until Toni looked lighter on her own.

"What?"

Leslie smiled, set her coffee on the table, and cleared her throat. "Just wondering how you're doing."

"I'm okay." Toni's eyes flitted from the newspaper she was reading to Leslie's eyes and then back to the article. "Why?"

"You seem—"

"I promise you I'm fine." It was Toni's turn to clear her throat. An attempt at dispersing the tension, no doubt, but the gesture was futile.

"Toni, honey, are you and Brittany..." Leslie paused. She didn't want to keep pushing. She knew Toni well enough not to push her when she was backed into a corner.

"Are me and Brittany what?"

Leslie sighed. "Oh, I don't know, maybe moving a little too fast?"

"Jesus..."

"Don't Jesus me," Leslie said, her voice stern as she stiffened her spine. "I'm worried about you. I'm allowed to be, y'know, and I make no apologies for it."

Toni's expression softened, and Leslie felt a wave of relief wash over her.

"I'm sorry, Aunty. You're right. I think maybe…" Toni stopped, folded the paper, pushed it away from her. "Maybe we did move a little too fast. I just…I really like her so much, and I feel this genuine connection with her, something I haven't felt in a really long time, and maybe, just maybe, this was what was supposed to happen to me on this island. I mean, it's a possibility."

"Yes, yes, it is." She smiled and reached across the table to place her hand on Toni's. "You're more than allowed to move on. I know you know that. But moving on too quickly when you're not ready? That can be a lot harder to deal with than maybe you realize."

"How would you even know that?"

"Well, after I filed for divorce from Bill, I tried to get Alice back, but she'd moved on with someone else by then. So eventually, I accepted that I'd lost her and went back to dating men to see if maybe I could get it to stick."

"Get what to stick?"

"Heterosexuality." Leslie laughed as she brought her coffee to her mouth. She took a sip, then another and gazed up at the ceiling as memories flooded back. "It obviously didn't work. I actually thought I might have been bisexual, but after Alice, it was no use. I sure gave it the ol' college try, though. I rushed myself into dating again, trying to push past the heartache."

Toni's eyes filled with tears, her chin started to quiver, and Leslie knew one false move and those tears were going to spill out onto those sun-kissed cheeks. She'd seen Toni grow from a stubborn little girl to a headstrong, beautiful woman. And now she was seeing her handle something she never thought they'd encounter together. Heartbreak and healing. Two things Leslie was a pro at. If only she could impart the wisdom of all of her years in one sitting. She knew that wasn't going to happen because growing up meant making mistakes and learning from them. Penn was Toni's biggest mistake. And she was definitely learning from it. However, the learning and the growth were sometimes harder than the mistake.

"I'm so sick of thinking about Penn. I'm so ready to get over her, Aunty."

"I know, baby. I know."

"And Brittany..." Toni pulled a deep breath in and held it for what felt like a solid minute. As she let it out slowly, she shook her head. "She's like no one I've ever met before. She has this way about her that just calms me, makes me feel desired, and also really important. You know that connection I'm talking about, don't you?"

"More than you realize." She shrugged before drinking again. "My connection with Alice was so intense and so wonderful. I never realized how much so until we were reunited. I thought it was just a fluke, and then...it wasn't."

"No offense, but I really don't want to lose this girl and have to find a way back to her somehow forty years later."

Leslie leaned her head back and laughed a hearty chuckle. "None taken, Antoinette. None taken."

"So what do I do?"

"Well, for starters," Alice said as she whisked into the kitchen wearing khaki cargo pants and a plaid short-sleeved button-down. "You take some deep breaths and try to remember this relationship is just as new for her as it is for you. You're both in similar places in your lives, so work with it. Go with your instincts on this one."

Leslie caught Toni's gaze and held it for a beat before she tilted her head. "She's right, y'know?"

"Sigh."

"Yeah, sigh." Alice leaned down and placed a kiss on Leslie's lips. "Good morning, beautiful."

"Good morning, my love." Leslie placed her hand on Alice's cheek and smoothed her hand over her soft skin. Morning kisses were always Leslie's favorite, for no other reason than she simply savored every single morning she got to spend with the love of her life. Saying she cherished every single second was the most cliché thing she'd ever uttered. Clichés existed for a reason, though, and it was hardly because they weren't true. "What would I have done if fate hadn't shined down on us not once, but twice?"

"Is it too obvious to say something about being miserable and alone?"

"Alice Burton," Leslie said as she playfully smacked Alice on the shoulder. "You're gonna get it."

"Okay, you two. You still haven't told me what to do with my situation. Can you focus on me, please?" Toni laughed as she downed the rest of her coffee and placed her mug on the table. "I don't want to lose this girl."

"Then don't lose her."

"Hold on to her with everything in you. But remember this," Alice said softly as she leaned down and looked directly at Toni. Leslie's heart swelled at the sight. She'd always loved how Alice handled her important relatives, but her relationship with Toni was, by far, Leslie's favorite to witness. "You are the only person who knows when you're ready. If you try to rush it, you'll know. I know it's scary, but you have to trust your heart."

The corner of Toni's mouth pulled up into a small smile. "Thanks, Alice. I needed to hear that."

"I know you did."

Leslie reached across the table again and placed her hand on Toni's forearm. She squeezed her gently and before she released her, she said quietly, "I love you."

"I love you, too. So much."

Talk about embarrassed. There had been a few times in Toni's life when she was made to feel like a complete idiot. Those times were in high school, of course, when doing a cartwheel across the quad and ripping her pants clean open was something she could recover from. But now? Now she was a grown woman who clearly didn't know how to handle her emotions, her heart, or herself, and now she'd dragged Brittany into her messy existence.

Chickening out wasn't something she handled lightly. She had never chickened out before. Not since she'd been dared to ride a bronco bareback and had succeeded. She'd vowed to never back down and to always face her fears head-on.

And then she went and got her heart broken and not only could she add "sad and pathetic" to the list of things she hated about herself, she could also add "chickened out at having sex with the fucking hottest woman she'd ever met" to it.

Despite her reassuring conversation with her aunts, her heart and her mind just weren't ready for some stupid reason, and all she wanted to do was crawl into a hole and waste away there until Brittany escaped back to California. The worst part was that she knew what it felt like to be denied. She knew the fucking heartbreak that occurred when someone said they couldn't...or wouldn't...and it wasn't easy to recover from. She was sad and stressed and even more upset when she woke up that morning to find her bed empty and that Brittany had taken off again on one of the bikes. She knew Brittany was researching a project or a story or a book or whatever the hell, but damn, all she wanted to do was apologize, and she couldn't.

She didn't want to text it.

She didn't want to call about it.

She wanted to see Brittany and tell her to her face that she was sorry. Embarrassed. Sad. Scared. But most of all, she wanted to tell Brittany that she was feeling so many things for her, deep, intense, crazy feelings, and that was almost as scary as healing had been.

Everything about life had been so simple, from the small town she grew up in, to the people she was still friends with, to how she knew everyone who stopped into the grocery store. She even joked that she was a simple girl with simple needs. But ever since she left Colorado with Penn, the simple girl with simple needs turned out to be someone who was easy to leave and wasn't at all needed.

It was such a blow to her self-esteem. She wasn't an ugly person. She knew that. But damn, Penn made her feel like a used hamburger wrapper. It did its job to begin with, but when it was no longer needed, Penn tossed it aside. Because if she meant more than that, why was she so fucking easy to leave in the middle of nowhere?

Toni picked up a rock from the beach and tossed it in the air. She caught it once, twice, three times before she threw it as hard as she could into the water. She waited until it splashed into the Atlantic before she plopped down onto the sand, arms propped on her bent knees, tears welling in her eyes. She blinked rapidly to release them. Maybe that's what she needed, a good cry.

"Because you're a big fucking cry baby," Toni said quietly as she took the sleeve of her shirt and wiped at her wet cheeks. "Just sitting by yourself, crying, like a stupid jerk. God. Why can't I just get over what that bitch did to me?" She looked up at the sky, at the dark clouds building, and groaned. "And now I'm fucking talking to myself. Just great."

"You realize you're not the only person who talks to herself, right?"

Toni whipped around. There stood Brittany, in all her goddamn beautiful glory, cutoff shorts and a San Francisco Giants T-shirt. She looked away and groaned. "Oh, of course, you had to hear all of that, didn't you?"

Brittany chuckled as she dropped her flip-flops in the sand, sat next to Toni, and leaned into her. When she nudged her gently, she said sincerely, "I'm glad I heard it. I think I needed to."

"No, you didn't need to hear that I'm a fucking basket case still not over a person who didn't give two shits about me. I should be over the heartache, and I sure the fuck should be over Penn. And you're right, what a stupid-ass name."

Brittany dug her toes into the sand, looking thoughtful. "You are not the only basket case in this relationship. I thought I told you that already."

"You did." Toni's response was quick, and she was trying to keep her composure, but Brittany's proximity combined with her scent, her lovely laughter, and her gorgeous legs were definitely causing Toni's facade to crack.

"Oh, hey there. Is that a smile I see?"

Toni shook her head. "No. You do not see a smile."

"I don't know…" Brittany leaned forward and looked at Toni. "I see something forming on those magnificent lips." She pointed playfully. "Riiiight there."

"Stop." Toni waved her hand. "You jerk." She felt herself giving in and before she knew it, she was smiling, and they were laughing together. *God, it feels so good to feel good again.* "I'm so sorry about last night, Britt."

"You have got to stop apologizing. For everything." Brittany draped her arm over Toni's shoulders and pulled her close. "Everybody is working on something, y'know? And I'm patient, as well as also working on my own somethings." She let out a small laugh. "Which makes me sound so appealing."

"Shush," Toni whispered.

"Just know I'm not mad at you, and I totally understand everything you're going through."

"Abandonment issues really are a fucking drag." Toni sighed. "I hope you know how much I like you, though. I mean, like, I like you so much it makes my hands ache."

"Oh, really?" Brittany pulled back and eyed Toni. "Please, tell me more."

Toni could feel the blush working its way up her chest onto her neck and across her face. "Have you ever felt that before? The aching...the way it can settle in your hands, in your stomach, in your chest..." Toni reached over and picked up Brittany's left hand. She turned it over and carefully drew a line down Brittany's thumb, pinky, ring, middle, index finger, to her palm. "The very thought of you, of your touch, your lips, the curve of your hips, the way your hair falls across your face before you casually push it behind your ear." She stopped, took a deep breath, and looked up into Brittany's eyes. "All of it makes my hands ache...ache to hold you, to touch you, to feel your wetness, to make you come undone underneath me...or on top of me..." She licked her lips and forced herself to slow her breathing. So much honesty was causing her to feel almost suffocated, but not in a bad way, which made absolutely no sense at all. She felt more alive than she had in months. Maybe she needed to get the wind knocked out of her in order to realize she was far from dead. "I am sure I want you. Because this ache? God...it isn't something that happens when these feelings aren't real."

"Toni..." Brittany's voice came out as a strained whisper.

"Take me back to the house."

"We do not have to do this. I don't want—"

"I'm ready."

"You weren't last night."

"I am now."

"Toni," Brittany said again, this time with more authority. "If at any moment you need me to stop—"

"I won't." Toni grabbed Brittany at the back of her neck and kissed her breathless.

She licked the moisture from her lips and brushed some stray hairs away from Toni's eyes. "Then let's go because I don't think I'll last much longer if I don't get to put my mouth on the rest of you."

Toni stood and held her hand out. "So you're admitting I gave you the ol' blue bean last night?"

Brittany burst into laughter. "Oh my God, did you just say 'blue bean'?"

Toni couldn't contain her laughter any longer. She doubled over as she said, "I did!"

"I swear, I will never recover from that." Brittany continued to laugh as they walked as quickly as possible back to the house. "Blue bean. I can't even..."

"It's true, though, isn't it?"

Again, Brittany started to laugh. She shook her head as they approached the front door, the first drops of rain starting to fall from the dark clouds. "You are a nut, you know that?"

"Am I wrong?"

Brittany pushed open the door and pulled Toni through it. "You are most definitely not wrong. Now, do you mind? I need some fucking release."

"I'll give you release. I'll give you so much release you won't know what to do with it all."

When they got to the top of the stairs, Brittany pulled Toni into her bedroom and immediately shut the door behind them. "I should have kept my rental."

"What? Why?"

"Because I plan on making you scream my name."

"Jesus Christ. That's so fucking hot."

"You're going to have to beg me to stop."

"*Fuck...*" Toni's mouth watered as she fumbled with the lock on the door. She turned, watched as Brittany closed the distance between them, and felt her entire being fill with hunger when Brittany's hands landed on her cheeks.

"Are you okay?"

She nodded, swallowed the rather large lump that had lodged itself in her throat, and licked her lips.

"Toni?"

"Hmm?"

"I won't hurt you," Brittany whispered, her thumbs lightly rubbing across Toni's cheeks. "I promise."

"Don't." Her tone was drenched with desire. "Don't promise that." Toni slid her hands down Brittany's sides, over her small hips, to the waistband of her shorts. She made quick work of undoing the button and zipper of the cutoffs. She slipped her hands under the material and pushed until they slid down Brittany's toned and tanned legs. "Just don't take off on me."

"Believe me," Brittany said, a sly smile on her full lips, "I'm not going anywhere."

Toni ran her hands under Brittany's T-shirt, dragged her fingers across her abdominal muscles around to her back. "Kiss me, please." When Brittany complied, their lips finally connecting, Toni could have sworn she tasted love in Brittany's kisses, in the way she so perfectly explored her mouth, in the fullness of her lips, in the smoothness of her tongue.

Breaking the kiss for a second, Brittany moved her hands to the hem of Toni's T-shirt and pulled it up and over her head. She tossed it over her shoulder and immediately continued the kiss. Every square inch of Toni's body was on fire. Her core throbbed against her tight khaki shorts. There wasn't a single fiber of her being that didn't want this. Something inside her had changed between last night and tonight. She was thrilled the shift finally happened, even if she wasn't sure exactly what had shifted, or why. Maybe it was acknowledging her own heartache? Or maybe it was figuring out how to handle being abandoned? Or maybe it was the simple fact that she loved having sex, and she knew she was going to absolutely fucking love having sex with Brittany.

Whatever it was, she knew she needed to speed this process up or they'd end up kissing for hours. Not that there was anything wrong with kissing for hours, but they both needed the release they'd teased each other with.

❖

Brittany's mind was racing. She was equal parts excited and scared. So much had happened between the two of them in the last thirty-six hours. She was getting what she wanted, and it was clear Toni was also on board, but were they allowing their need for release to drive this runaway freight train right off the tracks?

"What's wrong?" Toni's voice snapped Brittany back to the moment.

Busted... "Nothing. I promise."

"You're kissing weird." Toni smiled, giggled, and brushed her lips against Brittany's. "I may not be an expert on you yet, but I can certainly tell when something's going on in that head of yours." She pulled away. "Oh no, it's not a headache, is it?"

Brittany smirked as she hooked her thumbs into the waistband of Toni's panties and yanked them down her legs. The breath Toni released made her smile. "You're incredibly sweet thinking it's my head that's aching."

"Well, what else could be aching—" She stopped abruptly, her eyes widening. "Oh. I get it. You mean..." She trailed her finger down Brittany's sternum, over her still clasped bra, to her panties. She glided her hand under the cotton material and slid a solitary finger through to her wetness. "Take these off. Now."

Brittany's arousal was so uncomfortable, she did exactly as instructed. She was just as excited to get rid of the damp material as Toni seemed to be. "I'm glad you caught on." She held the panties up, draped across her index finger, then let them fall to the floor. "Now, if you don't mind, can we um...do this?"

"And here I thought I was with someone who had patience." Toni pushed her to the edge of the bed and they fell onto it, Toni on top. "I have a feeling," Toni pulled her hand from Brittany's panties, "you were just saying that," she bent down and placed a row of kisses along Brittany's neck, "to get me into bed."

Sweet Jesus. Brittany was ready to explode and they'd barely gotten started. She let out a laugh that sprang out of frustration coupled with desire. *Fuck this.* She needed to feel Toni, so she reached between her legs. The warm wetness she found reassured her there'd be no turning back.

Toni whimpered with pleasure, then sat up and straddled her. She grabbed Brittany's hands and pushed them against her breasts. How freeing it was being with a woman who actually showed Brittany what she wanted. Most of the time she found she was the one in charge, but being under Toni's command heightened Brittany's desire even further. Brittany cupped each of Toni's breasts in her hands, rubbing her hard nipples with her thumbs. She pushed the bra off Toni's shoulders as she watched, breathlessly. Toni's head was bent back, her eyes closed, as she rocked back and forth with the obvious pleasure of the nipple play.

She leaned forward, placed her mouth on a nipple, and sucked. Toni's moan was exactly what she'd hoped for. She bit down and received another low moan. She squeezed the other nipple, pinched it lightly, then did it again before Toni whimpered. With her mouth on Toni's nipple, Brittany moved her hand down, over Toni's flat stomach, to her warm center. She slid her hand down until she could glide her middle finger, softly and slowly over Toni's ready center.

"God, Brittany. I want you so bad," Toni whispered. "You feel so fucking good."

Brittany stood, lifting Toni to place her on her back near the foot of the bed. She was ready to make Toni come, but there was something to be said about her patience. She began devouring Toni's lips, nibbling, then biting them, rubbing her thigh into Toni's warm wetness. She then grabbed Toni's hands and hoisted them over her head, restraining her as she nibbled her neck.

"Brittany…" She let out a low groan. "I can't stand this teasing anymore. Please."

The urgency in her breathy whisper aroused Brittany even more. She had this gorgeous, sensual, sensitive woman beneath her begging her to satisfy her. The rush was almost too much. She trailed her mouth down Toni's neck, between her breasts, stopping just under her navel to tantalize her by brushing her lips over her skin.

When Toni clutched fistfuls of her hair, she ran her tongue over the spot Toni had been saving just for her. She worked her tongue like an artist crafting a masterpiece, careful to pay thorough attention to her every curve and contour. Toni's gasps and moans grew louder with every delicate swirl and flick. When she slid two fingers inside her, Toni moaned loudly, and Brittany cringed hoping Leslie and Alice were still out back sitting by the fire.

"Oh, God, Brittany, please don't stop."

Now it was Brittany who could no longer stand the teasing. She increased the pressure of her tongue and the speed of her thrusts. She could feel Toni's orgasm building, she could hear it in her breaths and moans. She curled her fingers slightly. Within seconds, she pulled an explosive orgasm from Toni, whose back arched as she practically levitated from the pile of sheets.

"Holy shit," Toni said through gaspy breaths.

When she reached down and pulled Brittany up to her, she held her tight. Brittany felt as satisfied at pleasuring Toni as she clearly seemed to have been to receive it. She gently kissed her face until Toni was ready for words.

"I can't believe how you made me feel."

"I can't believe how you made me feel," Brittany replied.

"But I didn't do anything to you yet."

"That's what you think." Brittany smiled and placed a soft kiss in the center of her forehead.

The way Toni was gazing into her eyes, Brittany was sure something seriously emotional was about to be said. She rolled off her lest, in her post-coital euphoria, Toni said something she wasn't ready for and freaked herself out.

"You're not trying to escape, are you?" Toni rolled on top and ran her hands through Brittany's hair as she looked down at her.

Brittany chuckled softly as she adjusted her body under Toni's weight. "Not that I could even if I wanted to, but I can assure you, I do not want to."

"That's good because you do something to me, Brittany. And I'm kind of hoping you'll stick around until I figure out what it is."

"Something more than making you scream like a banshee in bed?"

Toni giggled and sat up to straddle Brittany once more. She couldn't wait to get her mouth on every part of her beautiful body.

Struck with a naughty idea, she pulled the crumpled up top sheet out from the side of the mattress and felt her juices start flowing again. "Here's something else you bring out in me." She wound the sheet up like a rope, lifted Brittany's arms, and tied them together and to the poster at the foot of the bed.

"What are you doing?" Brittany said, her eyes reflecting a new height of arousal.

"I know you said you're not going anywhere, but I'm not gonna take any chances, at least not until I'm done having my way with your entire body."

When Toni stripped off Brittany's strapless bra, she drank in the vision of Brittany's curvaceous breasts and flexing abdominal muscles before she pressed her body back down on Brittany's, which by this point, was on fire.

"I hope you know this is absolute torture," Brittany said. "And I'm so turned on right now."

"I don't mean to torture you," Toni said seductively. "I'm just so in awe of you that I'm afraid I'll eat you alive if I don't pace myself."

"Go ahead. Eat me alive," Brittany whispered. "I dare you."

Toni accepted the challenge and began nibbling on Brittany's breasts, licking her nipples to a rock hard state. She watched as Brittany bit her bottom lip, trying to endure the exquisite torment. She slid her lips down Brittany's torso and bit at her stomach, watching her chest heave as she breathed harder and faster. She let her lips hover over Brittany's sex, grazing it ever so slightly, causing Brittany to groan and undulate with desire.

Toni had never done anything like this before. The control she had over Brittany at that moment, the control Brittany was allowing and trusting her to have, was empowering unlike anything she'd ever known.

Brittany's moans of anguished pleasure grew louder, and Toni couldn't imagine a more arousing sound.

"Toni," she whispered, still writhing.

"Yes, baby?"

"If you don't get down there, it's going to happen without you."

Toni stifled a laugh, then luxuriated in her taste and the sound of her calling out her name as she brought her to a shuddering climax.

She lay in Brittany's arms as they both recovered from the physical exertion. Toni gently traced circles around Brittany's stomach and across her ribcage. She wondered what was going through Brittany's mind but she also knew, whatever it was, it could vary greatly compared to her own. One of Toni's biggest faults was falling too hard, too fast, and she was aware of it, fully. In this particular circumstance, she could literally feel herself walking down that path. This time, though, she wasn't going to let herself get swept away so quickly.

Yes, she was definitely having deep feelings for Brittany. God, who wouldn't after the amazing sex they'd just had? But she wanted to make sure this was going to at least have some longevity this time. With Penn, she'd known almost instantly things were going to go nowhere fast, but she'd refused to let her heart believe her head. She didn't want to start another war between the two again.

Even if she knew her heart would win.

Again.

The next morning, Brittany awoke a little stiff. She'd apparently conked out with Toni's full weight on her arm and shoulder and hadn't moved for the rest of the night. She gently lifted Toni's arm stuck to her bare chest so she wouldn't wake her. But if the movement didn't wake her, surely her growling stomach would.

"Good morning," Toni said before opening her eyes. She stretched to reach Brittany and kissed her.

"Good morning. Sorry about my stomach. I'm starving."

"I'm hungry, too, but not for breakfast." Toni began kissing her neck and running her hand down Brittany's waist.

"Toni, honey. I'm smelling coffee downstairs. We better get up before your aunts bring us breakfast in bed. Without knocking first."

"Awkward," Toni said.

"Yeah. Totally." Brittany got up first and gathered her various garments that had been flung around the room the night before. "Hey, wanna take a jog out to the bluff and get breakfast in town after?"

"That sounds like a brilliantly strategic move." Toni nodded her approval.

After she'd brushed her teeth, splashed her face with cold water, and dressed in her running clothes, Brittany followed Toni down the stairs into the lair of curious aunts sitting at the breakfast table.

"Good morning, ladies," Leslie said with a suggestively lascivious grin.

Alice's was no better. "Coffee's on."

"Thanks," Toni said. "But we want to get a run in before it gets too hot out. We'll see you later."

Brittany waved and followed Toni out the door. They ran the main road heading up to the highest point overlooking the Atlantic, about four miles or so from the cottage. They were quiet for a lot of the run, but it wasn't an awkward silence. Brittany felt comfortable enough with Toni, especially after last night, that they could have stretches of silence and not feel pressured to fill them in with small talk. The longer they ran, exchanging warm, knowing smiles along the way, the more ready Brittany felt to let Toni in on the real reason she'd come to the island.

The end of the line was Babe's by the Sea, a breakfast and lunch shack surrounded by umbrella tables that had become trendy since the dawn of hashtagging. Babe herself had explained the phenomenon one night at the bar of the Second Wave. A rugged, buxom middle-aged butch, Babe had become a local celebrity among hungover lesbians of all ages for her greasy sausage, bacon, egg, and cheddar burrito drenched in Frank's Red Hot, guaranteed to remedy the queasy penance of the sins of the night before.

Since Brittany and Toni weren't hungover, they went with the healthier fare, veggie egg white and turkey bacon wraps and coffee.

Brittany finished her wrap fast, famished not only from their run but also from the extensive exercise of several rounds of lovemaking. She gazed at Toni as she more daintily ate her wrap, and silently adored the little blond fuzz on the side of her face lit by the morning sun.

"Stop staring. I look atrocious," Toni said. She attempted to fix the strands of sweaty hair that had escaped from her ponytail on their jog.

"You do not." Brittany squeezed her hand gently. "Most people would say it was a tie between what was more beautiful—the morning sun glistening on the waves or on your tanned, flushed face. But to me, it isn't even close."

"I don't want to freak you out or anything, but I can't stop thinking about last night," Toni said. "It was truly the best sex I've ever experienced in my life." Her voice was a hushed whisper and the blush on her cheeks only added to the sincerity.

"For me, too, Toni. And I'm not just saying it because you said it first."

"But the thing is, it wasn't the physical part alone. It was you, your vibe, the energy you gave off just made it—"

"Electric," Brittany said.

"Yes. That's the word," Toni said. "Is it weird that I felt like that, especially after all the protesting I did about getting involved with anyone again?"

"I don't think it's weird." Brittany absently chased a chunk of melon around the plate with her fork. "When I came here, the last thing on my mind was starting something with someone. I mean it wasn't even close to being on the radar."

Toni frowned. "I hope I haven't derailed your recovery process. I remember you saying you wanted a quiet place to ease back into a normal life after the accident."

"What's normal?" Brittany shrugged. "I don't think life will ever be how I knew it before the accident. I have no idea where this will lead us, Toni, but the one thing I know for sure is that whenever I'm near you, it's the closest to normal I've felt in a long time."

"They say that people come into our lives for a reason, a season, or a lifetime. Thanks to you, I've come to realize that Penn was only a reason, and that was to help me understand what I don't want in a person."

Brittany stared out the sailboats. "You wanna finish our coffees by the rocks?"

Toni nodded excitedly, and after Brittany left a tip on the table, they walked over to the entrance to the stairs that descended to the shore area. They found an outcropping of rocks above the beach and sat together, their shoulders touching.

"From my first morning here," Toni said, "I fell in love with New England summer mornings. When it isn't humid, the breeze off the Atlantic is fresh and crisp, and it's so quiet at the cottage. I think I can truly explain what Zen is after being here."

"Agreed," Brittany said. "I've never been anywhere like Swift Island. There is something different here, there's really no place like it."

"It's kind of wild that of all the locales you could've picked, you came here. I'm starting to believe serendipity might be an actual thing."

Brittany kissed Toni on her sweet coffee lips, just in case it was the last time she got to do it. "So speaking of serendipity, do you believe that can happen with other things?"

"I guess so. Like what?"

Brittany had to go for it. There would never be a better time or setting than now to tell her about her visions. "Like maybe I was directed here for more than just meeting you?"

Toni's nervous chuckle wasn't the response Brittany had hoped for. "Are you going to tell me that some higher power directed you here or something?" Toni finally asked.

Brittany felt her heart clench. "Uh, not exactly."

Now Toni appeared alarmed. "Okay, what's going on?"

"Nothing." It wasn't the right time. Toni's reaction made that clear. But maybe it would never be the right time.

"Please don't hold back now." Toni stared at her like something was starting to grow out of Brittany's forehead.

"Sorry. It's just, well, I have this aunt," Brittany started, quickly compensating. "She reads tarot cards, and she sort of persuaded me that I needed to pick a place and just jump headfirst into it."

The relief that flooded Toni's expression was almost palpable. "Oh, thank God."

"What?"

"I didn't know what you were going to say, but damn, I was nervous. I feel like I'm always waiting for the other shoe to drop. I'm sorry."

Brittany forced herself to chuckle along with Toni. "Of course. No, it's fine."

"So it's a tarot card reading that brought you here? That's pretty cool, actually."

"Yeah, it is." Brittany stared across the water and tried to calm down. She was so upset with herself. Of all the times to spring this on anyone, now wasn't the time. She wasn't even sure what the visions meant yet, so to tell someone else about them, someone she was feeling all sorts of feelings for, seemed counterintuitive. She took a deep breath and held it for one beat, two, three before she slowly released it. *It's fine. You didn't tell her. It's fine.*

But she feared it was only a matter of time before she'd have to say something. She was lying to Toni by not telling her the whole truth, and that realization burned in the back of her throat. She really hoped she could figure it all out before then.

Chapter Twenty-one

S urely you mean you want at least three kegs of U-Haul."
Leslie smiled. "Well, Quinn, I know you said it was going to sell really well." She paused and looked at Alice who gave her a nod. "But the ale is selling much better than the IPA. I hope you understand. We don't want to have kegs and kegs of something that we just can't move."

"Have you been trying to move it? Or is your niece over there only pushing the ale?" Quinn motioned to Toni.

Leslie felt herself get a little territorial. "She's doing a great job. We've sold out of every other beer you've brewed for us. You know that." She leaned across the table and patted Quinn's hand. Her expression softened instantly.

"Okay, okay. I'm sorry. Things have just been tense at the brewery. Lots of orders coming in and we just—" She glanced over at her new supply manager, Larry. "I didn't think I'd be this busy, but yeah, I'm just trying to show Larry here the ropes and—"

"Say no more, Quinn. We understand completely." Alice made a sweeping motion with her hand. Every table in the pub was full and every patron had pints of beer in front of them. "Our partnership is really blossoming."

Quinn's blue eyes sparkled. "Yes, you're right. It really is. I'm really glad I found you both." She folded her arms across her chest. "So, four kegs of ale, two of the blonde wheat, and one Kölsch?"

Larry rolled his eyes and scribbled in his book. "We're late for our next appointment."

"Perfect." Alice stood, hands on her hips.

"Meeting adjourned?" Quinn smiled as she held her hand out to Leslie. "Lovely doing business with you, as always, Leslie." She stood. "And Alice."

Larry barely looked up, but he did wave from the bar on his way out.

Once they were out of earshot, Alice leaned into Leslie and groaned. "She has the hots for you, and it just grinds my gears."

"Oh, Alice, honey, I could be her grandmother, for Pete's sake." She chuckled. She didn't completely disagree, though, and it sort of made her apprehensive around the young brew master. Leslie was no stranger to an unrequited crush but at this age, she had no energy for the drama it always caused. "I will put an end to it if you really think it's necessary."

Alice placed a hand on Leslie's cheek. "Don't you worry. I'll slug her if she gets too close."

"My hero." Leslie leaned forward and kissed Alice, a quick peck on the lips before they both stood and meandered through the pub. They stopped at tables, welcoming the guests, and asking how they were enjoying everything. Leslie stopped at the bar and turned to watch her beautiful wife as she laughed along with a couple of regulars, two gay men who absolutely loved the Kölsch. They'd brought in two growlers to get refilled just today, so Leslie was thrilled Quinn could deliver.

"Aunt Leslie?"

She turned. "Yes, dear?"

"I have a note for you, left by someone. It was on the bar."

"A note?" She took the envelope from Toni's outstretched hand. "Who in the world?" She tore into the envelope and quickly pulled out the nice stationery. Her heart leapt into her throat. Holding a hand to her chest, she smiled. "That Alice. She's always leaving me the sweetest notes." She gazed down at the "You're all I think about" on the paper, swooning the entire time. Moments like these were why she was so happy things worked out the way they did. After years and years together, some couples lost their spark. But not Leslie and Alice. A bouquet of flowers, simple notes like this one, and flirty looks from across the room kept their relationship fresh. She folded the paper and slipped it into her pocket, tapping it a couple of times before she glanced across the bar top at Toni. "You take a page from Alice's book, you hear me? She's a keeper, that one. And I feel like Brittany might be the same for you."

"Oh my God, Aunty, it has literally been like forty-eight hours since we, y'know," she paused, looked around, "slept together. Calm down." She lowered her voice on the last part, but she was grinning.

"Mm-hmm. Just so you know, I could read that lovesick look on your face from twenty paces."

"Yes," Toni said, "I hear you. But the rest of the bar doesn't need to." She turned her attention to an older gentleman, Mervin, seated a couple of stools away. He'd been a regular since they first opened their doors. He would come in every day and regale them with tales from the beginning of the LGBTQ+ movement on Swift Island. Before it was an accepting getaway for the oppressed, it was a very conservative island. "Hi ya, what can I get for you?"

"Maybe more of this juicy story," he said with a laugh. "You're bringing a lot of life to this pub, sweetie. I kind of enjoy it."

"Listen to ol' Mervin, sweetie. He'll help you with your heart concerns." Leslie patted Mervin on the back as she passed. "Tell her about the dawn of the gay movement on Swift Island. She'll love that."

Before she pushed through the door to the back of the pub, she heard Toni laugh and say, "Actually, I really would enjoy hearing about it."

It occurred to her that it was going to be mighty difficult when the time came for Toni to head back to Colorado. Maybe she would ask her to stay. Nothing was holding her down to the tiny town on the western slope, so maybe it was the perfect opportunity to get her to settle with them. As much as she enjoyed her time alone with Alice, they were both getting used to the presence both Toni and Brittany brought to the house.

She wasn't overly thrilled about the noise aspect, but maybe she'd start to lose her hearing.

God, hopefully one day soon... She chuckled to herself as she sat at the desk in her tiny office. What a whirlwind this season had been so far.

The wind blew through Brittany's hair as she sat in the same spot where she'd almost spilled her guts to Toni. She found herself thinking nonstop about how close she felt to Toni in that moment and how close she'd come to almost ruining it.

People understood the idea behind higher powers and fate, but when it came to visions and seeing things that aren't really there?

She shook her head and sighed. She needed to get to the bottom of what the hell these visions meant. She recalled the memories of when she sat outside a week or so ago. Even though her ability to pull a vision right out of the air frightened her, she'd been able to gather a little more information. She'd found a way to jump into the water without the headache, and it was liberating. She'd struggled to get back to that feeling, though. Being in control of whoever's mind was conjuring these visions was more than unsettling, and she wasn't exactly eager to try again. A small part of her wondered if maybe her connection to that part of herself was severed when she finally was able to release all that pent-up sexual tension she had with Toni.

And while that could be frustrating, given that she'd come here to get to the bottom of the visions, she was also super happy she was finally able to have multiple orgasms brought about by someone other than herself.

Masturbating was fine, sure, but when it was all you'd been doing for the past year or so? It started to be sort of boring.

Jesus, Britt, stop thinking about sex.

With Toni.

Brittany groaned as she pushed her hands into her sweaty hair. Running to the same spot where she and Toni went over the details of the night before was probably a bad idea. Now all she could think about was Toni, and her neck, and the soft side of her breasts, and the way she would fall against the mattress after each orgasm. Sweaty, panting, ready to go for round three, four, five…

Six.

"Stop." Brittany's voice sounded foreign, but she needed to get her head in the game. She needed to stop thinking about that and think about anything else so she could get another vision. The blood, the way she was always on the outside looking in, the eerie way she felt like she knew the person whose head she was always in.

And *bam*...

The daylight changed on the main drag, there were shadows on the outside of the pub...the Second Wave. Instantly, she switched into protection mode. She peered through the glass...saw a box labeled "Swift Island Stationery Shoppe." Then a letter. Nice thick stationery, the weight of the paper, the pen between her fingers, then the scribbling of "You're all I think about" with an antique fountain pen. Her heart was beating so hard. She wanted to slam her hands on the glass, burst through and find the person who was writing those words, which were vague but filled with growing vitriol, nonetheless. Why couldn't she? Why was she able to slip undetected into this person's mind, but she struggled controlling her own body? What the hell was this person doing? Why were they writing that? She could barely open her mouth, her tongue thick and her saliva all but gone.

And just like that, the vision ended. Brittany looked down and saw that she was gripping the bench she was sitting on. Her knuckles were white. She unclenched her hands and rubbed them. "Holy shit," she said softly. What the hell did any of that mean?

Her head hurt. This vision was definitely different as it caused a headache afterward, not before, and now her mind was swirling. Letters and more visions, and the rage, the deep-seated hatred the person felt, was growing, consuming them. It wouldn't be long before it erupted. Time was running out, and panic surged through her.

She stood, looked out across the Atlantic, and pulled a deep breath into her lungs. If she was going to get to the bottom of this, she knew what she was going to have to do.

Put herself into more visions.

More frequently.

And it wasn't going to be easy.

She pulled out her cell phone and dialed the only person who could help her. After a few rings, the other line picked up. "Hi, Aunt Patty."

"I was wondering when you'd call." Her aunt's voice made her feel instantly better. "What have you figured out?"

Brittany ran her hand through her hair. "Oh, you know, just that I'm a hot mess."

Her aunt shushed her. "None of that now. Tell me about your time there."

Brittany went into a detailed retelling of her last six weeks on the island. She didn't leave a single moment out, wanting her aunt to understand the full picture. Well, except the sex details.

Aunt Patty was so quiet, Brittany thought she might have lost her. "You still there?"

"Yes, of course. It doesn't sound like you need my help at all."

"I'm no closer to figuring out what's happening to me than I was two months ago." Brittany pinched the bridge of her nose.

"That's because you're looking at it all wrong. This isn't happening *to* you. You're a messenger. This is happening to someone else. You've been given a chance to stop it."

"Should I call the police?"

Aunt Patty laughed. "And tell them what? You need more information before they can help you. I can't fly out there to spring you from the mental hospital. I have bridge this weekend."

Brittany smiled at her aunt's sense of humor. "I don't know where to start."

"Do you remember the summer at the lake house where your cousin stole the whole box of Popsicles? You were so furious that you went around asking everyone questions. You built a reenactment of what could have taken place and used Barbies to represent where you all were. You proved that the only person who could've taken those damn things was Kenny." She laughed. "He was so mad."

"Of course, I remember. He wouldn't let me play flashlight tag with the rest of them for a week." Brittany leaned back and let the sun hit her face. It felt good to talk to her aunt.

"You know how to get to the bottom of this. You just have to stop being afraid."

"Easy for you to say. You aren't poking around in someone else's brain."

"That's true." Aunt Patty sighed. "But I also know you. And I can't imagine you letting this go without a fight. Even if danger might be lurking right around the corner. I just hope you're prepared for something like that. Be careful, and don't rush into anything without some sort of a plan." She was quiet for another few seconds. "I love you, baby girl. You can do this."

"Thanks. I love you, too." She clicked off and pulled out her notebook.

She opened the pages to the timeline she'd been diligently creating and added her most recent vision. She knew this person was involved in the local community. She also knew they had an affiliation with one of the breweries. But who were they watching? Writing letters to? Doing something that felt a lot like stalking? Was it Leslie and Alice they were after? Or had she simply focused on them through the person's eyes because she recognized them? What if she missed who the person was actually looking for? She'd gently probed Alice and Leslie about their relationships with the breweries and the employees who worked there. There didn't seem to be any relationships that reached beyond business. They hadn't been on the island long enough to make any dangerous enemies—not that she'd uncovered. She had no clear picture of motive.

Brittany rubbed her temples. *Okay, think.* She thought back to the overwhelming rage she felt each time she was able to slip into the person's thoughts. The anger—the need to hurt. It felt an awful lot like revenge. *Revenge.* But revenge for who? Or what? Well, this was at least something. She wrote down every single name that fit into her initial analysis and headed back to the house to do some research. Ten names was a lot, but it was better than nothing. This person had to have a history. Something had to be there, and nothing could hide forever on the internet.

Chapter Twenty-two

September 1st–Journal Entry 515

The headaches are getting more ferocious with each passing cycle. They go as fast as they come—millions of needles poking small holes inside my head. If my father were still alive, he would tell me that it's my vile nature, finally taking over my body. He would insist that I've brought this pain upon myself. He would laugh.

But it's not my vile nature that's causing my distress. My distress is brought on by the need to blend in, in order to complete what I came here to accomplish. All the small talk and idle chitchat is sedating my true nature. I read an article once about a wolf who'd been trapped by a hunter. To avoid its fate, the wolf gnawed its leg off to escape. I fear that is what my body is doing to itself to survive this mundane endeavor. I need to be free. I'm not sure how much longer I can endure the torment of living amongst these sheep. Nature dictates that sheep and wolves cannot coexist. Sheep are sustenance and nothing more. Wolves need to feed in order to survive. I am a wolf, and I've deprived myself of feeding for far too long.

I came so close to snatching you up today. It would have been easy. Luckily for you, there is one contributing factor that separates me from my four-legged brethren, and that is my intellect. I understand the consequences of taking you in the middle of the day. I understand that I cannot plan for every set of circumstances for every passerby. When I finally take you, I don't want to be rushed. I don't want to be looking over my shoulder. I want to enjoy my time with you. You are, after all, my most prized target. I can already taste the sweat from your cheeks. I know how your pheromones will shift ever so slightly, announcing to other animals your undeniable peril. But there will be no one to save you from me. I will be the last thing you see.

Chapter Twenty-three

Toni stopped on her way up the front steps of the house when she saw Brittany sitting at the table through the window. She looked intently focused on whatever she was reading as she held a pen between her teeth. Toni felt the warmth grow in her chest as she let herself consider what it would be like to come home to Brittany every day. It would be...wonderful? Maybe at first, but what would stop Brittany from changing her mind and leaving? Absolutely nothing. She could have everything she ever wanted one day, and the next, it could all be gone.

Toni rolled her shoulders and reprimanded herself. *Brittany is not Penn.* She took a deep breath and continued toward the door. She wasn't going to let her past dictate her future. She just needed to remind herself of that every day. Every single day.

She walked up behind Brittany and slid her arms around her, kissing her cheek. "Hi."

Brittany slipped her hand over Toni's wrist and continued to scroll through the images on the computer screen. "Hey, how was work?"

"The usual. Got another Swift Island history lesson from Mervin. I feel a connection to old Lucinda Swift. After being with men for years, she ultimately lived her best life with a woman. How was your day?"

Brittany finally looked away from her computer and pulled Toni down into her lap. "I've been thinking about you all day." She kissed her.

"Is it weird that I missed you?" Toni skimmed her lips over hers. "Actually, don't answer that. I don't want to know if you think I'm weird." She pressed her mouth against her again. "But do you think it's weird?"

Brittany laughed and kissed her forehead. "I missed you, too."

Toni searched her eyes, trying to determine if she was telling the truth. She saw no hint that Brittany was trying to placate her, so she allowed her comment to seep in. She needed to distract herself before she let her insecurities run wild.

"What are you working on?" Toni turned her attention to the computer.

"Doing some research for a story."

Toni scanned the screen. "On breweries?"

"It's actually a story I started working on back in San Francisco. Not about breweries, but on a person."

Toni watched Brittany's face. She seemed a bit nervous and wasn't making eye contact. "You came all the way out here to look for someone without knowing who?"

Brittany chewed on her lip. She seemed to be trying to make a decision, and Toni desperately wanted to be able to read her mind.

"Some weird stuff was going on back in San Francisco. Someone was hurting people, but it wasn't anything the police could get involved with because there wasn't enough information to go on. I got a tip that this person may be headed to Swift Island."

"Is this person male or female?"

Brittany sighed. "I don't know."

"But you know they came here to hurt someone. Do you know who?"

Brittany pinched the bridge of her nose. She seemed flustered. "I don't know any of that. I was following my gut by coming here. I don't even know if they're really here. I don't know if anyone is actually in trouble. I just don't know."

Toni put her hands on Brittany's cheeks. "Hey, it's okay. I want to help. Tell me how I can help you."

Brittany shook her head. "You do not want to get involved in this."

Toni smiled and kissed her lips, letting her mouth linger over Brittany's. "I'm already involved." She pulled her head back so she could look at Brittany. "Besides, you have no idea who this person is or what they're capable of doing. You can't be going rogue to find them without someone knowing where you are or without help. It's reckless." Toni tapped Brittany's nose with her finger. "I'm going to help whether you like it or not, so you may as well embrace it."

Brittany looked at her for what felt like an eternity. "Okay."

"Okay." Toni stood and pulled Brittany out of her seat toward the kitchen. "Now, let's eat something. I'm starving. You can fill me in as to how I can help while we eat."

Brittany was being agreeable, but Toni knew it wasn't because she wanted to be. She could tell by her facial expression that she didn't want Toni's help. She hadn't decided if she should be offended or hurt by that knowledge. But in the end, it didn't really matter. She wasn't going to let Brittany investigate a potentially violent individual without some assistance. That would be ludicrous. Toni might be a little crazy, but she wasn't foolish.

Brittany had no idea how she got herself into this situation. Well, she *knew*, but she didn't know why she just couldn't keep her mouth shut. It wasn't that she didn't want to tell Toni what was happening, but she had no way of explaining it without sounding like she'd come unhinged. Now she'd managed to involve Toni without telling her the whole truth and nothing but the truth. And telling Toni a lie like that was so not cool. *Omit is a better word.* Omit, lie, it didn't matter. She'd read enough books to know how this scenario played out. When the truth came out, Toni wouldn't care *why* she didn't tell her the truth; she would just care that she didn't. She was going to have to fill Toni in on everything as soon as the time was right. Once she had enough information, she would tell her the whole story. Maybe she'd be completely understanding. Or, and probably the more likely scenario, she could tell her to go to hell.

Perfect.

Toni handed her a plate with two pieces of pizza. "Your gourmet meal, madam."

"Thank you." Brittany wanted to act normal. She forced herself to smile, despite being terrified of having told her too much already.

"So, where do we start tomorrow? Are we going to stake out someone's house?"

Brittany took a bite of her pizza. "We're not cops. I have a few more names of people I want to go meet."

Toni's eyes got wide. "You're actually going to go speak to them?"

Brittany shrugged. "I need to be able to get a feeling for them. I want to know if they're telling the truth."

Toni shook her finger at her. "I like it."

"If you have to work, I can go by myself."

Toni smiled. "You're not getting out of this. I have the day off, so I'm all yours." She leaned across the table. "And who knows, if you play your cards right, you may even get lucky in the stakeout car."

Brittany leaned forward and kissed her. "It's not a stakeout, and it's not a car. I go on a bike."

Toni pulled her face in and kissed her again. "I'm sure we can figure something out."

Brittany let herself get lost in the moment, but it was short-lived.

Toni squinted. "What is it exactly that you think this person did or didn't do? How do you know they hurt people?"

Brittany pulled a piece of mushroom off her pizza and contemplated how to answer. "There were some pictures. Nothing concrete, just some blood, knives, and a few pictures of breweries. There were also a few pictures of some shops in this area."

"But you said it started in San Francisco—why would there be pictures of shops from here?"

Brittany felt her neck burning with nervousness. She hated lying, and she hated lying to Toni even more. "I found out about it in San Francisco, but it led me here."

Toni seemed satisfied. "Well, that's not a ton to go on, but let's see what we can find." She smiled. "How did you narrow down your suspect list?"

At least she could answer that honestly. "It all seems a bit stalker-like. This person seems like they're fixated. Usually, fixation is caused by revenge or entitlement. I've been looking into people who work at breweries who have something questionable in their past. So far, there hasn't been any criminal activity, but there are a few that seemed to drop in out of thin air."

"What do you mean?"

"I mean, they really don't have much of a back story. No social media presence, no property in their name, no previous addresses. It's like they just appeared here on the island."

Toni leaned back in her chair. "You could say the same about me. Am I on your list?" Her eyes got big. "Did you already check on me?"

Brittany tossed her napkin on her plate. "It never even occurred to me to check your background. Should I?"

Toni raised an eyebrow. "Do you want to check? I have a few places you can start."

Brittany's anxiety over the questioning rapidly dissipated, replaced by arousal. "Where should I start?"

Toni was kneeling between her legs before Brittany had a chance to process her moving. She put her hands on Brittany's waist and pulled her forward in the chair. She had to stop herself from gasping at the sudden shift. Toni lifted the bottom of her shirt and ran her mouth over her stomach. She kissed around her belly button and down to the button on her jean shorts.

She pulled on the button with her teeth and stopped before she unfastened it. "You want to continue this upstairs?"

Brittany nodded because she couldn't form any words. The sight of Toni perched between her legs with her mouth on her clothes and that look in her eyes was like nothing she'd ever experienced. She'd been with women who had clouded her mind. She'd been with women who made her want to tear their clothes off in public. She'd even been with women she thought she'd want to settle down with. None of them had the effect on her that Toni did. None of them could undo her with a simple look. Brittany was much deeper into this than she'd ever planned. *It may even be too late.* No matter what the outcome would be, Brittany knew she'd never rid her bloodstream of Toni. The remnants would remain coursing through her forever.

Brittany stood, picking Toni up with her as she moved. Toni wrapped her legs around Brittany's waist and looked quite pleased at Brittany's reaction.

"I like this side of you," Toni murmured against her ear.

Brittany continued up the stairs. The thought of putting Toni down never even occurred to her. She liked the way she felt wrapped around her body. She liked the way Toni continued to nip and kiss her neck. She loved how she could feel Toni's need growing as rapidly as her own with every step.

For the first time since her accident, Brittany felt alive. Her body felt electric, and it was all because of Toni. The connection she had with her, or whatever it was, was helping her find herself again, to ground herself in reality. And maybe it was selfish, but she was going to bask in every second of it. She could worry about the rest later.

Chapter Twenty-four

L eslie pushed herself up from the bed. She did her best to ignore the small aches and pains as she went to the closet to pull on some pants. As grateful as she was for her life in this portion of her journey, some things even love couldn't fix. Stiff muscles and creaky joints when she woke up were two of them.

"Where are you running off to so early?" Alice peered at her, still only half awake.

"I'm going to go get some pastries from the coffee shop." She sat on the bed and put her hand on Alice's face.

"May want to get extra the way those two were going at it last night." Alice smiled and her eyes sparkled in the early morning sun.

"We were never like that."

Leslie smacked her arm. "Oh, yes we were. The things you would do to me after our crochet klatches, in the supply closet at work, or in your Buick." She shook her head. "Thank the heavens my aunts weren't two bedroom doors away."

Alice sat up and kissed her. "We can still do those things."

Leslie stood. "Not with as much vigor as those two exuded last night."

"No, but I treasure the memories of when we had," Alice said. "I can't wait to tease them."

"Don't you dare," Leslie said before she shut the door behind her.

She chose to walk down the main drag rather than bike it to give her muscles some gentle, much-needed exercise. While most people enjoyed the quaint nightlife the small town had to offer, you'd never be able to convince her that there was a better time to be out and about than early morning. She liked being out just before the town woke up for the day. The number of people dashing about was at a minimum, and there was something about the smell of early morning ocean air. It brought a sense of contentment to her soul that nothing on the mainland could ever replicate.

"Hi, Mary," Leslie said to the barista who was busy cleaning the steam wand.

"Morning, Leslie." She stepped in front of the register. "What can I get you today?"

A voice from behind her spoke before she had the chance. "Four lattes, one with vanilla."

Leslie turned to see who would be so brazen as to order for her. She didn't recognize her immediately, so she turned her attention back to the barista to finish the order. "That's correct, and four bagels." She stepped back to look at the stranger after she paid. "Do I know you?"

She stuck her hand out. "Sorry, I thought you'd recognize me. I'm Shea Albright. I do sales for Nereids Brewery."

Leslie felt foolish. "Of course, I'm sorry, Shea. I do remember you." She put her hand over her face. "How did you know my order?"

Shea shrugged. "I've seen you in here a few times, and I just have a memory for things like that. It helps a lot being in sales."

Leslie didn't want to harp on what was ultimately a kind gesture, but she couldn't shake the weird feeling it gave her. "But how did you know I'd order four?"

Shea ordered before answering. "Your niece has been staying with you, and that new woman in town, Brittany. I was just making a guess with what they wanted." She shifted her weight back and forth. "I guess I thought I was being funny, but now I realize it came off as terribly creepy. I'm sorry about that."

Leslie didn't want her to feel foolish, and she felt bad for making her feel that way. "You know what, I'm sorry. It's early in the morning, and my brain isn't firing on all cylinders yet."

Mary pointed to the table next to the espresso machine. "Order's ready, Leslie."

Leslie grabbed the bag and the coffee carrier. "Thanks, Mary." She was walking out and stopped at Shea. "It was nice seeing you again. I hope you have a nice day."

Shea nodded but didn't say another word. As she walked back to the house, she replayed the scenario in her head. The more she dwelled on it, the more she felt as if her initial reaction was correct. It was a bit odd that she knew who was staying in her house. *That's okay. It's a small town. Word gets around fast, and Brittany is definitely noticeable.*

She got back to the house and was surprised everyone was already downstairs waiting at the kitchen table. She divvied up the coffees and kissed Alice on the cheek.

"You okay?" Alice cocked her head.

Leslie thought briefly of telling her about her encounter but decided she was simply overthinking. No use getting anyone else involved. "Yeah, everything is great." She kissed Alice and took a seat next to Toni. "What plans do you two have for today?"

Leslie let herself get lost in the idle chitchat of the people she loved most. She wasn't going to let one weird encounter color her day. She had far too much to be happy about.

After breakfast, Brittany and Toni told the aunts they were off for a beach day on the north side of the island. That would allow them to stay off the radar while they did what they needed to do. They walked their bikes around from the back of the cottage to the end of the crunchy shell driveway.

"You lead. I'll follow," Toni said. "Where's our first stop?"

Brittany smiled at what an awesome investigative partner Toni might be. "I like this," she teased. "An agreeable, insanely cute woman eager for my command."

"Don't let it go to your head," Toni replied. "The more I think about this mystery mission, the more exciting it sounds."

"I'd be more excited about it if I didn't get such a feeling of foreboding when I think of the pictures."

Brittany nodded. "Believe me when I tell you that I understand the sentiment. So, I'm thinking we should check out Nereids Brewing first. Then Riot Brewing. We need to take tours of both places. I was only able to get a peek inside Riot last time I was there. If we have time, I'd also like to check out Reputation."

"That'll be easy. I've met just about everyone at Nereids, so whatever questions come up, I'm sure they'll be glad to answer for you. Then we'll go from there."

"Onward we go," Brittany said, and they pedaled off down the road. While she was relieved that Toni was such a sport about this, she had a feeling that Toni wasn't fully on board with the validity of her claims. She didn't seem to take any of it with the level of caution the situation warranted. It seemed like she regarded this as an exciting little diversion amidst the calm of the island to reawaken that wild child inside her.

Brittany prayed that Toni was right.

They arrived at Nereids just in time to sign up for the eleven thirty a.m. tour. Brittany stuffed their tasting tickets in her pocket and stood near the door to the brewing room as Toni perused the merch hanging on the wall beside the bar.

When the door opened for the tour to begin, she heard Toni's voice before she'd had time to turn around.

"Hey, Quinn," Toni said excitedly. "You're our guide today?"

"Yeah," she said with a bit of a frown. "We all take turns, but this is my least favorite part of the job."

Toni nodded and walked over to Brittany. "This is perfect. Quinn is your inside source. We're all pretty sure she has the hots for Leslie. She'll be more than willing to answer any extra questions you may have."

"Damn. I hope I got game like your aunt when I'm in my early seventies."

Toni giggled. "Right? Imagine having a woman pine over you for forty years and still have women half your age chasing you later."

"I'd love to have what they have, but no way would I want to go through what they went through to get it."

"Preach, sister," Toni said.

They hung back at the end of the small group that followed Quinn into the warehouse area. Quinn's voice was so quiet Brittany heard only bits and pieces of the explanations about ingredients and the brewing process. She tuned out the chatter around her and tried to settle her mind so she'd be receptive to whatever occurred.

"Any of this ring alarm bells for what you found in San Francisco?" Toni whispered. "If you want me to ask any questions, I can sound really innocent when I want to."

Brittany grinned. "Why does that not surprise me? Thanks, but right now I just want to take in the surroundings and see if anything matches the things I've…found."

"Like the sketches you showed me?"

Brittany nodded. "Let's hope my artistic skills are better than I remember."

Toni walked alongside her silently. A few minutes into the tour, flashes of light flickered in Brittany's head. When they began obscuring her vision, she grabbed Toni's arm to steady herself and prayed she wouldn't notice anything was wrong.

"What's the matter?" Toni asked.

Brittany shook her head and raised her finger to her lips. She couldn't talk now for fear it would scare away whatever was going on in her head, or alert Toni that there was more than what she'd previously disclosed. Toni, thankfully, took the cue and walked along at Brittany's pace.

Again, the clouded imagery of beer kegs floated behind her eyes. The flashing light stopped, but now only a soft glow from a bare lightbulb in another part of the warehouse illuminated her surroundings. The acrid smell of hops and dried beer spillage on the cement floor assailed her nostrils. Was this the same brewery she'd seen before? Was it the one she was physically in? She couldn't tell now that the lighting in her mind's eye had become so weak.

Maybe it was the brewing area that she'd caught a glimpse of over at Riot Brewing. It was hard to tell as she tried to see through the low, amber light. The aroma around her almost cut off her other senses as she tried to focus in on specifics in her visions.

"Britt, are you okay?"

She recognized Toni's voice in close proximity, but she sounded muffled and echoey, like she was talking through an empty paper towel tube. She nodded but clutched Toni's upper arm tighter.

Her breath became labored as her physical senses took over. She felt constricted. Something was either on or near her body, but whatever it was, it was making her extremely uncomfortable. By now she would've fled from the place that had provoked these feelings, but she fought the urge to run, determined to see it through. She clasped her fingers in Toni's and held on waiting for the panic to subside. *I'm okay, I'm okay*, she repeated in her head. *This isn't really happening to me.*

The smells were there. The yeast, the hops.

The sounds were similar. The clanging, the *drip, drip, drop* of a leaky faucet.

The room, unfortunately, was different. And the deeper Brittany got into the vision, the more she realized the mission seemed futile. Of course the smells were the same. *It's a frigging brewery.* Of course the air felt the same. Everything on Swift Island had that same unyielding feeling thanks to the constant salty, moist air.

They were halfway through the tour when Toni pulled her away from the group. Behind the large fermentation vessel, Brittany's senses returned to normal, and the first sign of reality she saw were Toni's big eyes staring into hers.

"Why did you stop us?"

"Brittany, you were scaring the crap out of me. You had tremors worse than my grandfather used to and your lips were doing weird things. I didn't know what the hell was happening to you."

"I felt another headache coming on. I'm sorry," Brittany said, sounding as disappointed as she felt.

"I'm so sorry." Toni was almost pleading. "I didn't know what I should do, but I couldn't let you stroke out on me in the middle of a brewery tour."

Brittany looked at Toni's face, blanched white with near terror. How could she be mad at someone who showed such deep concern for her? "No, no, it's okay." She laid a calming hand on Toni's forearm. "It's weird, y'know, sometimes, when I'm researching something, I like to put myself completely into the scene in my head, so I can remember the details when I'm journaling about it... Does that make sense?"

Toni looked on the verge of tears, but she nodded anyway.

"It's strange, I know." Brittany shrugged and hoped her backpedaling was working.

Toni grabbed her and pulled her into a tight hug. "It's not. We'll get to the bottom of this and you're gonna be okay. I promise."

They scurried to catch up with the group for the final lap of the tour. When it was over everyone gathered at the bar in the tasting room to cash in their beer flight tickets. They stood at the corner of the bar away from the people in their tour group and sipped their beer samples.

Quinn meandered over with her hands in the pockets of her cargo shorts. "Sorry we don't have anything new out yet. You've tried all four of ours, but we traded two taps with Riot. Did you pick any of those?"

"Both," Brittany said. "Haven't had a bad one yet."

Quinn looked down with a shy, schoolboy smile.

"So have they made you a partner yet?" Toni asked.

"Not yet, but I'm working real hard at it." She looked away again, clearly unused to full-on eye contact.

"There're only three breweries on the island, right?" Brittany asked.

Quinn nodded. "Well, I better get back to work."

"Thanks for the tour," Toni said as Quinn shuffled off.

"By the way," Brittany said as she licked beer foam off her lip. "You knowing and understanding beer? That's so fucking hot." She wiggled her eyebrows to cast a little levity. Despite Toni's claims that all was cool, Brittany could see she was still a bit unnerved.

"We have to do this all over again at Riot, don't we?" Toni asked.

Brittany tried to hold in her mouthful of beer as she laughed. "Not at all. We can save it for tomorrow if you've had enough for today."

"Pfft. Me have enough of you? No way."

Brittany leaned into her and kissed her. "That's what I was hoping you'd say."

❖

Toni was extremely grateful they'd stayed at Nereids and finished their samples. She needed that dose of ten percent juicy IPA after what went down and assumed would go down again once they executed the same exact plan at Riot.

This time they didn't stick around to finish their samples that were part of the tour. Whatever Brittany was going through didn't seem as bad as what she went through during the Nereids tour. She still had the deep, pensive look on her face. She stumbled a few times over what seemed like nothing. And her shoulders stiffened again but she didn't go completely rigid, thank God. She was clearly drained after Riot's tour, though.

Toni hated to admit it, but whatever was happening with Brittany concerning the story she was researching was starting to worry her. It was clear it meant a great deal more to Brittany than she was letting on. That part didn't upset Toni as much as the fact that, deep down, something else was going on too. The headaches, the way she got all rigid when she was putting herself in the moment at the breweries, the glassy look in her eyes afterward…all of it was unnerving. But, at the same time, Toni was a bit of a basket case herself, so maybe she needed to just settle the fuck down and ride this out. Brittany was a journalist, after all, and she had to know what she was doing.

They pedaled away from Riot Brewing and stopped at a small public garden about a mile or so down the road. They strolled through the fragrant, colorful maze until they found a shaded bench. Toni was growing ever more concerned as Brittany wasn't snapping out of the experience as quickly as she had over at Nereids.

"Did you see anything you recognized at Riot?"

Brittany shook her head. "Unfortunately, no."

"Maybe we should see if there's a psychic medium on the island. I don't really believe in all that stuff and kind of think they're creepy, but maybe it's worth a shot?"

"Umm…"

"It was just a suggestion." Toni went quiet after Brittany's apparent disinterest.

"I'm sorry." Brittany draped her arm across Toni's shoulder. "I know you're only trying to help. It's all just so frustrating, and I can't figure it all out. What am I missing? Is there something I'm not paying attention to?"

"This must be so annoying, but you have to cut yourself some slack, Britt. I mean maybe once you sit down and map everything out again on your timeline, you'll figure it out."

"I guess."

Toni exhaled and stared into a multi-colored bank of asters and coneflowers jostling about in the breeze. She'd run out of comforting words and was losing with the logic spin, so silence would have to do for now.

"Toni." Brittany's hand clutched her knee, and when Toni looked at her, Brittany's face was alarmingly serious. "I feel like something bad is going to happen."

Toni felt the bottom drop out of her stomach. She placed her hand on top of Brittany's and hoped that Brittany's damaged brain was only playing tricks on her.

CHAPTER TWENTY-FIVE

That afternoon, when Toni got unexpectedly called in to help with the happy hour crowd at the pub, Brittany spent some time at the tiny little Swift Island library slash historical society to see if a combination of internet research on psychic phenomenon and some island history would help her piece together the fragments of information banging around inside her head. Other than some anecdotes about the "scandalous" life of the widow Swift and her African American "housekeeper" and how they became the matriarchs of this LGBTQ enclave, the history hadn't proved useful.

After a late dinner with Leslie and Alice in their backyard, Toni suggested they take a walk into town and enjoy the cool evening breeze now that the sun had set.

"What do you want to do? Check out the dance?" Brittany asked as they strolled hand in hand along the main drag.

Toni shook her head. "I'm too tired to fight off all the baby dykes who'll swarm you. You're mine tonight." She gave her a slow, sensual kiss in front of a handmade jewelry store.

"I can pass on the dance, too. But just so you know, you'd never have to fight for me. It wouldn't even be a competition." She returned the kiss and felt the arousal of being so close to Toni's mouth, smelling the sweetness of her skin stir inside her.

"How about a glass of pinot noir and something chocolatey?" Toni asked.

"Here or back in your room?" Brittany replied, loving their seduction games.

"Well…" Toni pretended she was thinking. "We can have dessert at the café and then work off the calories later in my room."

"Sounds like the perfect plan." Brittany allowed Toni to tow her along to the next block to the trendy café that specialized in tapas, desserts, and wine.

They chose to sit outside at a bistro table for two on the sidewalk. The evening crowd of street crawlers provided a plethora of people watching as they split a black forest cherry cheesecake and a bottle of red.

"Thank you for this perfect night." Brittany dabbed her mouth with her napkin after her last bite of cheesecake. "I really needed it after such a wild day."

"You and me both," Toni replied. "Was your trip to the library helpful at all?"

"A little. I found a few articles about the town's history which helped. It seems odd, I know, but learning about and appreciating the past sometimes helps me prepare for the future. It's like being grounded or connected beyond myself."

"Doesn't seem odd at all." Toni smiled, reached across the table, and ran her fingers along the top of Brittany's hand. "Nothing about you seems odd."

Yeah, well, if you knew the whole story, you might not feel that way. "That's good to know." Brittany forced a smile. If she came clean and Toni didn't take it well, what would she do? The idea of losing Toni because of something Brittany didn't fully understand herself was horrifying. She could tell deep down she was erecting parts of the wall Toni had already helped dismantle. It was for Toni's own good, though. It had to be. The look of fear on her face when the vision happened at the brewery was exactly what Brittany had feared. It was a look of fear mixed with far too much worry.

As Brittany stared at Toni's beautiful face, a shadowy figure appeared behind her at the corner of the building. She couldn't tell if it was a man or a woman as they were backlit by a streetlight. All she could make out was the person was in black pants and a black long-sleeve shirt. Not exactly an inconspicuous choice of outfits considering most people were dressed in light summer clothing or colorful evening wear.

Toni must've picked up that something other than their conversation had Brittany's attention. When she swung around to look behind her, the figure pulled back. Brittany jumped up and ran to the corner, not knowing what she'd say if she encountered the person. But when she looked up the narrow side street, all she saw was a woman in a white blouse and khaki shorts walking her dog.

What the hell? That definitely wasn't a vision. That was a real person lurking at the corner, staring at her and Toni. When she walked back to table Toni was obviously on high alert.

"What happened?"

"Nothing. I thought I saw someone who looked weird staring over at us. I must still be on edge from today."

"Hey," Toni said softly, her voice like warm honey.

Brittany pulled a breath in, held it for one count, two, before she released it and responded with, "Hmm?"

"You'll figure this all out. I know you will. You're one of the smartest people I know."

"Oh, yeah?"

"Yes. I mean, aside from my aunts and my mom. Well, and Elena, the ranch owner back home." Toni laughed. "You're definitely on the list."

"Gee, thanks," Brittany said, laughing along with Toni. "You really know how to woo a woman."

"Well, I could stop trying to woo you and just get to work on you, if you'd like." Toni pushed her chair away from the table and stood, hand outstretched. "What d'ya say?" She wagged her eyebrows, her eyes twinkling in the patio ambiance.

"I think I'd like that." Brittany took Toni's hand and stood. "Maybe you could rub my head tonight, too? You know those headaches can be killer."

"Oh? I think I could do that."

As they walked, they fell into an easy silence. Brittany squeezed Toni's hand, silently letting her know that she was happy, content, relaxed. Even though the exact opposite—scared, worried, stressed—were more accurate.

CHAPTER TWENTY-SIX

September 6th–Journal Entry 521

Labor Day Weekend. I hate these fun summer holidays. And these empty people who celebrate like they had anything at all to do with any of it. What did they know about having to "labor" over anything? Not in their lives of privilege. Just another excuse to drink and party. Shallow souls in their petty existences. Kids frolicking on the beach without a care in the world. Spoiled little shits from entitled families. I never had that. But I'm a better person for it. I'm strong mentally. I'm untouchable emotionally. My happiness is not contingent upon acceptance by any of these people. I am my greatest ally. They're all phonies. They cheat on their spouses, they lie to their parents, do drugs behind their parents' backs, and when they get into trouble, their clueless parents bail them out. My father never bailed me out of anything. When I did something wrong, I paid the consequences. Paid dearly. Were these kids ever truly punished? I'd hardly call a two-minute "time-out" in a corner punishment. That would've been a treat for me. No. I'd spend days in a crate like a dog nobody wanted to care for. I was a nuisance to him, and you allowed it to go on. You with your self-absorption, wanting, expecting to be worshipped by my father. And he, the weak fool, always gave in to you, so afraid you'd leave him. So afraid to be his own man. But he's dead now. Never had the guts to confront you as he should've. Once I came to realize it was his own weakness and failures as a man that prompted his death, I stopped grieving for him. Now all I feel for him is pity and the need to avenge him, to save face. You're not going to get away with what you did. You think you already have, but you haven't. I had to accept that my vengeance wouldn't be swift, but it's during this long wait that my strength, my resolve, my hatred have grown to the point where nothing and no one can stop me. I've learned to like waiting. It's different now, not like before when I had to wait to be fed or cleaned or get attention. Yes, now I like having something to look forward to. I like stalking you. I like watching you at the pub, knowing you have no idea who I am even when I'm looking you in the eye like everything is just fine. I like all of it. I love knowing that I've ignited a sizzling undercurrent of anxiety stirring in you. It's better than any sexual foreplay I've ever experienced. The vision of your blood spilling all over the place fills me with excitement. I can't wait to feel the warmth of your blood coating my hands.

CHAPTER TWENTY-SEVEN

After going back and forth what felt like a thousand times, Brittany decided to take Toni's advice about seeing a psychic. It wasn't a longshot like she had said it would be. It was exactly the right idea, and she felt rather stupid for not thinking of it first.

The only problem was that she didn't want Toni to come with her. What if the psychic could sense the visions and said something about them? What if the psychic outed Brittany before she was ready to out herself? Two scenarios she definitely didn't want to deal with. At all.

It wasn't easy escaping Toni, though, especially because she was genuinely invested in the research. Brittany scoffed. "Research," she said softly as she rounded the corner into the kitchen. There sat Alice, drinking her coffee. For some reason, Brittany felt caught as she pulled up short and smiled. "Good morning."

"Research, hmm?"

"You heard that?"

"I may be old, but I have hearing like a bat." Alice chuckled as she set her coffee mug on the table. "What are you researching? How to sneak out of a house? If that's the case, you need to do a little more before you master it."

"Ha ha ha." Brittany reached up and pulled her hair into a ponytail. She wrapped the band around it twice before she leaned onto the back of one of the kitchen table chairs. "Can I ask you something?"

"Of course. What's up?"

"Do you believe in psychic energy?"

"Absolutely."

"You do?" Brittany smiled. "So have you had a reading on the island?"

"I have. Leslie and I went when we first got here and even had the medium come to the pub. We wanted to make sure the energy was good."

"Okay then."

"Is that where you're headed?"

Brittany pushed off from the chair back. She shrugged, not wanting to let Alice in on everything in case she told Toni.

"Go to Madge's. Corner of Swift and Cornelia."

Brittany shook her head, smiled, and patted Alice on the shoulder before she moved to the back door. "You're a good woman, Alice."

"I know." Alice winked. "Be careful out there."

The ride into town was peaceful. She'd dressed a little warmer as the September morning air was chilly. She kept reading on the news that even though it was a little too early to call, it seemed Swift Island would escape yet another hurricane season without so much as a scratch. As a believer in fate, Brittany knew that was just tempting it, so she asked whatever higher power was listening that she could wrap this all up before some horrific storm blew into town.

She parked her bike at the rack on Cornelia Street. When she made her way up to the door of Madge's Mystical Musings, she noticed there were no business hours on the door. Rather there was a sign that read, *Open Only to Those Who are Open*. The cynical part of Brittany groaned while the part of her searching for answers heaved a sigh of relief.

The heavy door slowly closed behind her, leaving her in a dark room filled with smoking patchouli and incense. At eight in the morning. There was a hamsa mural on the wall, with a list of the five chakras next to it. Brittany was thankful for the knowledge, albeit limited, Aunt Patty bestowed upon her because otherwise, she'd feel as if she'd just stumbled into an awkward situation. A dark room filled with interesting smells was how some people ended up in a situation they weren't prepared for.

In this case, she was hoping like hell that this would help her answer her questions. Or, at the very least, help her figure out how to answer them.

"Hello there, young lady," came a voice from a smaller room before a buxom woman burst through a beaded curtain. "The name's Madge. You must be Brittany."

"Excuse me?" Brittany looked behind her then back to Madge. "How the hell did you know that?"

"I'm a psychic. I've been waiting for you." Madge glided gracefully through the small dark room and approached Brittany, placing her hands on Brittany's cheeks. "Alice called me. Told me you were coming."

Brittany let out a laugh, followed by an eye roll. "Had me fooled."

"Don't worry, I'll make sure the real magic comes during the reading." Madge spun her large frame, the tail of her paisley robe flowing behind her. "Your aura is a mess, darling." She sat, heaved a deep sigh, and motioned to the chair opposite the velvet covered table. She smoothed her hands over the material before she pulled a crystal ball from underneath, then a stack of tarot cards. "And the pièce de résistance…" she paused, then pulled out a Magic 8-Ball.

Brittany laughed. "Seriously?"

"Don't knock it till you've tried it, love." Madge motioned again to the chair. "Sit down. I ain't got all day." She smiled before lighting a cigarillo, puffing on it a few times, then, with the cigarillo firmly between her lips, said, "You have the gift, don't you?"

Brittany nearly flung herself into the chair. She leaned forward. "Are you serious? You can tell?"

"I could tell instantly." She pulled the cigarillo from her mouth and ashed it in the same tray where the incense was lit. "You're eager, yet scared. You're excited, yet conflicted. And you are one hundred percent," Madge leaned forward, "falling in love with someone." She waited one second, two, before she finished with, "Ya are, aren't you?"

Jesus Christ. "Yes."

"Interesting." Madge reached up and with her long fingernails scratched her scalp, causing her entire bushy black-haired wig to move. As she adjusted the hair back to its resting spot, she sighed. "Oh, love, you're just a mess."

"I know."

Madge placed the tarot deck in front of her. "Touch the cards. Really fondle them. Don't be shy. Finger the fuck out of them."

"I should be able to handle that."

Madge chuckled. "Ahh, yes, a woman who likes women. I had a feeling."

"Of course you did." She shuffled the cards numerous times and placed them back in front of Madge. She noticed as she pulled her hand away that she was shaking. She wasn't sure why. She wasn't nervous, but she felt a flutter inside, and if it wasn't nerves, the only other thing it could be was—

"*Fear* is not necessary."

Seriously?

Madge flipped over three cards in succession. "The Empress, the Lovers, and the Five of Cups. Hmm."

"What?"

"Well, it makes sense. The Empress is feminine in all the best ways. She gives of herself because she is protecting and mothering people in her life. The Lovers card is obvious. You're in love. But also, it could mean you're worried about the idea of opening yourself to love. Also, the lovers could be referring to other people in your life, not just yourself and whoever the lucky lady is."

She nodded as she thought of Leslie and Alice. "And the Five of Cups?"

"Regret and failure. But reversed like this?" Madge spun the card. "Self-forgiveness."

Brittany sighed. "Self-forgiveness can be a tall order."

Madge shrugged. "The cards say what they say." She rubbed her hands together. "Crystal ball time." Madge placed both of her hands on the orb. Her eyes grew wide, and she removed her hands instantly as if the ball burned her.

"What?"

"Nothing."

"That was not nothing."

"No, it's fine." Madge puffed on her cigarillo again. With it hanging between her pursed lips, she placed her hands on the ball again. The smoke billowed into Madge's eyes. She closed them, breathed in through her nose, then coughed a few times. She slid her hands over the smooth surface of the glass and peered into it. "Your visions brought you here. You're going to get to the bottom of whatever is haunting you." Madge leaned in closer. "Hunting. Not haunting. Although definitely interchangeable."

"How in the world—"

"The person in your life?"

"Yes?"

Madge removed her hands completely. "Be careful."

"What do you mean?"

"I see darkness and pain."

"Listen to me, Madge, this is not what I wanted you to tell me today."

"You cannot control what comes from the crystal. The cards? Sure. Your aura dictates those. But this ball?" The cigarillo was between Madge's chubby fore and middle fingers now. She reached up with her free hand and removed a piece of tobacco from her tongue. "This ball is simply indicating what your future holds."

If Brittany wasn't having visions of her own, she'd have gotten up and walked out because clearly this woman was a fucking hack. Except everything she said rang alarmingly true. "The visions?"

"Are you asking about them or are you going to tell me about them?"

"It's like I'm in someone else's body. Seeing through their eyes."

"Interesting."

"And I've only recently figured out how to trigger them."

Madge gasped and leaned forward. "You can *trigger* them?"

"Yes." Brittany breathed in deeply. "I think the person, whomever it is, is going to hurt someone. But I don't know anything more than that, and I'm basically failing, and I know if I tell anyone, especially Toni, she'll think I'm a fucking lunatic and honestly, up until two minutes ago, I sort of agreed with that, and now I'm just a bundle of fucking nerves and anxiety, which is so not like me, and how the hell do I handle all this?" Brittany took another breath. "Any ideas?"

"Well, first and foremost, you need to calm down." Madge pulled a box from under her table and handed over a packet of gummy bears. "Have one of these."

"What the hell is this?"

"It's CBD. No THC. I promise. Go on." She pushed them at Brittany. "Take them."

Brittany shook her head. "Maybe later." She slid them into the pocket of her jacket. "Second of all? Go on."

"Second, you need to remember that this is real. These visions are real. They are happening to you. Some people will never be able to understand it."

"Great."

"I know. I'm sorry." Madge smiled, this time revealing a gold tooth on the left side. "Third? And you might not like this one, but eventually you'll need to tell the people in your life what's going on. If for no other reason than to protect them."

"So you think these visions could be dangerous?"

"I do."

"Fuck."

"I'm telling you; this ball does not lie."

"Fuck."

"And the darkness I saw was real."

"Are you this honest with all of your clients? Because I have a feeling that might be why you're not super busy right now."

Madge leaned her head back and released a boisterous laugh. "It's ten in the morning. Swing by tonight and the line will be wrapped around the block."

Brittany sighed. "I'm sorry. That was rude of me."

"It's okay. You Californians are quick to fire off a witty barb."

"How did you know—"

"Lucky guess."

Another sigh escaped as Brittany rubbed her clammy palms over her yoga pant covered thighs. "How much do I owe you?"

"This one was on the house." Madge reached her hand out, a smile once again on her ruby red lips. "Good luck."

When Brittany took Madge's hand, the second their skin touched, a zap zipped through her body and images crowded her vision. The restaurant last night, a glass of wine in a home, a knife, a gun, a bundle of rope, zip ties, a mirror, a flash of someone's face.

Madge ripped her hand from Brittany's. Her eyes were as wide as saucers. "Holy mother of the spirits." Madge blinked rapidly, her other hand clutching her chest. "Is that…?"

Brittany tried to swallow, but her mouth was completely dry. She nodded, blinking her own disbelief from her eyes. She'd almost seen who it was. She'd almost seen the person in the mirror. "Touch me again."

"No way." Madge stood quickly and backed away from the table, her abrupt movements almost toppling the furniture. "That is not what I signed up for." She put her hands in the air.

"You have to, Madge. I almost saw the person!"

"You need to leave."

"Madge, please. You have no idea how insane I feel."

"Oh, yes I do."

"Madge, I'm begging you."

"Do not speak of this to anyone." Madge was wringing her hands. "I want you to let me sit with this. Okay?"

"But—"

"No. No buts. You hear me? I need to think. I haven't…" Madge scratched her head, the wig moving again, and cleared her throat. "I haven't felt this in quite some time. The kind of evil you're dealing with…" She shook her head. "Let me sit with it."

Brittany, finally accepting defeat, nodded again. She stood so fast that her chair tipped over. She rushed across the dark, smoke-filled room to the heavy door and pulled it open. Once she was safely outside and around the corner of the shop, she leaned against the building and started to cry.

Toni slapped a coaster on the bar top in front of Brittany. "So you went to the psychic without me?"

Brittany groaned. "Alice told you?"

"Yes, she did. She's my aunt. Why wouldn't she have told me?"

"Oh, come on. It's not that big of a deal."

"It's not?"

"I was going to tell you. I promise." Brittany reached for Toni, but she pulled herself away from the bar top.

She was too hurt to let Brittany's puppy dog eyes win that easily. "I would've gone with you." She folded her arms across her chest. "You acted like it was such a stupid idea, too."

"I know." Brittany pulled her hands away. "Listen, at first, I did think it was a stretch. But then, I thought about it and thought about it and thought about it some more, and I thought maybe it wasn't such a bad idea."

Toni wanted to reach for her and hated how quickly she gave in but she couldn't help but smile. "I come up with a few good ones now and then."

Brittany returned the grin. "I'm duly chastised."

She sighed as she moved closer to the bar top again. Brittany smiling at her like that made her irritation fade. So much for staying strong. "And? How did it go?"

"It went well."

"That's it?"

"Yeah, I mean, it was a normal session. Like, she told me a little about myself and that's about it."

"Hmm…"

"What?" Brittany sipped on her beer.

"I have a hard time believing that's all that happened, but okay." She wanted to shout at Brittany, tell her that she didn't believe her, but she had no *real* reason to not believe her. Brittany hadn't lied to her, and yet, it felt like something was off.

"Well, she was interested in the research portion."

Toni let out a laugh. "This is the lamest story I've ever heard. And you had to pay for this?"

Brittany's expression morphed from uninterested to relieved, and the voice in Toni's head telling her to trust Brittany started to argue with her again.

"Well, I mean, no. She said this first one was free because I know Alice. Friends and family discount or something."

"Mm-hmm." Toni studied Brittany's eyes. "You sure you're okay?"

"Honestly? I'm just super tired. I barely slept. Again. Because the woman I've been sleeping with likes to fuck at all hours of the night."

Toni let out a laugh and covered her mouth with her hand. The rest of the patrons at the bar top all looked over at her, and she waved apologetically. "You are full of lies," she said softly as she leaned in closer. "You're the one who woke me up at three this morning."

"Only because you woke me up at two."

"Oh? And then again at five?"

"That was definitely me again." Brittany laughed. "I could go again right now."

"Really?" Toni tilted her head, then looked around for their newest server, Erika. She waved her over and said she needed to take a quick break. She moved around the bar, grabbed Brittany's hand, and pulled her as nonchalantly as possible to the bathroom where she promptly pushed her into a stall and locked the door behind them. She turned and lunged at Brittany, who pulled Toni's skirt up to her waist.

A smile came to Brittany's full lips. "You aren't wearing panties."

"I didn't want panty lines."

"You fucking tease." Brittany slid her hand down then Toni felt her fingers as they slipped through her wetness before she lifted Toni's leg, propping it on her hip. "I'm going to fuck you," Brittany whispered against her ear. "You ready?"

"I'm so ready." Toni bit down on her lip, leaned her head back, and welcomed two of Brittany's fingers into her wetness. She heard herself moan, so she leaned back into Brittany and started to kiss her again as Brittany thrust into her.

"You're so wet," Brittany said against her lips.

"You do that to me." Toni could feel the heat from her own breath, and for some reason, it turned her on even more. This angle gave Brittany access to a spot Toni had only ever read about before. She dug her nails into Brittany's biceps. "Jesus Christ, Britt, I'm going to come."

"Good. Come for me."

"I am so close."

"Do it, baby."

Toni was so close, so very close, when all of a sudden, there was a throat clearing outside the door.

"Antoinette, that better not be you in there. And you either, Brittany."

Brittany's hand stopped moving, and Toni bit down on her lip. "Wrap it up, ladies. This isn't a brothel."

Toni waited until the door opened and closed again before she let out a laugh. "Of fucking course, Alice has to catch us."

"And you were so close…" Brittany's eyebrows were raised. "She did say to wrap it up."

"You're right. She did." Toni focused her gaze on Brittany's eyes. She felt Brittany pull her fingers from inside her, then focus her attention on her clit. She rubbed softly at first then increased her speed and intensity until Toni's orgasm finally crashed through her. She closed her eyes and bit her lip, holding in her moans and groans as Brittany continued to rub her clit. Then, as if trying to be quiet during an orgasm wasn't hard enough, Brittany pushed her fingers back inside. Toni literally felt like she was coming so hard she was going to pass out. When her orgasm subsided, and Brittany removed her fingers, Toni laid her head on Brittany's shoulder, panting the entire time. "Holy fuck. That was incredible."

"Tell me about it. I think I almost came just watching you." Brittany kissed the side of Toni's head. "I can't wait to get back to the house with you."

"God," Toni said as she picked her head up and looked at Brittany. "Same here. Two more hours of this shit shift and then we go fuck each other's brains out. Deal?"

"You don't have to ask me twice." Brittany laughed before she pulled Toni's face to hers and kissed her deeply.

And Toni noticed for the first time since Penn that her damaged heart wasn't as bandaged as it once had been. There wasn't an ounce of regret as it beat. There wasn't an ounce of sadness as she realized she had finally healed. And there was only love when she realized she had fallen completely for Brittany.

Chapter Twenty-eight

Brittany sat on the porch watching the rain pelt the quaint neighborhood. Her thoughts were a jumbled mess. It was as if she were currently existing in two places, and she was trying to reconcile them. Part of her brain was focused on what had transpired between her and Madge. Madge had been able to catch a glimpse of what she was experiencing. The realization demolished any thought Brittany had about losing her mind. The visions were real. The danger was real. It was all real, and she had no idea how to get ahead of it, much less stop it.

The other part of her mind was swirling around Toni. The feelings that Toni evoked, and how Brittany felt on the receiving end of her adoration. If and when she merged her two lives, she may very well lose Toni. The idea created a giant lump in her throat. They'd only known each other for seven weeks, and yet Brittany was having a difficult time imagining existing without her.

She looked down at her journal. Words, pictures, and different scribbles littered the pages. The small notebook was a startlingly accurate picture of her brain, and she groaned at the futility of it all. Figuring out who this person was and what they were after was no longer a mild obsession. It felt vital—as if her entire existence hinged on the outcome. *Maybe it does.*

"Hey," Toni said as she leaned against the doorframe. "You look miles away."

Brittany tried to plaster on a smile, but she knew it wasn't convincing. "Just thinking." She put out her hand to Toni. "Come sit with me. How was work?"

Toni sat in the seat next to her and took her hand. "Uneventful after you left."

"Did your aunts say anything?"

Toni rolled her eyes. "No. But they both were giving me odd smiles all night."

"Sorry. I didn't want to get you in any trouble."

Toni laughed. "Please do not apologize. It was hot, and it's not like it got me fired." She sighed and looked out onto the street. "I know I said we'd continue what we started, but I'm exhausted. Would you be terribly disappointed if I went to bed?"

"Not at all. I totally understand."

Toni kissed her cheek before going back in the house. "Come to bed soon?"

"Absolutely."

After Brittany was sure Toni had gone upstairs, she refocused on the sounds around her. She closed her eyes and took a deep breath. The tightness behind her eyes came first. With each attempt it was becoming easier to slip into this state. Her forehead started to throb, and pain tore through her receptors. Then came the light. Finally, the blurred light started to take shape.

Her mind was transported, and she tried to look around. They were sitting on the patio of a bar staring at the water. The person took a sip of dark brown liquid, and the ice cube clinked as they lowered the glass. Their focus shifted to a group of women laughing and yelling over one another, apparently trying to tell the same story. Brittany tried to force the person to look up. She wanted to see a bar sign, anything that could depict where they were. If she knew, she might have a chance of tracking the person down.

They slammed down their glass and pinched the bridge of their nose. Hands pressed to ears, hard.

A server walked over and put a hand on their shoulder. "Are you okay?"

She felt them nod. They quickly stood and walked over to the edge of the deck. The white tips of the waves seemed to scream as they crashed into the depths below. The ocean liked to punish itself by using its own ferocity against its very essence, just as the waves of aggression and despair crashed against themselves, creating a storm.

Get out. Get out. Get out. Get out.

Brittany jumped in her seat, thrown from the person's thoughts. Her body felt disjointed and heavy. She looked down at her own hands and blinked. Whoever's mind she'd been traipsing around in knew she was there. The thought was terrifying. Her only solace was that if she didn't know who this person was, the same was probably true for them.

Brittany stared at her notebook, and then slammed it shut. It was foolish to think the person would be able to find her through her scribbles, but she wasn't going to take any chances.

She leaned over in her seat and rubbed her hands over her face. The headaches didn't linger the way they had at first, but it was still an exhausting exercise. Her body felt depleted, and her nerves were ragged.

She walked into the house and poured herself four fingers of whiskey. By the time she made it back out onto the porch, her hands had stopped trembling.

"You doing okay?" Alice was leaning against the porch railing, sipping from a glass of her own.

"Yeah, I'm fine," Brittany said as she took her seat.

"I worked in insurance for…well, probably longer than you've been alive." Alive chuckled and took another sip. "Do you know the one truly usable skill I was able to master during my time there?"

Brittany sipped her whiskey. "Whether or not you should pay for the additional insurance on a rental car?"

Alice laughed. "That *is* often redundant if your actual policy is halfway decent, but no. I learned how to tell when someone is lying."

Brittany took another sip of her drink, avoiding eye contact. "I bet that is handy."

Alice nodded. "Something's going on with you, Brittany. I haven't pushed it because I can tell you're a good person who truly cares for Toni. But if you want to talk, I'm here."

Brittany tried to play out in her mind what it would look like to tell Alice about her visions. She had a distinct feeling that Alice would not only believe her but would be supportive. She opened her mouth to say something but stopped herself. If she told Alice, she'd also be harnessing her with the secret she'd been keeping from Toni.

She didn't want to put Alice in that position. She wouldn't put that kind of strain on her.

Brittany lifted her glass toward her. "Thank you, Alice. I appreciate it." She finished the liquid and stood. "I think I'm going to go to bed. See you in the morning."

Alice nodded. "I'll be here."

Brittany climbed the stairs knowing she'd made the right choice. She couldn't tell Alice what was going on before she told Toni. It didn't matter how much she felt she needed to unburden herself. Doing so would be selfish, and Brittany didn't want that as another mark against her when she was finally forced to expose everything, which, thanks to Madge, she hadn't been able to stop thinking about. She needed to come clean, but she had no idea how.

She stripped down to her tank top and underwear and slid into bed behind Toni, wrapping her hand around her waist. Even in her slumber, Toni intertwined their fingers. Brittany had to hold back a sob as she wondered how many more nights she'd get like this before Toni knew everything there was to know. It wouldn't be up to her at that point, and that thought was enough to make her squeeze Toni a little tighter.

Leslie put down the book she'd been reading when Alice came into their room. Her usually playful and carefree wife looked concerned as she moved around the room getting ready for bed.

"Everything okay, love?" Leslie took off her glasses and placed them on top of the book next to their bed.

Alice slid into bed next to her. "I'm worried about Brittany."

"What's going on? Is Toni okay?" Leslie fought the urge to go down the hall and check on her.

Alice kissed her cheek. "I think Brittany's dealing with something she doesn't want to share. I'm not an expert in a lot of things, but I know the toll that can take on a person."

"We're all dealing with something, sweetheart. I'm sure Brittany is no different."

Alice smiled at her, but Leslie knew it wasn't authentic. "I sent her to see Madge, and when I called Madge after to see what she thought, she was very short with me."

Leslie slid down in bed and rested her head against Alice, loving to hear the sound of her heartbeat. "Is she supposed to tell you? Isn't it an ethics violation to tell you what happened in their session?"

Alice laughed. "She's not a priest or a lawyer, honey." She kissed the top of her head. "I didn't want to know what they discussed. I just wanted to know her overall feelings about her."

"Should we be worried for Toni?" Leslie was weighing this information against how blissful Toni looked when she was around Brittany.

"No, I don't think so. I'm worried about Brittany as a friend of ours. I'm not worried about her intentions with Toni."

Leslie reached up and turned off the light, and then snuggled back into Alice. "All we can do is let her know we're here for her. The rest is up to her to decide."

Alice squeezed her. "You're right, darling. You're always right."

"I'm going to need that in writing."

"First thing tomorrow," Alice said with a slight chuckle.

Leslie listened to Alice's breathing level out as she fell asleep. She loved all the time they shared together, but these were some of her favorite moments. She'd longed for them in their years apart. There had been so many mistakes, so many missteps. None of that time wasted could ever be returned to either of them. Time. It was the most precious of the finite resources humans had at their disposal, too often squandered on meaningless arguments, endeavors, and stubbornness. She was guilty of all of that. She wondered how she could convey that to the two young women sleeping a few doors down from them. But that was the irony of the kind of hindsight she'd been able to achieve—it wasn't something you could explain to someone until they experienced it for themselves.

Leslie let herself drift into sleep reassuring herself she'd never squander another minute. The thought and belief carried her into slumber.

Chapter Twenty-nine

By the time they'd arrived at Reputation Brewery, the smallest and least well-known of the breweries on the island, the tour had already sold out. It was good for them, but bad for Brittany and Toni as that was what their day was supposed to consist of. Their server was pleasant and friendly, but Toni didn't miss the way she was shamelessly checking out Brittany. It shouldn't have bothered her, but Toni couldn't tamp down the surge of jealousy she felt.

In all fairness, Brittany seemed unaware of the attention and seemed to be trying to look beyond her at her surroundings.

"I recommend the sampler flight. There's a really good variety this week."

"That sounds perfect, thank you," Toni said but the server never took her eyes off Brittany.

The server placed a hand on Brittany's shoulder and Toni caught the extra squeeze she gave her. "I'll go grab that for you. If there's anything else I can get you, please don't hesitate to ask." She winked at her.

Brittany pulled her stool closer to Toni. "Are you okay?"

Toni pressed her thumb into her palm hard enough to leave a white pressure mark. "Yup. I love watching women fawn all over you. I've been meaning to work on my shortcomings, and you gave me the perfect opportunity."

Brittany looked confused. "Are you talking about the server? I don't think she meant anything by it."

Toni wasn't sure if Brittany was being intentionally obtuse or if she truly wasn't aware of the completely apparent flirting. "You can't be serious. She was ready to pull you into the back room and have her way with you."

Brittany raised her eyebrows and blinked at Toni. "Interesting."

"Excuse me? What's interesting?"

"It surprises me that you think you have anything to worry about. I haven't so much as looked at another woman since I've met you, and I thought I'd made that apparent. I guess I've fallen short."

Toni straightened her back. "Oh."

Brittany put her hand over Toni's. "Believe me when I tell you, no one I've met can hold a candle to you."

"I've heard similar words before," Toni said.

"I'm not interested in anyone but you, Toni. Not here, not in San Francisco. I don't want to be with anyone else."

Toni tilted her head and studied Brittany. Her face was earnest and her eyes were steady. "Are you saying I'm your girlfriend?"

Brittany laughed. "Do you want to be my girlfriend?"

Toni rolled her eyes and playfully smacked Brittany's arm. "I thought that was apparent the fifteenth time we had sex."

"I'm a slow learner sometimes."

Toni ran her hand through Brittany's hair. "I'm sorry I got a little crazy."

"I'm sorry I wasn't clear about what you meant to me."

Toni shrugged. "I may be a slow learner sometimes, too. I don't have the best track record."

The server brought the drinks over and set them on the table. "If you two need anything else, just let me know." She put a hand on Brittany's arm again before walking away.

Toni raised an eyebrow at Brittany to prove her point. "See."

Brittany waved her off. "What do you think of the beer?" She took a sip and sniffed the amber liquid.

"Terrible."

"I don't think it's that bad."

Toni finished the small glass in one gulp. "Agree to disagree."

Brittany chuckled. "You're a feisty one. I like it."

"What do you think of this place overall?" Toni leaned closer. "Anything tickle your journalist Spidey brain?"

Brittany sighed. "Not really. How many of the bars down by the water have outdoor seating near the water?"

"Pretty much all of them. Why?"

Brittany shook her head. "I figured as much." She took another sip of beer. "I was just wondering."

Toni looked at the time on her cell phone. "I have to get to the pub. What are your plans the rest of the day?"

"I'm going to head to the library and do some more research."

"Come by for a drink when you're done?" Toni leaned forward and kissed Brittany.

"You bet." Brittany grabbed her hand when she tried to walk away. "Try not to start any fights before I see you next."

"No promises." Toni kissed her one last time and headed out to her bike.

She maneuvered through the town on her way to the pub. She thought about all the good things her time in the small town had brought her. She was with family she loved and had met a wonderful woman. Maybe her luck really was turning around.

The library wasn't on Cornelia Street. Brittany told herself she was taking the long way to clear her head, but she was lying to herself. She parked her bike in front of Madge's Mystical Musings and debated her next move. She wanted to talk to her but was hesitant. Madge had practically thrown her out last time she was there before they'd gotten to the bottom of anything. She needed to know more, and Madge was the only one on the island who could possibly help. But first she'd have to gather the nerve to knock on her door.

The blinds moved and she saw Madge peering through the small slits. The slits were shut immediately, though so Madge must have seen who was standing on her doorstep.

Damn. She pulled on the bike and turned it in the direction of the library when suddenly, the front door to Madge's place opened and there she stood, in a billow of incense and patchouli scented smoke.

"You just gonna loiter, or are you coming inside?"

After swallowing the lump lodged in her throat, Brittany reparked her bike and hurried up the stairs, scooting by Madge's large body into the small entryway. "I didn't think you'd want to see me again."

Madge uncrossed her arms and waved for her to follow. "It was a lot to process; it's not like you gave me any warning."

"Yeah, um, I'm sorry about that. I didn't get any warning, either, if it makes you feel any better." She watched for a reaction from Madge. When she received none, she shrugged. "I had no idea it was going to happen, and I didn't really know what to say or how to say it."

Madge took the seat across from her and lit a cigarillo. "You haven't told Toni." Smoke billowed from her mouth and nostrils.

"I'm not even sure where to start. Given the way you reacted to the news, imagine what she might do."

Madge pulled a bottle of gin and two glasses from under her table. She filled them both more than was necessary for lunch time and slid one across to Brittany. "You should start by telling her that you love her."

"Love? I don't know if I'm in love with her or not."

Madge let the cigarillo hang from her lips as she spoke. "Who do you think you're dealing with right now?"

Brittany sipped the gin. She hated gin. She hated warm gin even more, but she needed a little mind lubrication. "I can't just tell her I love her. I haven't told her the whole truth about me. She could go screaming for the hills. And she probably should."

Madge ashed the cigarillo and crossed her arms. Her lips moved like she was chewing on a tiny piece of tobacco leaf. "Can't keep this up forever."

"You're very helpful, Captain Obvious. Thank you."

The deep laugh that poured from Madge was almost ominous. "You want someone to coddle your feelings and sugarcoat reality, get a puppy. That's not what I do here."

Brittany rubbed her temples. This meeting wasn't going in a good direction. "Can you help me with my visions? Can you help me decipher them?" She put her hand out for Madge to take.

Madge tapped her long fingernail against her lips, while staring at Brittany's hand without taking it. "You haven't had the sight long, right? Just since your accident?"

"How did you—" Brittany stopped her question abruptly when she noticed Madge's raised eyebrows. "Oh." Of course, Madge knew. "It started out of nowhere."

Madge shook her head. "You're linked to this person somehow. This isn't random. You may not know them personally, but you've come across them or vice versa. I would say sometime after the accident."

Brittany took another sip of the terrible alcohol. "I haven't really been around anyone before this started. I stayed at my friend Amy's house and went back and forth to the hospital. My other friends called a lot at first, but then it died off." She leaned forward on the table. "Take my hand, help me."

"I saw enough to know that what you're seeing is pure evil. I can't allow that type of energy into my aura without the proper guardians." She waved her hand around. "It would take me months of cleansing to get rid of it, and I can't afford that." She put out the cigarillo and immediately lit another. "If I were you, I'd find out who was in San Francisco at the time of your accident. That person is connected to you in some way, and that connection brought you here."

"Passenger lists are confidential. I can't just call the airline and ask."

"Hey, I'm not a legal expert. I'm just telling you that whoever you're anchored to has crossed paths with you, and the time frame it happened in."

"Can you use the expertise you do have and help me figure out how to control what the person is looking at so I can figure out where they are? Maybe even who they are? I know they can sense me there. Is there a way to—"

Madge put her hand up. "Stop. They can sense you?"

Brittany nodded. "Yes. When I channel them, they know I'm there. Or at least it feels like they know. And it's so strange. Sometimes it's almost as if I can smell what they're smelling. Taste what they're tasting. I sort of thought it was all related to the accident and my brain injury but it's been happening with more frequency. Like, the other day, I was eating fries and I swear I could taste some sort of fish." She swallowed the unsavory memory. "I thought I was hallucinating or something, but it makes sense now… I mean, it makes a little sense, I guess."

"Brittany, you need to be very careful. This person is dangerous. I could feel the hatred and death through your visions. Not only that, they're going to be smart and blend into regular life easily. If you aren't aware of everything going on around you, they may try to set a trap. People like that don't want someone poking around in their minds." She looked like she was going to grab her arms but changed her mind. "Please be careful. You need to do what you can to protect the people around you. Keeping them in the dark puts them in danger."

Brittany stood. "Thanks for your help and the drink." She walked to the door.

"Brittany," Madge said. "There's a storm coming, and I'm not just talking about a meteorological event." She pointed at her, waving her finger. "It will change and define the rest of your life. Please tread lightly."

"Gee thanks, Madge."

"I'm just the messenger." Madge shrugged and started turning over tarot cards.

Brittany walked back outside to her bike and looked up at the sky. A storm was definitely coming. The clouds were moving swiftly, and the pressure in the air had changed. She wasn't sure what was coming next and whether or not she could handle it. All she knew for certain was that she should take Madge's warning to heart about a metaphorical storm coming her way. She'd likely need all the positive forces she could assemble.

She exhaled deeply, resolute in her decision to tell Toni everything tomorrow and let the chips fall where they may.

CHAPTER THIRTY

Leslie was in bed watching TV trying to stay awake for the weather forecast on the eleven o'clock news. Folks in the bar were talking about the hurricane stirring out in the Atlantic, and she was concerned about preparations for the island. Alice turned off the bathroom light and rubbed in hand lotion on her way to bed. "Honey, you're so sleepy. Let's turn off the TV."

Leslie popped her eyes open and sat up. "I'm awake, I'm awake. I want to see the weather. They're calling for a hurricane."

"I heard the kids talking about it in the kitchen today," Alice said as she climbed into bed. "I wanted to look it up on my phone, but I got busy with other things."

"It's a category two now, but last I heard it was gathering strength off Bermuda."

"Turn it up," Alice said.

As soon as the weather segment began, the meteorologist excitedly explained that Hurricane Karlie was on a steady track to make landfall in New England in about forty-eight hours, brushing by Martha's Vineyard and Swift Island on its way. He added that the New England Weather Service was issuing a storm watch because it was only a Cat 2 at the moment, and the storm's direction could change course and head north, in which case it would bypass land. However, residents and vacationers alike on the islands and Massachusetts shores should stay vigilant and sign up for weather updates on their phones.

"How do we sign up for the updates?" Leslie asked.

"We have to download their weather app first and then sign up," Alice said.

"Great. Can't I just watch the news? Lord knows it's on every hour of the day."

Alice giggled. "You could do that, too. But I think with two tech savvy women in the house, we'll have no trouble staying up to date."

"When should we start boarding everything up? Should we close the pub?"

"I think when they issue a warning that they're confident it's going to hit. Gosh, I hope they don't issue an evacuation."

"You think they will?"

"It's entirely possible if this thing increases in strength, which it probably will since the oceans are so much warmer now."

"That'll be awful. What'll we do with the girls? The house in Connecticut's closed for the summer. We're not prepared."

Alice grabbed Leslie's hand and gave it a comforting squeeze. "Honey, relax. Nobody said anything about an evacuation yet. We'll handle it if it happens, but more times than not, the weather forecasters hype these things up way more than necessary."

"That's true," Leslie said. "And as long as we're all together and safe, so what if we only have cans of baked beans to eat."

"I think we have more in the pantry at home than that," Alice said. She extended her arm for Leslie to snuggle under. "Now settle your mind and get some sleep."

Leslie clicked off the TV, happy to do as Alice advised. One of the things she'd always loved about Alice was the way she could take charge of a difficult situation. She'd learned how to be more self-confident and not so anxious about every little thing thanks to her wife. They were both born in an era where women were taught to be reliant on men and that their gender defined both their roles and capabilities in life. Thankfully, Alice and her feminist crochet group friends from the seventies had helped undo some of the traditional middle-class indoctrination Leslie had grown up with.

As Alice gently caressed her back in the dark, Leslie listened to the light wind whistling through the window. While the rest of the cottage had air conditioners in various rooms, they chose to cool theirs by the ever-reliable ocean breeze. Tonight, it was stronger than usual. Once Leslie's eyes adjusted to the half-moon light peering in through their bay window, she gazed up at Alice's profile. Sometimes she just needed to stare at her, really stare hard at her face to absorb every last little contour and line. For years, all she'd had of Alice was a photo of them at a company party in the seventies. With its edges torn and the surface dulled with fingerprints, Leslie carried that old photo of them, at times her lifeline, in her wallet to this day, an enduring memento of how deeply she loved her and how truly complete her life finally felt.

"Alice," she whispered. "Are you awake?"

"Hmm? What is it?" she replied, seeming to rouse herself from sleep.

"Don't you think it would be a shame to waste this breezy, breathtaking, moonlit night sleeping?"

That seemed to wake Alice up pronto. She turned on her side and gently stroked Leslie's upper arm. "There will never come a day in my life where I'd waste one wonderful moment with you." She leaned over and began kissing Leslie's neck.

Leslie sighed. How exquisite it was to still feel attractive and desired at her age, long after society had written women off as old grandmas. She and Alice enjoyed the rare magic of still discovering the ways their love and affection for each other reminded them they were still vital, sexual beings.

"You make me feel wonderful, my love."

"You are wonderful," Alice said before she kissed her lips. "And beautiful. And sexy."

Leslie giggled. "Those two down the hall got nothing on us."

They wrapped each other in their arms, skin to skin, and made love to the beat of the waves crashing louder and louder into the shore below.

❖

The next morning Toni sat at the island counter in the kitchen eating cold cereal as she watched funny TikTok videos. The house was quiet as everyone in it but her seemed calm enough about the storm not to let it affect their sleep. After tossing and turning all night, she decided to get up and leave Brittany a final hour or so where the bed didn't feel like a rowboat on rough seas.

She put her phone down and listened to the weather outside. The ocean sounded rowdier than usual, and the tulle curtains in the kitchen and family room were flouncing about in a blustery breeze. A hurricane was coming. She wanted to be annoyed, but it was the heart of hurricane season in New England, so she couldn't be too pissed at Mother Nature.

She checked out the local weather forecast on her phone as she finished eating and didn't like what she read. A creak at the top of the wooden staircase preceded Leslie and Alice as they padded down from the second floor.

"Good morning, sunshine," Leslie announced, then toned it down. "Ooh, is Brittany still sleeping?"

Toni nodded as she watched Leslie and Alice dance around each in other in the kitchen as Alice made their coffees and Leslie pulled out the eggs and avocados.

"Who's up for an omelet?" Leslie asked, her face as vibrant as a gameshow contestant.

"What got into you this morning?" Toni asked, ruling out any old lady aches and pains from last night.

Alice wheeled around to Toni, her eyes gleaming. "I did, only it wasn't this morning. It was last night."

Toni's coffee mug seemed to freeze suspended at her lips while Leslie, standing in the corner, blushed as red as the cluster of poppies in front of the house.

"Alice," Leslie said in a singsong, clearly her way of scolding her.

"Come on. Toni's used to me by now."

Toni giggled. "It's true. I am."

"Well, I'm not," Leslie said.

Alice came up behind Leslie, wrapped her arms around her, and addressed Toni. "For as much progress as your dear old aunt's made in becoming a feminist, she's still uptight about openly discussing sex as a part of a healthy woman's life."

Leslie glanced over her shoulder at Alice. "It's not that I have a problem discussing sex. I just don't think it appropriate to discuss it in front of my little sister's daughter."

"It's all good, Aunt Leslie. I think it's awesome that you and your lady love are still active in your seventies. It fills me with optimism for the future." Toni relaxed, proud of herself that she'd gotten over the ick factor involved in realizing her aunts were still having sex.

Leslie shook her head, still blushing despite the reassurances. "Good God. Where is Brittany when we need her?"

"Right here," Brittany said as she descended the staircase. She made her way into the kitchen with her neck bent toward her phone. "They're saying that hurricane hasn't veered off course yet."

Toni sat on the stool with her lips puckered, waiting.

"Oh. Good morning." Brittany leaned down and gave her a kiss.

"So that means we need to prepare for a direct hit?" Leslie asked.

"We certainly need to keep an even closer eye on it," Alice said. She looked to Brittany. "Would you want to help me down at the hardware store?"

"Sure," she replied. "It's a good idea to get there before everyone starts panic buying up all the plywood sheets."

Leslie started to look worried. "Do you think we're going to get a direct hit?" she asked again.

"I've never had to endure a hurricane before. Winter storms in the Rockies with six feet of snow? Sure. But this?" Toni knew it'd be okay in the end, but it still worried her.

"Oh, you two, we'll be fine. I promise you." Alice was the most levelheaded when it came to a crisis. "Even if it completely bypasses us, we should have all that stuff on hand for the next storm because I assure you, there will be one."

"Right," Brittany said. "And even if it hits, a category three isn't that dangerous if you prepare for it. According to the meteorologists on the news, anyway."

Toni was in love with how self-assured and rational Brittany's tone was as she tried to ease Leslie's worry.

Brittany continued. "You should have the plywood, extra batteries, candles, all that stuff. As long as we prepare, we'll be fine."

"This kid knows her stuff," Alice said. She kissed Leslie on the cheek and released her from her grip. "I'm gonna grab a shower, and when you're ready we'll head out."

"Want me to come with you guys?" Toni asked.

Alice stopped before she rounded the corner. "You and Leslie should head over to the pub and make a list of everything we'll need to secure it. Brittany and I will get it all at the store."

"Okay," Toni said. "We're on it."

"Doesn't anyone want an avocado and cheese omelet?" Leslie asked.

"I will," Toni said. "They can take theirs to go."

Alice and Brittany headed upstairs to get ready.

After her shower, Brittany stared at herself in the mirror as she brushed her teeth, her hair wrapped in a towel turban. She was sort of hoping Alice would've sent Toni and her to the hardware store together and handled the pub with Leslie, but Alice clearly wasn't the kind of woman who needed others to make decisions for her.

With all the hurricane hype dragging a pall of negativity over the island like a wet beach towel, Brittany's emotions were being pulled in multiple directions. She liked having something important to focus on aside from the visions, but at the same time, she needed to stay in tune with them, especially after her trip to the psychic. If something bad really was churning among them, she needed to keep her mind clear to receive and interpret the warnings. Of course a hurricane had to pick just now to stir up. The last thing this shit pot needed was more stirring.

In Alice's SUV, on the way to the hardware store, Brittany was quiet as she tried to open the channels in her mind. With snatches of gray-green sky, torrents of rain, and exceptionally rough white caps on the water flashing through her mind, she didn't need a meteorologist to tell her the hurricane had no intention of blowing out to sea. The person she was attached to was watching it come at them, too.

"I can't tell you how glad I am that you're here," Alice said.

Brittany snapped out of her musings and turned to Alice. "Me too. I'm glad I can help out. I knew I was led to this island for a reason."

"I don't just mean because of the storm. Toni is such a different person since meeting you. I haven't known her all her life, but till now, she's always seemed brooding and discontented, like she was restless to find some space where she felt like she fit. All of that seems like it's gone now. She's coming into her own."

Brittany smiled. "I feel that way about Toni, too—my life seems fuller with her in it. Actually, all of you have made me feel like I found a space to feel comfortable in. I appreciate that a lot."

"You've been a pleasure to have around, Brittany. I know you've gone through some incredible struggles over the last year, and I'm happy we could be part of your healing journey. I think you and Toni have found something that could be really special."

"I think so, too, but I have to say, after seeing the dynamic between you and Leslie, that's a tough act to follow. We should all be as lucky. It sucks that you guys had to wait so long to find your way back to each other."

"The important thing is that we did. At this stage in my life, I'm absolutely okay with quality over quantity."

"Rock on, sister," Brittany said and held up her fist for a bump.

She returned to her thoughts, kicking around her approach to how she'd let Toni in on the truth about her visions. Today, as they all began preparing for the big storm, was as good a day as any to do it.

They pulled into the parking lot at the hardware store, which was already bustling with activity. In another couple of hours, the place would probably be cleaned out. They went inside and headed down different aisles to pick up items on their lists. Brittany turned down aisle three and saw the girl who gave them the tour at Nereids Brewing.

"Crazy times, huh?" Brittany said as she checked out duct tape.

Quinn jumped, then smiled at Brittany. "Yes. The ladies sent me out for some supplies. I just heard the weather service bumped up the hurricane to a category three."

"Oh, shit," Brittany said. "I thought you were gonna say they canceled the storm watch."

Quinn gave a goofy chuckle. "Nah. I wish. I guess we still have time for it to turn out into the Atlantic."

"I'm keeping my fingers crossed," Brittany said. "And hey, keep that place safe. You guys make some incredible beer."

"Yeah, you, too. Batten down the hatches at the Second Wave," Quinn said. "That's my favorite place to eat."

Brittany gave her a thumbs up and continued shopping. I'll bet it is, she thought with a smile as she recalled Toni's accusation that she had the hots for Leslie. Quinn was so cute but soooo awkward. It would be just like her to have a crush on a sweet, attractive old lady. Although Brittany had to admit that if she had seen a younger Leslie walking down the street, she might catch her eye for a moment.

By early afternoon, Brittany, Toni, and Alice had stacked the plywood against the house in the front and back, ready at a moment's notice to begin boarding up windows if the situation required. Leslie was relegated to maintaining inside supplies like batteries, candles, and food staples that would last for at least three days. Brittany began wondering if a three-day supply would be enough after Alice mentioned how ferry service between there and the mainland was going to be stopped for at least a day once the official storm warning was released. That meant if store shelves were emptied, they'd stay that way until service resumed.

Toni walked over to Brittany and handed her a bottle of cold water. "This humidity is killing me. I don't know about California, but Colorado rarely gets this sticky." She used the bottom of her tank top to wipe the sweat from under her nose.

Brittany agreed. "I don't think I've ever felt air this thick before. It's like you can chew it."

"It's gross," Toni said. "Alice says that's how you can tell the hurricane's coming. She also said if we see animals start boarding the ferry out, we better follow them," she added with a chuckle.

"There's a whole weird vibe going on out here. It's more than just the pre-storm atmosphere." Brittany watched Toni's reaction carefully, trying to gauge how receptive she'd be if Brittany just happened to throw in her dark, sinister visions along with the storm talk.

Toni nodded as she faced the ocean to catch a kicked up breeze. "It's gotta be all the negative juju everyone's throwing off as they switch into survivalist mode."

"Panic spreads faster than germs in small enclaves." Brittany watched Toni redo her ponytail and smooth back the excess strands of hair. God, she looked sexy as hell all sweaty in that tank top. "So speaking of negative juju, I wanted to—"

Alice appeared around the corner of the house. "Are you gals ready to head over to the pub? We can grab a bite to eat before getting things organized there."

"Yeah," Toni said. "I'm starving." She grabbed Brittany's hand and tugged her along behind Alice.

Brittany trotted along behind them. Dammit. That was the perfect moment to lay it on Toni. At the pub, there would be too many people around. She had no choice but to wait till tonight when they were settling in back at the house.

CHAPTER THIRTY-ONE

Toni was no stranger to hard work. After the numerous times she had to help with the herding season at the Bennett Ranch, she understood the term "daylight's burnin'" better than most. Just because she understood the reason behind the sweat and dirt, didn't mean she particularly liked it, though. And as much as she was in shape, she was so not the type of person to lift heavy plywood and hammer nails. Every bone and muscle in her body was starting to feel the effects of manual labor. When she lifted the mushroom and Swiss burger she ordered to her lips, she felt her muscles shaking. "I haven't been this sore in a really long time," she said with a laugh as she took a greedy bite of the amazing burger.

"Oh, I refuse to believe that," Brittany said around a mouthful of fries.

Toni could tell her eyes were wide, and she covered her mouth as she chewed, trying to contain a laugh. She swallowed, nudging Brittany with her elbow.

"What? You know it's true."

"Leslie, looks like Toni is the same as you, embarrassed to discuss sex."

"Jesus." Toni chuckled before she took a long drink of the U-Haul IPA. She hated it at first, but it grew on her and now she couldn't get enough of it.

"Look, I'm just saying." Brittany winked. "Don't worry. I'll help massage those tired muscles later."

"I swear to God, you are absolutely going to get it."

"Pipe down, you two," Leslie said, followed by a sweeping motion with her arm. "The news is on." She waved at Erika the bartender and shouted, "Turn it up!"

"Hurricane Karlie is officially a category three storm off the coast of Massachusetts. It looks to make landfall in the next forty-eight hours. The spaghetti models show at least ten different landfall locations. The most prevalent seems to be Karlie blasting onto the coast of Swift Island, with winds upward of eighty-five miles per hour. The only thing standing in the way of Karlie slamming into Boston is the tiny island. So far, the storm is moving at a record speed, which is good news for the island. The rain and flooding won't be as much of a problem as the winds. As they say, batten down the hatches, Swiftonians. Karlie is comin' for ya."

Toni's mouth was completely dry. She didn't want to admit it because she was far from a fraidy-cat, but the impending storm was starting to freak her out. The rest of the inhabitants of the island were calm, cool, and collected, which, truth be told, freaked her out even more. The idea of being stranded on the island wasn't her idea of a good time. Claustrophobia was settling in, threatening to choke her.

"Hey."

Toni looked down at Brittany's hand in hers. "Huh?"

"Are you okay?"

"Sure." Toni licked her dry lips. "Sure." She continued to stare at the hand over hers. "Just, y'know, never been through this before."

"Toni, honey, this is nothing big. Your aunt and I have weathered storms before. Big storms. We're going to be okay." Alice's voice was soothing, but it wasn't helping much.

"Sweetheart, look at me."

Toni blinked a couple of times before she turned to look at Leslie.

"We're going to be okay. I promise. If you're really that nervous, though, we can get you on the next ferry." Toni watched Leslie check her old Seiko watch. "It leaves in two hours."

The idea sort of soothed her. She was seconds away from saying okay when old Mervin bent down between Leslie and Alice. "Just letting you all know that the ferry has canceled its last trips today. The waters are simply too rough. It's not safe."

Toni's stomach dropped.

"Oh. Okay." Alice seemed upset by this news. "Thanks, Merv."

"Anytime, ladies. You need any help boarding up the pub? I can have my sons come over."

"No, no. We're fine. The shutters on the outside close up easy enough—" Alice stood and walked away with Mervin.

Toni immediately turned to her aunt. "Now what?"

Leslie's small chuckle wasn't comforting. "Toni, we're going to be okay. I would not tell you that if it wasn't true."

"You're sure?"

"Yes."

Toni looked to her left at Brittany. "Why aren't you freaked out by this?"

Brittany shrugged. "I dunno…"

There was something underneath that answer, some sort of truth that Brittany clearly didn't want Toni to know. In the last couple of weeks, Toni was starting to sense more and more that Brittany wasn't being completely honest about something, and up until now, she was able to push the irritation away. But now, as her anxiety surged because of the impending doom of a category three hurricane, she could feel the irritation stirring, not unlike how the sea felt the hurricane building. She hoped it was just the stress of everything and not some other sign that things weren't as wonderful with Brittany as she assumed. She couldn't handle the idea that Brittany was anything like Penn, a giant planet of disappointment orbited by a million smaller ones.

"You've dealt with storms before, Toni. The only difference is you won't be shoveling yourself out." Leslie smoothed her hand over Toni's, squeezed lightly, then smiled. "Trust me, okay?"

Toni nodded and took a deep breath, eyeing Brittany the entire time. But Brittany was somewhere else. Her mind, her eyes, everything. Now was not the time for Toni to start sensing something horrible about this amazing woman she'd somehow found in the middle of the storm of her life. Finding Brittany and then subsequently losing her in another storm wouldn't be a shining moment. She needed to calm down. She needed to get a grip, so Brittany knew she wasn't really a basket case who couldn't handle a little wind.

❖

Brittany should have told Toni the truth. Not just about the visions but about her anxiety surrounding the storm. She wanted to keep her stress level down because she needed her stamina to help with the preparations for the storm. There was no way she could leave Alice and Leslie high and dry. Or maybe the more appropriate term was low and soaked. Either way, she needed to be on her A game.

She also wanted to try to remain calm for Toni, who seemed quite literally on the edge of a mental breakdown about the storm. Brittany understood the nerves. It was scary knowing a hurricane was out in the ocean heading straight toward them. Preparing for impending doom was never easy.

Everything that'd happened since meeting with Madge was beginning to consume all of her brain capacity. She was almost always connected to this other person now. She could sense their movements, their own senses, their feelings of hatred, desire, jealousy. Even in moments when she was pretty much present, she felt the other person lurking in the shadows of her mind, confusing things.

Or was that her own jealousy?

And hatred?

And desire?

Fuck. I am such a mess.

"Okay then. All the windows are shuttered. The back door is boarded. I even went up into the attic and boarded those windows. From the inside but still. At least you won't get wetness and debris in there." Brittany laid the hammer on the bar top and wiped her brow with her sleeve. She sat and accepted the beer Toni set in front of her, gripping the pint glass like a lifeline. The entire pub had cleared out, leaving just the four of them to get things done.

"You've outdone yourself, Britt," Toni said with a smile. She reached across the bar. "I don't know what we would have done without you."

"Oh, I know. You would have had to get those hands a little dirtier and helped out, missy." Alice chuckled before drinking from her own beer. "You really have been amazing, Brittany. Thank you so much."

"Yeah, well, you all have been so wonderful to me." Brittany smiled, then a light flashed and a vision displayed before her eyes, except this time, she could see Alice, Leslie, Toni, herself, all in the same outfits, positions... The anger, the loathing, the jealousy tasted like bile. Then she saw herself turn on the stool she was sitting on. "Holy shit." Brittany realized once she snapped herself from the vision that she had seen herself turn, almost as if she had no memory of actually doing the movement. She jumped from the stool, moving so fast she spilled her beer; the pint glass rolled off the bar and shattered. Without stopping to explain, she bolted through the open door as she felt the person running off.

She sprinted into the street, a golf cart narrowly missing her.

"Hey! Watch it!" the elderly man said with a gruff voice.

"Sorry," she shouted back as she ran, her Nikes carrying her as she ran after whomever had been watching them. She could no longer see a person running, but her mind's eye told her the person was still sprinting, still breathing hard, still frantically trying to escape after being spotted. Brittany turned onto Kloss Drive and, without warning, the vision ended. She slowed to a jog, then to a walk, before she stopped and, hands in the air, screamed, "I fucking hate you," into the dark, churning northeastern sky.

As Brittany made her way back through town, more and more of what her nemesis had been feeling started to take up residence in her head. There was hatred, yes, but it was deeper, more intense, and it seemed to be the only thing they were able to think about. The jealousy and, holy shit, the unfettered *rage* the person was feeling. It was shocking. Brittany had never felt such intensity before in her entire life. She was no stranger to anger, but this was on a whole different level.

The part inside of her that was truly terrified wondered if she should get the authorities involved. Of course she'd have to come clean to them about the visions, which would only make her a laughing stock. The only person on the island who knew was Madge, and Brittany knew psychics were hardly considered reliable sources. Even if, in this case, it all happened to be true.

When Brittany walked up the crushed shell driveway to the house, Alice, Leslie, and Toni were on the front porch waiting for her. A warmth washed over her knowing they were worried about her. These wonderful people were worried about her. These wonderful people the visions had led her to. These wonderful people who she felt like she'd been lying to. These wonderful people who weren't going to understand what she'd been going through, but she knew she needed to tell them.

"Brittany, oh my God, are you okay?" Toni rushed up to her and threw her arms around her neck. "You scared the shit out of us."

"I'm sorry."

"What is going on?" Leslie's voice was laced with worry. "You lit out of here like a crazy person."

Brittany cringed. *Crazy person. Of course.* "I know. I'm really sorry."

"Do you want to tell us what the heck is going on?" Alice moved closer and, arms folded across her chest, tapped her foot on the crushed shell.

"Okay, fine. You want to know what's been going on? I'll tell you." Brittany paced to the left three steps, then back to the right three steps. "After my accident, the one you all know about, I started…" Her words fell off the cliff she was standing so close to.

Toni took a step toward her. "Started what?"

"Tell us, honey," Leslie said softly.

Brittany stopped pacing. She looked at Leslie, then Alice, and last, but certainly not least, she looked at Toni. She held Toni's gaze, her dark brown eyes, her gentle soul, and felt a lump form in her throat. "I started having visions."

"I'm sorry, what?" Toni's tone was everything Brittany feared about this moment.

"Visions. I started seeing things. And that's what brought me here. To you all." Brittany looked at each of them again. "I was drawn to you all, and I didn't know exactly why."

"Visions?"

"Yes. Visions."

"You were seeing things?" Toni moved closer to Leslie.

Brittany nodded. "Until tonight, I didn't really understand what these visions were supposed to mean. I'm still not positive, but.... and I wanted to tell you earlier, because I think you're in danger, all of you, but I just couldn't bring myself to…but the vision I just had was really bad. Like, something bad is going to happen, and I wasn't totally sure it was about you guys before, but now I am…I think. Everything I've seen has had this undercurrent of hatred and anger and rage, and I just didn't know how to tell you all this. I didn't know what to say. Or even if you would believe me, which it seems like maybe you don't, but I swear, I am telling the truth—"

"Stop. Stop right this instant."

It was the first time Brittany had heard Toni's voice reach a shrill tone. It ripped a hole inside her heart. She'd known this would happen. "Toni, I'm not lying. I know it seems far-fetched—"

Toni's eyes started welling with tears. "I should've known something like this would happen. I knew you were too good to be true."

"What are you talking about?" Brittany took a step in Toni's direction, but she immediately backed away. "Toni, stop, please."

"You lied to me. I kept asking you and you lied to me."

"Look at how you're reacting. Why would I have told you the truth? Why would I have told any of you the truth?" She eyed Leslie and Alice. "Would you have believed me?" Their silence was deafening. "Would you have believed me?" No one answered her. She wanted to throw up. She wanted to turn and run again, but she knew exactly where the danger was directed so it wasn't possible to simply disappear, even if that was the only thing she wanted to do.

"I don't know if you should continue to stay with us." Toni's words smacked Brittany across the face.

"Toni, I don't have anywhere to go."

"Yeah, well, maybe you should have thought about that before you stalked us. Before you started playing some kind of weird game."

"Stalked you? Are you serious? I'm trying to help you." Brittany moved again toward Toni, and when she again backed away, she stopped and held her hands up in surrender. "Toni, please. Don't…I'm not going to hurt you. I would never hurt you."

"Sure. That's why you made me fall for you without being honest with me."

Toni's shoulders were shuddering. All Brittany wanted to do was swoop her up and apologize for everything, even though she knew she hadn't done anything wrong. She was simply trying to protect herself and her relationship, along with people she'd come to care about.

"I don't want to see you anymore. Just stay away from me." Toni covered her mouth with her hand and ran into the house, the screen door slamming behind her.

Leslie looked at Brittany and heaved a heavy sigh. She shook her head slowly, a look of pure disappointment on her beautiful features. Brittany could feel the emotion rising in her throat, and it was making her light-headed. When Leslie turned and followed Toni into the house, Brittany felt her knees start to wobble. She was getting ready to pass out. She could feel it. And apparently, Alice could sense it because like a flash she was there to catch Brittany before she hit the ground.

Chapter Thirty-two

Leslie watched as Toni crept into the living room and sat on the couch. She propped her feet on the ottoman and sighed, the entire time not making eye contact with Leslie. She knew exactly what Toni was going through. The feeling of being lied to was one of the worst feelings ever in a relationship. This she knew from her own situation decades earlier when she'd tried to manage her passion for her co-worker, Alice within the context of her marriage to Bill. When he'd finally confronted her, she'd confessed; she had to. The emotional devastation from Alice moving away was simply too powerful to conceal behind a happy homemaker smile. After that, trust was hard to rebuild. It must be especially so in a new relationship.

Poor Toni. Proposed to and then abandoned. It didn't seem like she'd ever bounce back from that. And then in waltzed Brittany with her cute body and her vivacious personality. Turned out Brittany was exactly what Toni needed, until she wasn't.

"You doing okay, sweetheart?"

Toni still didn't make eye contact. She sighed, which was more than Leslie had been able to get out of her for the past twelve hours since Brittany had left. Leslie wondered where Brittany found to stay, especially with the hurricane right off the coast. She was definitely worried about Brittany, especially because she'd grown to care for her.

"Have you considered that Brittany really isn't that bad?"

Toni finally looked at Leslie, her dark eyes even darker. "No."

Yikes. "Okay then."

"Don't try to talk me out of this." Toni grimaced as she sat up. "I've made up my mind."

"Good to see stubborn runs in the family," Alice mumbled under her breath as she meandered through the living room from the tiny office to the kitchen.

"Did she just say what I think she said?"

Leslie rolled her lips in, forcing herself not to smile. "Mm-hmm."

Toni rolled her eyes. "Whatever. I'm not being stubborn."

"Oh, yes you are," Alice mumbled again on her way back to the office.

Leslie stifled a chuckle.

"Stop, Alice. Please."

"I'm not saying another word," Alice shouted from the office.

Leslie snapped the magazine she was reading and brought it back to eye level. She heard Toni sigh again, so she lowered the magazine. "What is it?"

"Do you think I'm being stubborn?"

"Absolutely not." Leslie rubbed Toni's knee.

"Told you, it runs in the family," Alice said as she emerged from the office. This time she moved around the couch and sat next to Toni.

Toni glared at Alice, then looked back to Leslie. "Why did you marry this woman?"

"Because she's right about almost everything." Leslie smiled when Alice beamed and puffed her chest. "And because she's stubborn, as well, and honestly, it takes one to know one."

"Touché." Alice winked before she patted Toni on the knee. "Listen up, buttercup."

"Ugh."

"I'm being serious, Antoinette."

"Fine. What?"

Alice sighed. "I believe Brittany. I know you don't, but I do. And I told her as much because look at how she's been acting. Something has been going on with her from the start. Toni, dear, I don't think you're being entirely fair. Especially kicking her out when there's a hurricane on the way. It's not like she knows anyone who could take her in, and you just booted her. Not super nice."

"She lied to me."

"Did she? Or did she just not tell you the entire truth?"

"She told me she was researching a story."

"That wasn't a lie." Alice shrugged. "She was researching something for sure."

"Alice, honey, I don't know if now's the right time."

Toni snapped her attention to Leslie. "Do you believe her, too?"

"I didn't say that." Leslie straightened her back.

"But you aren't *not* saying that."

"Toni, don't put words in my mouth, please. You're upset and I get it. I do. But we're just looking out for your best interests."

"And you think my best interests lie with a woman who lied to me?"

"She *didn't* lie to you," Alice said. "She simply…hedged her bet. Like she said, it wasn't as if you were going to believe her. I can't blame her for keeping mum."

"Okay, a woman who has visions, though? You think that's where my best interests are? Like, how fucking crazy is that?"

"You have clearly never had your tarot cards read." Leslie laughed and Alice joined in.

Toni stood abruptly. "Great. Now I'm the bad guy because I don't believe some lunatic woman who came into my life and was absolutely perfect, but now believes we're all in danger because of *visions* she's having?"

She took a deep breath and Leslie could see the emotion bubbling beneath the surface. One little push and Toni was going to crack and the tears would start and it'd be all over.

"I know I allowed myself to get swept off my feet again, and I allowed my heart to get broken again but so what? I don't have to keep falling for her. Okay?"

"Okay, okay. But she wasn't trying to deceive you. Sometimes it takes a while for people to open up about things they're pretty sure people won't understand. Just try to remember that."

"Yep, I'm the bad guy. Simply fucking great. Thanks, Aunts. Thanks. I'm going upstairs." Toni rushed to the stairs, taking two at a time until she disappeared to the second level.

Leslie sighed. "I told you it wasn't the right time."

"I know, but I'm stubborn. Apparently." Alice chuckled and leaned her head back on the couch. "I do believe Brittany. She had no reason to lie to us, and if one of us is actually in danger, I'm glad she decided to say something—despite the outcome."

"I know, love. It just all seems a little out there." Leslie wasn't sure what she believed. She wanted to think Brittany wasn't a raving lunatic who would lie about something as serious as frightening visions of them being in danger. There was a spot inside her that trusted what Brittany said, but she didn't want to put stock into something when she didn't feel as if she were in danger. She was safe and sound on Swift Island and with Alice to protect her, there was literally no one who could hurt her.

"No going anywhere alone until things settle down. Okay?"

"I'm not going anywhere alone with a hurricane on the way. No worries there, my love."

Alice smiled and closed her eyes, her afternoon nap on the horizon. Leslie took a deep breath and reminded herself again that there was nothing to worry about. Even though the more she thought about it, the more a part of her was unnerved by the thought that maybe one of them really was in danger.

CHAPTER THIRTY-THREE

September 13th–Journal Entry 576

I know you can see me. I feel you there, watching. My head splinters announcing your intrusion. I've suspected as much for a while, and then you gave yourself away. You turned to chase me. But what would you have done had you caught me? Would you have let violence consume you? Would you have attempted to hold me there and alert the authorities? To tell them what exactly? There are no options for you. There is no way for you to prevent what will happen because you aren't capable, Brittany. I saw the fear in your body when you turned. I practically smelled it oozing off you. Your weakness, your downfall, your personal betrayal is that you cannot do what needs to be done. You cannot execute. You cannot bring yourself to stop me because your social construct won't allow it. I don't fear you—I pity you. You and I are not equals. I am the predator, and you are nothing more than the jackal that'll pick through the remains of my kill.

It would be easy for me to eliminate you from the equation. I could extinguish your life any one of a thousand ways. But I won't do that to you. We're connected, you and I. I recognized you as soon as the look of sheer panic consumed your expression when you turned to find me. You were the woman I saw lying on the damp street in San Francisco. The motorcycle crash didn't claim your life. I'm glad for that. It is a gift to me. I have been afforded the opportunity to torment you, as you have done to me. See, I had only come here for Leslie, but now…now there is so much more to take. I wonder how it will feel for you to look upon Toni's lifeless body. Will it shatter your heart? Will it kill your proverbial will? Will it suffocate whatever shred of normalcy you've been clinging to?

Perhaps this is my chance to create. I can make you in my image. Sculpt your fury into something productive. I'll finish taking what is mine, and you will be left to deal with your choices and regrets. It will be easy to blame me. But we both know that when you lay your head down to rest, it will be your regrets that fester. They will eat away at your skin and blood. They will gnaw at your subconscious and beg you to answer why you didn't indulge your animal instinct. Why didn't you keep running after me? Why did you let me get away? Why didn't you put a stop to it before it was too late?

Sweet dreams, Brittany—a fiery hell awaits you.

Chapter Thirty-four

Toni tried to shield her face from the apocalyptic rain, but there was no point. The wind was howling with a vengeance that she'd never experienced. She and Leslie had come to the Second Wave to finish shoring up the place, while Alice stayed behind to secure their house. But now that they were here, she wasn't sure it was the best choice. The weather was rapidly transforming from powerful to dangerous, and she hated the idea of being separated. *Separated.* That was exactly what she'd done to Brittany. She'd cast her out of the house and out of her life. She'd be lying to herself if she didn't admit she regretted it.

She'd let her hurt and anger, the weight of her emotional baggage, make choices for her that now she couldn't take back. With no cell service, she had no idea where Brittany had gone. It wasn't that her pain and sense of betrayal had dissipated—it hadn't. Brittany had hundreds of opportunities to come clean, and she hadn't. She hadn't trusted her enough to tell her the truth, and that was what plagued her now.

Once they finally got inside Toni and her aunt took everything they could off the floor. Toni immediately got to work placing sandbags by the doors in the hopes to protect the bar from flooding. Her mind raced with all the potential bad things that could transpire over the course of the next day or two, but it was nothing compared to the concern she had for Brittany.

"You okay?" Leslie wiped sweat from her forehead, and she looked exhausted.

"I'm not sure I should've thrown her out, especially with this." Toni waved her hand around to indicate the approaching hurricane.

"You know, I should've spoke up on her behalf when you threw her out, but my only instinct at the time was to protect you."

Toni heaved another sandbag. "She hurt me. Deeply."

Aunt Leslie nodded. "You know, no one has ever said you're guaranteed pain-free relationships. It's how you deal with the pain that dictates your success with each other."

"You believe her, don't you?" Toni shivered even though the humidity was stifling.

"The question you should be asking is if you think she'd hurt you intentionally. Once you know the answer to that, you know the answer to the other."

Before Toni had a chance to answer, the door swung open and crashed into the wall behind it. "Do you guys need some help?" Quinn shook off the water sliding down her raincoat. "I was driving by and saw the lights on. I have some extra plywood in my van. We can board up the rest of the windows in the back and get out of here."

Toni practically fell over with relief. "Thank you. I'll come back there in a second. Let me just finish putting these sandbags in place."

After placing the remaining sandbags in front of the entrance, Toni made her way back through the kitchen to where Aunt Leslie was with Quinn. The back door was wide open, rhythmically thumping against the wall behind it. Despite the storm raging around her, everything was eerily quiet. She expected to hear hammering or shouting over the wind. But there was nothing. Toni rubbed her arms as she took a step closer to the back door.

"Aunt Leslie? Quinn? Where are you guys?" Toni took another step.

A tall frame took up the expanse of the doorway when she appeared. Toni was relieved at first. "Oh, Quinn, thank God, I was calling for you and Aunt Leslie. Is everything okay?" And then she saw Quinn's eyes. It wasn't the emotion she saw that terrified her—it was the absence of it. Quinn's eyes seemed black, and Toni took a step backward. Every nerve ending in her body seemed to scream out a warning to get out. She took another step backward.

Quinn wiped the back of her hand against her chin, and that's when Toni saw it—blood. She turned to run, and Quinn grabbed her arm. She tried to pull away, but Quinn squeezed harder.

"You're coming home with me," Quinn said.

The last thing Toni saw was the butt of a gun coming down against her face before she plunged into darkness.

❖

Brittany had nowhere else to go but to Madge. She wasn't familiar with anyone else on the island, and she needed to be with someone who not only understood her but unequivocally believed her. The look on Toni's face when she'd told her the truth had torn a hole through Brittany's heart, and it was all she could see every time she tried to focus. The hurt in her heart had slid into numbness and she danced on the edge of exhaustion. It wasn't that she hadn't known how Toni was going to react—she'd just hoped she was wrong. A small part of her had hoped that Toni would've surprised her.

The wind and rain beat against the small house. Brittany stared into the cup of coffee Madge had handed her before the power had gone out. She should've been frightened. She should've been trying to make her way to the community shelter like everyone else. She should've been counting down the minutes until this was over, and she could find the psycho that seemed tethered to her mind. But all she could do was stare at the black liquid that sat idly in the cup with no comfort to give.

"Not everyone is going to understand," Madge said softly from her stool at her tarot reading table. "Most people live on the surface-level of consciousness." Her tone was sprinkled with support but also a dusting of *I kind of knew this would happen.* "The only thing you can do now is—"

"Oh, I know what I have to do. I have to find this lunatic and stop them. I don't care if Toni never wants to see me again. I can't let anything happen to her."

Madge seemed single-minded as she continued to flip over the tarot cards. Her shoulders were pulled back, her purple bifocals perched on the tip of her nose. She looked as if she was in a zone somewhere between comfortable and anxious. Brittany, unfortunately, knew the area all too well. It was somewhat calming that the impending hurricane didn't seem to dampen her spirits. Or maybe Madge was as crazy as her. Either way, she appreciated Madge taking her in.

Brittany leaned back in the chair and took a deep breath. She needed to push the melancholy away by focusing on getting another glimpse into the lunatic's mind. She needed to make sure they were still here. She needed to know she hadn't missed her chance to find this person and ruin their chances of hurting the people she had grown to care for. But when she closed her eyes and tried to focus, all she saw was the look on Toni's face—the look that solidified her previous assumption. She'd lost Toni by being honest with her. The truth sat like a ten-pound weight in the pit of her stomach, a perpetual reminder of how badly she'd fucked things up.

As tears started to form in her eyes, there was suddenly a crash, shaking her from her focus. The door to Madge's shop had swung open and in burst Alice, drenched with rain and terror. She ran straight for Brittany and grabbed her shoulders.

"I can't find them," Alice shouted between ragged breathing. "They were supposed to be at the pub. I went to check on them. There was blood on the floor. And the back door was wide open. I don't…I don't know where they are."

The numbness Brittany felt fell away, replaced by terror. "What do you mean you can't find them?"

Alice wiped her hands over her face and started pacing. "You have to help me. You said we were in danger. Does this person have them? You can see into his mind, right?" She turned and shook Brittany again. "Please. I won't lose her again. I can't."

Brittany felt dizzy. "I don't—I don't know. I've been trying to see it again, but I can't. I can't concentrate."

"Brittany," Alice said, her voice shaking. "You're the only chance I have to find them."

Brittany nodded her understanding. Her heart felt like it was in a vise. Fear and worry and panic clenched her chest, forcing the air from her lungs. A small part of her was relieved to think that she wasn't crazy after all. But the rest of her was wholeheartedly terrified that she'd been right. This person was there to do harm. All of the anger, betrayal, and the desire for vengeance she'd felt whenever she entered this person's mind would be inflicted on Toni and Leslie if they didn't find them.

Madge nudged Alice away from Brittany. "Give her some room. She needs to concentrate."

Brittany closed her eyes, trying to center her thoughts on the person like she'd done before. She ignored the wind, the rain, and she even managed to push the trembling Alice from her mind. She let her mind fall away from the present moment and trudge through the unknown—searching for the opening. Her head started to pound. It felt as if it were splitting itself open, allowing Brittany to peek through a crack in a wall. She felt the person before she saw anything. The all-consuming blanket of rage and hatred draped itself over Brittany's psyche, confirming she was in the right spot. This person wanted vengeance, and Brittany knew there would be nothing swift about it.

This voyage into the abyss wasn't like the others. She couldn't see anything. Nothing but complete blackness surrounded her. She heard voices, but Brittany couldn't tune them in with any clarity. She couldn't be sure if it was Leslie and Toni, and she couldn't tell where they were. She didn't understand how to fix it or what she was doing wrong. The person was pushing against her. Whoever they were, they were fully aware of Brittany's intrusion, and they wanted her gone.

Brittany felt a shove, and then she was falling backward. She wasn't sure if it was real or in her mind until she hit the floor. Madge was beside her, dabbing her face with a tissue. The minimal light offered in the room from the lanterns burned her eyes and made her head ache more. Brittany touched her nose, not understanding why Madge looked so concerned. When she pulled her hand away, she tasted the blood as it slid onto her lips.

"Can you see them? Where are they?" Alice was more frantic now.

"I'm not sure." Brittany shook her head and winced. The movement made her want to vomit. "They knew I was there. The person was blocking me somehow."

Madge helped her onto the chair. "I was afraid of this. You need to take a break."

"No!" Alice lurched forward. "We don't know how much time we have. We have to find them. Brittany is our only chance."

Madge straightened her back. "You don't understand what is happening. If this person pushes against her too hard, it could *harm* her." She took a deep breath. "She won't be any good to you if she's dead."

Brittany grabbed Madge's arm in an attempt to reassure her. "I'm okay. Alice is right. I need you to help me. Will you? Please?"

Madge looked as if she might protest as she reached up to adjust her wig. She took another deep breath as she moved across the room to her table. She pulled out a cigarillo from a small wooden box, lit it, inhaled for one beat, two, before she said under her exhale of smoke, "I picked the wrong day to cut back on these babies."

"Madge, please. I need you—"

"I know." Madge sighed and inhaled another long pull from her cigarillo. She pulled an old leatherbound book from under her table and dropped it onto the table with a thud, the earlier tarot reading scattering to the ground. The death card landed face-up at Brittany's feet.

"You're gonna be the death of me, kid."

Brittany forced herself to smile. "Thank you." It came out as a whisper but Madge's understanding look had to mean she was welcome.

Alice sat next to her, her leg tapping furiously. "It's not that I don't care what happens to you. It's just that—"

"I get it," Brittany said. "I wouldn't be able to live with myself if I didn't do everything I could."

Brittany wasn't sure how to beat this person at whatever game they were playing, but she knew she'd let herself die before she stopped trying to find Toni. Maybe if she risked her life it would help Toni see she never meant to keep things from her or hurt her. She never wanted any of this to unfold like it had. All she'd wanted was to understand what the visions meant. And now, all she wanted was to keep Toni safe and if it meant staring death in the face, she was going to without any hesitation, even if it really did kill her.

CHAPTER THIRTY-FIVE

Toni's vision was blurry and her head pounded like a kettle drum. Her thoughts were hazy as she tried to put the pieces together. She tried to remember the last thing that happened. They were getting the pub ready for the hurricane. Sandbags and sweat and loud banging and...Quinn...she came to *help*. Except it wasn't help she had offered. Toni felt a surge of urgency rush through her body as she looked around for her aunt. Leslie was sitting next to her, tied to a wooden chair. She was in men's clothing. The clothes looked several sizes too big, and Toni couldn't put the information together in her head. She wanted it to make sense. She tried to reach out and touch her aunt. She needed to make sure she was okay, but her hands were stuck. The more she pulled the more the rough material dug into her wrists. *Fuck.* She was tied up, too.

Toni looked down at her clothing. She was in spandex pants and a strange top made of lace. It was as if someone had transported her into the eighties. She wanted to find a way to wake her aunt. She needed to make sure she was okay, but she didn't want to alert their abductor. Her body worked against her, threatening to vomit whatever contents remained in her stomach. *What is happening? Why are we here?* Then another realization—Brittany. Guilt and regret flooded through her. She never should have doubted her. If she'd listened, they wouldn't be in this situation now. Toni had let her own bullshit cloud what she knew and felt about Brittany deep in her heart, a horrendous miscalculation that had landed them here.

Her aunt moaned beside her, and her head fell over to the side.

"Open your eyes, Aunt Leslie," Toni said with a hushed tone. "I need you to wake up."

Leslie's head rolled back and forth a few more times before she finally opened her eyes. The terror on her face when she looked over at Toni and then down at her clothing was something straight out of a horror film. Her aunt was ghostly white as fear enveloped her expression.

"Focus on me," Toni urged her. "Can you hear my voice? Stay focused on me."

A laugh came from a darkened corner of the room. "You two are *sickeningly* sweet."

The way the voice accentuated the syllables made Toni want to vomit. "What do you want from us?" she asked, then clamped her teeth together, the pain from the ropes almost unbearable.

Another laugh dripped out before Quinn stepped into the minimal light. She sauntered to the table in front of them, a gross sense of pride oozing from her, and leaned against the edge. "I've never had two at once before. This should be interesting."

Fury rose in Toni's chest. "You fucking psychotic lunatic. What the fuck do you want with—" Toni was instantly shut up by Quinn's backhand across her face. Her head throbbed and her cheek burned.

"You shut your whore mouth."

"Don't you *dare* hurt her." Aunt Leslie's voice was shaky but forceful and it made Toni want to cry.

"Or what?" Quinn's attention was focused on Aunt Leslie now. She unsheathed a knife and as she bent over Leslie, she placed the tip of the knife on her chest. "Old. Tied up. Helpless. You think you're in a position to do anything about it?"

Toni could do nothing but watch in horror. She saw her aunt gulp, then lift her chin with defiance. "I am not afraid of you," Aunt Leslie said and if it wasn't for the tears streaming down her face, Toni would have believed her.

"You should be." Quinn pointed the knife at Leslie's face as she spoke, her voice low and full of hatred. "You *should* be."

"Why are you doing this?" The fear in Toni's voice was secondary only to her anger. She wanted Quinn's attention on her, though, if only to make sure her aunt was safe from Quinn's fury.

Quinn moved and placed her hands on the arms of Toni's chair. She leaned down until the sides of their faces were touching. "Leslie owes a debt to me." Quinn tilted her head so that her lips were against Toni's ear. "I'm going to watch her kill you." She must have found the shudder that went through Toni's body funny because she laughed and said, "You don't like it when I'm this close to you, hmm? What's the matter? Only find your dyke girlfriend attractive?" She took the knife and ran the tip over Toni's cheek. "You're not my type anyway. I like them older and frail, preferably with a cane." The smirk on Quinn's face made the anger flare inside Toni to a point of near combustion.

"Get away from her!"

Quinn snapped her head to Aunt Leslie. "You're awfully pushy for a woman who is going to die at the end of this."

"Leave her alone. If it's me that you want, then fine, but leave Toni alone."

Toni swallowed the disgust bubbling up into her throat. "Quinn?" She waited until Quinn looked at her and when she did, she spit in her face.

Quinn laughed as she licked the spit from her lips. Toni's stomach churned. She was going to vomit if this kept up. She didn't want Quinn to know she was getting to her, but her body wasn't cooperating.

Quinn stood up straight and wiped her face with a rag from the table. She stalked over to Leslie, keeping her eyes on Toni the entire time. "Your whore niece is going to make this so much more fun." She leaned over Leslie and dragged the tip of the knife down the side of her neck, to the loosely tied necktie. "Do you remember me?" Quinn's voice was a whisper now. "I can't image that you would, but I'm sure you remember my father."

"What are you talking about?" Toni was surprised by how calm her aunt sounded.

"Harry West." Quinn stabbed the knife into the arm of the wooden chair and grabbed the lapels on the suit Leslie was wearing, jerking her forward as much as the restraints allowed. "You ruined him." Quinn let Leslie fall back into her seat, and she flattened out the rumpled material. "You killed him."

Leslie looked baffled. "I didn't kill Harry. And I didn't know he had any children either."

Quinn took a step backward and put her fingers against her lips. A low, sadistic rumble of laughter came out, full of rage and disbelief. It lasted far too long.

Quinn swiped a photo off the table and shoved it into Leslie's face. "There we are." She pointed to the figures on the paper. "He didn't want you to know about me. He thought it would scare you off." Her anger was palpable, spit flying from her mouth as she spoke. "He kept me hidden in the basement whenever you visited, but I could hear everything. I could hear you laughing. I could hear you eating. I could hear you fucking." She crumpled up the photograph and threw it onto the ground. "He killed himself two months after you left him. I went to twenty-two foster homes after that." Quinn changed direction and grabbed Toni. She gripped the back of her neck and pulled her forward so that their foreheads were touching. "What do you think the ratio of good to bad caregivers is in twenty-two foster homes?"

Toni shook her head because she didn't know what else to do. "Not good?"

The veins in Quinn's neck were bulging. "I'm going to watch your aunt kill you so she learns what real loss feels like."

"Please don't do this," Leslie said, her voice wavering.

Quinn's head whipped toward Leslie.

"I'm so very sorry. I had no idea you existed," Leslie said, her voice soft and nurturing. "I didn't know what you were going through, but I didn't kill your dad. He was sick. He had a drug problem, he had an alcohol problem, and he was abusive. I left him after he hit me. If I'd known there was a child, I would've told someone. I would've helped you. I would have taken you away."

Quinn stumbled backward holding her head. "Fuck. Fuck. Fuck." She beat the sides of her skull with her fists. "Get out, get out, get out."

Toni realized something was starting to go awry with Quinn's plan. The headaches. *Oh, my God, the headaches.* Brittany was trying to find them. Brittany knew they were missing. If she could point Brittany in the right direction, maybe they could get out of this alive. She could talk to Brittany through Quinn. Toni just needed to get Quinn calm enough to allow it.

"That must have been horrible," Toni said. She didn't continue until Quinn had turned her attention back to her. "I can't imagine how scary all of that was for you. I wouldn't have been strong enough to survive."

Quinn glared at her. "It all could've been avoided if she had paid attention." Quinn pointed the knife at Leslie.

"But she didn't know she had to. I know you hate her, but are you really going to kill her? Kill me? For your father's actions?"

Quinn stared at her for so long, Toni shifted in her seat. "Leslie is in my father's clothing. I have you in something that looks like what she used to wear. I want her to kill you, like my father should've killed her. Instead, he took his own life, and I was left with what?"

"You're insane," Leslie said. "I won't do it. I'll die before I harm my niece."

Quinn shook her head. "Do you know how many times I've heard people say they won't do something? Do you know how many times I've watched people commit the unthinkable? Do you know what people are willing to do when the thresholds of pain are reached? I do. I've seen it dozens of times. I've watched people continue to beg for their lives as the last few ounces of their blood dripped onto the floor. I've listened to people tell me they'll trade the love of their life if only I'll spare them." She smiled at Leslie. "You'll do the same."

Outside, the storm continued its unmerciful battering, causing windows above them to rattle and whistle as the wind fought its way into every exposed crevice. Toni looked at the wall and saw water sliding down the concrete. They were in a basement or cellar somewhere, and she felt slightly relieved to have a new piece of information.

Quinn crossed her arms and once again turned her attention to Toni. "I saw Brittany a year ago in San Francisco, you know. She'd just crashed her motorcycle. There were pieces everywhere, and her body was completely broken. There was so much blood." Quinn seemed nostalgic thinking about it. "I looked into her eyes as she lay in the road. She'd made peace with dying. She'd accepted her fate, I could tell. The emergency crews were too far away. And she knew it." Quinn walked over and put her hand on the side of Toni's face. "You can imagine my surprise when I saw her here." She moved her grip around Toni's jaw and squeezed. "I was even more surprised when I noticed her traipsing around inside my head." She squeezed harder. "Could you feel me watching you, Leslie? Did you enjoy having my eyes on you?" Quinn looked at Leslie as she squeezed Toni harder and harder. "Answer me!" Then she winced and put her free hand up to her head.

Toni knew this was her chance. The pain caused by Quinn squeezing her was relentless, but it could be Toni's only opportunity to speak through Quinn without her realizing. She was trying to find something to say that could help lead Brittany to where they were. She needed something. She thought about the water on the wall and focused on anything else her senses could provide. The air was cool in the room—much cooler than it should've been with the humidity. She glanced down at the floor and realized that it too was concrete. They were definitely in a cellar. Something this size would have to be in a building, not a house. Toni made the best guess she could with the information she had and hoped she was right. More than that, she pleaded with whatever god who was listening that it would be enough.

Toni mustered every bit of courage she had and made eye contact with Quinn. "Brittany didn't tell me anything. If I'd known, I would've never come to Nereids with her. I would've taken my aunt and left, and we wouldn't be tied up in this cold, dank storage basement in some godforsaken building with you and your knives."

Quinn released her and walked back to the table. She pulled the knife from the arm of the chair and cut the ties around Leslie's hands, then stabbed it into the table before taking several steps back. She pulled a gun from the back of her waistband and pointed it at Leslie. "Take that knife and kill her." She motioned to Toni. "Kill her or I will force you to do it."

Leslie didn't move from the chair as her lips quivered. "No."

"Do you have any idea what I'm capable of? This all ends with her dead. I'm letting you decide how painful that has to be. I assure you; it is an act of mercy that I'm letting you do it." Quinn grabbed her head with both hands again, hitting it with the butt of the gun. "Get out of my head, you bitch."

"Let us out of this basement, Quinn!"

A sharp slap across the face silenced her once more. The hit stung less this time. She wondered, fleetingly, if it meant she was numb from adrenaline or fear. Either way, she hoped Brittany had heard her, if such a thing was possible. She had no way of knowing if she'd gotten through. All she could do was wait and hope her aunt could hold out long enough.

The last flash of light and thunder through Brittany's head had nothing to do with the hurricane raging outside. The intensity knocked her to the floor. She was able to get to her knees just before another flash of visions consumed her. In her mind's eye, she saw a cement floor and walls, smelled damp, stagnant air, and felt the intense pleasure of gratification pulse through her veins. Toni's face came into view. She was tied to a chair, and her face was etched in pain. She watched her mouth move as words fell from her lips. And instantly she pulled herself out of the vision. Alice grabbed under Brittany's arm as she struggled to her feet, panting, and struggling against the way the vision made her feel. "They're at Nereids," Brittany said, sucking in her breath. "I'm seeing a cellar of some kind and stacks of kegs. I saw the logo on one of the kegs."

"Are you sure it's not the pub?" Alice said. "They were just there."

Brittany shook her head. "I saw Toni in the vision and…she, um, she said a name, Alice. I think it might be Quinn." She took a deep breath as she saw the acknowledgement wash over Alice's face. "I need to go now." The rage Brittany felt from Quinn's mind drifted along the skin on her arms and neck. Something was poking Quinn, prodding, and taunting her. "They're in physical danger, maybe pain. I have to find them." Still unsteady, she staggered to the door and grabbed the handle.

"I'm coming with you," Alice said.

"No. It's too dangerous. Call the police. Tell them to send officers." She tried to open the door, but Alice had her arm stretched over Brittany's shoulder holding it closed.

"Madge, call the constable's station," Alice said. "I'm going with Brittany." She reached around Brittany, opened the door, and they headed out into the driving wind and rain.

Madge grabbed Brittany's arm before she made it to the door. "You're going to need more than your good looks for this one." Madge opened a small wooden box and handed her a .38 pistol.

Brittany was surprised, and it must have shown on her face.

"Hey," Madge said. "Sometimes crystals won't cut it." She squeezed Brittany's shoulder. "I felt the rage engulfing this person. You need to protect yourself."

Madge was right, and she appreciated the help. Brittany hadn't fired a weapon since she was a teenager at the family lake house with her father, but it was like riding a bike, right?

They stopped between Brittany's scooter and Alice's bicycle, both parked at the entrance, Alice appearing ready to hop on the back of the scooter.

"Alice, please. You're not coming with me. You could get seriously hurt. Go to the police department, fill them in on the details, and send them over to the brewery."

Alice shouted through the storm noise. "I hate to break this to you now, but Swift Island doesn't have a police department. We have a tiny little substation with a handful of constables who I'm sure are completely tied up with hurricane-related stuff." She climbed onto the back of the scooter. "Now get on. We're wasting valuable time."

"But, Alice—"

"Brittany," Alice shouted frantically. "I lost Leslie once. I'm not losing her again. Now either get on this bike and drive me there, or I'll run alongside you until my legs give out."

Completely out of persuasive arguments, Brittany slid between Alice and the handlebars, and they jetted off toward Nereids Brewing. The rain pelted her face and obstructed her vision at points along the way, but her psychic vision was fully 20/20 as an onslaught of physical pain, emotional terror, and guttural rage plowed through her. Her heart ached to see and hold Toni again, to feel her tucked safely in her arms. She couldn't begin to imagine the abject horror and helplessness Alice must've felt knowing the woman she'd loved all her life was in peril.

❖

Quinn's pacing had increased. She squinted and frowned as she seemed lost in anxious thought. Was she second-guessing her plan and about to become reckless before Leslie could figure out another way to try to talk her down? Leslie's heart was pounding so hard inside her chest she hoped her body was strong enough to withstand it. Her throat was parched and scratchy, and she struggled to hold her urine as panic whirled inside her. Compounding it was her desire to remain calm on the outside for Toni, who sat beside her with her eyes closed doing some kind of breathing exercise to self-soothe.

Quinn had wandered off behind a stack of kegs, apparently taking a breather from taunting her and Toni with jabs from the tip of her knife, digging the barrel of her handgun into their stomachs or foreheads, and shoving pictures of herself when she was a kid in the late eighties into Leslie's face.

Harry West. Leslie thought back to that brief yet disturbing period in her life. She'd finally gotten the courage to divorce Bill and tell Alice she wanted her back, but by then, she'd waited too long. Alice had moved on with another woman and wasn't willing to risk a healthy relationship for a second chance with the woman who'd torn her heart out and made her wait almost ten years to leave her husband. By that point, Leslie couldn't blame her. She'd decided it would be too selfish of her to interfere further with Alice's newfound happiness, and she let her ride off into the sunset without further intrusion.

Eventually, she began dating men again as the idea of another woman replacing Alice was inconceivable. A friend of a friend's husband had introduced her to Harold T. West, a business executive who'd recently moved to Connecticut. His outgoing personality and expensive, tailored suits made him appear attractive, despite a pockmarked face and a scar near his eye. But his outward positive traits belied the deeply troubled man hiding behind the facade. He'd treated Leslie like a queen at first but had grown increasingly demanding of her time and obedience. It only took one slap across her face after too much Jack for Leslie to leave him, but that was when the stalking started, the menacing phone calls, and the shadowy figure appearing outside her home. It abruptly ended when Leslie got the restraining order after a couple of months of his harassment. She'd believed it was over and hadn't thought of him in years. How could he have hidden away a child? His own child. She shuddered in revulsion toward him and, strangely, allowed a moment of pity for the monster Quinn had become due to his unconscionable actions.

She tried to muster enough saliva to swallow, but the action caused a fit of coughing instead.

"Are you okay?" Toni whispered.

Quinn wheeled around the stack of kegs and headed back to them. "What do you think you're doing? You two think you can plot some kind of escape plan when my back is turned? That's never gonna happen. You're an old woman with a fucking limp." She leaned over Toni and stuck the gun under Toni's chin, glancing over at Leslie to make sure she was watching. "You're a pathetic shit. You think you're this young, hot lesbian it-girl since you showed up on this island, but you're just a shallow, snotty little bitch. I may decide that it'll be more fun to kill you myself. And I'll do it with way more enthusiasm than Grandma Moses over there."

Leslie trembled with anger at Quinn for tormenting Toni, the pity replaced with desperation. She thought maybe she could burst from the chair with enough force if she could just get her bearings. She adjusted her position in the chair. The movement caused the wood to creak.

Quinn lurched like an animal into her face, startling Leslie backward. "And what the fuck do you think you're gonna accomplish over here, you old bag? You can barely walk without a cane, how do you think you'll be able to take me down? Now just sit tight until I decide which method of putting you both out of your misery will bring me the most pleasure."

"Quinn." Leslie hoped her soft, motherly tone could reach whatever shred of humanity was left in her, if there ever was any in a person who could talk of killing others so casually. "It doesn't have to be like this. Your father is gone. What good will come of avenging his death if it ruins your own life?"

"That's where you're mistaken, Leslie. Searching for you has been a labor of love for many years. And those people I killed in the past, women who reminded me of you—selfish women who took what they wanted and left only scraps for weak, pitiful men to peck at? Well, they were just practice, dress rehearsals for the final, glorious act of me taking you out of this world. And what a good riddance that's gonna be."

Leslie's stomach plummeted. This woman wasn't just mentally unstable; she was pure evil, a true psychopath. How on earth would she even begin to break through such a hardened shell of malice? However futile her attempts might be, she had to keep trying. "Quinn, isn't there anyone we can call for you to help you through this? It's not too late to turn things around. How about your mom? Is she still living?"

"Don't you mention that bitch to me ever again!" Quinn's eyes flashed with maniacal brilliance as in one fluid move, she grabbed the knife from the table, leaned over Leslie and pressed the knife's sharp, glistening edge into the skin above Leslie's collarbone. "She was the first one who left me."

Leslie shrieked in pain at the tear the knife made in her thin skin. A line of warm blood trickled down her chest.

"Stop it!" Toni yelled. "Leave her alone. She hasn't done anything to you." As she frenetically attempted to free herself, the chair moved beneath her almost as though she were about to get up and drag it with her.

"Shut the fuck up, both of you!" Quinn shouted back. "I've had enough of your shit." With her free hand, she cocked the gun at Toni's temple.

"Quinn, please," Leslie said, tears streaming down her face. "Let her go. She's innocent. I'm the one you have the gripe with."

When Quinn pulled the gun back, Toni shook her sweaty hair off her face. "You may succeed in killing us both, but there's no way you'll get away with it. No one's getting off this island for at least another day or two. You'll be caught by then. People are out looking for us as we speak."

Quinn uttered a chilling laugh. "What people? Another frail old woman and your nutty girlfriend?" She scoffed as she slowly circled them. "You know what I love about Edgar Allan Poe's stories?" She paused, looking into the air pensively. "His murderers always get away with it, except for the poor bastards whose consciences eat them up with guilt. Weak, fallible men, that's what they were. Lucky for me, I don't have a conscience. I don't give a fuck about how my actions make you feel." She stopped behind Leslie and spoke directly into her ear. "You took my father from me and didn't care who it affected. You think I give a shit about your niece?"

She then turned and leaned over face-to-face with Toni. "You're nothing but collateral damage, a bonus prize, really. You act like it's your God-given right to make people feel like dog shit under your shoe because you were born beautiful. Well, you won't be so beautiful when I'm through with you." She stood up straight, tucked the gun back into her waistband, and waved the knife between Leslie and Toni. "So don't tell me I won't get away with it. I know exactly what I'm doing."

"Go fuck yourself," Toni said with a reckless cool Leslie had no idea she possessed.

Quinn clenched her jaw and kicked Toni's chair so hard, it went over. Toni hit her head on the concrete floor with a loud, sickening thud. Toni let out a soft whimper and rolled her head to the side, her eyes closed. Blood pooled around Toni's hair.

"Toni," Leslie yelled in horror. She made frantic, jerky motions to try to loosen the bindings, almost rocking her chair over onto the floor. "Quinn, please. You can't let her bleed to death!"

Quinn stood over Leslie with her arms crossed over her chest and an eerie, satisfied grin. "Who says I can't?"

Chapter Thirty-six

The ride to Nereids Brewing was dicey and delayed. The main road was closed due to a fallen tree that took out a powerline on its way down. Brittany and Alice had to backtrack about a half mile and go down a flooded side street. Brittany drove the scooter on the sidewalk to bypass the flood and continued toward the brewery, careful to dodge storm debris gathering in the road as the cold, heavy rain stung her face and obstructed her view.

When they finally arrived, Brittany pulled in Nereids' lot and parked the scooter toward the side of the building to avoid having it seen in case the kidnappers were inside looking out for potential rescuers.

Alice climbed off first. "Check to see if Madge texted you back. I'm going to try calling the constable station again." She pressed their number in her recent calls, but it rang several times before a recorded message went on advising anyone who stayed on the island to shelter in place until the storm subsided. "Goddammit. Still a recording."

"Nothing from Madge either," Brittany said as she stuffed her phone back in her pocket. "Look, we can't wait any longer. This has to be the place. Let's do a loop around the building and look for an entrance."

Alice nodded and went around the left side of the building while Brittany took the right. From what she could see from the outside, the building was dark. Maybe they'd lost power or kept the lights off on purpose. Or worse, maybe nobody was in there, and this was a waste of time. *Time.* Each minute that ticked by that they hadn't found Toni and Leslie could mean they were that much closer to… Brittany stopped herself before that train of thought went any further. Her head felt weird, throbbing and humming, but not like she usually felt before a vision. It was like she was being sucked into a vortex pulling her toward the back of the building. Was it the wind? The unstable air pressure from the storm?

She rounded the corner and found Alice standing over Bilco doors that led to a basement area. "Everything is boarded up from the outside," Alice said. "I didn't see any way in. Except maybe here."

Brittany's throat seemed like it wanted to close as she and Alice stared expectantly at each other for a second that felt like a year. "If they're down there, they'll hear the door. There's no way to open those doors quietly. Let me go first."

"Wait." Alice looked around and grabbed a thick, wet branch from the ground, held it at an angle, and kicked it until it snapped in half. "It's almost as thick as a baseball bat."

"It's gonna have to do," Brittany said. Her hand trembled as she reached toward the door handle. "Stay behind me until we know what we're dealing with."

"You're gonna need me either way," Alice said. "I'm right beside you."

Brittany didn't think she could admire Alice any more than she did—until now. This woman was willing to risk her own life to save the woman she loved. Actually, so was Brittany. She pulled at the heavy steel door, clutching it tightly against the gusting wind. She lifted it slowly in an attempt to avoid alerting anyone inside with a sudden shriek of metal hinges. Looking in, she saw mostly darkness except for a glow of either a candle or flashlight coming from the far right. She nodded at Alice, and they crept down the steps into the basement.

Once inside, they stopped behind a brick chimney base. Brittany pulled the small pistol from her jacket pocket and held it by her side. She wanted to be ready for anything, but she didn't want to make a mistake either. She could hear a voice shouting orders, and she wanted to get a better look.

"Tell her you're sorry it had to be this way. Tell her you're sorry that you have to kill her."

Leslie choked out words between sobs. "I won't kill my niece. I don't care what you do to me, I won't do it."

Brittany wiped the sweat mixing with rainwater dripping from her hairline with the crook of her elbow. She gripped the gun a little tighter, worried the humidity would work against her already trembling hands when she needed them most. They took a step closer to the voices.

"Can you see what's happening?" Alice whispered. "It sounds like Leslie is in trouble," Alice said. "I'm going to her."

"No," Brittany said, clutching Alice's thin arm hard. "When we move, we're moving together. We can't do a thing until we know what we're up against. Otherwise, we're just two more easy targets."

Alice nodded, her pupils dilated with fear. Brittany chewed on her lip, eyeing where their next covert move would be. She needed to get closer to see if Quinn had any weapons trained on Leslie and Toni. If they charged over there like the heroes Alice wanted them to be, that could easily result in Leslie and Toni being hurt—or worse.

She nodded to Alice, and they crept over to a pallet full of highly stacked boxes. From there Brittany could see figures in the corner. She squinted at the tall figure standing, making jerky arm motions in front of Leslie. It really was Quinn. A part of Brittany wanted to take a page from Alice's book and charge in there, but then she saw Toni on the floor, strapped to a chair, motionless.

Suddenly, Leslie's voice rang out. "Please don't do this, Quinn. I'm sorry for what happened to you. I'm sorry you were hurt. I'm sorry you thought I knew and didn't care, but that simply isn't true! Please, Toni needs help. It's not too late to do the right thing."

Brittany burned with anger. How many times had they been in the same room with Quinn? How many times had they spoken? How many times did Brittany ignore the weird sensations she'd felt around her? She should have paid more attention. She could have stopped this before it started. Damnit.

"It's too late to do anything for her," the now familiar voice said. "You put yourself in this position, Leslie. You did this."

"I'm sorry." Leslie sobbed softly.

"Shut up!" Quinn yelled. "Shut your fucking mouth right now before I shut it for you."

Quinn was unraveling, no question. She looked at Alice to indicate it was time to prepare to charge. But before they could launch their sneak attack, a gust of wind blew the heavy Bilco door from Brittany's grip, causing it to slam shut with a resounding smash of metal against metal.

"Who's there?" Quinn shouted. "Come out right now or I'll kill them both." She held the gun to Leslie's head.

Brittany stepped out from behind the boxes with her gun trained on Quinn. "It doesn't have to be like this, Quinn. I can help you."

Quinn stared at her for a long moment before laughter erupted. "Help me? You think you can help me? You couldn't even help them, and you've been wandering around my head for months." She cocked the gun, and Leslie whimpered.

Brittany took a step closer, keeping her gun trained on Quinn. Alice scurried over to Toni and freed her from the chair. Quinn's rage was apparent, but her options were few. If she moved to stop Alice, she'd have to leave Leslie free to move. She'd also leave herself vulnerable to Brittany. Quinn may be psychotic, but she clearly understood her choices.

"That was a big mistake," Quinn screamed at Alice. "Leslie is going to pay for your choice."

"I'll tell our story." Brittany interrupted. "If you let Leslie go, I will tell our story."

"She is *my* story." Quinn's voice was shaking now. "My circle ends with her. Don't you see that? She has to die."

Brittany shook her head. "No one has to die. But if you kill her, if you make that choice, two people will be dead. And it won't be Leslie and Toni, I swear to you."

Quinn laughed. "You don't have the balls to kill me. If you had the stomach for it, you would've already done it."

"You have no idea who you're talking to." Brittany breathed in deep as she pulled the hammer back on the gun.

"Oh, yes, I do." Quinn's smile was almost as chilling as her tone. "A scared, washed up journalist who is so fucked up from an accident that she infiltrated a serial killer's mind. I know exactly who I'm talking to."

"Yeah, well, I'd rather be in your mind than you in mine."

"And why's that?"

"Because you would know what's going to happen next."

"Yes, yes, I do. I'm going to splatter this woman's brains all over." Quinn pushed the gun harder into Leslie's temple.

"No, no you're not." Brittany made eye contact with Alice, who was still crouching next to Toni. As if on command, Alice popped up, shoved Quinn hard, and knocked the gun from her hand. It fired as it hit the ground. Toni stood, swinging a metal pipe, and hit Quinn square in the back of the head, knocking her to the ground. Brittany moved quickly to snatch the weapons that had fallen beside her. She placed her fingers along the pulse on her neck and felt it thump. Quinn was alive, albeit unconscious. She worked with speed as she grabbed the discarded rope on the table and tied Quinn's hands behind her back.

Toni's pupils were dilated, and her skin was ashen. Brittany grabbed her and set her down on the ground. She touched her head where blood still seeped from her injury. "It's going to be okay. We're going to get you help."

Toni's eyes were going in and out of focus as she looked up at her. She looked like she was going to say something, but before she had the chance, she passed out.

"I finally got through." Alice held up her cell phone with one hand as she held Leslie's head to her shoulder with the other. "They're on the way."

❖

Toni gasped as she came to, the throbbing inside her head harsh and nauseating. Everything hurt, including her eyelids.

"Toni? Can you hear me?"

"Yes, I can hear you. Please stop shouting." Toni blinked a few times to clear the darkness from her vision until she was surrounded by white lights. She looked around frantically, trying to get her bearings and saw Brittany hovering over her. "Where am I?"

"Oh my God, you're okay," Brittany said.

Toni focused on Brittany's expression, so full of concern and relief. And so damn beautiful.

"You're at the clinic. Your head…you were bleeding and lost so much blood."

"I tried to talk to you," Toni said. "Quinn was having the same headaches as you, and I tried to talk to you through her."

Brittany smiled as she sat on the edge of the bed and smoothed her hand over the side of Toni's face. "You did great. You're very persistent." Brittany smiled. "I thought persistent was a better word than reckless."

Toni tried to laugh but it made her entire body ache. "Stop. It hurts to laugh." She breathed in through clenched teeth when she stretched her legs out. "What happened?"

"How much do you remember?"

She shuddered. "I remember Quinn taking us. She knocked us out, and I woke up in different clothes. I remember the yelling, the threats, the anger. I remember you showing up. I think I hit her?" She was equal parts relieved and worried over the loss of memory.

"You have a pretty bad cut on the side of your head from where it slammed into the concrete. And a gash over your eye from where she hit you with the gun, I'm assuming."

"Jesus." Toni winced in pain once again. "I'm a mess."

"You're remembering correctly though. You hit her. Hard. So hard in fact, you knocked her out." Brittany gripped Toni's hand. "You are gonna have a pretty cool scar."

"Great. I always thought my face needed some street cred." Toni forced herself to smile through the pain. "Thank you for coming to save us. Thank you for not giving up on me, especially after I was so horrific to you."

"I did it for all of you, Toni. But I never would've given up on you."

Toni nodded. "I should've known that."

Brittany didn't respond and Toni's heart ached at the pain she knew she'd caused.

"Listen," Toni said and immediately regretted raising her voice. Her head started to throb again. "I'm sorry. I really am. I should've believed you."

"I know it's crazy, so I understand why it was hard to believe." Brittany looked down at her lap. "I would never intentionally hurt you, though, Toni. I hope you know that."

"I know that. I don't even know why I questioned it. I guess I am far more messed up than I realized." Toni reached for Brittany's hand and squeezed it softly. In the past, she'd trusted people who hadn't earned it, and it cost her. But this person in front of her? Brittany, who had such integrity and empathy and courage? She'd more than proven she was worthy of Toni's trust.

She needed to make things right with Brittany somehow. But now all she could focus on was how much pain she was in and the lingering images of terror on her aunt's face. "How's Aunt Leslie?"

Brittany's features shifted, a soft smile appearing. "She's actually doing well. She is one hell of a woman."

"Oh, thank God." The relief Toni felt was indescribable.

"Well, well, well, look who's up."

Toni peered around Brittany to see her aunts in the doorway. "Aunt Leslie, why are you in a wheelchair?"

"This dumb thing?" Leslie popped up from the chair after Alice wheeled her closer to the bed. "Stupid clinic protocol. They'll make us wheel you out of here in one, too." Leslie bent down and kissed Toni on the forehead, then looked into her eyes. "You gave us a real fright."

"I'm so sorry this happened, Aunt Leslie." Toni tried to stop the tears, but her efforts were futile. "I should have known something was wrong with how Quinn was acting. I should have known."

"Shhh," Leslie said softly. She sat where Brittany had been sitting moments earlier. "You stop right now. I should be the one apologizing to you."

"I'm just so happy you're okay. She didn't hurt you at all?"

"I have a few cuts and scrapes, but for the most part, I'll survive."

Alice appeared next to Leslie. "That was a genius move, talking to Brittany through the visions."

Toni looked at Brittany, who had removed herself to the back of the room. "Yeah, I definitely should have believed her." Brittany's eyes locked onto hers and she smiled. "I hope she forgives me for being so stupid."

"I'm pretty sure she already has," Leslie said as she leaned down. "We'll leave you two alone. Make sure you tell her what she needs to hear."

Toni smiled. "And what's that?"

Leslie looked over at Brittany then back at her. "Life doesn't always give us second chances. Don't waste this one." Her voice was a loud whisper, and she ended the sentence with a deliberate, unsubtle wink.

She watched them as they wheeled out of the room, then turned her attention back to Brittany. "Come here, please."

Brittany's movements were tentative and had been since Toni woke up. She knew it was because of how she'd treated Brittany not even twenty-four hours earlier. It broke her heart to see how badly she'd hurt her. She had some serious apologizing to do.

"I forgive you," Brittany said softly. "You know that, right?"

"No, wait." Toni tried to situate herself so she was sitting more upright. A zap of pain shot through her and she pulled a breath in sharply. "I want to say something, and I need you to just let me talk, okay?" She watched as Brittany nodded, her hazel eyes sparkling. The sides of her hair were pulled away from her face into a barrette. There was something about Brittany in that moment and a million moments before that made Toni wish she could go back in time and believe in Brittany when she confided in them. And her clothes being splattered with blood also hardened her resolve. "Obviously, you know that I've had some shit heaped onto me in the last six months. I ran away from it all to come here, to heal wounds that I thought I'd have to some degree, forever. I mean, I really thought I knew what love was. I thought I was in love. But then you came into my life and everything changed. And I mean everything." Toni reached out and took Brittany's hand. "I don't know why this happened to you. But, at the risk of sounding sort of inconsiderate, I am really glad it did because it brought you to me. And as much as I've fought how I'm feeling about you, I'm so very thankful for you."

"Toni—"

"Hold on, please." Toni squeezed Brittany's hand.

This was her chance. She should tell Brittany she loved her. She should put it all on the line. She should say those three words. But then what? So much had happened. Could it ever be fully repaired? Could she ever be fully repaired?

She paused, pulled in a breath, and shrugged. "I know you're probably going to leave, and things will be different and maybe that will be the end of us. I don't know what the future holds, clearly, at least, not like you do." The smile that appeared on Brittany's lips brought a wave of comfort to her as she danced around what she really wanted to say. "You saved me. And I don't even mean from Quinn. I mean from myself. And I can't thank you enough—"

Brittany lunged forward, took Toni's face in her hands, pressed her lips into Toni's, and kissed her.

And finally, Toni's world clicked back into place.

Chapter Thirty-seven

B rittany?"
She snapped her attention to one of the FBI agents who were now on the island investigating the crimes. "Yes?"

"I'm Special Agent Agron and I have a few questions for you. If you wouldn't mind coming with me."

She stood and followed the agent through the corridors of the constable's small office on Swift Island. She'd been called in for questioning two days after Quinn had been arrested, and even though she'd had to answer questions before during other investigations, this time she was really nervous. As she sat at the table in the tiny gray room, she breathed deep and worked at calming herself down. "I really don't think I have many answers for you, Special Agent."

The agent pushed her blond hair over her shoulder and smiled. "Don't worry, Brittany, you aren't in trouble. I wondered if you knew this has been someone the FBI has been after for quite some time?"

Brittany swallowed around the large lump lodged in her throat. "No, I didn't know that."

"Quinn West is one of the most prolific serial killers in the United States. The Vengeance Killer. She's been hunting women for quite some time. She's left a brutal and bloody trail in her wake. She seems to target women as a punishment for what she perceives as misdeeds. Leslie Burton's was dating and dumping her father years earlier."

"And supposedly causing his suicide." Brittany shook her head. "This is so unreal."

"Ms. West had been after her for quite some time. The other murders were less methodical, more like a quick fix. Her true vendetta was against Mrs. Burton."

"Leslie said she hadn't even known this person existed. It's amazing she survived."

"That brings me to my questions for you," Agent Agron said softly. "How did you manage to put it all together?"

Brittany swallowed again. She couldn't be completely honest. There was no way. "I, um, I mean, I didn't really know for sure. I guess I just followed my instincts."

Special Agent Agron narrowed her eyes. "I can understand that. You're a journalist. I'm sure you have a lot of instincts."

"Yeah. Exactly."

"And the visions?"

Brittany blinked, once, twice, then let out a laugh. "Oh, the visions."

"Mm-hmm."

"I didn't come in here to be made fun of. So if that's what this is all about, then I'd like to go." Brittany pushed away from the table and stood, then watched as Special Agent Agron smiled. "What?"

"I didn't plan on making fun of you. I simply asked because the visions were mentioned by the others. And, much to her chagrin, it was also mentioned by Quinn that she was only caught because you hacked into her brain."

"Oh."

"So?"

Brittany sat twisting her ring around and around. "I don't know how to explain them. All I can really say is that I was connected to her somehow and I needed it to end. It was exhausting, dealing with all her hatred and rage."

"I can imagine. Listen," Agent Agron said softly, then paused as she leaned forward. "Quinn has agreed to plead guilty to all thirteen of her murders, as well as the kidnapping of Leslie and Toni. The problem was that we only knew of nine murders. We need to give those other families closure. But in order for Quinn to tell us where the other bodies are buried, she struck a deal." She grabbed a banker's box from under the table and set it on the Formica surface. "The deal was two-fold. The first stipulation was that the death penalty be taken off the table. The second was that we give *you* copies of all the journals we found in her apartment. It's some disturbing shit." Agron slid a piece of paper in front of her and pointed to the bottom line. "I need you to sign this form, indicating that you've received these journals."

Brittany blinked at the FBI letterhead. "Why? Why would she do that?"

The Special Agent shrugged. "She said you two were connected. She said she wanted the circle to be closed, whatever that means."

Brittany signed the form and slid it back. "I told her I would tell our story. When I was trying to stop her, I said I'd tell our story so people understood."

Special Agent Agron stood, her chair making a horrible screech as it scooted across the old tile. "Have a good day, Brittany."

She left the room, leaving Brittany holding a box of journal entries and an idea.

Leslie rounded the corner into the kitchen and pulled up short when she saw Brittany sitting there, stacks of papers laid out in front of her. "What are you reading?" She leaned over Brittany's shoulder and started to read.

"Quinn's journals. Special Agent Agron gave them to me. It was part of the deal she made to tell them about the other people she killed." Brittany looked up at Leslie. "Is it okay that I'm here with them? If it's too much for you, I can go somewhere else. I just…feel better being closer to you and Toni."

Leslie rested her hands on Brittany's shoulders, moved by her desire to protect them. "You really are a great gal, aren't you?"

"I try to be, but I understand why you may have had your doubts."

"It had nothing to do with the visions, Brittany. I hope you know that." Leslie pulled out a chair and sat next to Brittany at the table. "Listen to me, okay?" She reached over and placed her hand on Brittany's arm. "Toni is as close to me as a daughter, a granddaughter. I have been in her life since birth and I am insanely protective. When

I heard about Penn breaking her heart, Alice had to practically tie me down so I didn't go after the woman." Leslie saw the corners of Brittany's mouth tick upward. "I believe in whatever you felt. Visions, premonitions, whatever. I believe because you do and that's all it takes for me. But Toni? She was fragile, *is* fragile, and the devastation she felt at being lied to came out through me. Does that make sense?" She waited for Brittany's response, a gentle nod of her head. "Look at me." Brittany did as requested, her hazel eyes shining with tears. "Alice and I love you. We all care about you. We have enjoyed having you around. And I hope, I really do, that you plan on sticking around because things just won't be the same without you."

Brittany sat in silence, seemingly taking it all in. After a few deep breaths, she turned her attention to Leslie. "Thank you for saying that. I didn't think I would ever find another family that I clicked so well with. And hurting Toni was never my intention. It physically pained me to know she thought I would do that, because I would never. I just never figured out how to tell her, and we saw what happened when I did."

"I know, sweetheart. I know." Leslie placed her arm over Brittany's shoulders and hugged her close. "You two will find your way. If anyone knows how a bird set free can find its way back, it's me."

Brittany accepted a hug and Leslie, for the first time since the kidnapping, felt as if things might return to normal. At least she hoped they would, because the disconnection wasn't just between Toni and Brittany, but also between Brittany, Alice, and Leslie.

Toni skipped a rock across the calm water. She was amazed at the difference between how angry the water was four days ago and how restful it seemed now, especially since just the opposite seemed to be true for her. Four days ago, she'd thought her life was going to be absolutely wonderful. Then she let her heart get broken, she was kidnapped, she cracked her head open, had to get thirteen stiches above her eye, and twenty-seven along the side of her skull. Life really did know how to deal her an awful hand.

The only good thing was she finally apologized to Brittany. She really hoped the apology came through as sincerely as she meant it. She still felt awful for not believing Brittany, regardless of how nutty it sounded. The fact that she didn't trust Brittany said a lot more about Toni than it did about her relationship. Trust was always the hardest to come by in her relationships. For some reason, though, trusting Brittany came as easy to her as breathing and when she thought she'd been duped, she figured it was just the other shoe finally dropping. When in all actuality, it was her needing to come to terms with her trust issues.

"Care if I join you?"

Toni glanced up at the sound of Brittany's voice. "Please, I'd love the company." She watched as Brittany took tentative steps and sat next to her in the sand, promptly digging her toes into the cool moistness. "How was your meeting with the FBI?"

Brittany stared out into the water, the wind tripping through her hair. Her face looked relaxed, as if the rescue and capture of Quinn had released tension wires holding her taut since before they'd met. Toni wondered if she would have been able to notice it before if Brittany hadn't told her about the visions.

"It went really well, actually. Special Agent Agron was very supportive."

"That's good. Really, really good."

"Yeah, I guess." Brittany turned so she was looking into Toni's eyes. "I guess you all mentioned the visions?"

"Well, yeah, I mean, they seemed pretty prominent to the story."

"I'm not mad. It just felt odd…to be believed."

"Is that jab at me?"

"Honestly?" Brittany smiled. "No, but I sort of wish it was because it was perfect comedic timing."

"Ha ha ha." Toni winced slightly. "I'm glad you feel better. You look lighter, if that makes sense."

"It does." Brittany looked back across the ocean, a small smile on her full lips. "I, um, I'm going to write a book, I think. About this whole experience." She paused, licked her lips. "Quinn kept a journal that she had given to me. And it's part of the deal for me to write her story, or whatever." Brittany shrugged, then wrapped her arms around her bent knees, propping her chin on them. "I'm really sorry for how this all went."

"Britt," Toni said, followed by a sigh. "Please do not apologize to me. This is not your fault. You didn't do anything wrong. I mean, you saved me and my aunt, for Christ's sake." She chuckled as she nudged Brittany's side with her shoulder. "I know our love affair was swift, but you were everything I didn't know I needed."

"Past tense, hmm?" Brittany glanced over at Toni, her eyes sad. "No longer present?"

"Need. Absolutely, without a doubt, need. Desire. Long for." Toni smiled as she slid her hand down Brittany's legs to where her hands were linked together. "There are so many things I want to say. There's so much I feel that I wish I could explain. It's all just so messy right now. My mind is all over the place, and I'm not sure how to make sense of it all."

"I understand. You've been through a lot. More than anyone should have to go through." Brittany rubbed her face. "The last time I told someone how I really felt, it just…didn't end well. And then…" Brittany took a breath and the way the air seemed to fill her lungs made Toni's heart ache.

"Brittany, listen, I was wrong. I should've been able to believe you, or at the very least, accepted that you believed it. This is all my fault. All of it. I'm not going to blame anyone else." Toni knew, deep down, that her reaction to everything was part of why Brittany hesitated. The whole relationship had been a dream come true, but then there were the visions and Quinn and Leslie…and all of it had just been a royal pain in the ass. No wonder Brittany had been skittish. And Toni's reaction to everything had been the worst that it could be. She never realized how truly messed up she was until now. She really had some more healing to do.

"Toni, baby, I know. I get it. I probably should've told you a lot sooner, but as you can see, it was hard to talk about."

"Well, you know what's harder to talk about? You going back to San Francisco. That's fucking brutal to talk about."

"I know." Brittany's eyes were filled with tears and it made Toni's heart clench.

Another opportunity. She was being given another chance to lay her heart on the line. She should tell Brittany to stay. She should tell her that she couldn't imagine a single day without her. "Is there a way for us to, I don't know…make this work somehow?"

"A long-distance relationship?"

"Yeah, I mean, could it work?"

Brittany sighed. "I don't know."

"What's causing you to hesitate?"

"Honestly?" Brittany shrugged. "Maybe because you didn't trust me when I was right in front of you. Who's to say you'll trust me when I'm across the country on the opposite coast?"

Toni hated that answer because she was absolutely right. "So, we have to break up? Why can't you stay?"

"Because San Francisco is my home. My family is there. Why can't you leave?"

"Because I'm a fucking mess, Brittany. I'm a mess. I was kidnapped. Held at gunpoint. Beat. I mean, seriously, Britt. Is it that hard to believe that I don't want to leave my aunts, especially after what Leslie has been through? I came here to heal. And now I'm even more fucked up. And I can't keep leaving every time the going gets tough."

"Sounds to me like maybe this time, getting the fuck out of here might be exactly what you need." Brittany's tone should have been dripping with irritation, but it wasn't. She was calm, collected, everything Toni wasn't.

"So I just leave? And leave my aunts to deal with everything without me?"

"They *are* grown women, Toni."

Toni let out a puff of air. "That's… I mean… That's not what I mean."

"I know." Brittany smiled a small smile as their eyes locked. "As much as you might want to love me, you need to find a way to love yourself first. You have some healing to do before we can figure out how to move forward together. I get it."

"Goddammit," Toni said quietly as she wiped at her tears. "Why are you so fucking wonderful to me?"

"Because," Brittany whispered. "You're really *fucking* important to me."

Tears instantly stung Toni's eyes. She looked away from Brittany's beautiful face and willed herself to not let those tears escape. She wanted Brittany to stay so badly. But she didn't have the right to beg for that. She couldn't ask Brittany to give up her life in San Francisco, or put her dreams on hold just because she couldn't find the courage to leave. Not when everything in her mind, body, and soul felt as if she was on the cusp of a breakdown.

"Can I ask you something? Sort of off-topic?" Brittany sighed deeply.

"Of course." Toni looked at Brittany as she gathered her thoughts. She studied the gentle slope of her nose, the beautiful soft pink of her cheeks, the fullness of her lovely lips. Everything about Brittany was exactly what Toni wanted, including the incredible way she handled every eccentricity Toni had. Her ups, her downs, her crazy moods— Brittany knew how to deal with it all, and for the first time ever, Toni felt like maybe she really had found the soul mate she'd been looking for. And now her soul mate was going to leave because Toni didn't have what it took, yet, to be with her. The reality of the situation was starting to choke off her air.

"Do you think it's a good idea for me to even be thinking about writing this story?"

"Brittany, oh my God, of course I think you should do it." Toni situated herself so she was facing Brittany. "When you and I had our first meaningful conversation, you mentioned searching for something that had a higher meaning. I thought I understood what you meant then, but holy cow, now I completely get it. You were searching for a way to heal, for a way to get yourself out of the rut the accident threw you into. Now you have an awesome way to get past all of that. You need to leave, go back to San Francisco, find an agent and get a contract. You can write, which is what you love to do, but you can also exorcise any demons that might still be haunting you from the accident. I am very proud of you."

Brittany's smile was exactly what Toni needed in that moment. And when Brittany pulled Toni into a long, sensual kiss, it reminded her why she loved Brittany so much. There was so much Toni needed to deal with, but the one thing she knew without a shadow of a doubt was Brittany had come into her life at exactly the right moment. A few days earlier and Toni wouldn't have been ready. A few days later and Toni would have been too far into her own depression to want a way out. Even though their future was uncertain, Toni knew her love for Brittany wasn't. And she hoped her kisses would be enough to relay that message to Brittany.

Chapter Thirty-eight

Brittany tossed her bag into the trunk of the car. "Thanks for driving me, Alice. I really don't mind taking the ferry."

Alice slammed the trunk. "Don't be ridiculous. The schedule is a bit hit and miss right now with one of the boats still being down from the hurricane. And now that the bridge has been reopened, I don't mind at all."

Brittany had been dreading this moment for the last four days. Toni hadn't wanted to talk about her impending departure date, and now here they were. There was so much to say, so many thoughts to articulate, but now they were out of time. Every tear sliding down Toni's cheeks created a new crack in Brittany's heart. She hated to see her in pain, and more, she hated to be the cause of that pain.

"Hey," Brittany said. She pushed Toni's chin up with her finger, needing to see her eyes. "Everything is going to be okay. I'll call you as soon as I land."

Toni nervously bit her bottom lip. "I'm sorry I can't go with you. I just can't bear the thought of watching you walk into that airport."

Brittany was having a hard time understanding. She wanted Toni to come with her. In fact, she wanted Toni with her in San Francisco. But Toni had been through so much, and she felt safe with her aunts—comfortable. Brittany wasn't about to take any of that from her or push her any harder to give it up for her. Deep down, she knew things were going to be okay, even if it hurt like the devil now.

Brittany pulled her into a hug. "I understand." She kissed her forehead. "I'm going to miss you."

Toni rested her face against her shoulder. Her body was trembling from the silent tears Brittany knew were falling. She did the only thing she could do and squeezed her harder.

Toni abruptly kissed her cheek. "Good-bye, Brittany." She turned and disappeared into the house.

The loss was immediate, and Brittany fought the urge to go after her for one more embrace, one more taste of her lips. She knew it would just prolong the inevitable. San Francisco was home, and Toni had made it clear she needed time to figure herself out.

Leslie wrapped her in a hug. "Take care of yourself out there."

Brittany nodded. "Thank you for everything. Both of you."

Madge squeezed her arms and placed a necklace around her neck. "The clear quartz is for healing. The rose quartz is to help restore trust and harmony. The jasper helps with courage, quick thinking, and confidence." She put her hand on Brittany's face and sighed. "Much better energy now. You're going to do great things, honey."

Brittany touched the stones. "Thanks, Madge. Stay out of trouble."

Madge raised an eyebrow. "What fun would that be?"

Brittany stared at the house. This was it. She was leaving, and no one was protesting. No one was trying to stop her. She knew then she was making the right choice. She loved Toni. She knew that with every fiber of her being, but sometimes that wasn't enough. Maybe she wasn't enough. Toni had been through so much, they all had. She just wasn't ready, and Brittany had to be okay with that. What other choice did she have?

Thirty-six days had passed since Brittany had left the island. Eight-hundred and seventy-two hours. Toni got up every day. She went to the pub to work since they decided to keep it open through the winter months. She took long walks, bundled in her parka, hat, and gloves. She sat and stared at the ocean. Her aunts reminded her to eat. They forced her to sit with them and watch the news. She did the bare minimum required to exist, which fortunately, also included going to a therapist to unpack the feelings she'd been struggling with.

The best part about that was she was finally able to say the name Quinn without immediately wanting to cry. She could discuss the events without needing to take a nap afterward. And she was able to be by herself without constantly checking over her shoulder. She even had sessions with Aunt Leslie. Together they were able to work through some of their shared trauma. It felt really, really good. And it also felt good to work through the damage Penn had done, as well. Overall, she really loved her new therapist and their three times a week sessions.

The hardest part of her daily tasks was ignoring the phone calls from Brittany. She ignored them because it hurt so much to talk to her. It hurt to remember what they shared, and it hurt to think about what they could've been. She'd wanted to get on the plane with her, but she couldn't. The trauma of Penn, of being kidnapped, of being afraid to leave her aunts—it was all too much. So she stayed where she was. She reminded herself to breathe in and out, and she wished for the pain to subside. It wasn't fair to Brittany, she knew that, but she didn't want to undo all the work she was doing by jumping on a plane and joining her in San Francisco before she was ready. And it was possible Brittany might not want her to, given the way she was handling things. But it felt like one more thing on her plate would crack it altogether.

It had been raining for almost three straight days, and she was jealous. It wasn't fair that the skies could cry without anyone questioning their stability or their intention. No one asked the clouds why their color looked off, or why they let the water pour from their insides. They just existed exactly how they were, with no interference.

"You need a refill on your coffee?" Alice and Leslie had both been hovering lately.

Toni shook her head and continued to look out the window. "No, thank you."

Alice held out her cell phone. "Looks like you have a few missed calls."

Toni closed her eyes and concentrated on her breathing. She knew who they were from.

"I think she misses you." Alice sat in the chair next to her. "Did something else happen? Is that why you won't talk to her?"

Did something else happen? How was she supposed to answer that? The answer should've been easy—no. Nothing else happened. Brittany did exactly what she expected her to do, more so, what she'd told her to do, and left. Toni hadn't been brave enough to tell her how she felt, and now this was what she had left. Memories and regrets. Brittany was everything she'd ever wanted, and she still couldn't force herself to take the plunge. She couldn't let herself follow another woman to an unknown place without knowing for sure how it would end.

"Nothing else happened."

Alice sighed. "You know I've been around since Christ was a corporal, right?" She smiled. "I've seen my fair share of failed relationships, successful relationships, and just about everything in between. Do you know what all the successful ones had in common?"

"No," Toni said.

"Faith—when one person loses it, if the other can hold on tight enough for both, then you know it's real. And worth the struggle."

Toni sat quietly as she processed Alice's words.

"Sometimes life is fucking hard. On good days, the really lucky folks are only breaking even. Life is riddled with obstacles. People, work, economic standing, liars, cheaters, manipulators—these are all things you have to navigate daily. But if you have that one person who gives you a little bit of faith, the rest is bearable. That's not because they can make those other things go away; no, those things are the tolls we pay for living. But they make the rest of it seem worth it." She sipped her coffee.

Toni hadn't really wanted to listen but now she was intrigued. "Faith in like, a higher power?"

Alice rubbed her shoulder. "Faith in yourself. Faith that you can be a better person. Faith that you can eventually be the person they see in you. Faith that the world is a better place because you are in it."

"Brittany makes me a better person." Toni had meant to think it, but it spilled out of her mouth like a confession.

Alice stood. "Then have some faith in what you have and go get her."

Toni's neck flushed at the thought of leaving the island and her aunts. "What if I can't?"

Alice shrugged. "What if you can?"

Toni watched the rain for several more minutes. She let Alice's words play through her mind. *What if you can?* It was time to have faith. To stop being a coward and letting the past determine her future. Toni grabbed her laptop before she had a chance to change her mind. She opened a tab and started searching for flights.

Chapter Thirty-nine

Brittany clinked her beer bottle against Amy's. "Thank you again for helping me move. You're the best."

"It was like eight bags and a computer. It wasn't exactly a hardship." Amy winked. "This really is a great place. How did you find it?"

"My aunt Patty, actually. I'm subleasing it from her friend's niece. It's only for six months, but that should be enough time for me to find my own place."

Amy took a sip from the beer bottle, looking like she was trying to keep herself from saying anything.

"What?"

Amy narrowed her eyes slightly. "Are you sure this is where you want to be?"

"Don't."

She held her hands up. "Listen, it's not that I don't want you here, you know that. It's just that you haven't seemed all that happy since you've gotten back."

Brittany pushed herself up on the counter. "I love Toni. I miss her so much I ache every day. But she hasn't returned any of my calls. She won't even text me back. She's the asshole who said we could try long-distance and now she won't pick up the phone. What am I supposed to do with that?" She shook her head and sipped her beer. "All I can do now is write this book and focus on what's ahead."

"Can you, though? Can you just let her go that easily?"

"Easily? Amy, there is nothing easy about this. I think about her all day long. I wonder what she's doing, if she's okay, if she's happy. I can't stop thinking about her. But it can't be a one-way street. I don't feel right pressuring her right now. I know what it's like those days and weeks after a trauma."

"This has to be hard on her too. I mean, she has a lot going on. Like, a lot."

"Amy, she won't talk to me. There's nothing else I can do."

Amy opened the freezer and pulled out a bottle of vodka. "There's something we can do. Let's drink about it."

Brittany laughed, thankful for the reprieve. "I can do that."

Amy poured the liquid into two glasses. "How is the book coming?"

Brittany swirled the alcohol around in the glass. "Really well. I have an interview lined up with a couple of psychiatrists so I can fully understand Quinn's frame of mind. The first one is going to help me unpack some of the shit in the journals."

Amy sipped the vodka. "Are the visions gone?"

"Yeah. I mean, I feel like I can still sense more, like something opened inside of me. But I don't see through Quinn anymore."

Amy's eyes got wide. "Sense more? Like what?"

Brittany tilted her glass at Amy. "Like that you aren't twenty-five anymore, and you're going to be hungover tomorrow."

Amy downed the rest of her drink. "Ain't that the truth?" She laughed. "But seriously, like what?"

Brittany thought about how to explain it. "Like I was passing by this woman in the park the other day, and I could sense her anxiety. She seemed worried about her husband. Then this morning, I got coffee down the street, and I could tell the barista was thinking about something other than my caramel macchiato, like how to pay for tuition next semester. It's not concrete. I can just feel things now. I get glimpses into people."

"That seems exhausting," Amy said.

"Sometimes." Brittany shrugged. "But I also kind of like it. I feel connected to people."

"Can you sense Toni?"

Brittany had tried to do it so many times over the last several weeks. When she realized what her extra senses were capable of, she'd tried to channel Toni. She wanted to feel that connection to her again, at the very least to know that she was okay. But she came up empty every time.

"No. I don't think I can pick when it happens or with who."

Amy's phone buzzed. "Okay, my Lyft is here. I have to get over to Lands End to meet Lena. Are you going to be okay?"

Brittany hopped off the counter and hugged her. "Yes, I'll be fine. I'm going to put up a few pictures, and some books. Anything to make me feel more settled. Thanks again for your help. Make sure to say hi to Lena for me."

Amy kissed her cheek. "See you soon."

She didn't tell Amy, but she could sense her as well. Amy emitted happiness and peace. Brittany could feel the love she had for Lena and the life they shared. She was happy for her.

She wandered around her new apartment. She examined all the furniture and electronics. Nothing here belonged to her. She was glad to have a place to stay, but it wasn't home. Nothing about it was familiar or brought her peace. She wasn't sure she'd ever find what she'd had at Swift Island with Toni, Alice, and Leslie. The sense of home and belonging was strong there, and Brittany wasn't sure she'd ever be able to duplicate it if she stayed in California. She felt untethered without Toni, and she knew it would be an emotion she'd have to learn to live with—whether she liked it or not.

Toni stood at baggage claim inside the San Francisco Airport and berated herself. *You really didn't think this through.* She'd thought of calling Brittany to tell her she was coming, but it didn't seem like enough. She'd let too much time go by, and now she felt like she needed a grand gesture. If she called her and told her she was there, it would be easy for Brittany to hang up on her. She couldn't take that chance. Her heart couldn't handle it. She needed to see Brittany face-to-face. She needed to tell her exactly how she felt without the possibility of her simply hanging up.

The cab driver stared at her in the rearview mirror. "Where to?" Toni stared at him. "You already asked me that, didn't you?" He nodded. "A few times now."

Toni took a deep breath and requested the only place she knew she'd have a chance to see Brittany. "Lands End."

He put the car in drive. "Great restaurant. I asked my wife to marry me there."

She smiled at him because she knew it was the polite thing to do, but her insides were screaming with anxiety. What was she going to do once she got there? Sit out front and wait like a stalker? *No. You went over this already. You're going to ask for Amy. Amy loves Brittany. Amy will tell you where to find her.* Yes, that was the plan. It was a good plan. *Unless Amy hates you because Brittany now hates you. Why wouldn't she hate you? You haven't returned a single call or text in a month and a half. You're the worst.*

The cab ride was much faster than she'd expected. Maybe it was faster than she'd hoped. She still hadn't completely devised a plan of how to talk to Amy when the cab dropped her off. She thought she heard the driver mumble something about her being crazy after she paid him, but she couldn't be sure.

Toni took a deep breath and looked around. Brittany had described this place perfectly. It was set on the farthest tip of San Francisco, and she could see Alcatraz and the Bay Bridge from its location. The Pacific Ocean was beautiful and sparkled magically against the setting sun. She jiggled the bag in her hand and stared at the door. She could do this. She needed to do this. She needed Brittany.

The hostess who greeted her was extremely pleasant. She practically shouted her welcome. "Hi! Welcome to Lands End. Table for one?"

Toni's mouth was so dry, she had to lick her lips to speak. "Is Amy Kline here?"

The hostess looked around for a moment, and then pointed to a corner of the restaurant. "There she is. I'll go grab her."

Toni thought about telling her to stop. But the vibrant young woman disappeared before she could cough out a word. A few minutes later, an extremely attractive woman approached with the hostess in tow. *Jesus. This was who Brittany was dating before me?*

Amy looked confused at first, before her eyes widened. "You're Toni, aren't you?"

"How did you know?"

"Brittany described you perfectly."

Toni's heart skipped a beat. "Do you have a minute?"

Amy's face split into a wide smile. "I have several. Please, come sit down."

Brittany had been very clear about two things—Lands End had the best crab chowder in the world, and Amy was a wonderful person. But she'd underplayed both. The crab chowder was phenomenal, and Amy was even more wonderful than she'd expected. Amy had listened intently while Toni had rehashed what brought her here, and why she stopped to find her before Brittany.

"I'm so happy you decided to come here. Brittany has seemed a bit out of sorts since she returned," Amy said, as she refilled Toni's wine glass. "You've been through a lot together. Maybe you found your way clear across country because there's still more for you guys to experience."

"Thanks." Toni sipped the wine. "I was worried about ambushing you, but from the way Britt always spoke about you, this seemed a good place to start."

A good-looking dark-haired woman walked up and placed her hands on Amy's shoulders. Amy smiled and reached for her hand. Toni could see the resemblance between her and Brittany. Amy definitely had a type, and it was clearly a type she shared with Toni.

"Hey, honey. The dinner rush is almost over. Why don't you sit down and talk to us? This is Toni. Toni, this is Lena."

Lena put her hand out. "It's so nice to finally meet you, Toni. We've heard a lot about you."

Based on her use of the world "nice," what they'd heard from Brittany couldn't have been all bad. "Your restaurant is incredible. Brittany raved about it, but she didn't do it justice."

Lena sat down. "I'm glad you're enjoying yourself. Can I get you anything else?"

Amy rubbed Lena's arm. "Have any of that chocolate cheesecake left?"

Lena beamed. "I saved you a few pieces. I'll have someone bring them out."

Amy turned her attention back to Toni. "When are you going to tell Brittany you're here?"

Toni squirmed in her seat. "I was hoping you could tell me where to find her. I don't really want to just call. I owe her more than that."

"Grand gestures. I like it." Lena pointed at her, seeming excited.

Amy pulled out her cell phone. "Let me see where she is."

Toni's heart was pounding in her stomach. This was what she wanted. It's what she flew across the country for. She'd spent days planning this, and now it could possibly come to fruition with a simple text. *I think I'm going to throw up.* Her whole body felt hot. What if Brittany didn't want to see her? What if she told her to go away? Or worse, what if she didn't feel the same way anymore?

Amy grabbed her hand. "Hey, everything is going to be okay. I don't know what's going on in that head of yours right now, but it will be okay. Brittany misses you."

Toni shook her head. "I think I messed everything up."

Amy's back straightened, and she looked over Toni's shoulder. "Well, it's too late to turn back. Brittany is here."

Amy's words echoed in Toni's head. *Brittany is here.* She turned in her seat hoping and terrified that she'd heard her correctly. She had. Brittany's face was a beautiful tapestry of confusion, excitement, and caution as she walked toward the table. She was wearing her black leather jacket and her silk black tank top. Her jeans were tight around her perfect hips, and just the sight of her shifted Toni's libido into high gear.

Everything Toni had ever felt for Brittany flooded through her in waves. She knew how much she desperately missed her while they'd been apart, but it was crystalized in that moment. She loved Brittany. She wanted Brittany. She needed Brittany.

"Toni?" Brittany crossed her arms when she got to the table.

That hadn't been the reaction Toni had been hoping for exactly, but what did she really expect?

There were thousands of words she could and should say. There were poems others had written that could articulate what she was feeling, love songs that echoed promises of forever and destiny. But they all escaped her now. She did the only thing she could think of to express how she felt. She stood up, put her hands on Brittany's face and kissed her.

She kissed her like it was the last thing in her life she could do that would mean something. She kissed her to convey the loss she'd felt since they'd been apart, and to apologize for not being brave enough to say how she felt. She kissed her as a promise that she would kiss her every day, for as long as Brittany would let her.

Brittany seemed to hesitate at first. She didn't move when their lips connected, but that only lasted a fleeting moment. Brittany kissed her the way Toni had always wanted to be kissed. She kissed her with so much passion, Toni knew that everything would be okay. She had made the right choice in coming here, and she'd fallen in love with the person she was meant to be with. Everything else in her life that led to this moment, this kiss, had been worth it.

When Brittany finally had her fill, she gently nudged Toni back so she could drink in the sight of her. She looked as beautiful as ever, but her eyes were tinged with melancholy. It was the last thing she'd remembered about her since that morning when she left the cottage.

"I see you've met Amy and Lena," Brittany said, finally letting Toni out of her grip.

"I have. They're as amazing as you said they were."

"They make a mean chowder, too, no?"

Toni nodded. "Alice's New England clam chowder has some serious competition."

Brittany looked over at Amy and Lena. "We're gonna take a walk outside for a bit. Would you excuse us?"

"Wait," Amy said. She went around the corner and came back with another wine glass for Brittany. "Here. Take this with you." She handed Toni the bucket her bottle of white was chilling in.

"Thanks." Brittany gave her a loving smile and led Toni outside. They walked down to the private area of the property where Amy and Lena kept two Adirondack chairs pointed toward the ocean for nights when the sunset was especially brilliant, and they could steal away from the restaurant bustle.

"You know what's funny?" Toni said as Brittany handed her a glass of wine. "I spent six hours on an airplane thinking about all the things I wanted to say to you, and now that I'm here, next to you, I'm just speechless."

Brittany smiled as she sipped her wine. "This view will do that to a person."

"It's not the view." Toni shifted in her chair to face Brittany. "Do you hate me now?"

Brittany smirked as she lowered her glass from her mouth. "Did it feel like I hated you when I kissed you? I couldn't possibly hate you, Toni. Yeah, it hurt when you didn't answer my calls or texts. But I've spent the last month and a half daydreaming of ways we could arrive at this moment. And you made it happen."

Toni ran her hand through her hair after the ocean breeze tousled it. "I wanted to go with you, you know."

"Looking back, I'm glad you didn't. Airport good-byes are the absolute worst."

"I don't mean to the airport. In my heart, I wanted to jump in your suitcase and go wherever you wanted to take me. But…"

"I know." Brittany reached over and tapped her forearm. "Even though I wanted you to come with me, I knew I couldn't ask that of you. I've had a while to reflect now, and I see that it was actually the best thing for both of us."

"So you don't resent me for ignoring your calls? I mean, I had to. I knew if I heard your voice, I'd never be able to pull myself together."

"You don't have to explain—"

"I do, Britt, because I want you to know it was never about me questioning my feelings for you. When you'd told me you were leaving, I needed to know that if I went with you, it would be out of love for you and not just the fear of losing you. I think that's where I went wrong with Penn. She'd presented me with an offer to escape my life, and I said yes without even thinking because I was afraid of losing that chance."

"That makes perfect sense, Toni. You and I both landed on Swift Island because of our own individual baggage. Then we meet, connect, and then experience the grandmamma of all traumas together. It was really smart of you to question if our connection was born out of trauma or a healthy mutual respect and appreciation of each other."

"Wow. You mean I actually made a thoughtful, rational choice in a relationship?" Toni's eyes were big and bright, and Brittany laughed, unsure if Toni's dramatic awe was ironic or sincere.

"Yes, and I want you to know, all of this is unfolding exactly how it's supposed to. Life is messy sometimes. But I'm here for you. For all of it."

"We may not have known each other for a long time, but something led me back to you, Brittany. Something about you, about us, made its way through the clutter and chaos in my head to make me buy a plane ticket and fly out to you." Toni's lips parted then closed again. Finally, she said, "So, this is something you think you still want?"

Brittany refilled their glasses then looked Toni in the eye. "No."

Poor Toni looked like she'd witnessed a demon dancing over Brittany's head. Brittany realized her attempt at a little dramatic flair had missed the mark. "I don't *think* I want it. I know I do."

Toni closed her eyes and exhaled.

"Too soon?" Brittany said.

"Let's take a walk and watch the famous Pacific sunset, you jerk."

When they stood, they were facing each other. Brittany caressed Toni's chin and kissed her tenderly as a breeze blew across them. They walked up the street, hand in hand, carrying their wine glasses to a scenic area that had a few benches. But instead of sitting they leaned over the railing, shoulders touching, and gazed out at the mango sun lowering onto the water.

"So I know you believe in visions," Toni said. "But do you believe in fate?"

"There are lots of things I believe in now that I didn't before," Brittany said, dangling her empty wine glass over the railing. "How about you? You were the skeptic."

"I'm at the point now where if someone told me aliens had a plan to put seeds in America's food supply so we'd poop out an army of extraterrestrials, I'd believe it."

Brittany giggled. "Well, let's hope that's not on the horizon."

"Tell me about it," Toni said.

"Seriously, though. Are you okay that I get visions? Since I had them once, I'm assuming it'll happen again at some point. Does that possibility freak you out?"

Toni turned to face her. "Nothing freaks me out more than the possibility of losing you, Britt. If they happen again, at least we'll know what they are, and you'll definitely have a better handle on how to deal with it."

"For sure, especially if I know I won't have to hide them from you."

"Let's make a pact, right here in front of the majestic Pacific Ocean…no more hiding things from each other, no matter how awful or embarrassing it may be."

Brittany exhaled. "Amen to that." She reached around and began rubbing Toni's back, savoring the picturesque view.

"So now that I'm here," Toni said. "I need a place to stay. Can you recommend any good hotels or Airbnbs?"

"Everything around here is so overpriced," Brittany said, enjoying the light banter. "You can crash at my place if you'd like. My rates are quite reasonable."

"If it won't be an inconvenience…" Toni leaned over and pecked her on the lips.

"On the contrary. It'll be my pleasure to have you." Brittany kissed her back.

"It'll be my pleasure to be had by you." Toni smiled as she nibbled Brittany's lip.

Brittany swept her into her arms, and they kissed passionately, sensually in the glow of the setting sun. With the taste of Toni on her tongue, the feel of her soft, warm skin against her, all she wanted to do was whisk her away to a private bungalow and make love to her until dawn. But for now, her apartment would do just fine.

"I'm going to text Amy and Lena that we'll take a raincheck on cocktails with them."

As Toni's smile temporarily eclipsed the sun, Brittany noticed that the melancholy she'd begun to think was part of Toni's essence was gone from her eyes. She relaxed into a serenity she hadn't felt in years. Or ever. She wanted to consume Toni, protect her, nurture her, to keep her as close to her as she was at that moment. Forever. And she was prepared to take things at whatever pace Toni felt comfortable with.

❖

By the time Brittany had taken her back to her newly sublet apartment, Toni wasn't interested in a tour, no matter how quick it would be. After their talk she felt so much better about everything, about Brittany's feelings for her and her own feelings about herself. Brittany helped her realize that even if she hadn't had everything in her life figured out and functional, that was okay. That was life—the journey to figure it all out with the help of the beautiful people you meet along the way.

She felt lighter and freer than she'd ever felt, and the sight of Brittany's delicious shoulders and chest in her tank top as the leather jacket dropped from her shoulders was as life-affirming as it got.

"This is it," Brittany said with a shrug. "It's not much, but it's home for now." She started toward the window. "Actually, the view is pretty—"

"Where's the bedroom?" Toni said.

Brittany whirled around with a surprised-as-hell grin. "Right there."

Toni grabbed her hand and dragged her into the room. "Do you mind if I freshen up first?"

"Of course not." Brittany pointed to the adjoining bathroom.

Toni again grabbed her hand and towed her along. She turned on the water and began kissing Brittany passionately as she unfastened her belt and jeans. Brittany followed her cue and stripped Toni out of her clothes, and they stepped into the shower stall together.

They took turns letting the water wash over them, soaking their hair as they kissed. Toni grabbed the cucumber shower gel from the window shelf, squirted it over Brittany's chest, and began sliding her soapy hands over her back, down her waist, and over her hips.

Brittany pressed her against the cold wall and massaged Toni's breasts and teased her as she slid her slippery fingers between Toni's legs. She began grinding up against her as they devoured each other in steamy kisses mingled with water dripping down their faces.

Toni grabbed Brittany's hand and slid it between her legs, then reached for Brittany's swollen clit. Words weren't needed as their gasps and moans of pleasure guided the speed and pressure of their soapy fingers as they brought each other to powerfully intense climaxes that weakened Toni's thighs. She leaned all her weight against Brittany as they caught their breath and savored the physical pleasure gazing into each other's eyes.

"I'm sorry. I couldn't wait," Toni said, licking a droplet of water from her lips. "I hope I didn't ruin any plan you might've had."

Brittany giggled. "I couldn't have planned this any better if I tried." She turned off the water and reached for a towel on the rack beside the shower. She draped it around Toni like a cloak and patted her face dry. "You're adorable, you know that?"

Toni felt herself blush. Or was it being flushed after an amazing orgasm? "Here. You're gonna freeze." She wrapped Brittany in a towel and followed her to the bed.

"After a hot shower like that, there's no way I'm going to freeze," Brittany said. She turned down the bed, dropped her towel, and climbed in.

Toni did the same and snuggled up to her. "You smell delicious."

"It's the cucumber. You must be hungry. Have you eaten anything today?"

"An egg sandwich at the airport in Boston and some crab chowder at Lands End."

Brittany reached for her phone on the nightstand. "We need to get some Chinese food up in here. Pronto. Cantonese or Szechuan?"

"Uh…surprise me."

Brittany looked at her. "You have no idea which one's which, do you?"

"None whatsoever."

Brittany laughed and dialed the number.

After they enjoyed a feast of delivery and a bottle of wine, they made love again. This time it was slow and sensual, nothing rushed or urgent, every inch of skin touched and kissed, every breath and every glance as meaningful as a grain of sand in an hourglass.

Once their physical desires were finally satiated, Brittany crawled back up to face Toni. Her hair was spread messily across the pillow, her eyes heavy and dreamy, her eyelids lazily opening and closing. "How do you feel?"

Toni opened her eyes and smiled. "In love," she whispered. "Completely, totally, head over heels in love."

"Me, too, baby." Brittany gently brushed a few strands of hair off Toni's forehead. "I love you, Toni, and I don't ever want to lose you again."

"You're the one who helped find me and I promise, I will never get lost again."

"At least send up a flare next time, so I know where to find you." Brittany chuckled and leaned down to kiss Toni.

Toni smiled into the kiss. "You'd better buy me a flare gun."

"Oh sure, I'll get right on that."

"In all seriousness, Britt," Toni said, then paused as she bit her lip. "You've shown me what it feels like to be loved. It's the best feeling I've ever known."

Brittany sighed. "I can't wait to see what's on the horizon for us next."

"I'm hoping for a guided tour of San Francisco. And of course, a stop at a flare gun shop," Toni replied.

"That's a great idea." Brittany laughed. "But you'll have to stay for a couple of weeks if you want the works."

"Hmm, a couple of weeks of Chinese food in bed, hot showers, and waking up to you every morning? This Airbnb is gonna get the best Yelp review ever."

Brittany wrapped Toni in her arms and fell into the best sleep of her life.

The next day was a free day for Brittany, aside from the therapy appointment she said she couldn't miss. Once Brittany explained the background, and why it was so important, Toni understood. Going over all of the journal entries with a professional was something Brittany was passionate about. And when she brought up Quinn's name, it didn't even make Toni flinch. Not exactly. She flinched. But only a little. But who could blame her? The last time Toni saw Quinn, she was tied up and begging for her life.

Quinn.

Ugh.

Toni took a deep breath and let it out slowly as she digested the thoughts about her kidnapper. Right after it all happened, Toni made it a point not to think about it, not to think about her, and not to call her by her name. But as time went on, she realized that was the wrong approach. She needed to think about it and process it so she could heal. Even though the name still made Toni shudder, she had done a lot of soul searching since the event took place.

The lighting in Brittany's apartment was magnificent. Toni had spent the month and a half dealing with the impending season change on the island, and while the weather had been mild, she was loving the change brought by being on the West Coast.

As Toni meandered her way through Brittany's place, she made a mental note of all the different pictures on the walls. Brittany really made the space her own. Toni loved everything about the way she decorated, too. Brittany had a boho style, rugs, tapestries, and plants, which struck Toni as odd at first. Brittany didn't seem like the kind to have time for plants. Nevertheless, there were small house plants all throughout the living room. And she also had three different bookshelves, filled, of course, with books, but also different knickknacks. Toni smiled, feeling a deeper sense of who Brittany was as she observed the things she'd collected and the style with which she'd arranged her space.

After she pulled a few photo albums from one of the shelves, she positioned herself on the color rug next to the large bay window. As she thumbed through the first album, she was struck by how Brittany seemed never to change, she just got more beautiful. There were pictures of her in high school playing sports, working on the yearbook, writing for the school newspaper. There were pictures of her in college, hanging out with friends, holding hands with guys, girls—all of it. A couple of the pictures were of her with family. She was the spitting image of who Toni assumed was Brittany's mom. There were pictures of an older man, probably Brittany's dad, and some with Amy and Lena.

Before she had the chance to look through anymore, the door to the apartment opened, and in walked Brittany. The sight caused Toni's mouth to water. It'd been too long since she was able to simply sit there and admire Brittany's beauty. And it had also been too long since she had been able to see Brittany's ass in those tight skinny jeans.

"Well, shit. I thought I'd hidden those albums better."

Toni chuckled and waved Brittany over. "Help me up. I'll put them away, and we can go to lunch."

"Mm-hmm. You'd better not make fun of how dorky I was in high school." Brittany gently pulled Toni from the floor, then placed a loving kiss on her lips. "You know I'll eventually find pics of you, right?"

Toni leaned into Brittany and kissed her again. "The only thing you should know is I haven't gotten better with age as you have. I was a badass years ago. I used to have streaks in my hair. I wore combat boots. I even had a belly-button ring."

Brittany's eyes were wide. "Excuse me?"

"Oh, yeah. I was a real looker."

Toni followed Brittany out of the apartment and down the stairs to the street toward Golden Gate Park. Brittany pointed out a few things as they walked, but Toni was enjoying her view as she gazed at Brittany's profile. How grateful she was that she'd come to her senses and allowed herself the gift of healing. And the gift of Brittany.

"This restaurant is one of my favorites," Brittany said as she held open the door to a Mexican restaurant called Nopalito.

Toni loved it instantly. Behind the bar, there was a large mural with colorful flowers and birds. The liquor shelf was stocked with numerous kinds of tequila. And as soon as they sat down, Brittany smiled.

"Do you mind if I order for us? I promise it won't disappoint you."

Toni nodded and watched as Brittany interacted with the server. He knew her by name, and when she stood to hug him, they both laughed and exchanged pleasantries. Toni was really enjoying watching Brittany in her element. The Brittany she'd met on Swift Island was exciting, yes, but it was obvious there was something she was holding back. This Brittany seated before her had figured herself out, and she was no longer confined. She was free. And it was amazing.

"Okay, so margaritas are ordered, and chips, salsa, and guacamole are on the way. I hope you're hungry."

Toni laughed. "I feel like I haven't had a substantial meal in days. And then you worked me out like an athlete last night, so yes, I'm famished."

"An athlete, hmm?"

"Yes. Some of the muscles aching today I didn't even realize I had."

Brittany leaned forward, her eyebrows raised, and said, "I'm sure I can rub out any cramps you may get."

"Jesus," Toni whispered.

The margaritas were promptly delivered, and thankfully so because Toni's cheeks were on fire. And she was happy to experience the familiar feeling of excitement and longing coursing through her veins again. After she took her first sip, she reached across the table and took Brittany's hand. "Do you mind if I tell you something?"

"Toni, my love, you can tell me anything."

She smiled, another wave of desire washing over her. "I feel like I need to explain. I mean, I know you said I don't have to, but I want to. I want to tell you."

"Okay." Brittany propped her elbow on the table and cradled her chin in the palm of her hand. Her eyes were sparkling, and Toni wanted to lunge over the table and kiss her.

"Obviously, you know I struggled with what happened."

Brittany nodded.

"It was horrifying. All of it. From the hurricane preparation to not believing you to the kidnapping to the fucking fear engulfing me. All of it was the worst thing I had ever been through. And I thought Penn leaving me was bad." Toni sipped on her margarita. The drink was delicious, and she wanted to down it to calm her nerves. "And then you left. And even though I was the one who told you to leave, I felt abandoned."

"Toni—"

"I know. I know. Let me finish." Toni held her finger up. "It was me. All of it. You have to believe me when I say that. You know the traumatic part of being kidnapped isn't always just the kidnapping. It's the post-traumatic stress, and the depression that follows that is sometimes worse. I've done a lot of research about it and have talked for hours and hours about it with my therapist during the time we've been apart. The idea of surviving spurs you on when you're taken, but once you're returned? You feel held back by the fact that you could have died. Even though I didn't die." She took a breath and held it as she looked out the window of the restaurant. "You saved me, but afterward, I feel like a part of me stayed behind in that basement."

"Toni..." Brittany's hushed tone caused Toni's chest to clench. "You went through so much—"

"I went to see Madge a month ago."

Brittany blinked a couple of times, quickly, and she pressed her lips together.

"And she was super helpful. As well as encouraging..." Toni paused and looked into Brittany's eyes. "Especially about you. And how much I meant to you."

"*Mean* to me," Brittany whispered.

Toni nodded. "Yes, *mean* to you." She shrugged. "You have to realize how fucked up I was. I still am. I mean, I've come a long way in the last month and a half, but I still have some pretty vivid dreams, or nightmares, but I know how to ground myself. And they're getting less frequent."

"I am so sorry, Toni. I am."

Toni took her hand and pressed it to her cheek. "Listen to me, Britt. You do *not* need to apologize. Okay? You are everything I needed, everything I wanted, and unfortunately, the island had different plans for us. Madge actually said she figured some higher power would bring us back together. Especially after she read my cards and flipped over the Lovers card and then the fucking Death card."

The laugh that poured out of Brittany was exactly what Toni needed to hear. "You know the Death card doesn't actually mean death, right?"

"Well, I know now, thank you very much. But I definitely did not know then. I looked at Madge when she flipped it over and told her I had already escaped death once, what the hell else was going to happen now?" Toni laughed along with Brittany. "Seriously, though, y'know? Like, I better never be kidnapped again, goddammit." She smoothed her hands over the wood-topped table. "I ended up having weekly sessions with Madge. She encouraged it, and she refused to take money. She's not my only therapist, obviously, but she sure is lovely to speak with. I cannot even begin to explain to you how much she helped me. She grounded me and made me see everything differently. Sort of like, instead of being pissed off that everything happens for a reason, she made me happy that's the case."

"So when did you make the decision to come here?"

"Honestly?"

Brittany nodded, a small smile on her full pink lips.

"After a deep talk with Madge. She even nudged me into scheduling my flight right then because I was worried you wouldn't appreciate me showing up on your doorstep without warning."

"You could never go wrong surprising me like that."

"Good." Toni took a deep breath, then asked softly, "I know you said you forgave me, but can you see where I was coming from now?"

Brittany waited a second before she responded. It seemed as if she was gathering her words. "All I want to say is this…" She sighed. "I think we should talk about the future. We're both done living in the past, right?"

Toni smiled. "Yes, right."

"Then? What should we do? Where should we live? I mean, San Francisco is lovely and it's where my family is but I sort of…"

"You fell in love with the island, didn't you?"

Brittany nodded, but smiled and said, "Nope."

"Lies, all lies." Toni's heart was so happy. "So, are you considering Swift Island a possible place for you to live?"

Brittany rolled her eyes. "I guess," she said playfully. "I mean, I sort of love Leslie and Alice now, too, so what the hell?"

"Brittany, listen, we can make the decision in a few weeks." Toni shrugged. "There's no rush, as long as we're together." She cleared her throat and added, "And I promise you, I will not shut you out again."

"Toni, you were terrified. *I* was terrified. We each had to deal with it all from different angles, but we were fighting the same villain. Y'know what I mean?"

"I do. I promise." Toni reached across the table again and took Brittany's hand in hers. "If I'm struggling to talk about it, at the very least, I'll tell you that. Okay?"

"That's all I ask."

"I love you. You know that, right?" Toni squeezed Brittany's hand. "I love you so much. I didn't know how deeply until you were gone. Do you have any idea how much you've changed my life?"

"Toni." Brittany's eyes glistened with emotion. "Oh, baby, I love you, too." She smiled, tears rolling down her cheeks.

"*Senorita*, are you okay?" the server asked as he placed a large bowl of chips between them and slid the salsa and guacamole onto the table. "You need more margaritas to take the edge off?"

They both started to laugh. Brittany shook her head. "I promise you, for the first time in a long time, I am absolutely okay."

And Toni believed her without a second thought. For the first time in what felt like forever, Toni was able to put her entire heart into someone else's hands. She was at ease, completely. And she loved being loved and being in love. Two things she never thought were going to happen after she was abandoned in Montana. She was so happy she finally healed from a wound she never thought would even form a scab.

CHAPTER FORTY

One Year Later

Leslie sat at the bar as a gentle, Indian-summer breeze sailed in through the open garage door on the south side of the building. The taproom was buzzing with customers there to celebrate the closing of another Swift Island vacation season. She picked at a salad as she waited for Alice to finish up some financial analysis on the profits over the last five months. After this wildly successful second season, Alice had predicted their net profit would be impressive to say the least. Leslie had no doubt about it. While the kidnapping may have left her and Toni a bit more cynical, if not altogether wary about human nature, it sure helped boost business. Sort of a silver lining?

Their harrowing story of survival had made national headlines, and their encounter with the now infamous serial killer Quinn West was even the subject of a late winter *20/20* episode. In addition, Brittany's book detailing her experience in the tragedy sold surprisingly well for a debut nonfiction author. Naturally, by the start of the following tourist season, rooms and rentals were hard to come by. Regulars had flocked back to Swift Island in droves to support their favorite pub owners, while a new wave of vacationers seeking a vicarious brush with the sensational packed the island in hopes of running into the band of unlikely heroines.

Leslie sipped her lager as she gazed at Toni and Brittany across the room at their favorite high-top table by a window facing the street. They were magical to watch. So in love, so in tune with each other.

So solidly healthy. She couldn't help smiling whenever she stole a glance at them.

"What a difference a year makes." Alice's voice floated in from behind as she brushed her arm across Leslie's back.

Leslie turned and rested her head on Alice's shoulder briefly then nodded toward the outside. "Can you believe this weather? It couldn't possibly be any more gorgeous."

"We have so much to be grateful for," Alice said. She squeezed her thin frame between Leslie and a customer, and leaned against the bar. "We can make a healthy down payment on the bungalow in Siesta Key." A smile illuminated her face along with an entire ten-foot radius around them.

"We're really doing this," Leslie said, feeding off Alice's enthusiasm.

"We deserve a long and happy retirement, my love. The Second Wave thrived in its second year, so we're on solid footing. Plus, we'll have no worries with your daughter and Toni in charge."

Leslie nodded. "I'm so thrilled Rebecca and Toni are going to be working together. Our dream will be in very capable hands, and it'll be nice to have our family here with us."

"Speaking of Toni, what's she up to?" Alice smirked as she indicated Toni sauntering toward the bar.

Leslie watched in anticipation as Toni rang their newly installed ship bell and climbed up on top of the bar.

"Hey, hey! Everyone, listen up!" The bar patrons settled down, but soft murmurs still rumbled throughout the taproom. "On behalf of the proprietors of the Second Wave, my thoroughly badass aunts, Leslie and Alice Burton..." The crowd interrupted with loud cheers. "We want to thank each and every one of you who came out and supported our modest little brewpub all season long. It's been an amazing second year, and we're beyond excited about what the future has in store for us here on Swift Island. Leslie and Alice have poured their hearts and souls into this place, and I, along with my cousin Rebecca, plan to carry the legacy on for many seasons to come." More cheers echoed throughout the pub. "So thank you again, and we can't wait to see you all next year when we'll have a whole new lineup of local brews on tap. I promise you, we will support you by being here whenever you're thirsty—"

"Yeah!" came the ovations.

"Whenever you're hungry!"

"Yeah!"

"And whenever you're too drunk to walk, ride a bike, or drive home!"

The entire establishment exploded in riotous *woot-woots* and shouts.

"Thank you all so much! The bar is *open!*" Toni rang the ship bell one more time as the bartenders scrambled to fill drink orders. People were crowded in every direction, shouting drink and burger orders.

Toni hopped off the bar top and looked at Aunt Leslie, who was beaming at her with glassy eyes.

"I'm so proud of you," Leslie said, clutching Toni's hands. "For so many reasons, not the least of which is the strong, confident woman you've become."

"I don't know if I'm fully there yet," Toni said, "but I'm definitely trying." She absorbed her aunt's aura for a moment, studying her soft features on a face that showed the triumphs and tragedies endured and overcome over the decades. "And for sure, I have the best role model in the world."

Once Leslie released her from the massively-strong-for-an-old-woman embrace, she rushed back to the table where Brittany was seated, typing something into her phone. "How'd I do?"

"You're hot as fuck right now, and I can't wait to get into your pants later."

"Hmm. I'll have to make sure they're as open as the bar is...only to you of course."

"Of course." Brittany leaned forward as she pulled on the homemade V-neck of Toni's black shirt. "How about you make sure they're not even on," she whispered against her lips before they met in a sensual kiss. Toni heard a few random customers cheer. As they pulled away, Brittany let out a soft chuckle. "These old gays sure do love us."

"Hell yeah, they do," Alice said as she slid out a tall chair and jumped onto it with an *umph*. "You two are exactly what this placed needed last year, and you're more than worthy of the fanfare this year."

"Especially since our Brittany here is well on her way to being a famous author now." Leslie beamed. "I never thought I'd live to see the day that someone I know is famous."

"I am far from famous."

"Oh, come on now," Toni said with a laugh. "You were recognized when we flew into the Boston airport. I think you're famous."

"Pish-posh." Brittany winked at Toni.

"What's on your agenda now, Brittany? Still writing?" Leslie asked.

Brittany put her phone down and cleared her throat. "I'm writing a few freelance articles for the *Boston Globe*. And I have a really great story lined up for the *New Yorker*. I've been working on a couple of other things here and there, nothing crazy. But aside from that? I think I might start writing another book. I really loved doing it. It was intense, it stretched my writer's muscles, and hell, I'm definitely not complaining about the royalties."

Leslie smiled. "Every bit of good news coming your way is well deserved. Your book is captivating right from the first paragraph. Hell, the first *sentence*. You did a remarkable job."

"She's not lying. It's quality storytelling. That's for sure." Alice nudged Leslie. "I had to make her put the damn thing down some nights. She didn't want to go to sleep."

"And not because it was causing flashbacks," Leslie explained. "It was just really, really good. I'm so impressed."

Toni laughed. "See? Famous for a reason."

"Stop," Brittany said, followed by a sheepish grin.

"And the visions? How are those going?" Aunt Leslie leaned in closer and nudged Brittany.

"Well, let's just say, I am way more connected spiritually to people than I ever have been. No visions. Just…hmm…intuition?"

"Intuition sounds like a great way to put it." Madge's voice cut through the crowd-filled silence.

"Madge!" Brittany popped up and wrapped her arms around Madge. "It's so good to see you."

"And you, too, my dear."

"I heard you've been helping Toni here."

Madge chuckled a deep hearty laugh. "Well, the one who didn't believe is always the one who believes the most at the end, am I right?"

"You certainly are," Brittany said, echoing Madge's laugh.

"Oh shush, you two. At least I am a believer." Toni draped her arm over Brittany's shoulders. "And I'm just happy you believe in me enough to want to spend the rest of your life with me."

"Whoa, whoa, whoa." Leslie poked Toni with the end of her cane.

Madge moved closer to Leslie and Alice. "Excuse me?"

Toni slid her hand across the table and wiggled her fingers, revealing a princess cut engagement ring. "She asked, and I said yes." She squealed, and Alice echoed her.

"Hmph, I didn't see that one coming," Madge said with a grin.

"Wow! Now that's a rock! Don't jump into the sound. You'll sink." Alice laughed as she patted Brittany on the back. "You have a good eye."

Brittany's cheeks blushed a light shade of pink, and she ducked her head. "I knew I needed to lock her down before some other woman swept her off her feet."

"Not gonna happen," Toni said as she kissed Brittany on the cheek, smoothing her thumb over the soft pink skin. "Besides, you're famous now. Why would I leave that?"

"Ha ha ha." Brittany rolled her eyes, but Toni was quick to gently take her face and pull her in for another kiss.

"I love you, Brittany. More than anything." She kissed Brittany deeply. "Thank you so much for *seeing* me. Even when I refused to believe anyone would want to see me, you cared enough to keep trying."

Brittany kissed Toni softly before she pulled away and said, "I will never stop seeing you."

And Toni knew it was true. It was the one thing in her life she didn't question anymore. She was convinced that she was destined to meet Brittany. Every single moment was meant to help her grow, to help her let go of her past demons, to help her see the beauty of loving herself before loving someone else. Finally, she was where she was supposed to be. And she was going to marry the woman she was meant to be with. She trusted Brittany with every fiber of her being. And she knew, without a shadow of a doubt, that Brittany felt the same way.

Nothing was going to get in their way.

Not fear.

Not another person.

They were stronger together, held tightly by their hopes, their dreams, and their love.

Forever.

About the Authors

Jean Copeland

Jean Copeland is an author and English/language arts teacher at an alternative high school in Connecticut. For her first novel, *The Revelation of Beatrice Darby*, she won the Alice B. Readers Lavender Certificate and the 2016 GCLS Goldie Award for debut author and was a Goldie finalist in the historical fiction category. In addition to her novels, Jean has published numerous works of short fiction and essays online and in print anthologies. When not exploring the world of lesbian fiction, she enjoys watching her students discover their talents in creative writing and poetry, traveling, relaxing by the shore, and good wine and conversation with friends. Organ donation and shelter animal adoption are causes dear to her heart.

Jackie D

Jackie D was born and raised in the San Francisco, East Bay Area of California. She earned a bachelor's degree in recreation administration and a dual master's degree in management and public administration. She is a Navy veteran and served in Operation Iraqi Freedom as a flight deck director onboard the USS *Abraham Lincoln*.

She spends her free time with her wife, son, friends, family, and their incredibly needy dogs. She enjoys playing golf but is resigned to the fact she would equally enjoy any sport where drinking beer is encouraged during game play. Her first book, *Infiltration*, was a finalist for a Lambda Literary Award.

Erin Zak

Erin Zak grew up on the Western Slope of Colorado in a town with a population of 2,500, a solitary Subway, and one stoplight. She started writing at a young age and has always had a very active imagination. Erin later transplanted to Indiana where she attended college, started writing a book, and had dreams of one day actually finding the courage to try to get it published.

Erin now resides in Florida, away from the snow and cold, near the Gulf Coast with her family. She enjoys the sun, sand, writing, and spoiling her cocker spaniel, Hanna. When she's not writing, she's obsessively collecting Star Wars memorabilia, planning the next trip to Disney World, or whipping up something delicious to eat in the kitchen.

Books Available from Bold Strokes Books

A Turn of Fate by Ronica Black. Will Nev and Kinsley finally face their painful past and relent to their powerful, forbidden attraction? Or will facing their past be too much to fight through? (978-1-63555-930-9)

Desires After Dark by MJ Williamz. When her human lover falls deathly ill, Alex, a vampire, must decide which is worse, letting her go or condemning her to everlasting life. (978-1-63555-940-8)

Her Consigliere by Carsen Taite. FBI agent Royal Scott swore an oath to uphold the law, and criminal defense attorney Siobhan Collins pledged her loyalty to the only family she's ever known, but will their love be stronger than the bonds they've vowed to others, or will their competing allegiances tear them apart? (978-1-63555-924-8)

In Our Words: Queer Stories from Black, Indigenous, and People of Color Writers. Stories Selected by Anne Shade and Edited by Victoria Villaseñor. Comprising both the renowned and emerging voices of Black, Indigenous, and People of Color authors, this thoughtfully curated collection of short stories explores the intersection of racial and queer identity. (978-1-63555-936-1)

Measure of Devotion by CF Frizzell. Disguised as her late twin brother, Catherine Samson enters the Civil War to defend the Constitution as a Union soldier, never expecting her life to be altered by a Gettysburg farmer's daughter. (978-1-63555-951-4)

Not Guilty by Brit Ryder. Claire Weaver and Emery Pearson's day jobs clash, even as their desire for each other burns, and a discreet sex-only arrangement is the only option. (978-1-63555-896-8)

Opposites Attract: Butch/Femme Romances by Meghan O'Brien, Aurora Rey, Angie Williams. Sometimes opposites really do attract. Fall in love with these butch/femme romance novellas. (978-1-63555-784-8)

Swift Vengeance by Jean Copeland, Jackie D, Erin Zak. A journalist becomes the subject of her own investigation when sudden strange, violent visions summon her to a summer retreat and into the arms of a killer's possible next victim. (978-1-63555-880-7)

Under Her Influence by Amanda Radley. On their path to #truelove, will Beth and Jemma discover that reality is even better than illusion? (978-1-63555-963-7)

Wasteland by Kristin Keppler & Allisa Bahney. Danielle Clark is fighting against the National Armed Forces and finds peace as a scavenger, until the NAF general's daughter, Katelyn Turner, shows up on her doorstep and brings the fight right back to her. (978-1-63555-935-4)

When in Doubt by VK Powell. Police officer Jeri Wylder thinks she committed a crime in the line of duty but can't remember, until details emerge pointing to a cover-up by those close to her. (978-1-63555-955-2)

A Woman to Treasure by Ali Vali. An ancient scroll isn't the only treasure Levi Montbard finds as she starts her hunt for the truth—all she has to do is prove to Yasmine Hassani that there's more to her than an adventurous soul. (978-1-63555-890-6)

Before. After. Always. by Morgan Lee Miller. Still reeling from her tragic past, Eliza Walsh has sworn off taking risks, until Blake Navarro turns her world right-side up, making her question if falling in love again is worth it. (978-1-63555-845-6)

Bet the Farm by Fiona Riley. Lauren Calloway's luxury real estate sale of the century comes to a screeching halt when dairy farm heiress, and one-night stand, Thea Boudreaux calls her bluff. (978-1-63555-731-2)

Cowgirl by Nance Sparks. The last thing Aren expects is to fall for Carol. Sharing her home is one thing, but sharing her heart means sharing the demons in her past and risking everything to keep Carol safe. (978-1-63555-877-7)

Give In to Me by Elle Spencer. Gabriela Talbot never expected to sleep with her favorite author—certainly not after the scathing review she'd given Whitney Ainsworth's latest book. (978-1-63555-910-1)

Hidden Dreams by Shelley Thrasher. A lethal virus and its resulting vision send Texan Barbara Allan and her lovely guide, Dara, on a journey up Cambodia's Mekong River in search of Barbara's mother's mystifying past. (978-1-63555-856-2)

In the Spotlight by Lesley Davis. For actresses Cole Calder and Eris Whyte, their chance at love runs out fast when a fan's adoration turns to obsession. (978-1-63555-926-2)

Origins by Jen Jensen. Jamis Bachman is pulled into a dangerous mystery that becomes personal when she learns the truth of her origins as a ghost hunter. (978-1-63555-837-1)

Pursuit: A Victorian Entertainment by Felice Picano. An intelligent, handsome, ruthlessly ambitious young man who rose from the slums to become the right-hand man of the Lord Exchequer of England will stop at nothing as he pursues his Lord's vanished wife across Continental Europe. (978-1-63555-870-8)

Unrivaled by Radclyffe. Zoey Cohen will never accept second place in matters of the heart, even when her rival is a career, and Declan Black has nothing left to give of herself or her heart. (978-1-63679-013-8)

A Fae Tale by Genevieve McCluer. Dovana comes to terms with her changing feelings for her lifelong best friend and fae, Roze. (978-1-63555-918-7)

Accidental Desperados by Lee Lynch. Life is clobbering Berry, Jaudon, and their long romance. The arrival of directionless baby dyke MJ doesn't help. Can they find their passion again—and keep it? (978-1-63555-482-3)

Always Believe by Aimée. Greyson Walsden is pursuing ordination as an Anglican priest. Angela Arlingham doesn't believe in God. Do they follow their vocation or their hearts? (978-1-63555-912-5)

Best of the Wrong Reasons by Sander Santiago. For Fin Ness and Orion Starr, it takes a funeral to remind them that love is worth living for. (978-1-63555-867-8)

Courage by Jesse J. Thoma. No matter how often Natasha Parsons and Tommy Finch clash on the job, an undeniable attraction simmers just beneath the surface. Can they find the courage to change so love has room to grow? (978-1-63555-802-9)

I Am Chris by R Kent. There's one saving grace to losing everything and moving away. Nobody knows her as Chrissy Taylor. Now Chris can live who he truly is. (978-1-63555-904-0)

The Princess and the Odium by Sam Ledel. Jastyn and Princess Aurelia return to Venostes and join their families in a battle against the dark force to take back their homeland for a chance at a better tomorrow. (978-1-63555-894-4)

The Queen Has a Cold by Jane Kolven. What happens when the heir to the throne isn't a prince or a princess? (978-1-63555-878-4)

The Secret Poet by Georgia Beers. Agreeing to help her brother woo Zoe Blake seemed like a good idea to Morgan Thompson at first…until she realizes she's actually wooing Zoe for herself… (978-1-63555-858-6)

You Again by Aurora Rey. For high school sweethearts Kate Cormier and Sutton Guidry, the second chance might be the only one that matters. (978-1-63555-791-6)

Coming to Life on South High by Lee Patton. Twenty-one-year-old gay virgin Gabe Rafferty's first adult decade unfolds as an unpredictable journey into sex, love, and livelihood. (978-1-63555-906-4)

Love's Falling Star by B.D. Grayson. For country music megastar Lochlan Paige, can love conquer her fear of losing the one thing she's worked so hard to protect? (978-1-63555-873-9)

Love's Truth by C.A. Popovich. Can Lynette and Barb make love work when unhealed wounds of betrayed trust and a secret could change everything? (978-1-63555-755-8)

Next Exit Home by Dena Blake. Home may be where the heart is, but for Harper Sims and Addison Foster, is the journey back worth the pain? (978-1-63555-727-5)

Not Broken by Lyn Hemphill. Falling in love is hard enough—even more so for Rose who's carrying her ex's baby. (978-1-63555-869-2)

The Noble and the Nightingale by Barbara Ann Wright. Two women on opposite sides of empires at war risk all for a chance at love. (978-1-63555-812-8)

What a Tangled Web by Melissa Brayden. Clementine Monroe has the chance to buy the café she's managed for years, but Madison LeGrange swoops in and buys it first. Now Clementine is forced to work for the enemy and ignore her former crush. (978-1-63555-749-7)

A Far Better Thing by JD Wilburn. When needs of her family and wants of her heart clash, Cass Halliburton is faced with the ultimate sacrifice. (978-1-63555-834-0)

Body Language by Renee Roman. When Mika offers to provide Jen erotic tutoring, will sex drive them into a deeper relationship or tear them apart? (978-1-63555-800-5)

Carrie and Hope by Joy Argento. For Carrie and Hope loss brings them together but secrets and fear may tear them apart. (978-1-63555-827-2)

Death's Prelude by David S. Pederson. In this prequel to the Detective Heath Barrington Mystery series, Heath discovers that first love changes you forever and drives you to become the person you're destined to be. (978-1-63555-786-2)

Ice Queen by Gun Brooke. School counselor Aislin Kennedy wants to help standoffish CEO Susanna Durr and her troubled teenage daughter become closer—even if it means risking her own heart in the process. (978-1-63555-721-3)

Masquerade by Anne Shade. In 1925 Harlem, New York, a notorious gangster sets her sights on seducing Celine, and new lovers Dinah and Celine are forced to risk their hearts, and lives, for love. (978-1-63555-831-9)

Royal Family by Jenny Frame. Loss has defined both Clay's and Katya's lives, but guarding their hearts may prove to be the biggest heartbreak of all. (978-1-63555-745-9)

Share the Moon by Toni Logan. Three best friends, an inherited vineyard and a resident ghost come together for fun, romance and a touch of magic. (978-1-63555-844-9)

Spirit of the Law by Carsen Taite. Attorney Owen Lassiter will do almost anything to put a murderer behind bars, but can she get past her reluctance to rely on unconventional help from the alluring Summer Byrne and keep from falling in love in the process? (978-1-63555-766-4)

The Devil Incarnate by Ali Vali. Cain Casey has so much to live for, but enemies who lurk in the shadows threaten to unravel it all. (978-1-63555-534-9)